Archie®

CYBER ADVENTURES

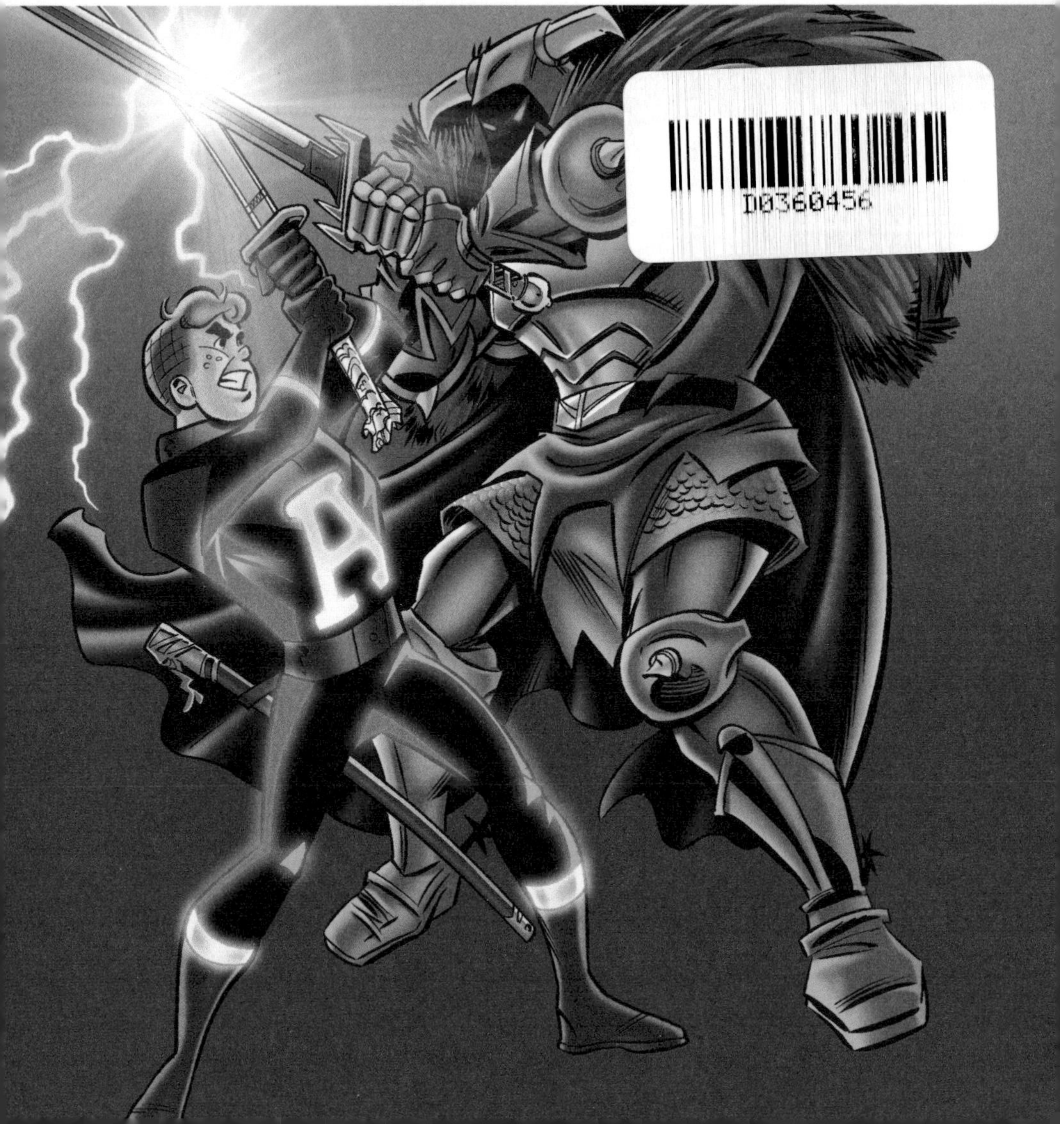

Archie Adventure Series Vol. 2
Archie: Cyber Adventures
Published by Archie Comic Publications, Inc.
325 Fayette Avenue, Mamaroneck, New York 10543-2318.

ArchieComics.com

ISBN: 978-1-879794-83-2

10 9 8 7 6 5 4 3 2 1

Printed in U.S.A.

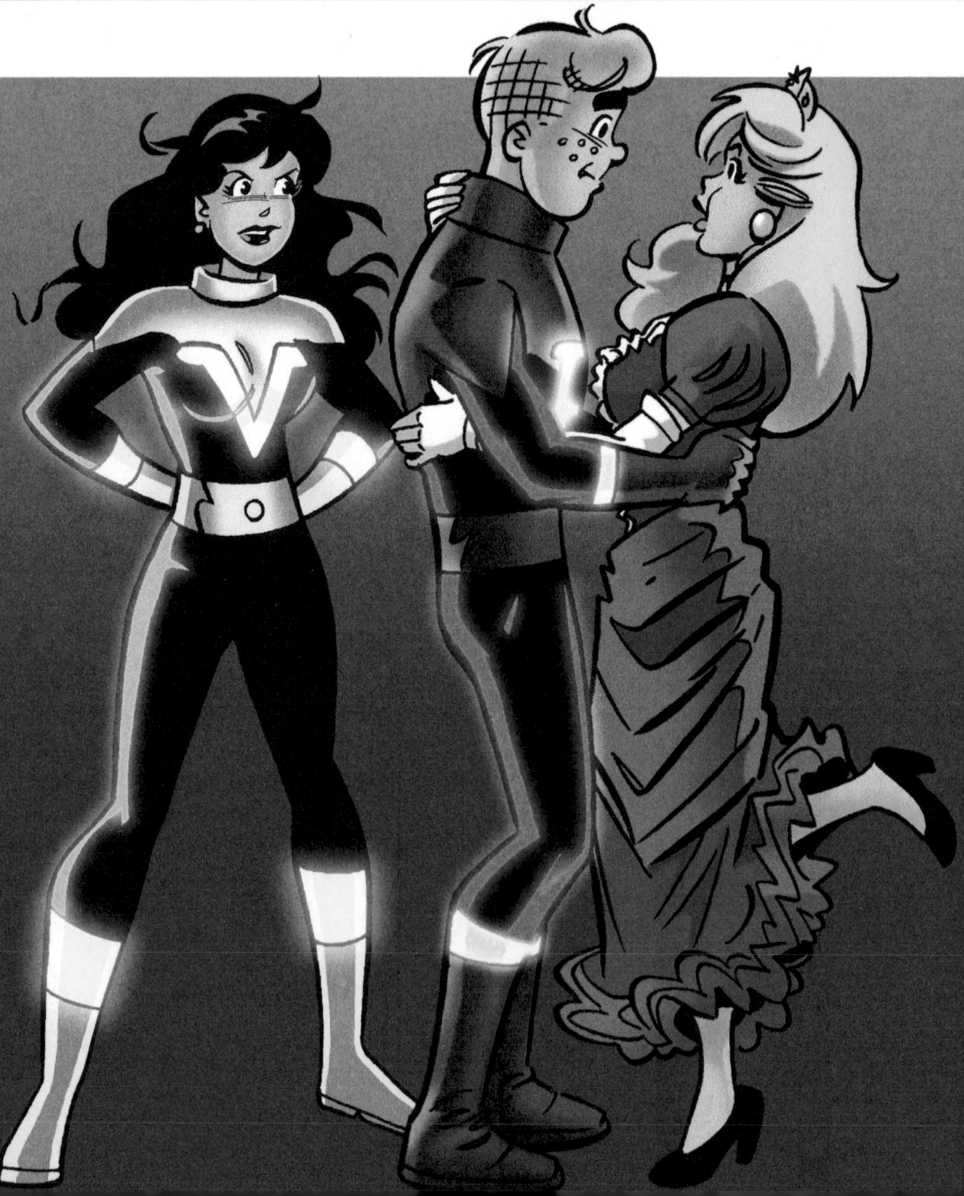

Archie®

CYBER ADVENTURES

Story by: STEPHEN OSWALD

Pencils by: JOE STATON

Inks by: BOB SMITH

Letters by: JACK MORELLI

Colors by:
ROSARIO "TITO" PEÑA
JASON JENSEN
JOE MORCIGLIO

Co-CEO: Jon Goldwater
Co-CEO: Nancy Silberkleit
President: Mike Pellerito
Co-President/Editor-In-Chief: Victor Gorelick
Director of Circulation: Bill Horan
Executive Director of Publicity & Marketing: Alex Segura
Executive Director of Publishing/Operations: Harold Buchholz
Project Coordinator & Book Design: Joe Morciglio
Production Manager: Stephen Oswald
Production: Jon Gray, Duncan McLachlan
Proofreader: Jamie Rotante

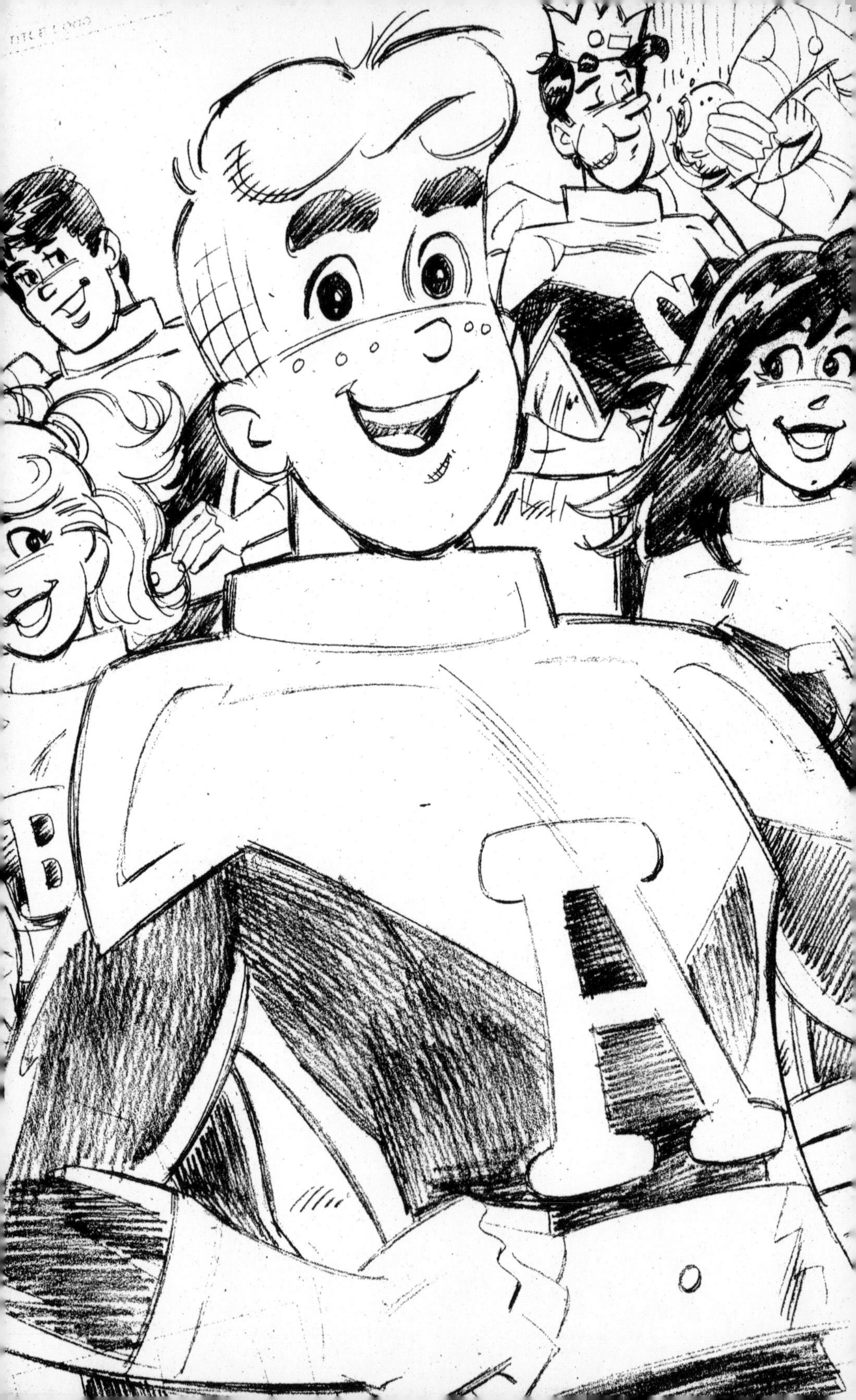

CHAPTER ONE

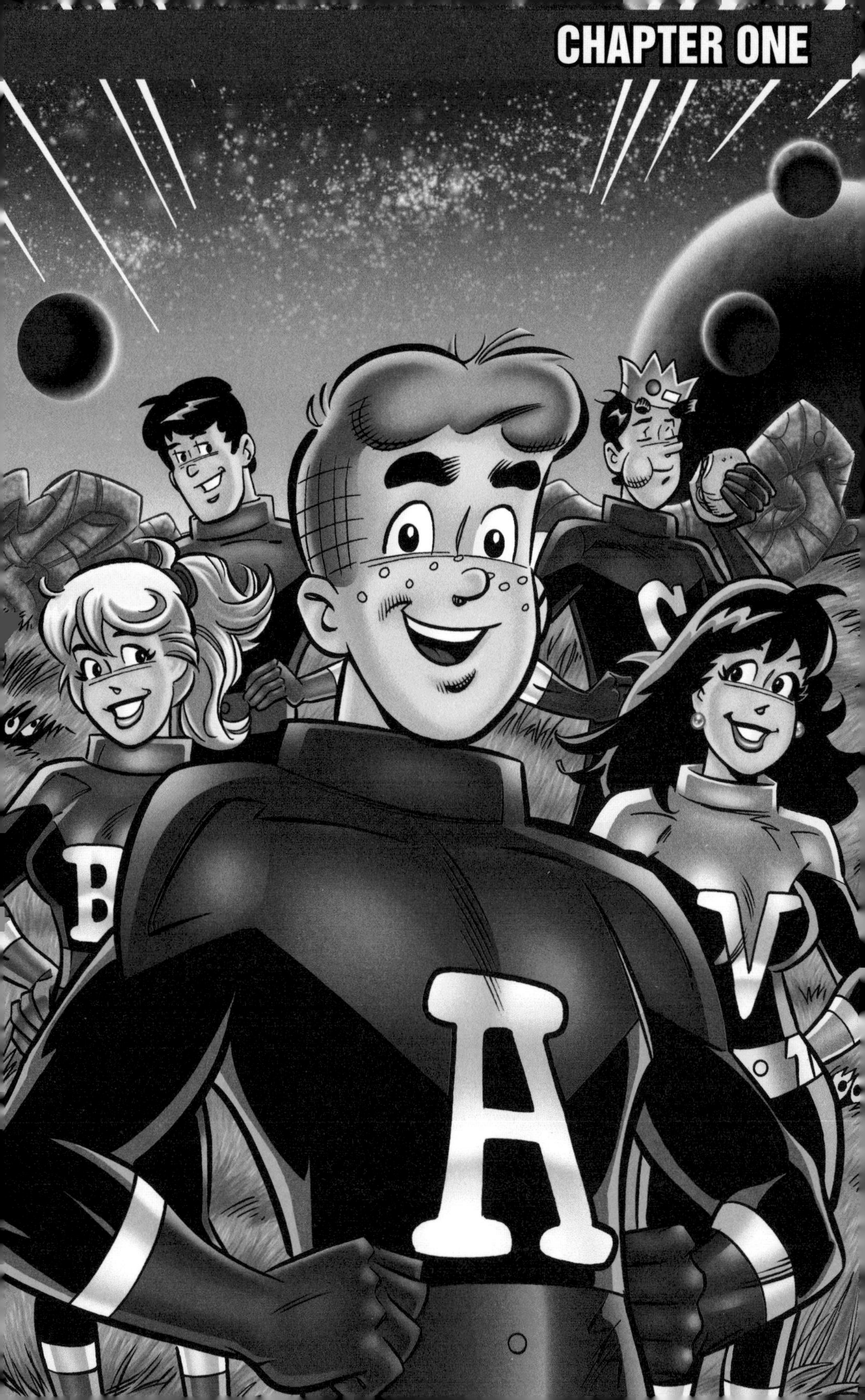

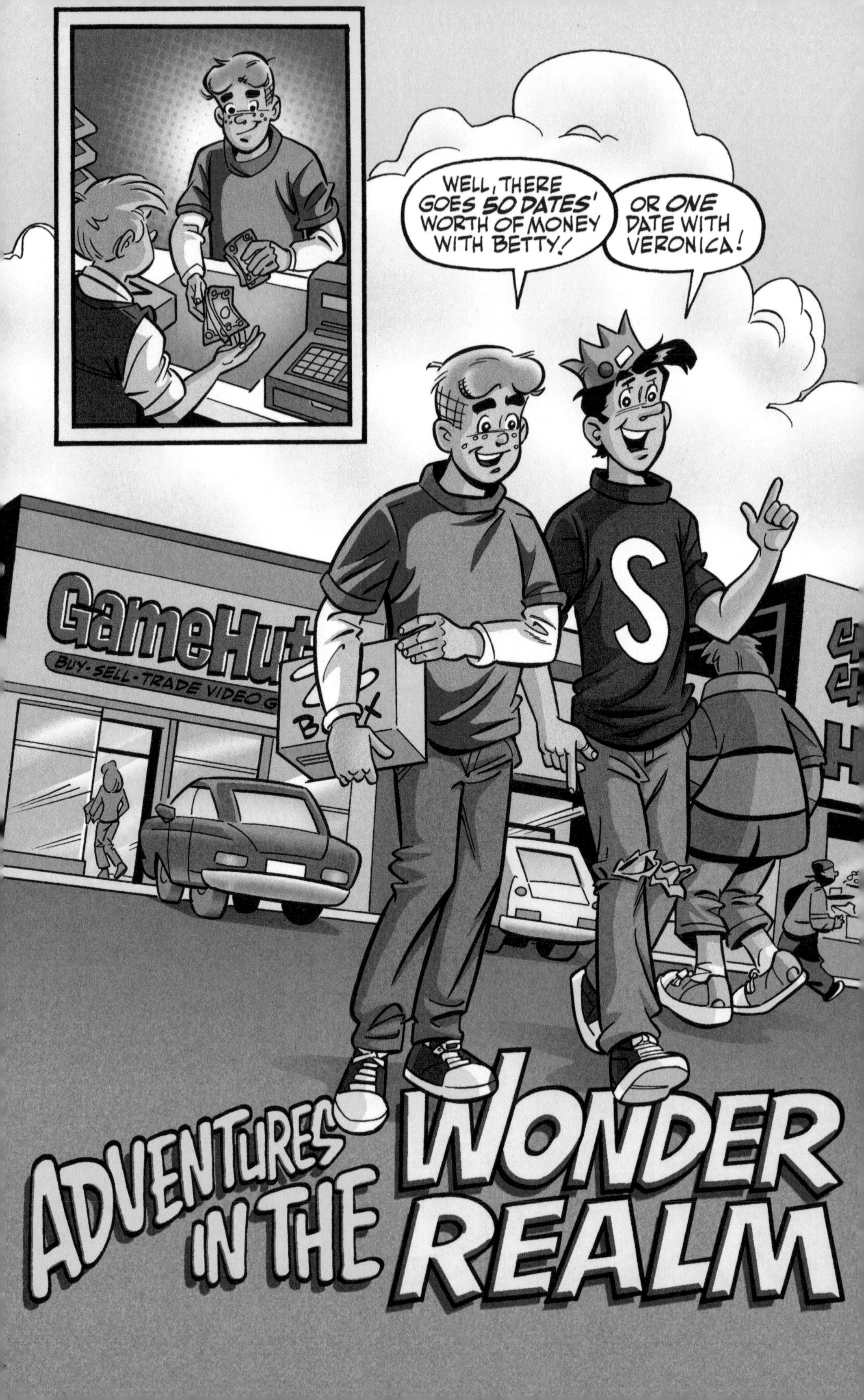
WELL, THERE GOES 50 DATES' WORTH OF MONEY WITH BETTY!
OR ONE DATE WITH VERONICA!
ADVENTURES IN THE WONDER REALM

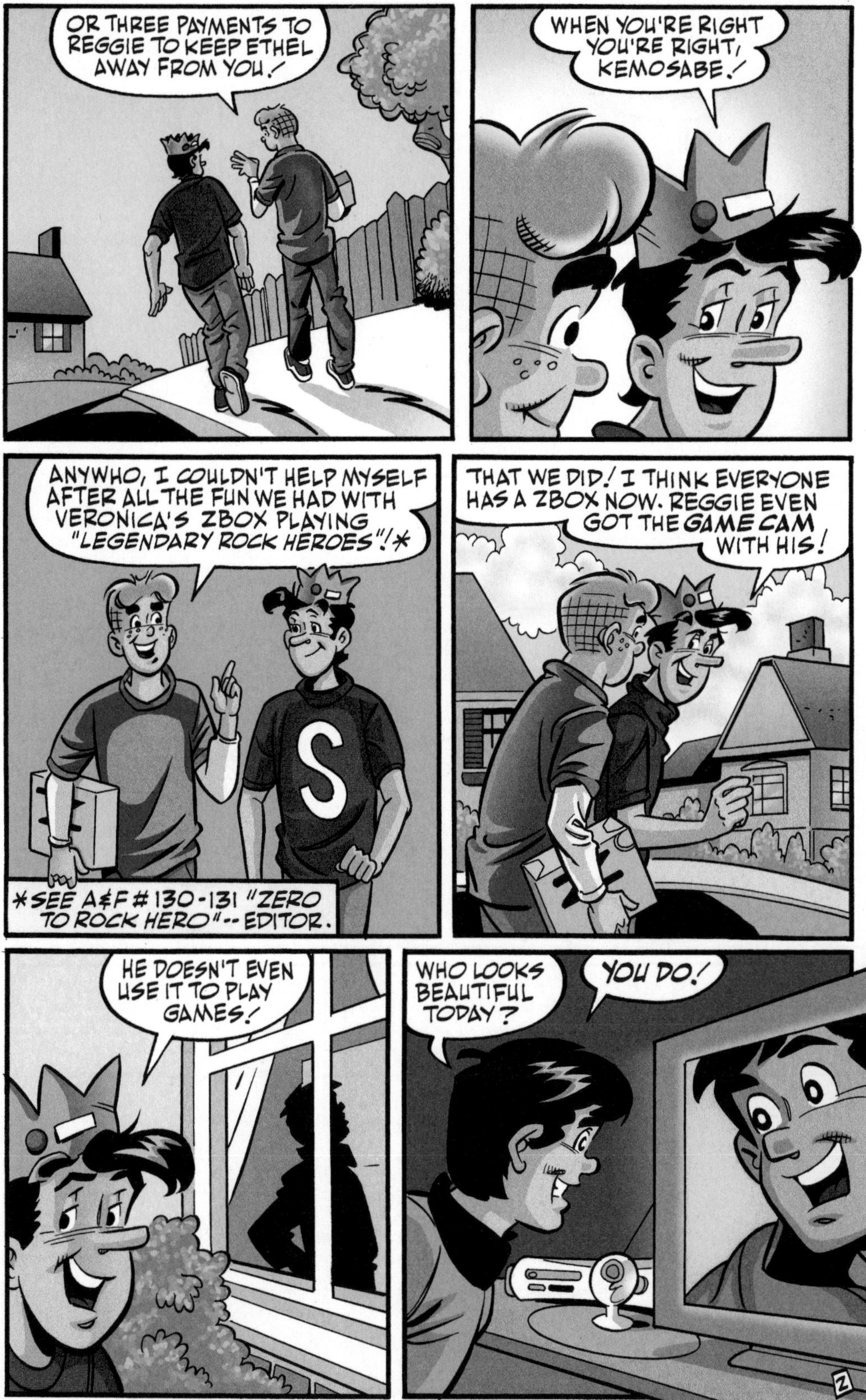
OR THREE PAYMENTS TO REGGIE TO KEEP ETHEL AWAY FROM YOU!
WHEN YOU'RE RIGHT YOU'RE RIGHT, KEMOSABE.!
ANYWHO, I COULDN'T HELP MYSELF AFTER ALL THE FUN WE HAD WITH VERONICA'S ZBOX PLAYING "LEGENDARY ROCK HEROES"! *
*SEE A&F #130-131 "ZERO TO ROCK HERO"-- EDITOR.
THAT WE DID! I THINK EVERYONE HAS A ZBOX NOW. REGGIE EVEN GOT THE GAME CAM WITH HIS!
HE DOESN'T EVEN USE IT TO PLAY GAMES!
WHO LOOKS BEAUTIFUL TODAY?
YOU DO!
2

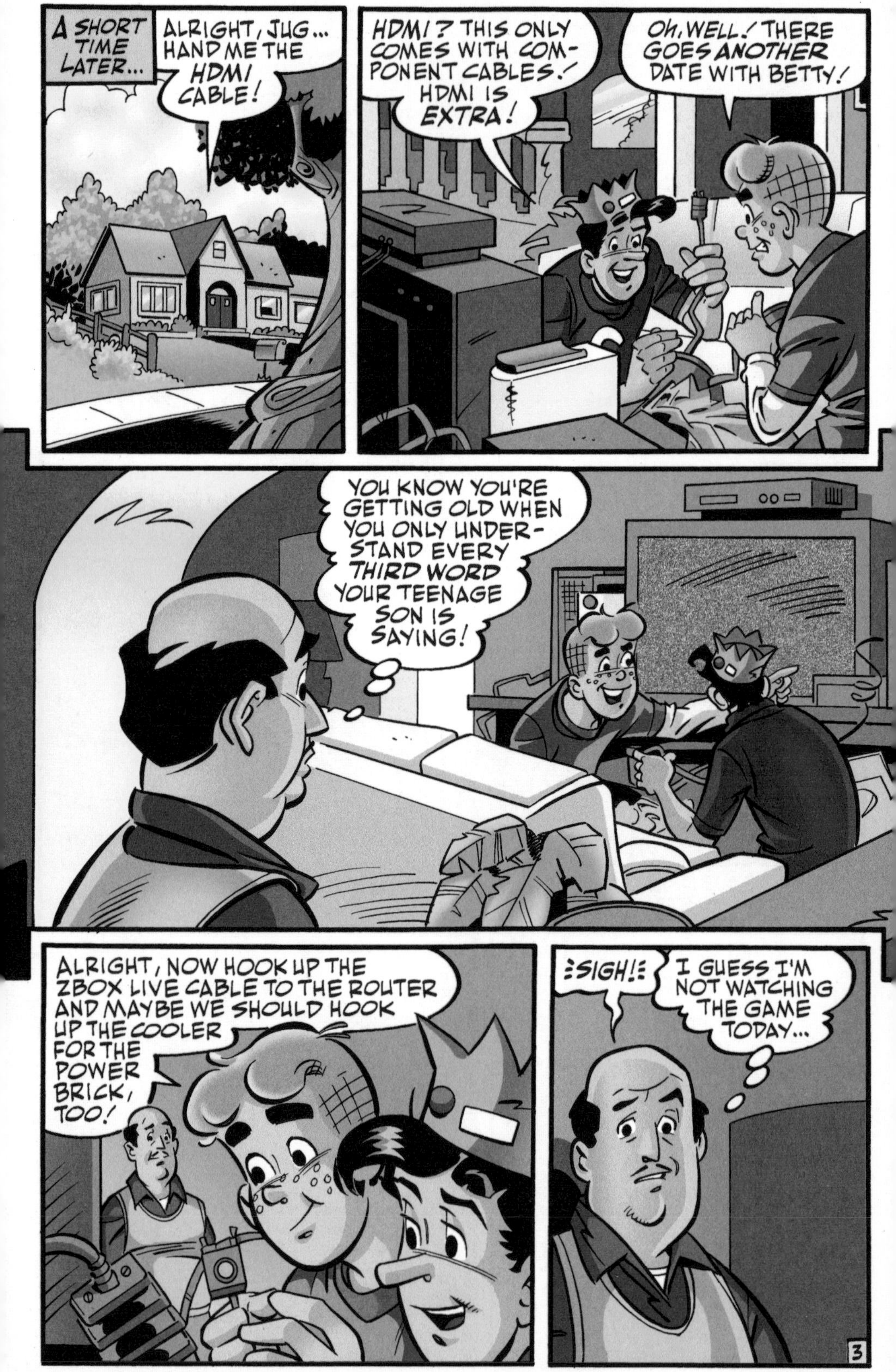
A SHORT TIME LATER...
ALRIGHT, JUG... HAND ME THE HDMI CABLE!
HDMI? THIS ONLY COMES WITH COMPONENT CABLES! HDMI IS EXTRA!
Oh, WELL! THERE GOES ANOTHER DATE WITH BETTY!
YOU KNOW YOU'RE GETTING OLD WHEN YOU ONLY UNDERSTAND EVERY THIRD WORD YOUR TEENAGE SON IS SAYING!
ALRIGHT, NOW HOOK UP THE ZBOX LIVE CABLE TO THE ROUTER AND MAYBE WE SHOULD HOOK UP THE COOLER FOR THE POWER BRICK, TOO!
SIGH!
I GUESS I'M NOT WATCHING THE GAME TODAY...
3

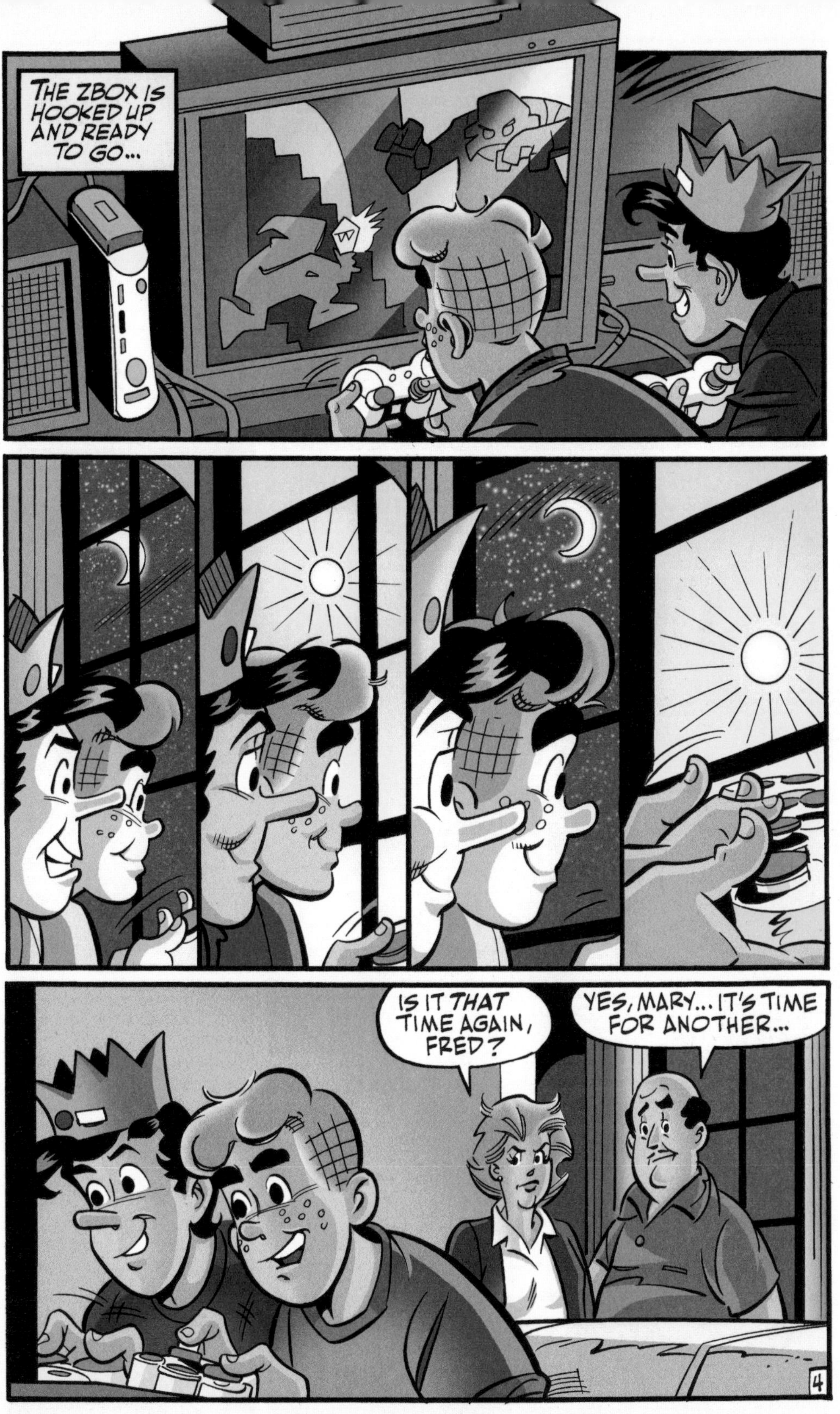
THE ZBOX IS HOOKED UP AND READY TO GO...
IS IT *THAT* TIME AGAIN, FRED?
YES, MARY... IT'S TIME FOR ANOTHER...

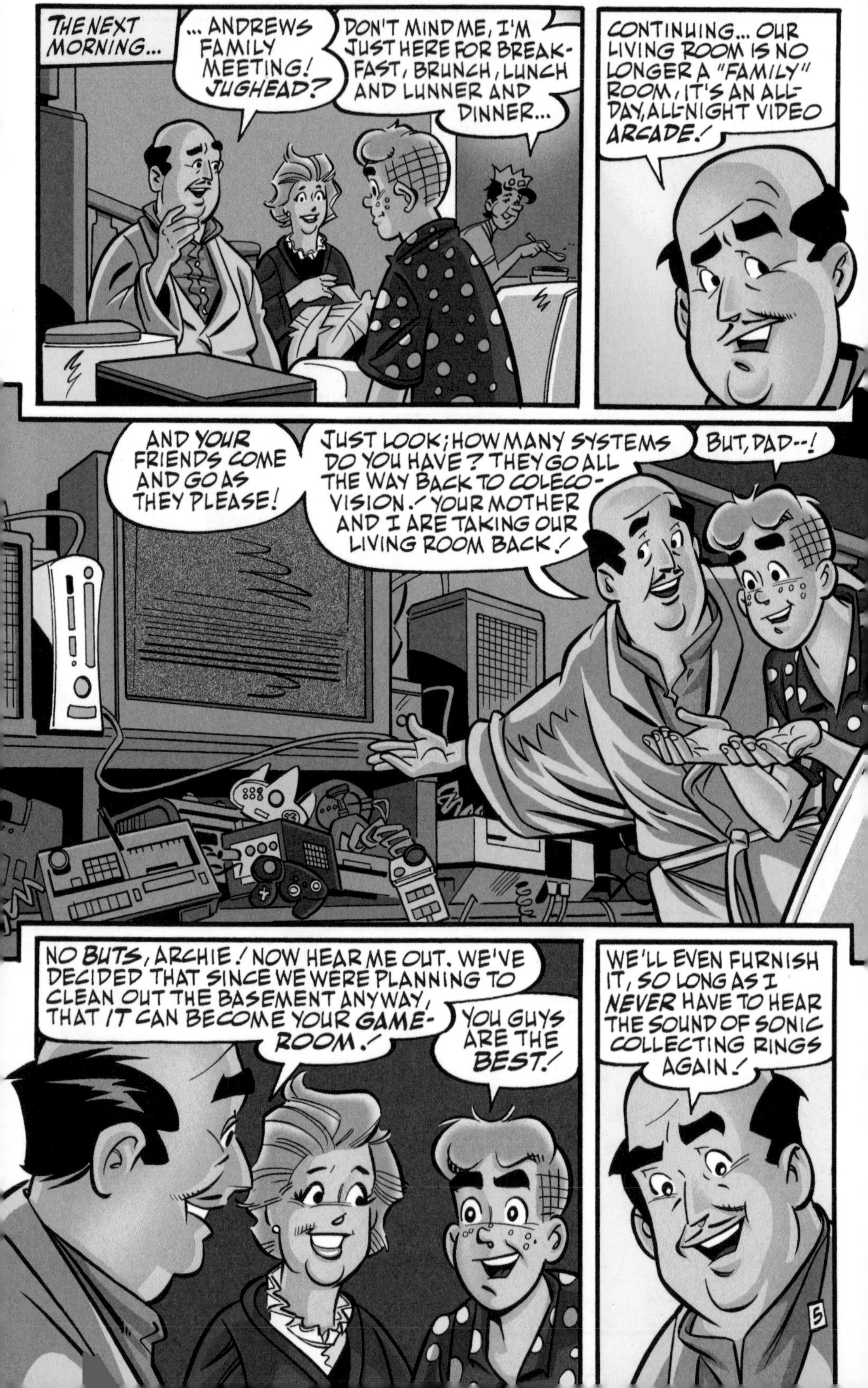
THE NEXT MORNING...
... ANDREWS FAMILY MEETING! JUGHEAD?
DON'T MIND ME, I'M JUST HERE FOR BREAK-FAST, BRUNCH, LUNCH AND LUNNER AND DINNER...
CONTINUING... OUR LIVING ROOM IS NO LONGER A "FAMILY" ROOM, IT'S AN ALL-DAY, ALL-NIGHT VIDEO ARCADE!
AND YOUR FRIENDS COME AND GO AS THEY PLEASE!
JUST LOOK; HOW MANY SYSTEMS DO YOU HAVE? THEY GO ALL THE WAY BACK TO COLECO-VISION! YOUR MOTHER AND I ARE TAKING OUR LIVING ROOM BACK!
BUT, DAD--!
NO BUTS, ARCHIE! NOW HEAR ME OUT. WE'VE DECIDED THAT SINCE WE WERE PLANNING TO CLEAN OUT THE BASEMENT ANYWAY, THAT IT CAN BECOME YOUR GAME-ROOM!
YOU GUYS ARE THE BEST!
WE'LL EVEN FURNISH IT, SO LONG AS I NEVER HAVE TO HEAR THE SOUND OF SONIC COLLECTING RINGS AGAIN!
5

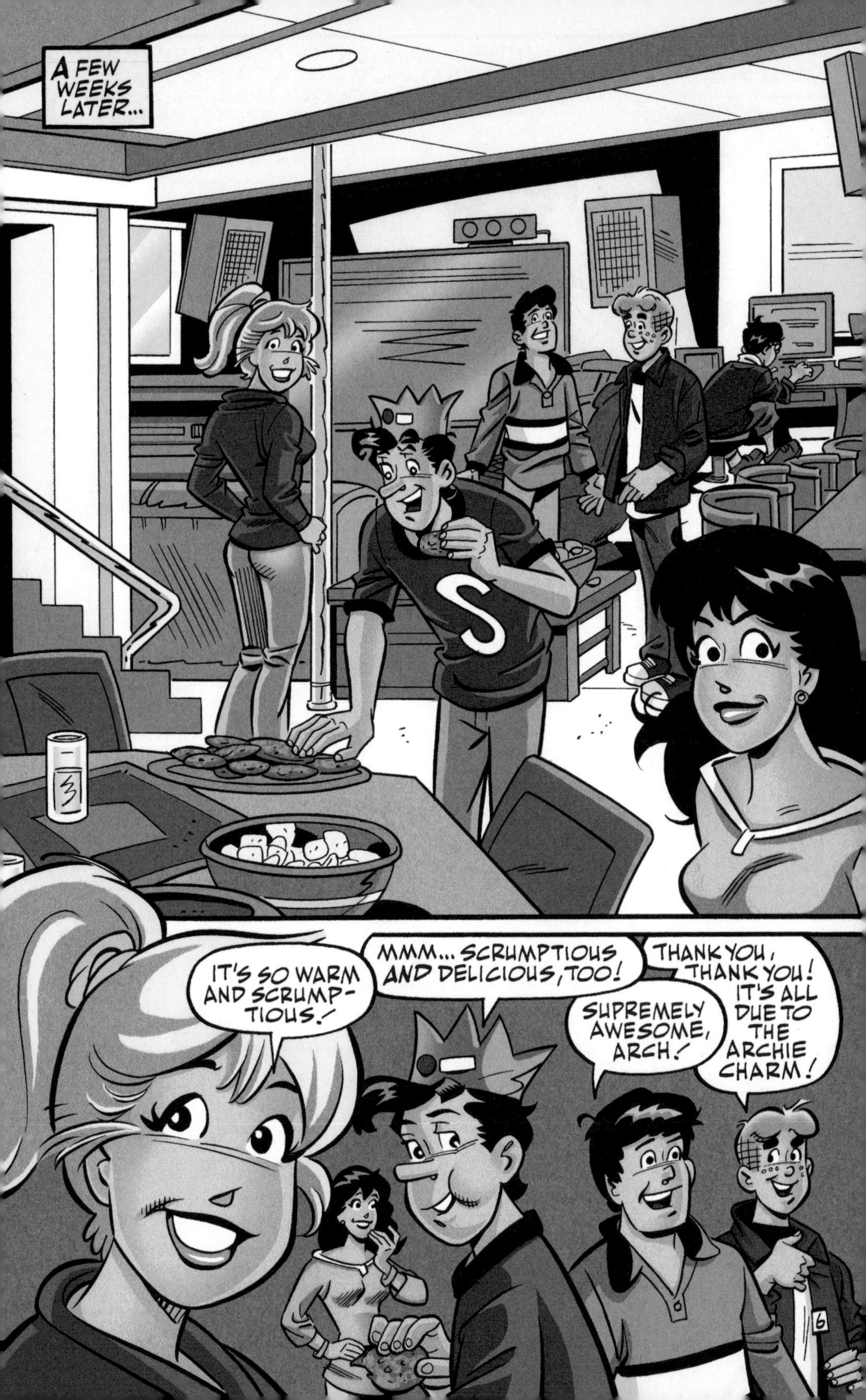
A FEW WEEKS LATER...
IT'S SO WARM AND SCRUMPTIOUS!
MMM... SCRUMPTIOUS AND DELICIOUS, TOO!
SUPREMELY AWESOME, ARCH!
THANK YOU, THANK YOU! IT'S ALL DUE TO THE ARCHIE CHARM!

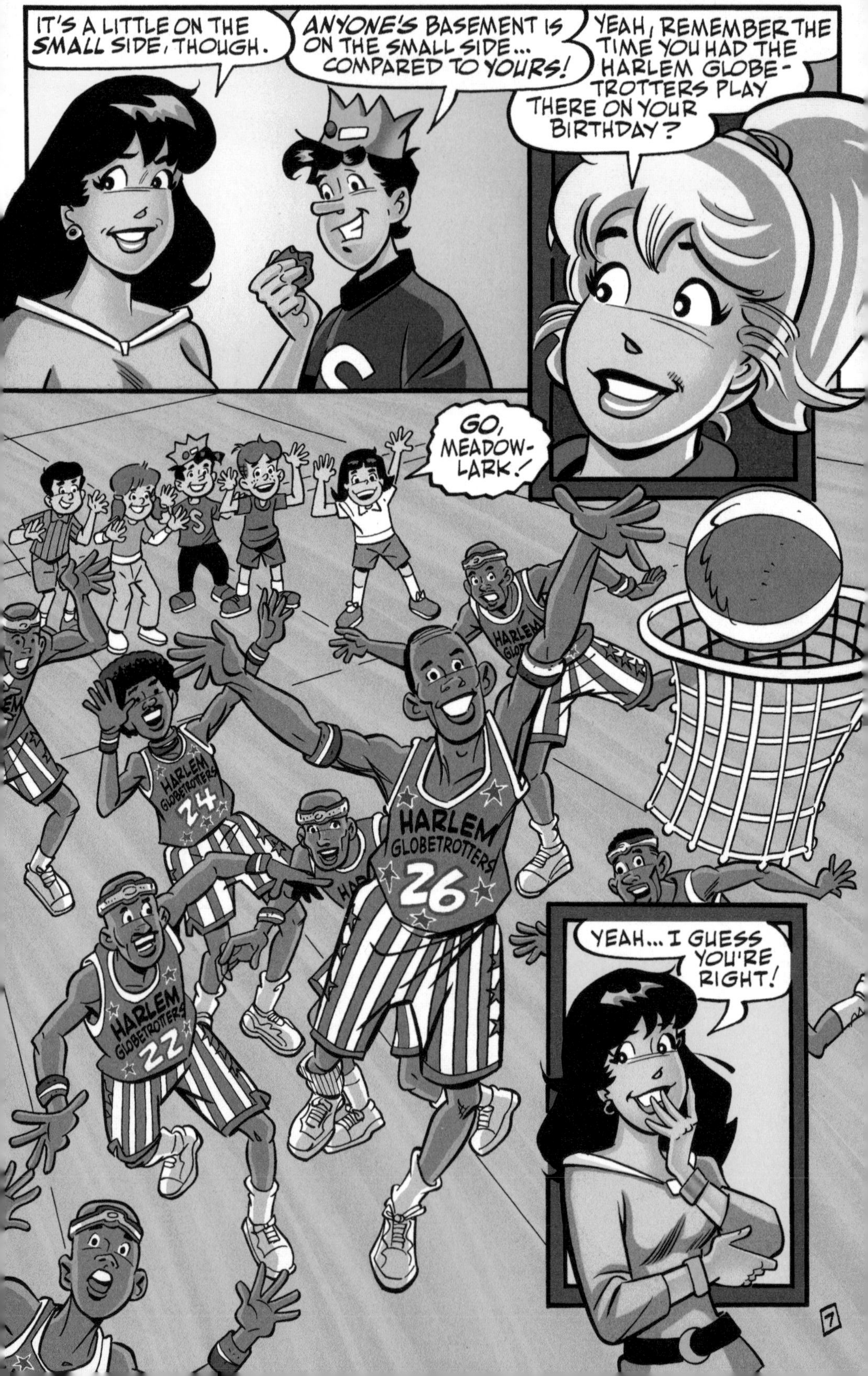
IT'S A LITTLE ON THE SMALL SIDE, THOUGH.
ANYONE'S BASEMENT IS ON THE SMALL SIDE... COMPARED TO YOURS!
YEAH, REMEMBER THE TIME YOU HAD THE HARLEM GLOBE-TROTTERS PLAY THERE ON YOUR BIRTHDAY?
GO, MEADOW-LARK!
HARLEM GLOBETROTTERS 26
HARLEM GLOBETROTTERS 24
HARLEM GLOBETROTTERS 22
YEAH... I GUESS YOU'RE RIGHT!

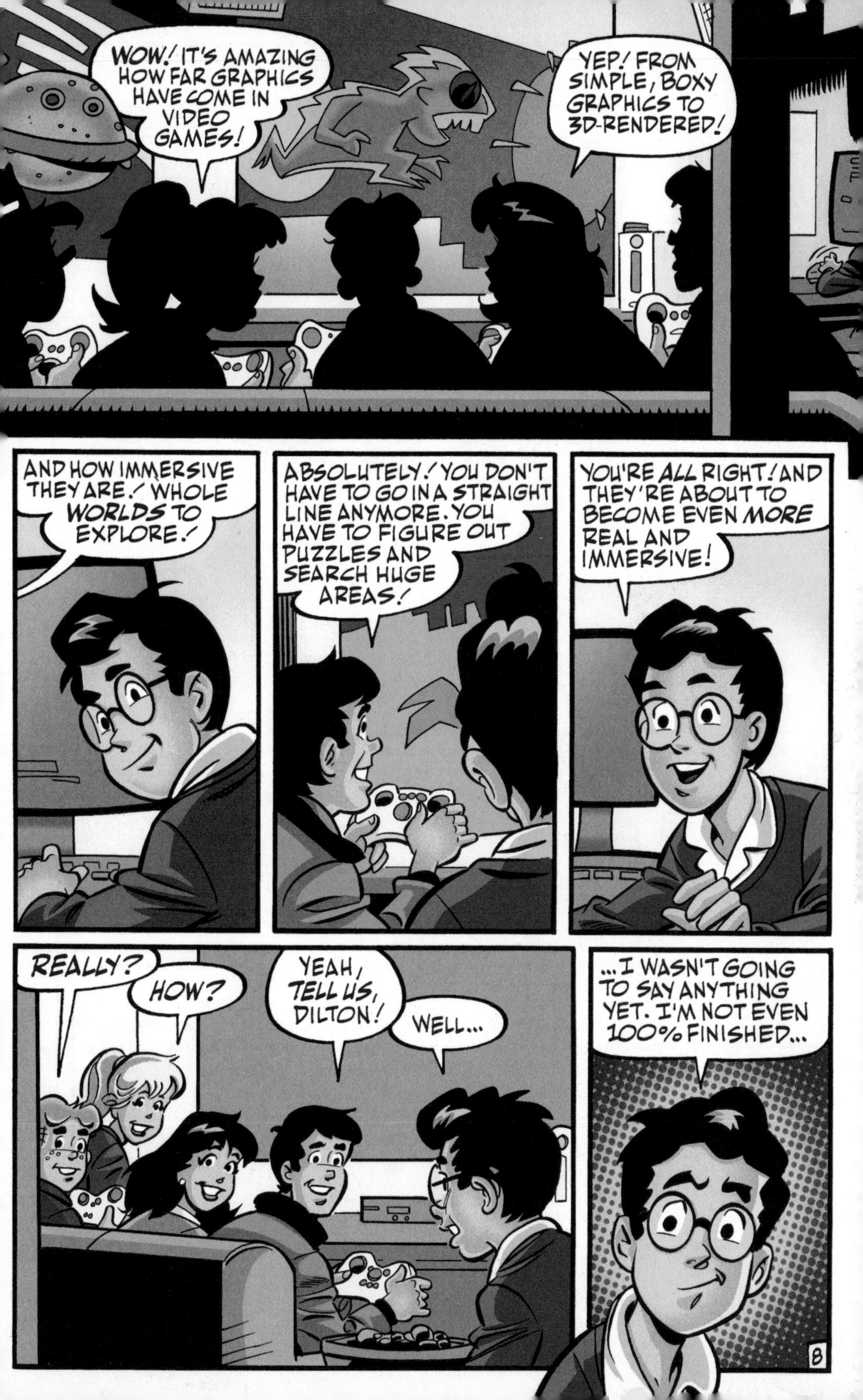
WOW! IT'S AMAZING HOW FAR GRAPHICS HAVE COME IN VIDEO GAMES!
YEP! FROM SIMPLE, BOXY GRAPHICS TO 3D-RENDERED!
AND HOW IMMERSIVE THEY ARE! WHOLE WORLDS TO EXPLORE!
ABSOLUTELY! YOU DON'T HAVE TO GO IN A STRAIGHT LINE ANYMORE. YOU HAVE TO FIGURE OUT PUZZLES AND SEARCH HUGE AREAS!
YOU'RE ALL RIGHT! AND THEY'RE ABOUT TO BECOME EVEN MORE REAL AND IMMERSIVE!
REALLY?
HOW?
YEAH, TELL US, DILTON!
WELL...
...I WASN'T GOING TO SAY ANYTHING YET. I'M NOT EVEN 100% FINISHED...

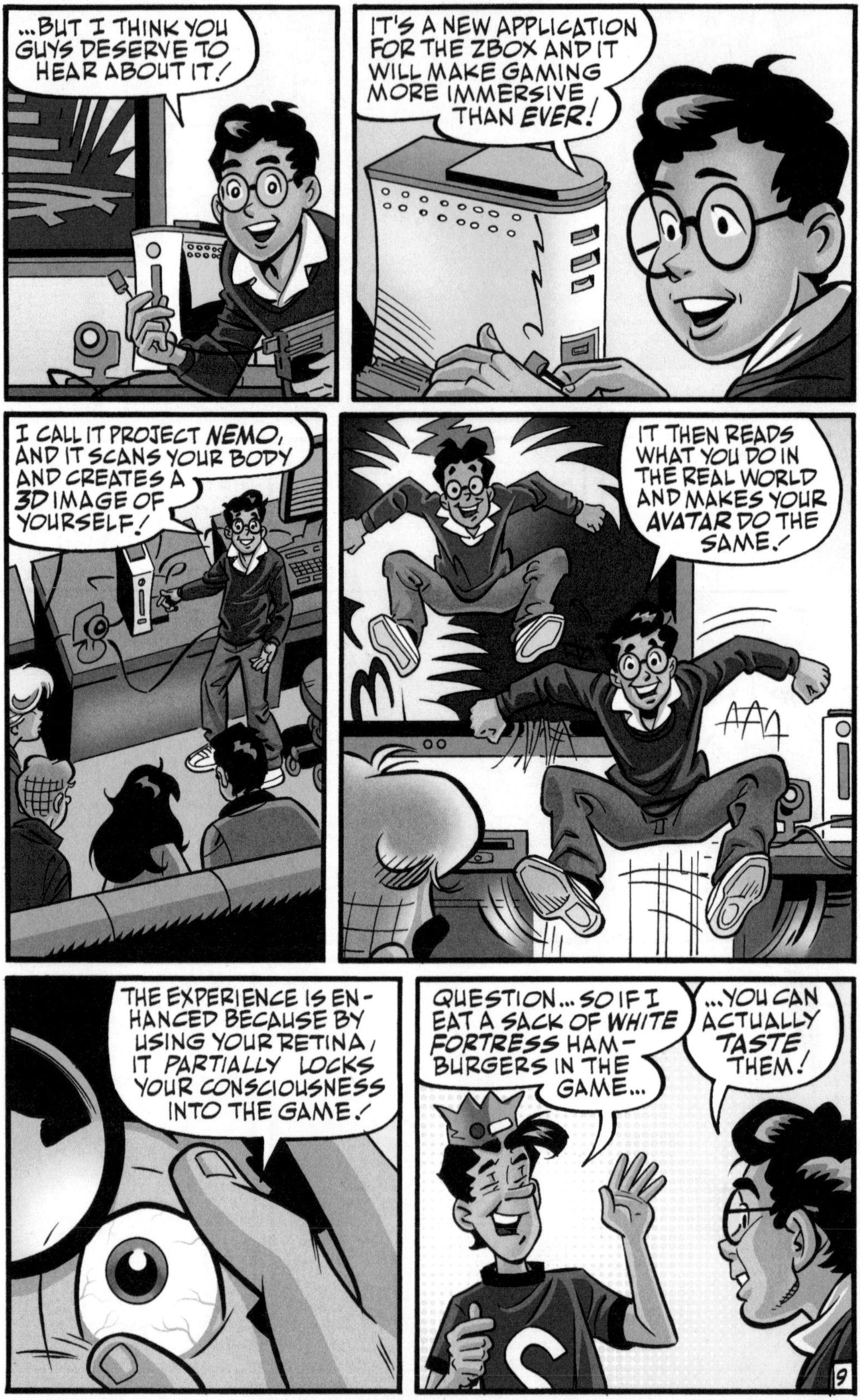
...BUT I THINK YOU GUYS DESERVE TO HEAR ABOUT IT!
IT'S A NEW APPLICATION FOR THE ZBOX AND IT WILL MAKE GAMING MORE IMMERSIVE THAN EVER!
I CALL IT PROJECT NEMO, AND IT SCANS YOUR BODY AND CREATES A 3D IMAGE OF YOURSELF!
IT THEN READS WHAT YOU DO IN THE REAL WORLD AND MAKES YOUR AVATAR DO THE SAME!
THE EXPERIENCE IS EN-HANCED BECAUSE BY USING YOUR RETINA, IT PARTIALLY LOCKS YOUR CONSCIOUSNESS INTO THE GAME!
QUESTION... SO IF I EAT A SACK OF WHITE FORTRESS HAM-BURGERS IN THE GAME...
...YOU CAN ACTUALLY TASTE THEM!
9

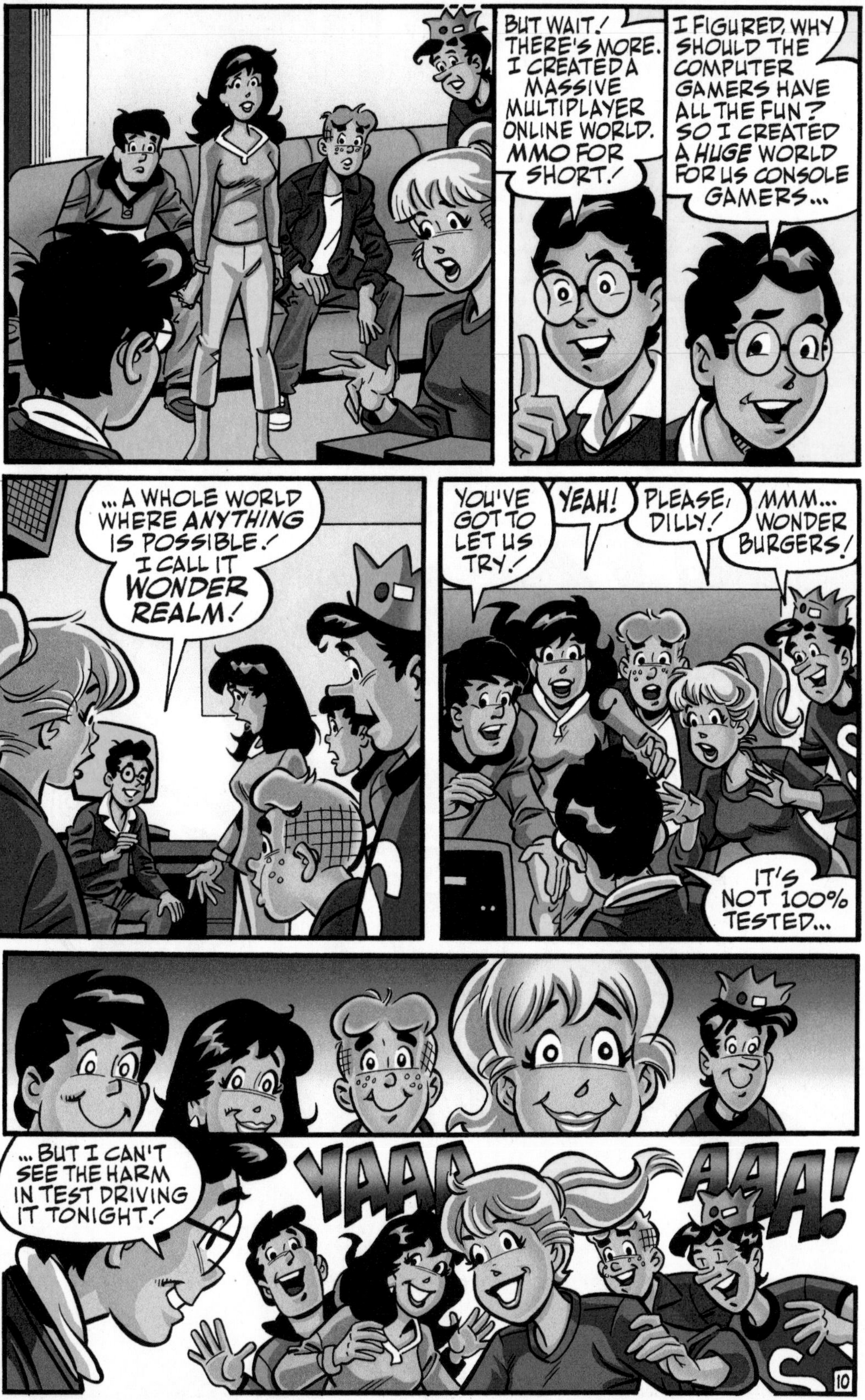

BUT WAIT! THERE'S MORE. I CREATED A MASSIVE MULTIPLAYER ONLINE WORLD. MMO FOR SHORT!
I FIGURED, WHY SHOULD THE COMPUTER GAMERS HAVE ALL THE FUN? SO I CREATED A HUGE WORLD FOR US CONSOLE GAMERS...
...A WHOLE WORLD WHERE ANYTHING IS POSSIBLE! I CALL IT WONDER REALM!
YOU'VE GOT TO LET US TRY!
YEAH!
PLEASE, DILLY!
MMM... WONDER BURGERS!
IT'S NOT 100% TESTED...
...BUT I CAN'T SEE THE HARM IN TEST DRIVING IT TONIGHT!
YAAAAAA!

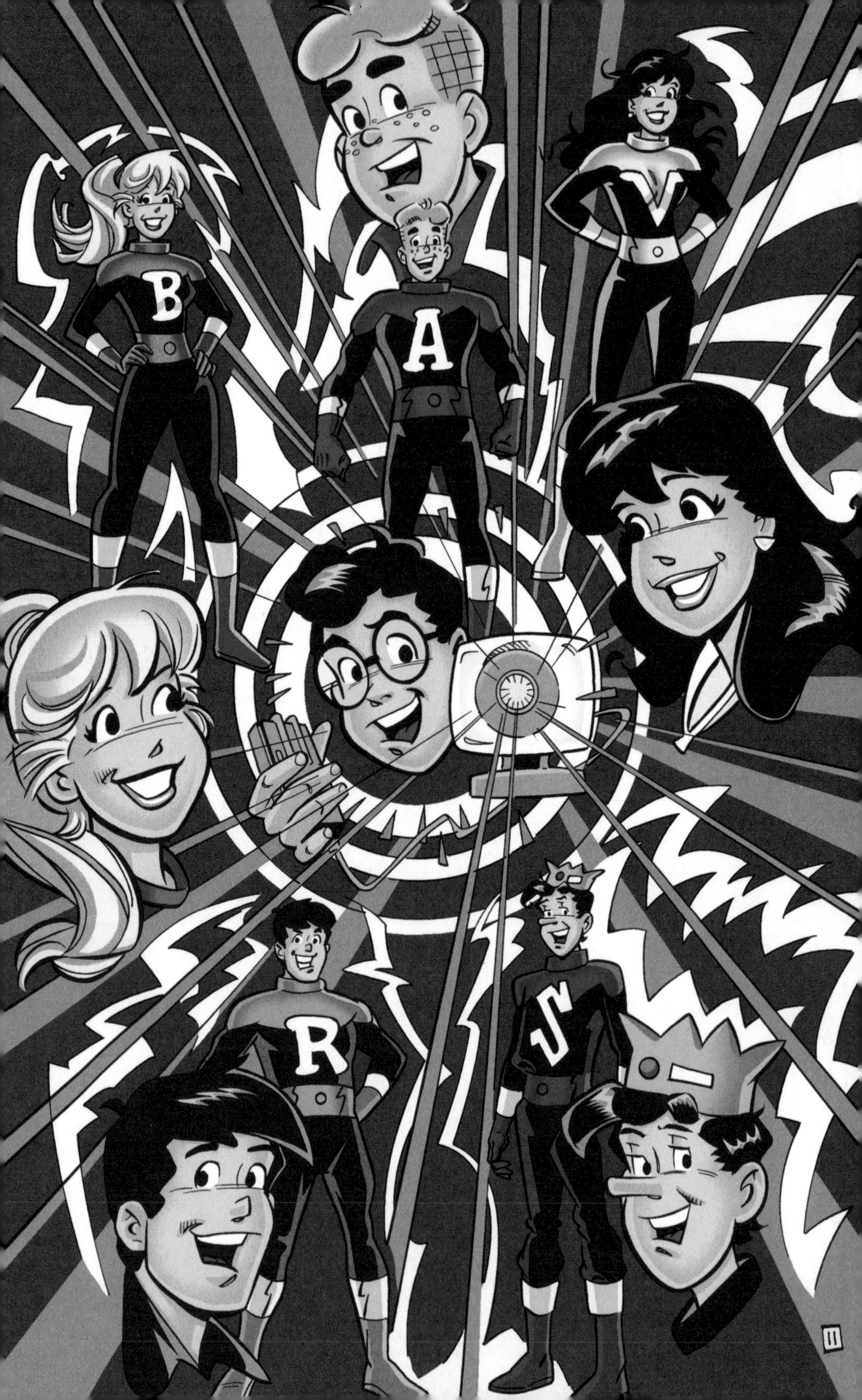

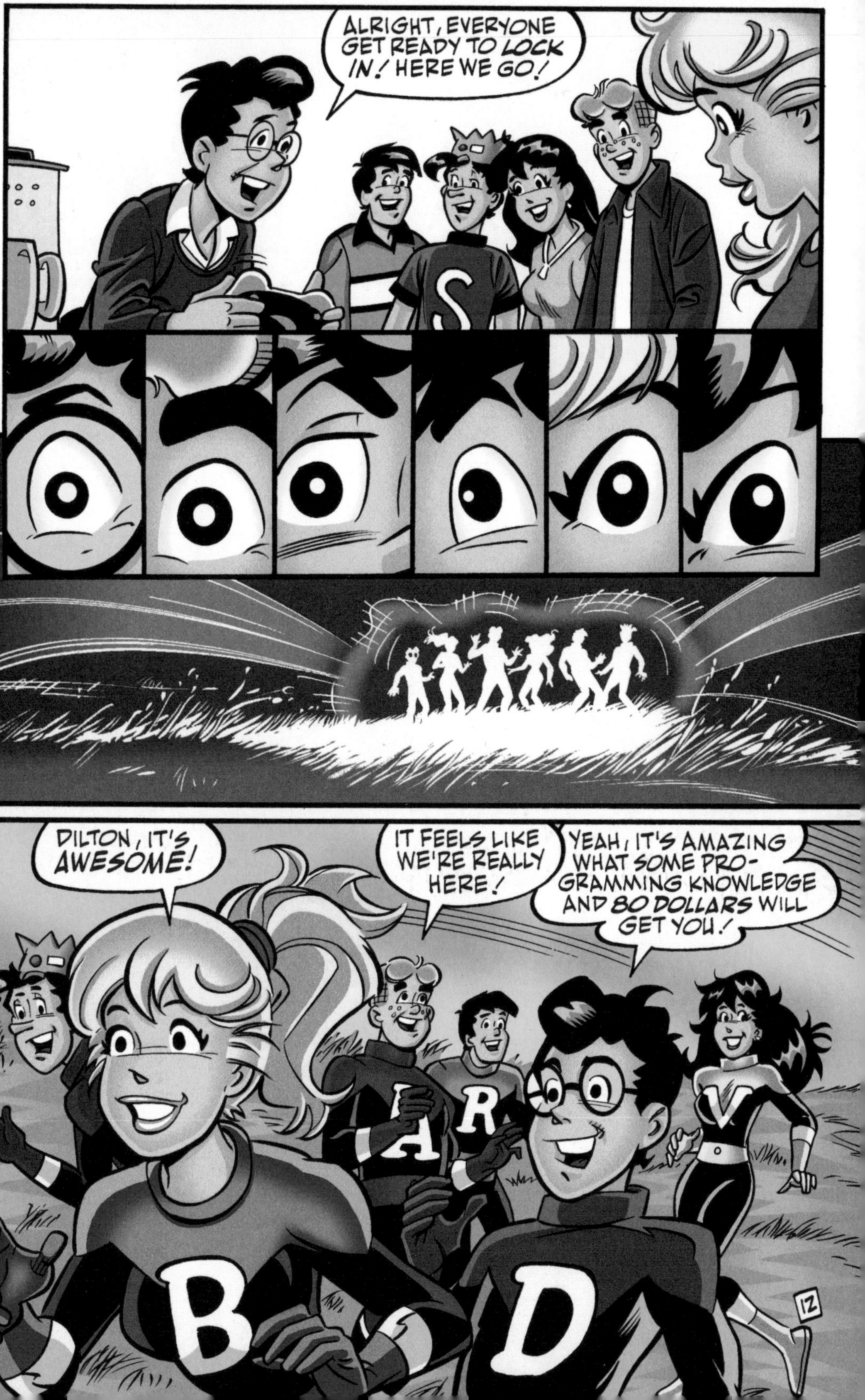
ALRIGHT, EVERYONE GET READY TO LOCK IN! HERE WE GO!
DILTON, IT'S AWESOME!
IT FEELS LIKE WE'RE REALLY HERE!
YEAH, IT'S AMAZING WHAT SOME PRO-GRAMMING KNOWLEDGE AND 80 DOLLARS WILL GET YOU!
12

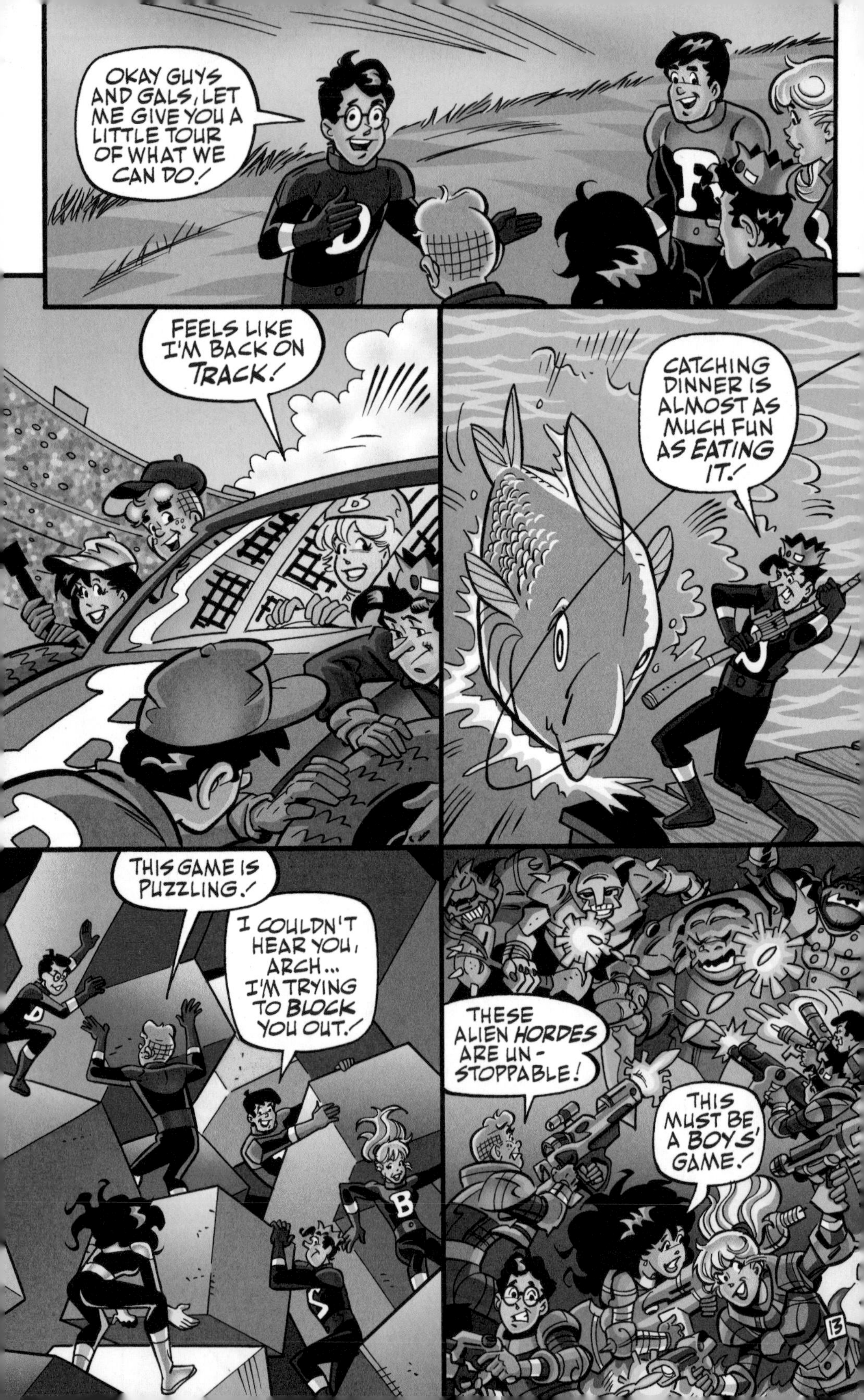
OKAY GUYS AND GALS, LET ME GIVE YOU A LITTLE TOUR OF WHAT WE CAN DO!
FEELS LIKE I'M BACK ON TRACK!
CATCHING DINNER IS ALMOST AS MUCH FUN AS EATING IT!
THIS GAME IS PUZZLING!
I COULDN'T HEAR YOU, ARCH... I'M TRYING TO BLOCK YOU OUT!
THESE ALIEN HORDES ARE UN-STOPPABLE!
THIS MUST BE A BOYS' GAME!
13

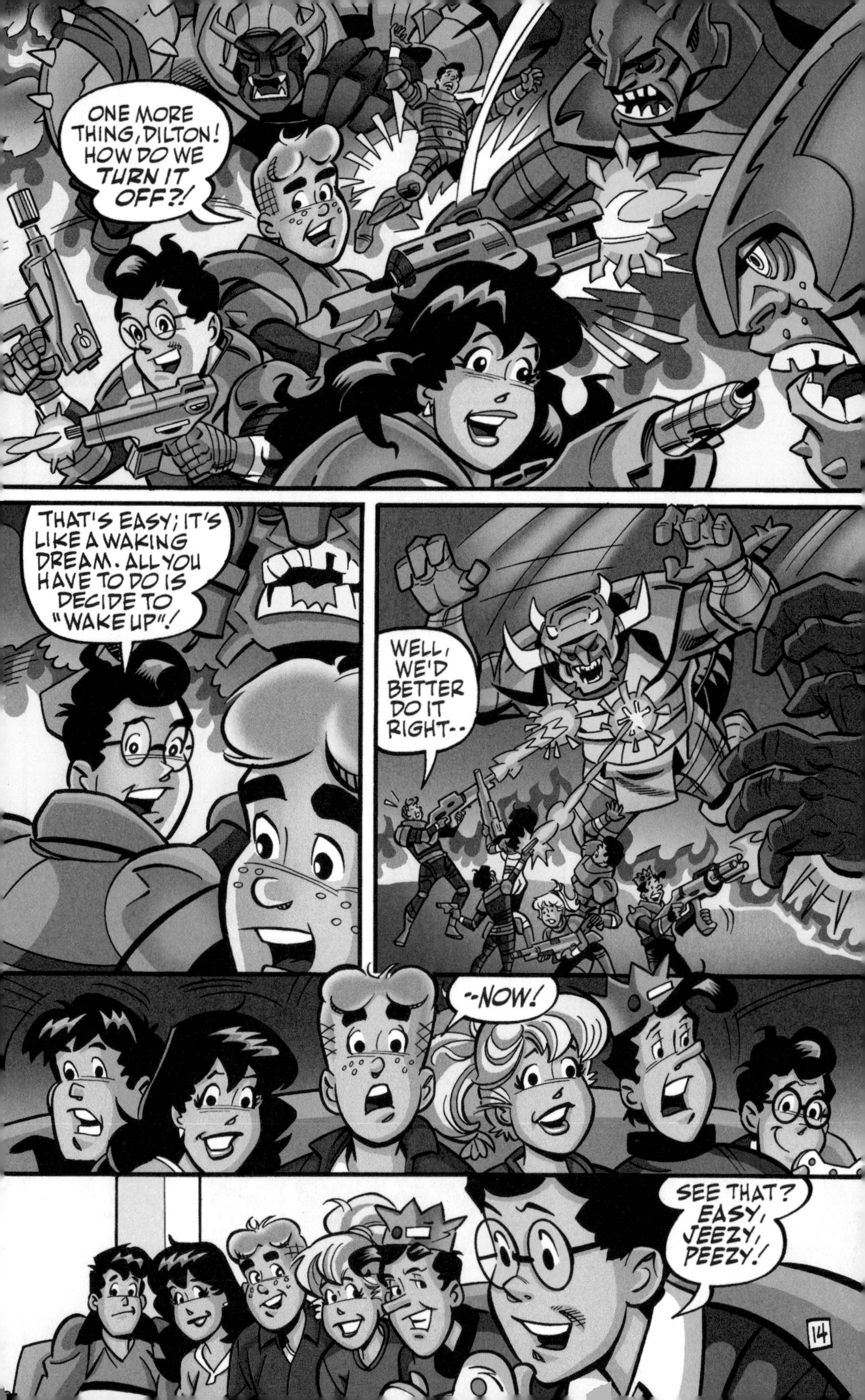

ONE MORE THING, DILTON! HOW DO WE TURN IT OFF?!
THAT'S EASY; IT'S LIKE A WAKING DREAM. ALL YOU HAVE TO DO IS DECIDE TO "WAKE UP"!
WELL, WE'D BETTER DO IT RIGHT--
--NOW!
SEE THAT? EASY, JEEZY, PEEZY!

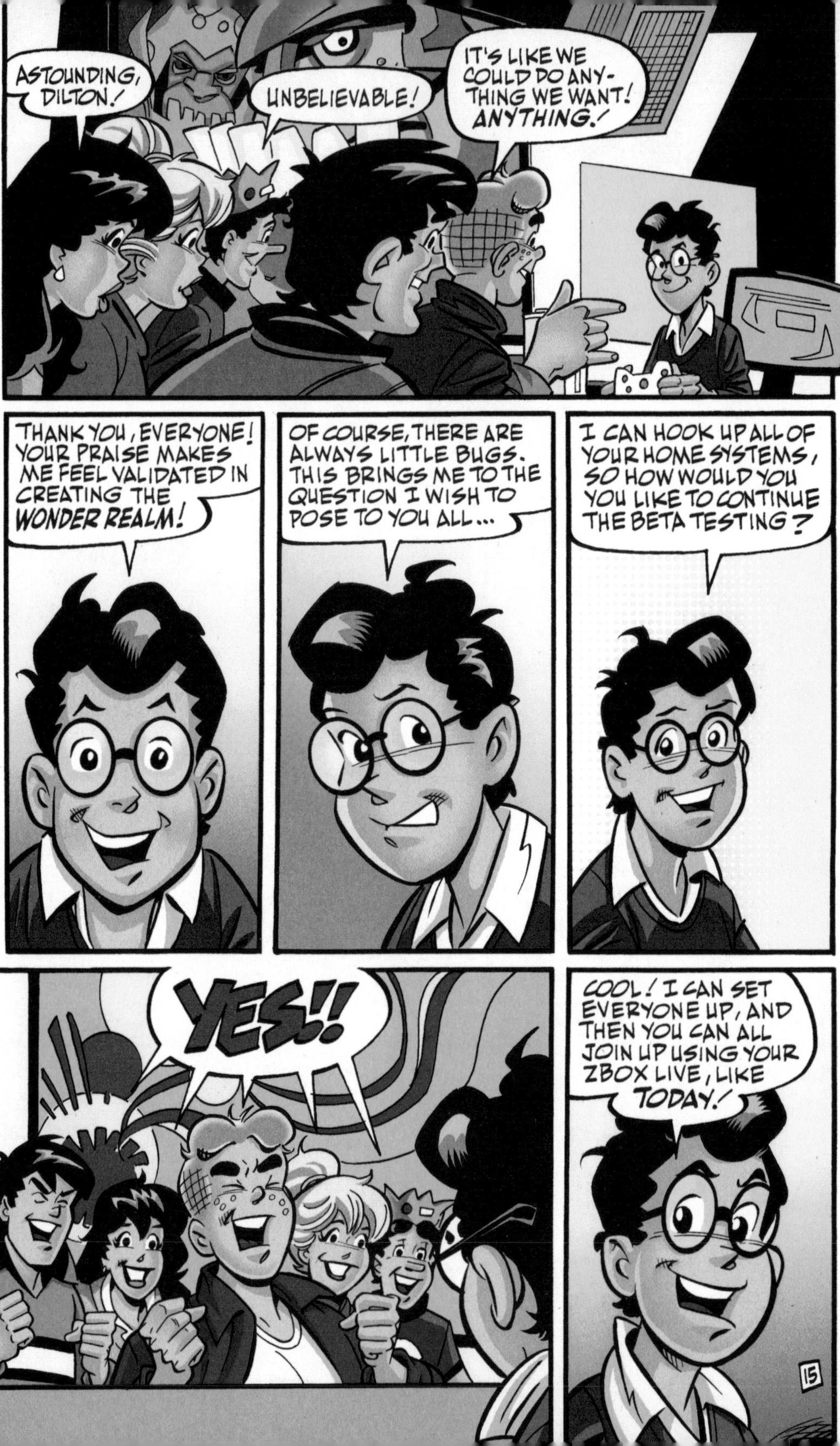
ASTOUNDING, DILTON!
UNBELIEVABLE!
IT'S LIKE WE COULD DO ANY-THING WE WANT! ANYTHING!
THANK YOU, EVERYONE! YOUR PRAISE MAKES ME FEEL VALIDATED IN CREATING THE WONDER REALM!
OF COURSE, THERE ARE ALWAYS LITTLE BUGS. THIS BRINGS ME TO THE QUESTION I WISH TO POSE TO YOU ALL...
I CAN HOOK UP ALL OF YOUR HOME SYSTEMS, SO HOW WOULD YOU YOU LIKE TO CONTINUE THE BETA TESTING?
YES!!
COOL! I CAN SET EVERYONE UP, AND THEN YOU CAN ALL JOIN UP USING YOUR ZBOX LIVE, LIKE TODAY!
15

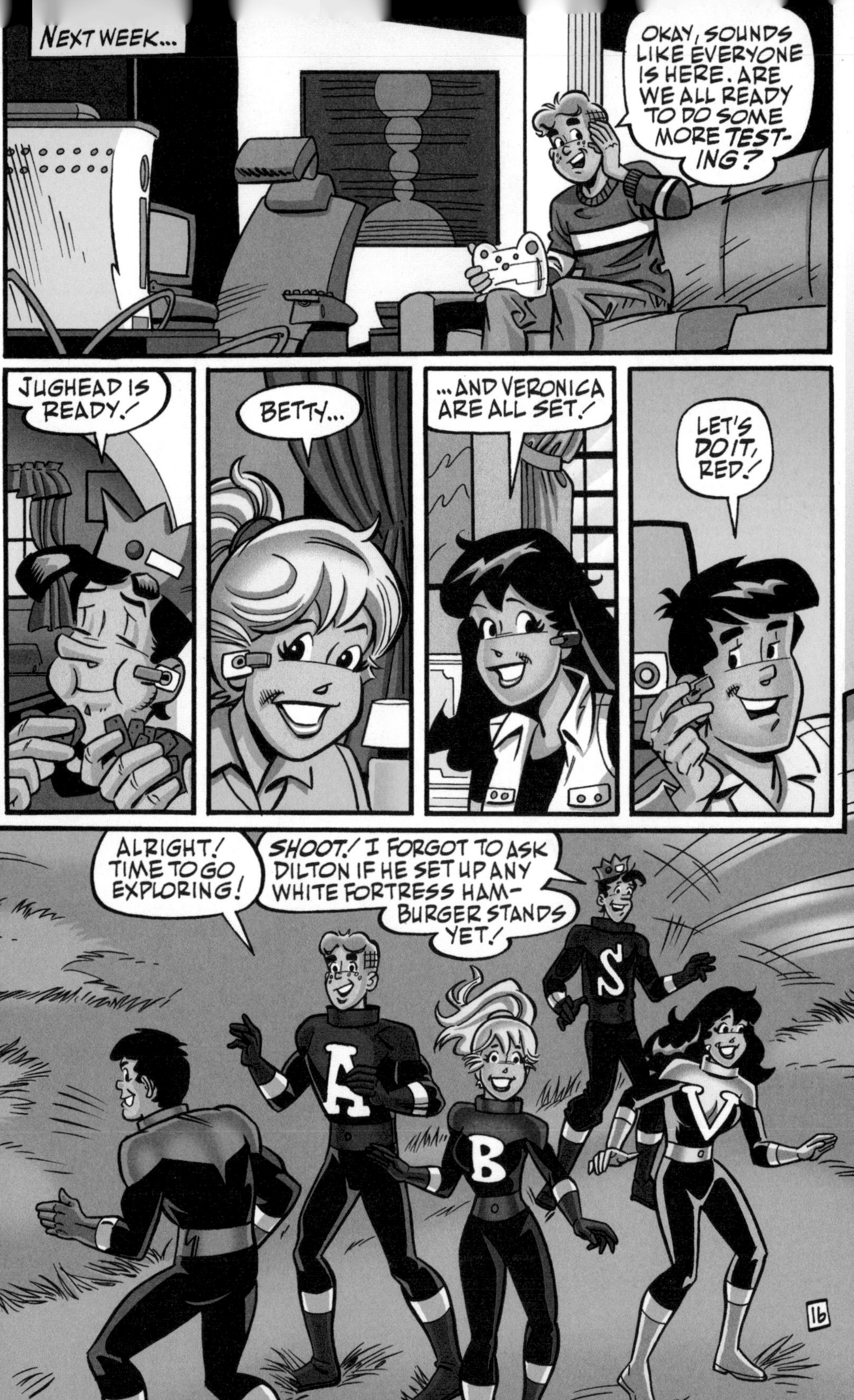
NEXT WEEK...
OKAY, SOUNDS LIKE EVERYONE IS HERE. ARE WE ALL READY TO DO SOME MORE TESTING?
JUGHEAD IS READY!
BETTY...
...AND VERONICA ARE ALL SET!
LET'S DO IT, RED!
ALRIGHT! TIME TO GO EXPLORING!
SHOOT! I FORGOT TO ASK DILTON IF HE SET UP ANY WHITE FORTRESS HAMBURGER STANDS YET!
16

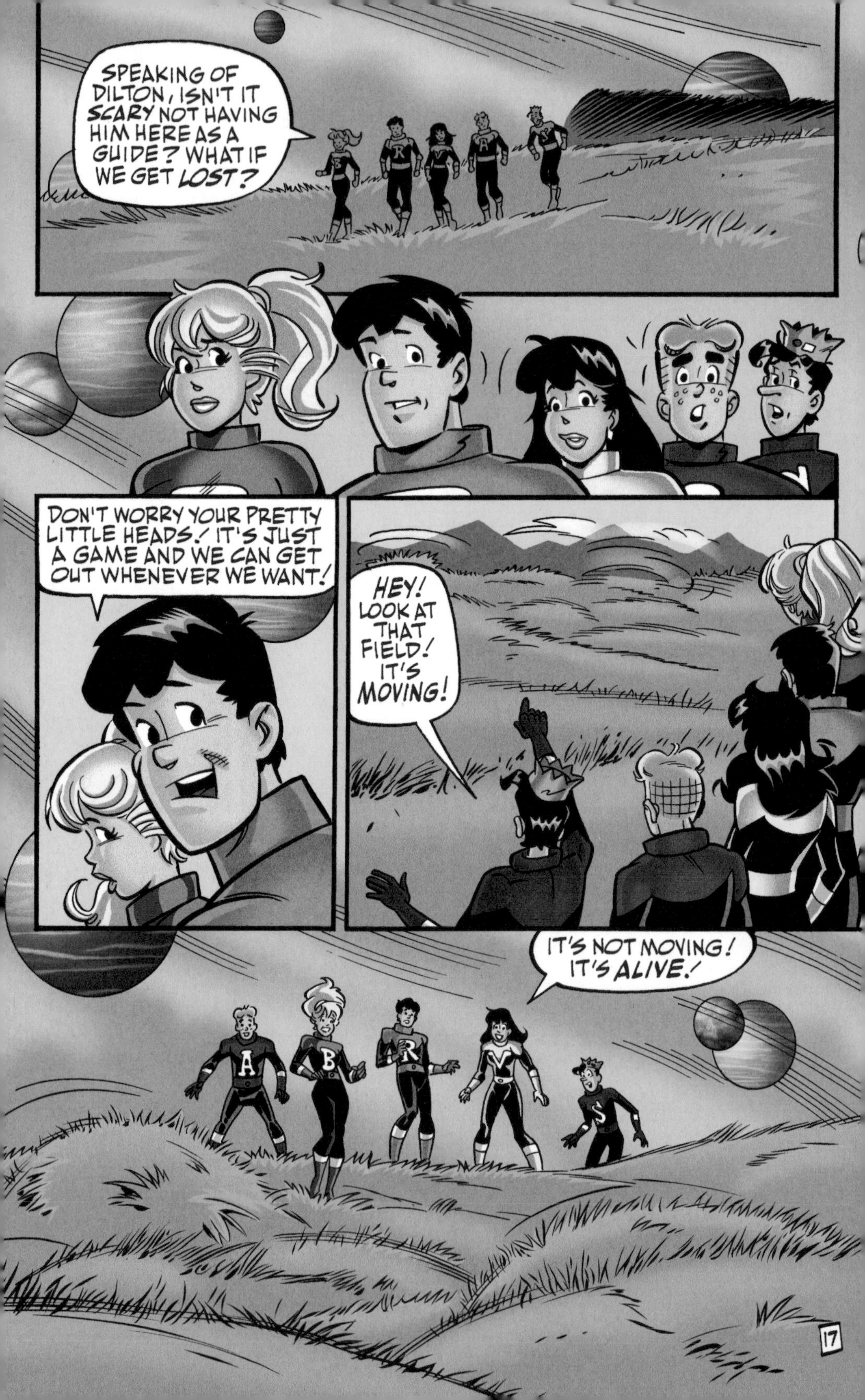
SPEAKING OF DILTON, ISN'T IT SCARY NOT HAVING HIM HERE AS A GUIDE? WHAT IF WE GET LOST?
DON'T WORRY YOUR PRETTY LITTLE HEADS! IT'S JUST A GAME AND WE CAN GET OUT WHENEVER WE WANT!
HEY! LOOK AT THAT FIELD! IT'S MOVING!
IT'S NOT MOVING! IT'S ALIVE!

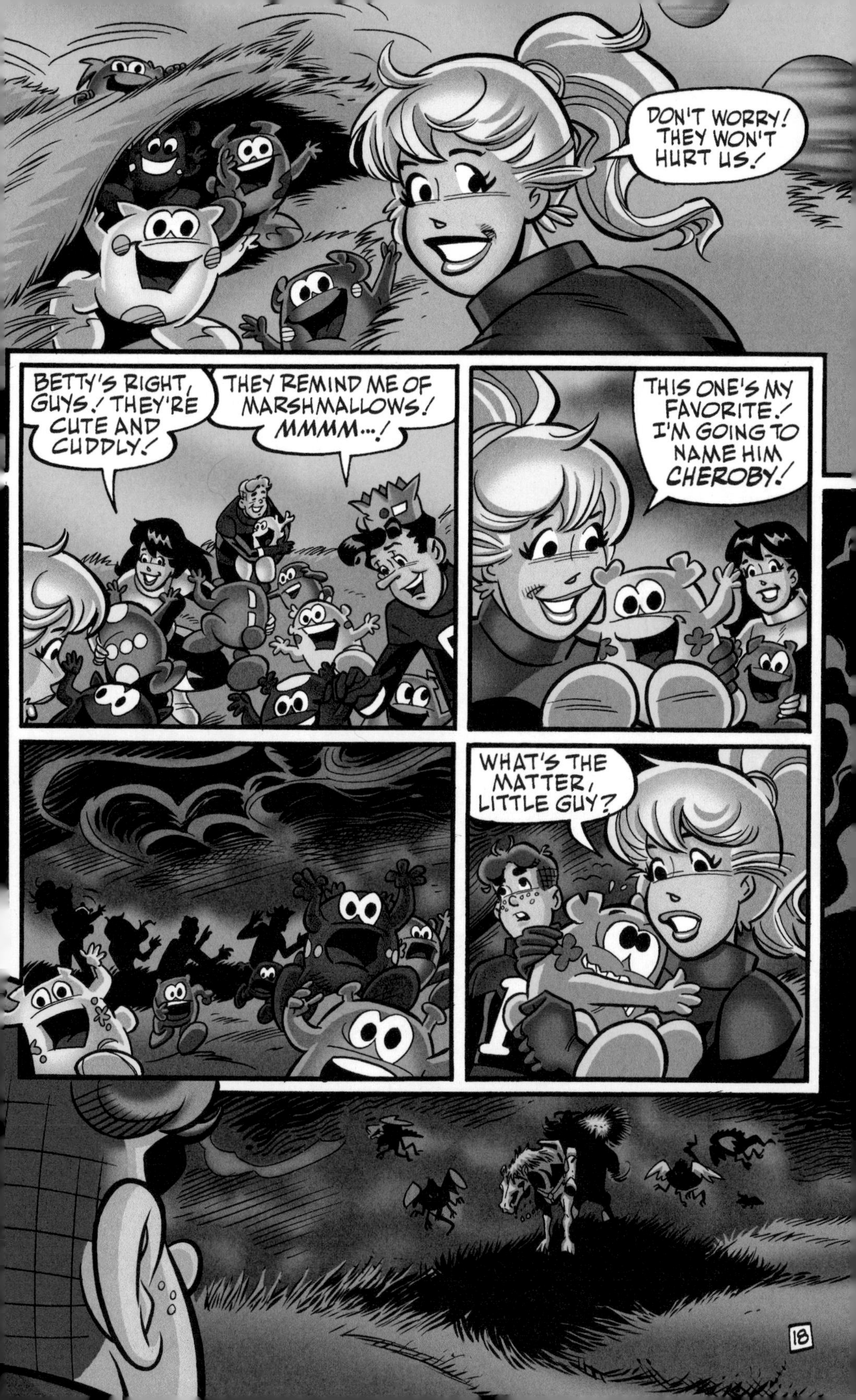
DON'T WORRY! THEY WON'T HURT US!
BETTY'S RIGHT, GUYS! THEY'RE CUTE AND CUDDLY!
THEY REMIND ME OF MARSHMALLOWS! MMMM...!
THIS ONE'S MY FAVORITE! I'M GOING TO NAME HIM CHEROBY!
WHAT'S THE MATTER, LITTLE GUY?

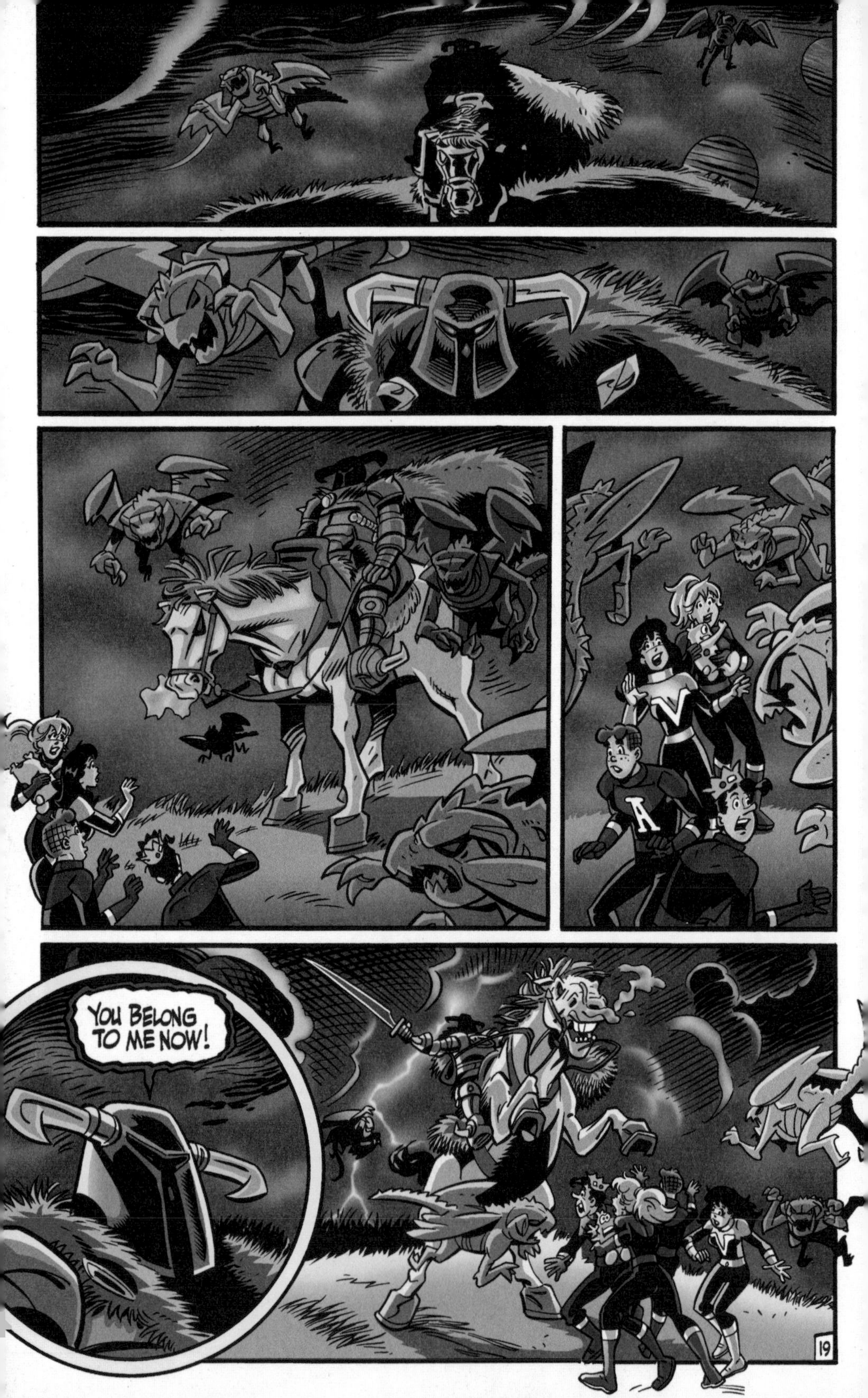
YOU BELONG TO ME NOW!

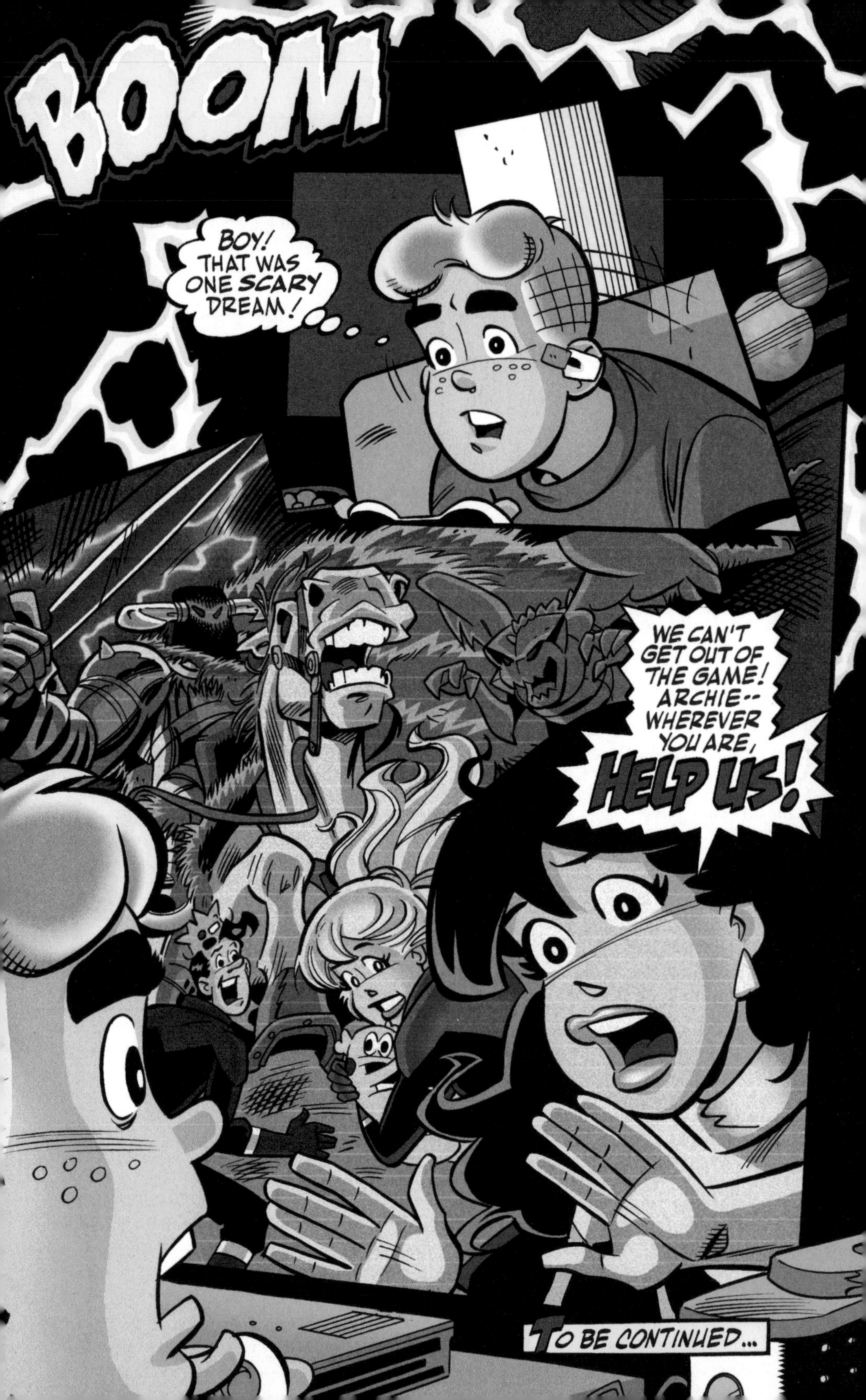
BOOM
BOY! THAT WAS ONE SCARY DREAM!
WE CAN'T GET OUT OF THE GAME! ARCHIE-- WHEREVER YOU ARE, HELP US!
TO BE CONTINUED...

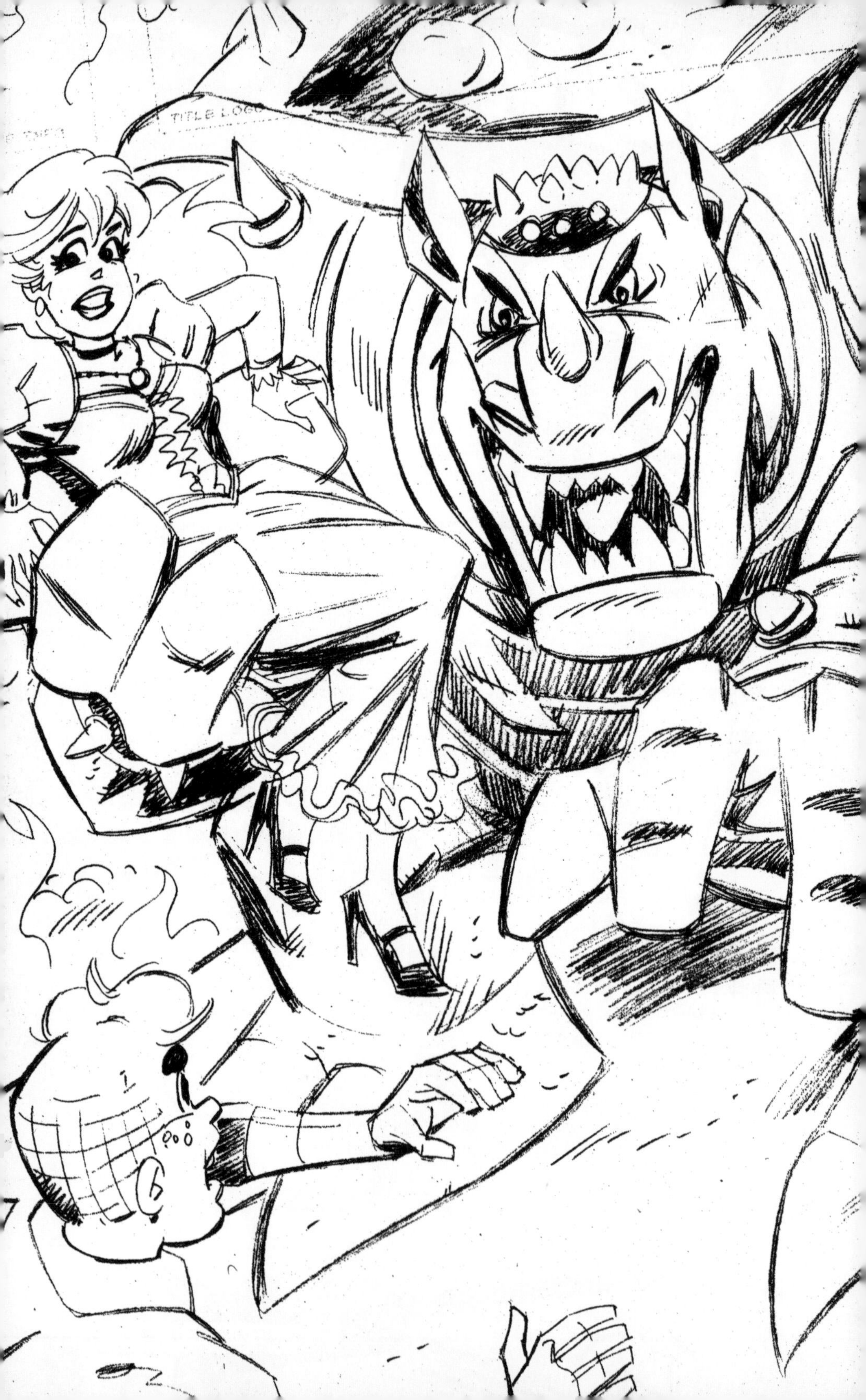
TITLE LOGO

CHAPTER TWO

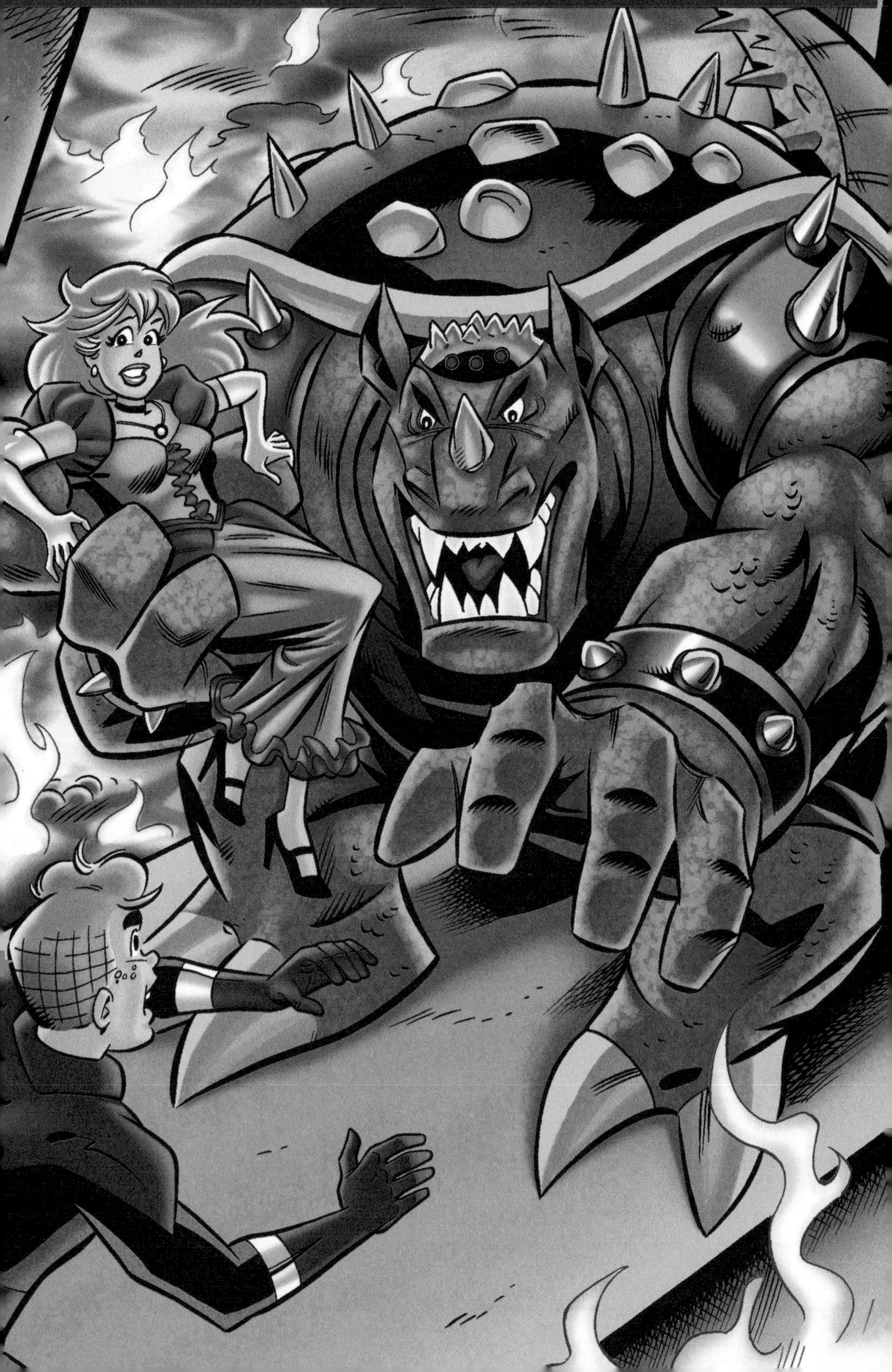

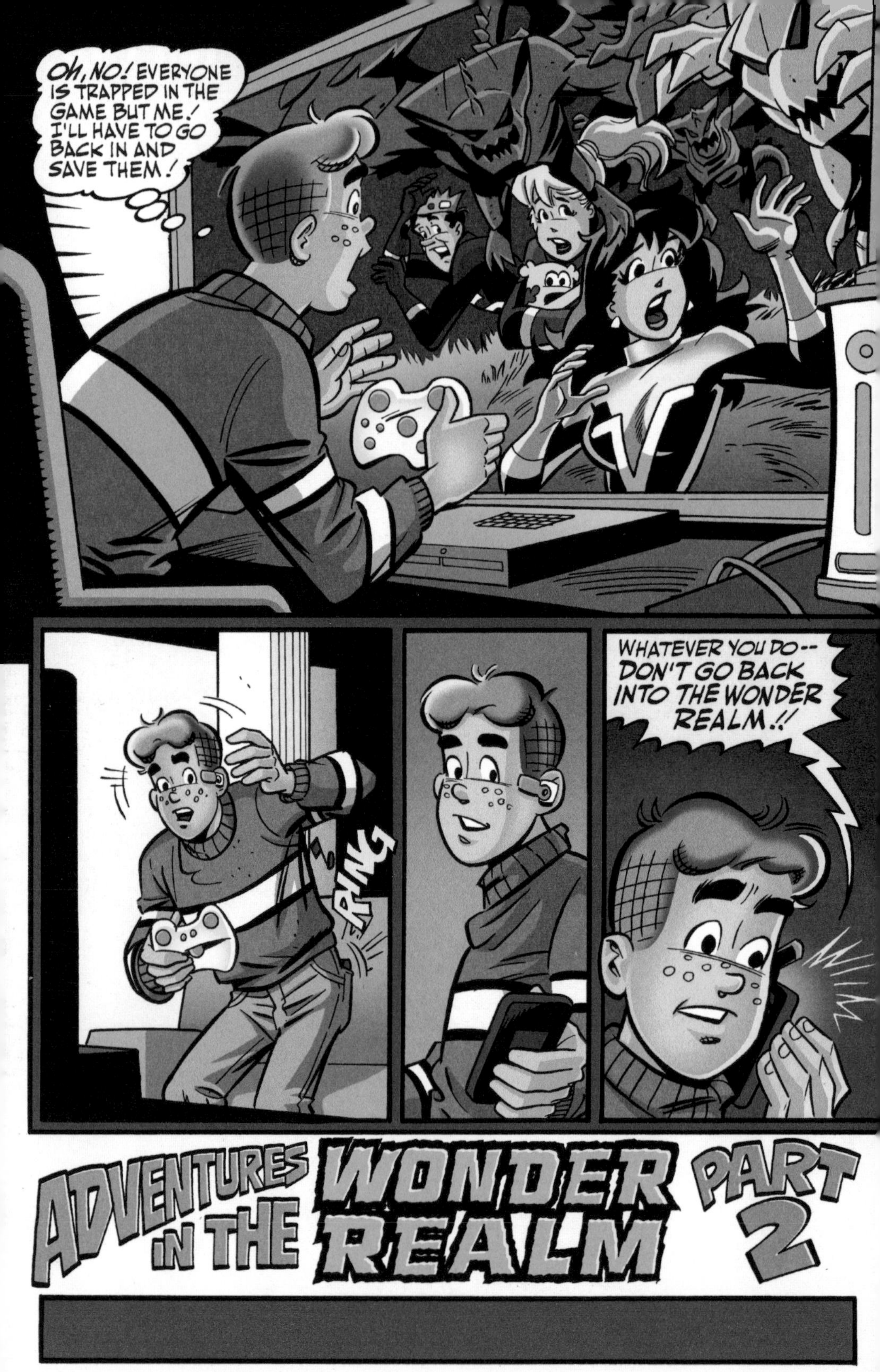
OH, NO! EVERYONE IS TRAPPED IN THE GAME BUT ME! I'LL HAVE TO GO BACK IN AND SAVE THEM!
RING
WHATEVER YOU DO-- DON'T GO BACK INTO THE WONDER REALM!!

ADVENTURES IN THE WONDER REALM PART 2

[redacted]

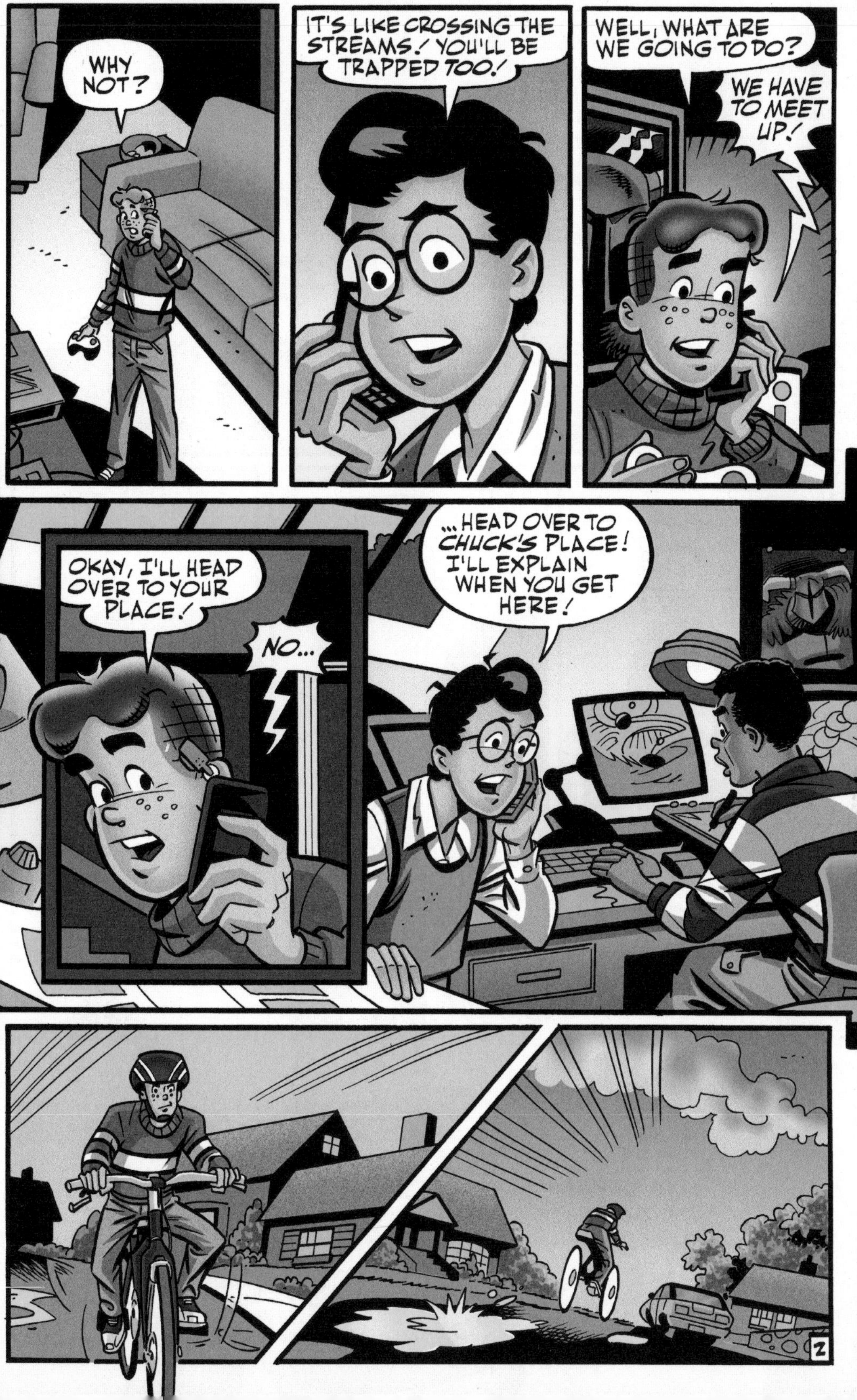
WHY NOT?
IT'S LIKE CROSSING THE STREAMS! YOU'LL BE TRAPPED TOO!
WELL, WHAT ARE WE GOING TO DO?
WE HAVE TO MEET UP!
OKAY, I'LL HEAD OVER TO YOUR PLACE!
NO...
...HEAD OVER TO CHUCK'S PLACE! I'LL EXPLAIN WHEN YOU GET HERE!
2

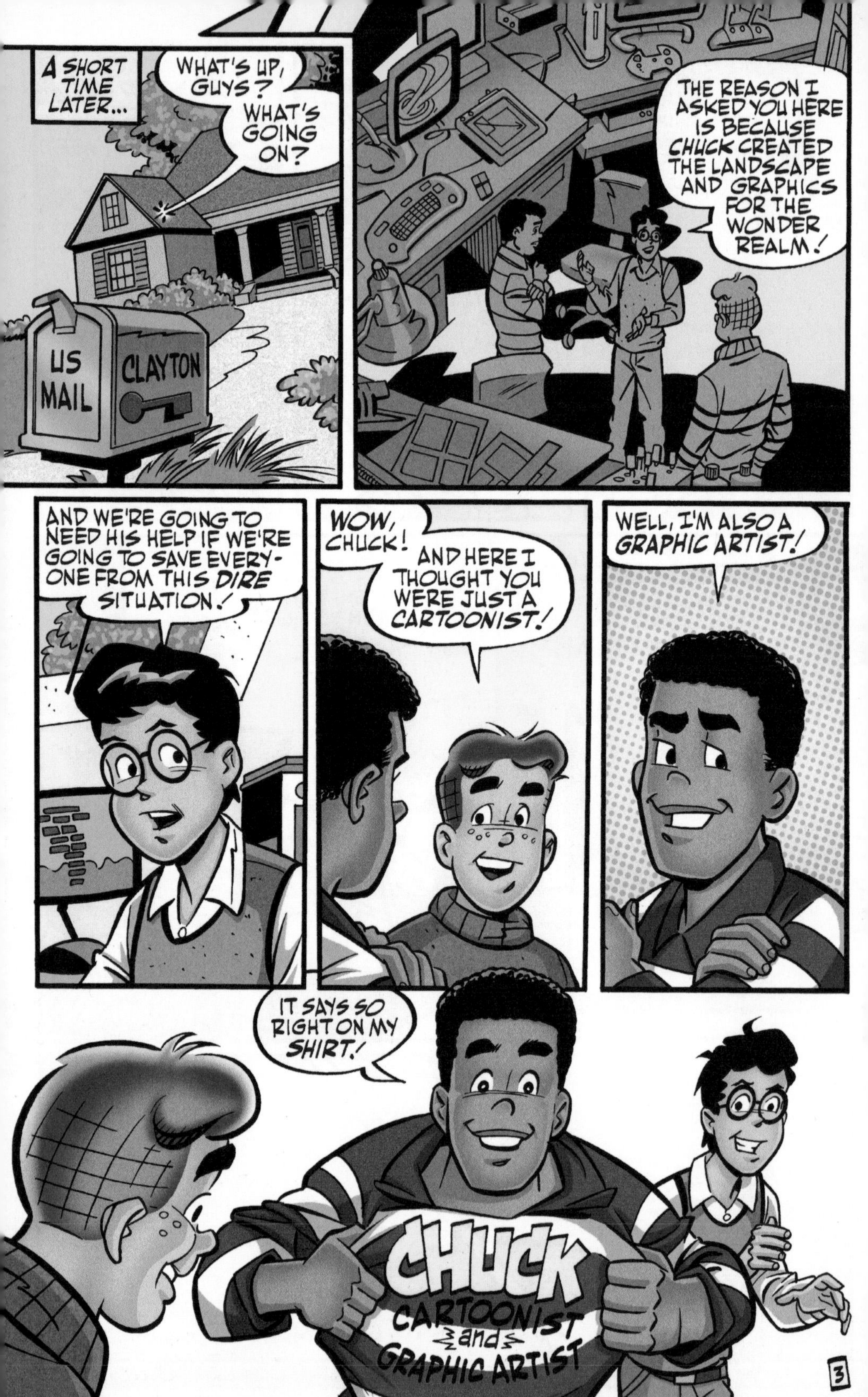
A SHORT TIME LATER...
WHAT'S UP, GUYS?
WHAT'S GOING ON?
US MAIL
CLAYTON
THE REASON I ASKED YOU HERE IS BECAUSE CHUCK CREATED THE LANDSCAPE AND GRAPHICS FOR THE WONDER REALM!
AND WE'RE GOING TO NEED HIS HELP IF WE'RE GOING TO SAVE EVERY-ONE FROM THIS DIRE SITUATION!
WOW, CHUCK!
AND HERE I THOUGHT YOU WERE JUST A CARTOONIST!
WELL, I'M ALSO A GRAPHIC ARTIST!
IT SAYS SO RIGHT ON MY SHIRT!
CHUCK
CARTOONIST and GRAPHIC ARTIST

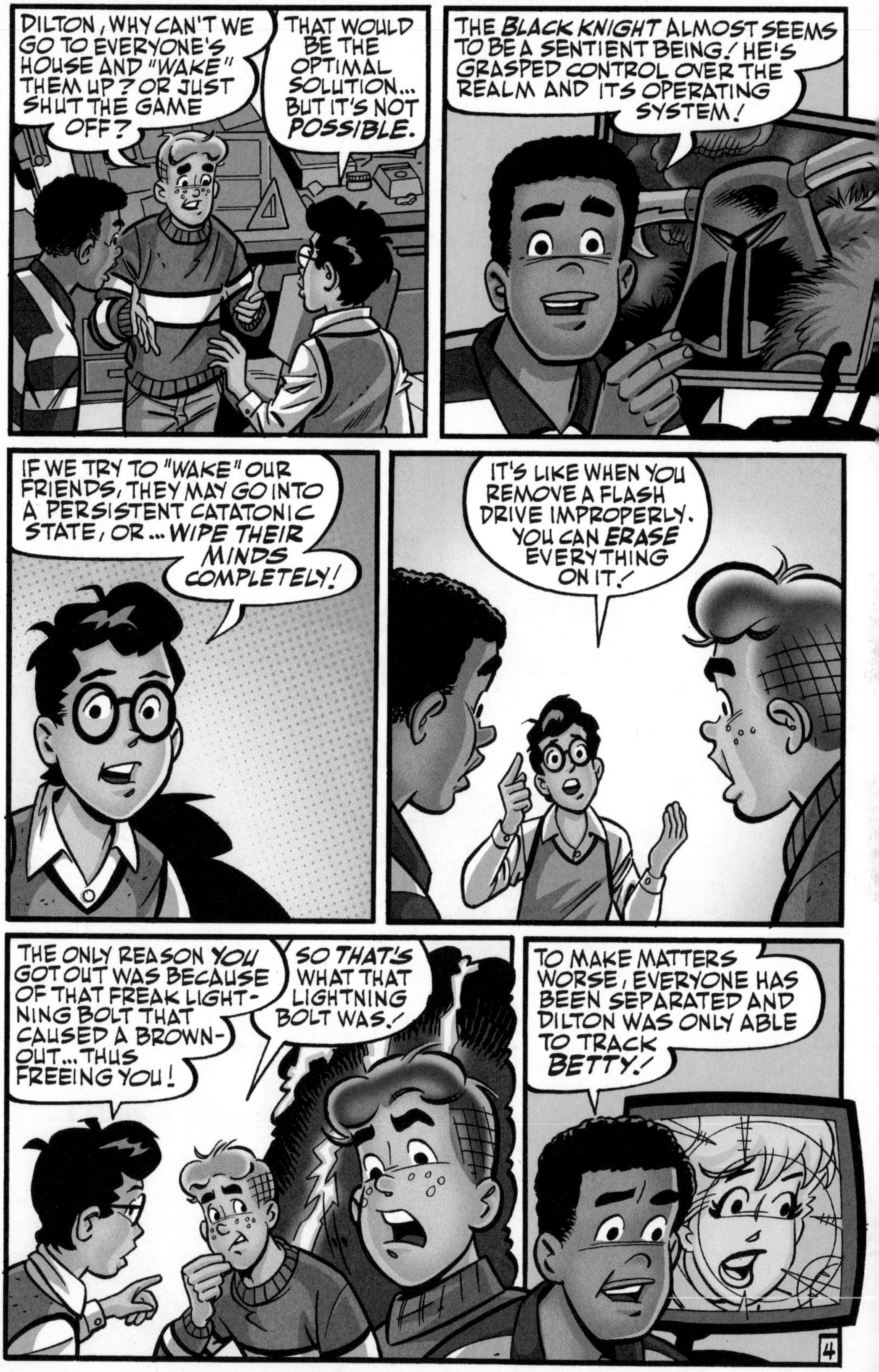
DILTON, WHY CAN'T WE GO TO EVERYONE'S HOUSE AND "WAKE" THEM UP? OR JUST SHUT THE GAME OFF?
THAT WOULD BE THE OPTIMAL SOLUTION... BUT IT'S NOT POSSIBLE.
THE BLACK KNIGHT ALMOST SEEMS TO BE A SENTIENT BEING! HE'S GRASPED CONTROL OVER THE REALM AND ITS OPERATING SYSTEM!
IF WE TRY TO "WAKE" OUR FRIENDS, THEY MAY GO INTO A PERSISTENT CATATONIC STATE, OR... WIPE THEIR MINDS COMPLETELY!
IT'S LIKE WHEN YOU REMOVE A FLASH DRIVE IMPROPERLY. YOU CAN ERASE EVERYTHING ON IT!
THE ONLY REASON YOU GOT OUT WAS BECAUSE OF THAT FREAK LIGHTNING BOLT THAT CAUSED A BROWN-OUT... THUS FREEING YOU!
SO THAT'S WHAT THAT LIGHTNING BOLT WAS!
TO MAKE MATTERS WORSE, EVERYONE HAS BEEN SEPARATED AND DILTON WAS ONLY ABLE TO TRACK BETTY!
4

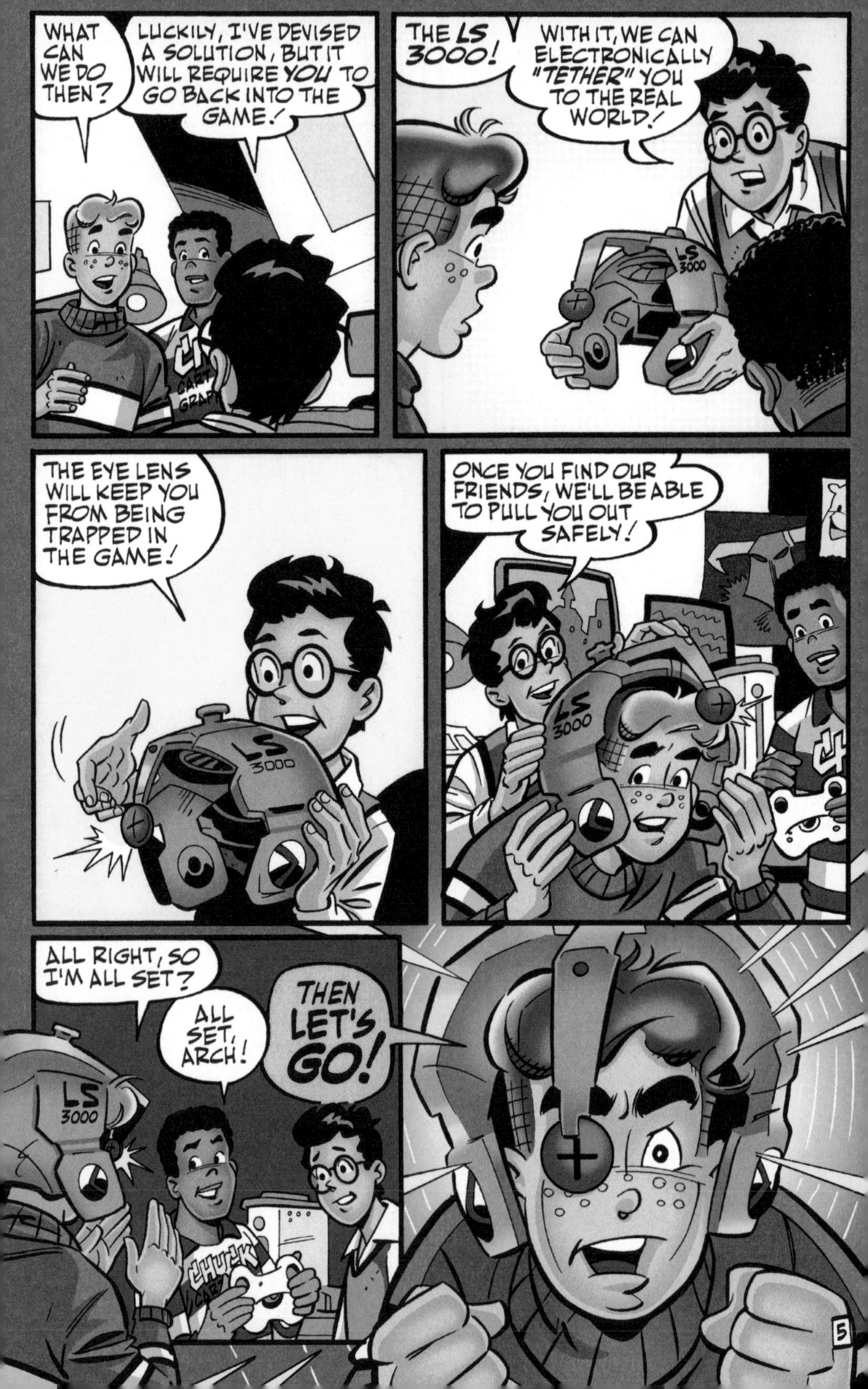
WHAT CAN WE DO THEN?
LUCKILY, I'VE DEVISED A SOLUTION, BUT IT WILL REQUIRE YOU TO GO BACK INTO THE GAME!
THE LS 3000!
WITH IT, WE CAN ELECTRONICALLY "TETHER" YOU TO THE REAL WORLD!
LS 3000
THE EYE LENS WILL KEEP YOU FROM BEING TRAPPED IN THE GAME!
LS 3000
ONCE YOU FIND OUR FRIENDS, WE'LL BE ABLE TO PULL YOU OUT SAFELY!
LS 3000
ALL RIGHT, SO I'M ALL SET?
ALL SET, ARCH!
THEN LET'S GO!
LS 3000
CHUCK

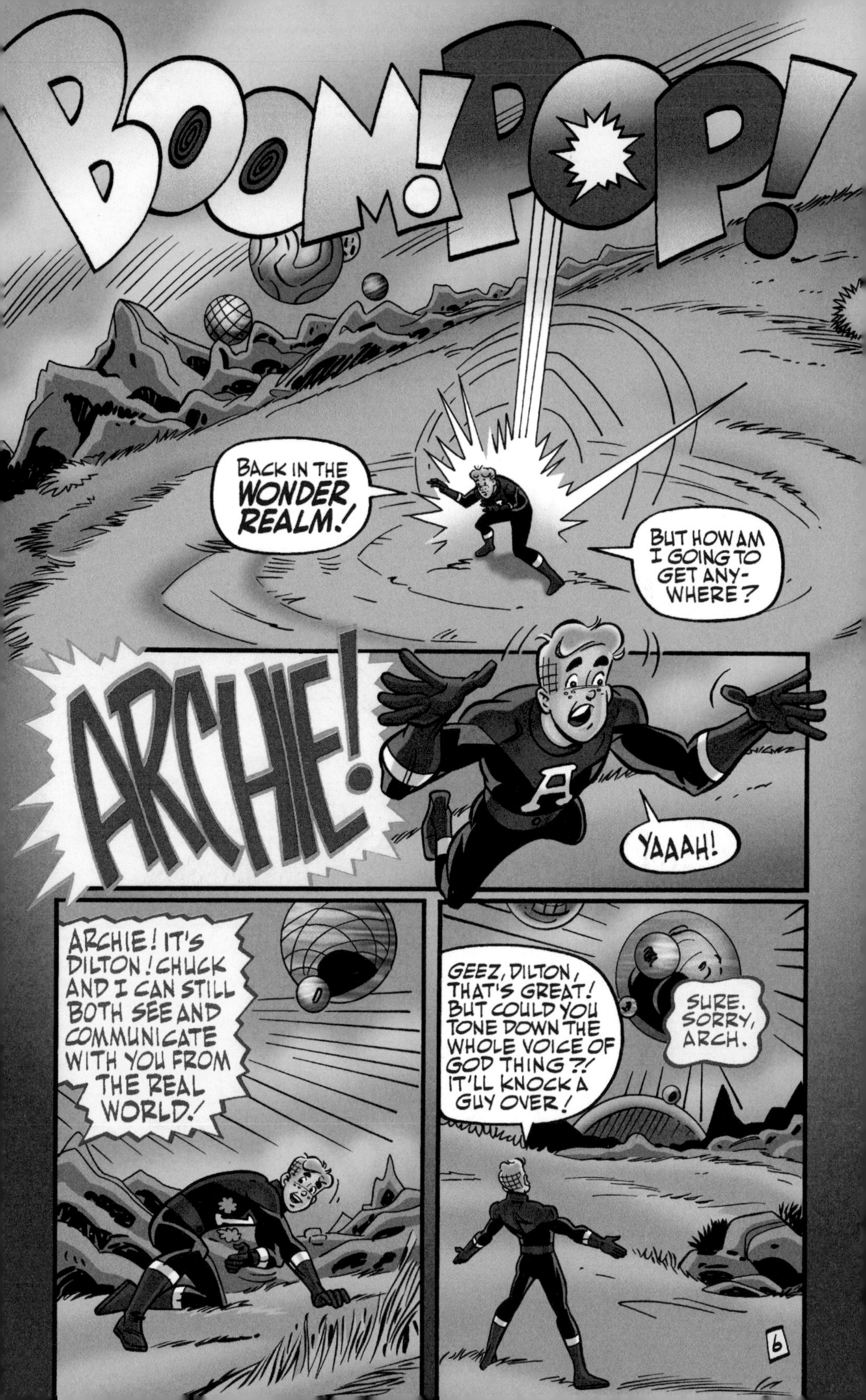
BOOM!
POP!
BACK IN THE WONDER REALM!
BUT HOW AM I GOING TO GET ANY-WHERE?
ARCHIE!
YAAAH!
ARCHIE! IT'S DILTON! CHUCK AND I CAN STILL BOTH SEE AND COMMUNICATE WITH YOU FROM THE REAL WORLD!
GEEZ, DILTON, THAT'S GREAT! BUT COULD YOU TONE DOWN THE WHOLE VOICE OF GOD THING?! IT'LL KNOCK A GUY OVER!
SURE. SORRY, ARCH.
6

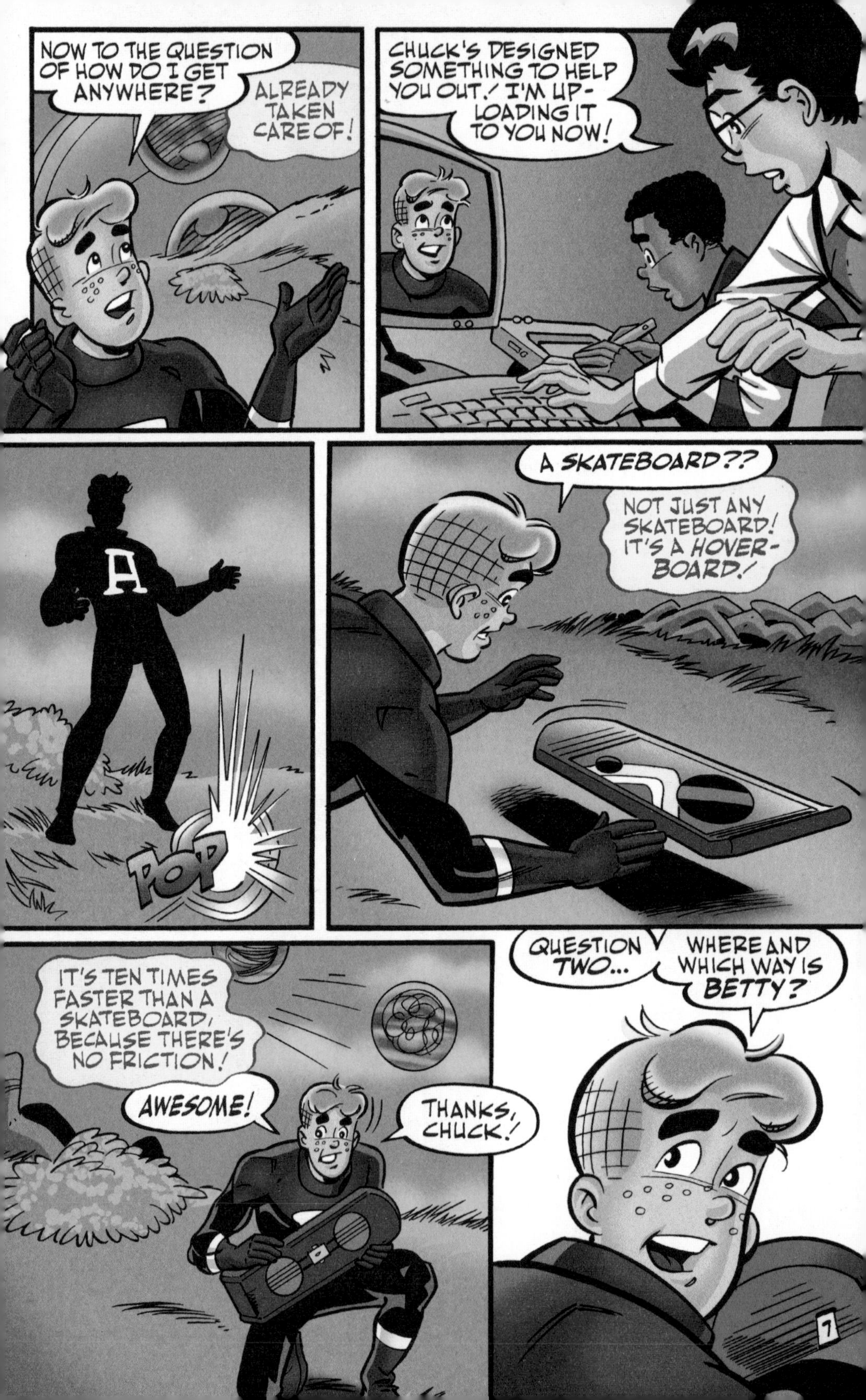
NOW TO THE QUESTION OF HOW DO I GET ANYWHERE?
ALREADY TAKEN CARE OF!
CHUCK'S DESIGNED SOMETHING TO HELP YOU OUT! I'M UP-LOADING IT TO YOU NOW!
POP
A SKATEBOARD??
NOT JUST ANY SKATEBOARD! IT'S A HOVER-BOARD!
IT'S TEN TIMES FASTER THAN A SKATEBOARD, BECAUSE THERE'S NO FRICTION!
AWESOME!
THANKS, CHUCK!
QUESTION TWO...
WHERE AND WHICH WAY IS BETTY?

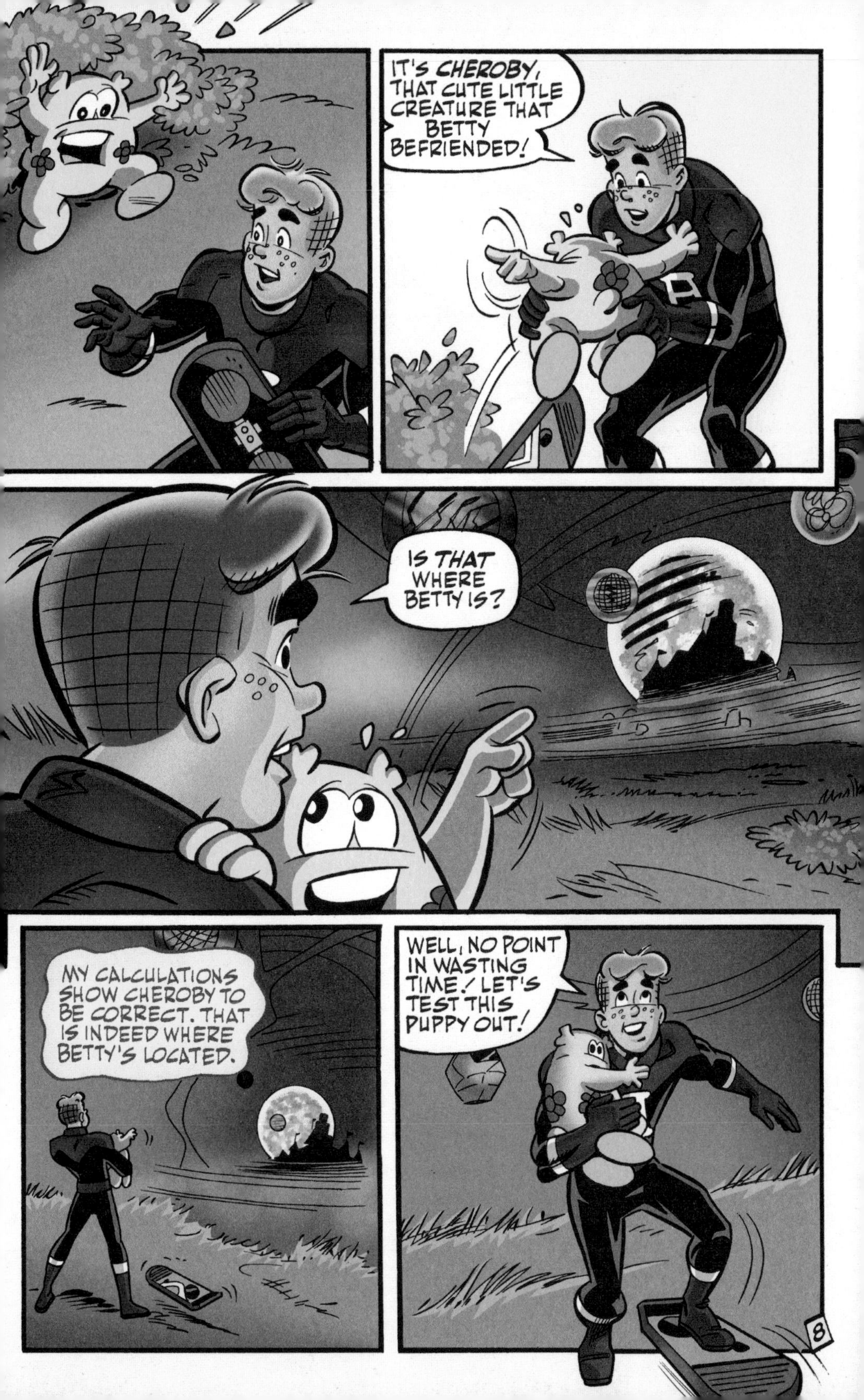
IT'S CHEROBY, THAT CUTE LITTLE CREATURE THAT BETTY BEFRIENDED!
IS THAT WHERE BETTY IS?
MY CALCULATIONS SHOW CHEROBY TO BE CORRECT. THAT IS INDEED WHERE BETTY'S LOCATED.
WELL, NO POINT IN WASTING TIME! LET'S TEST THIS PUPPY OUT!
8

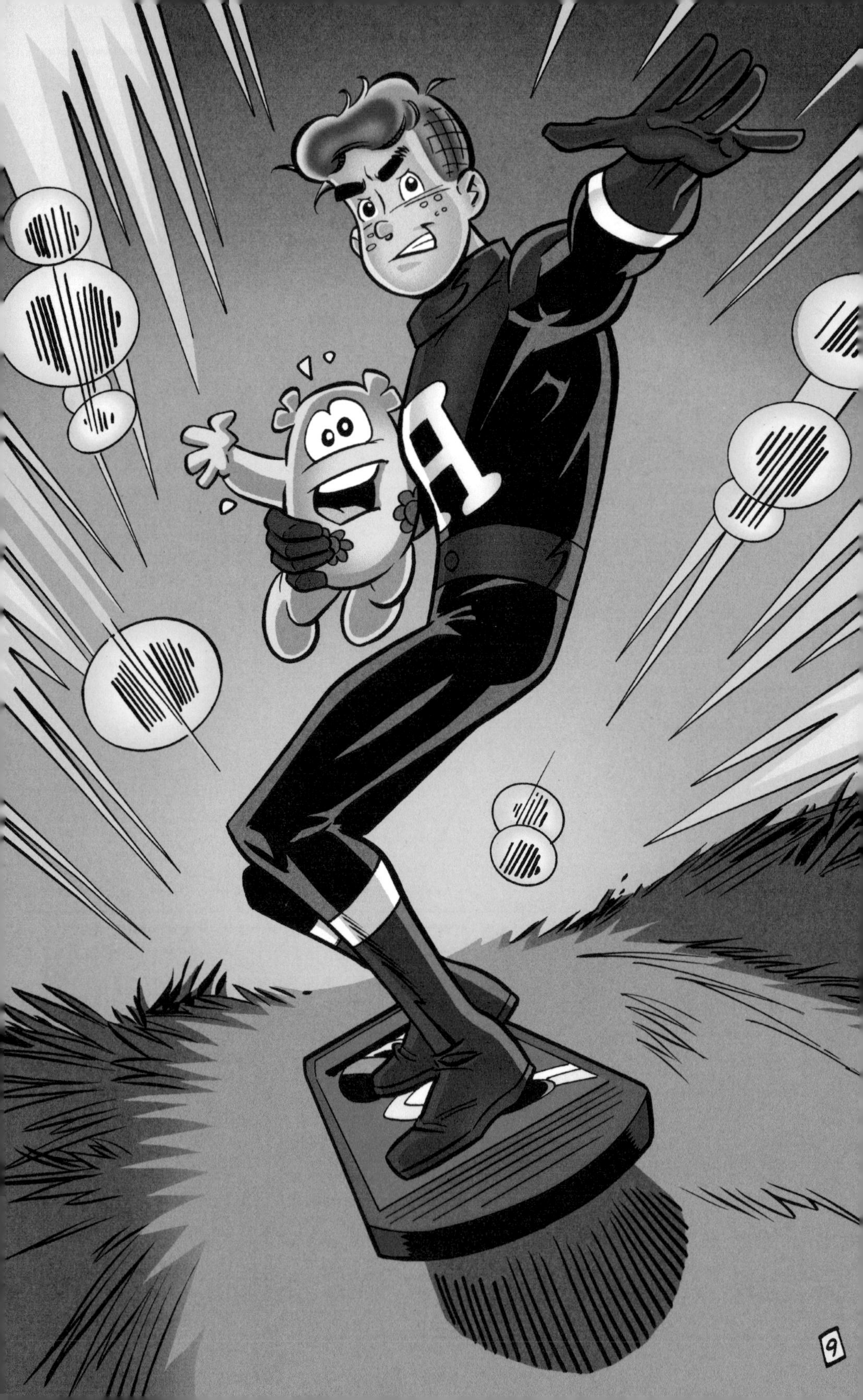

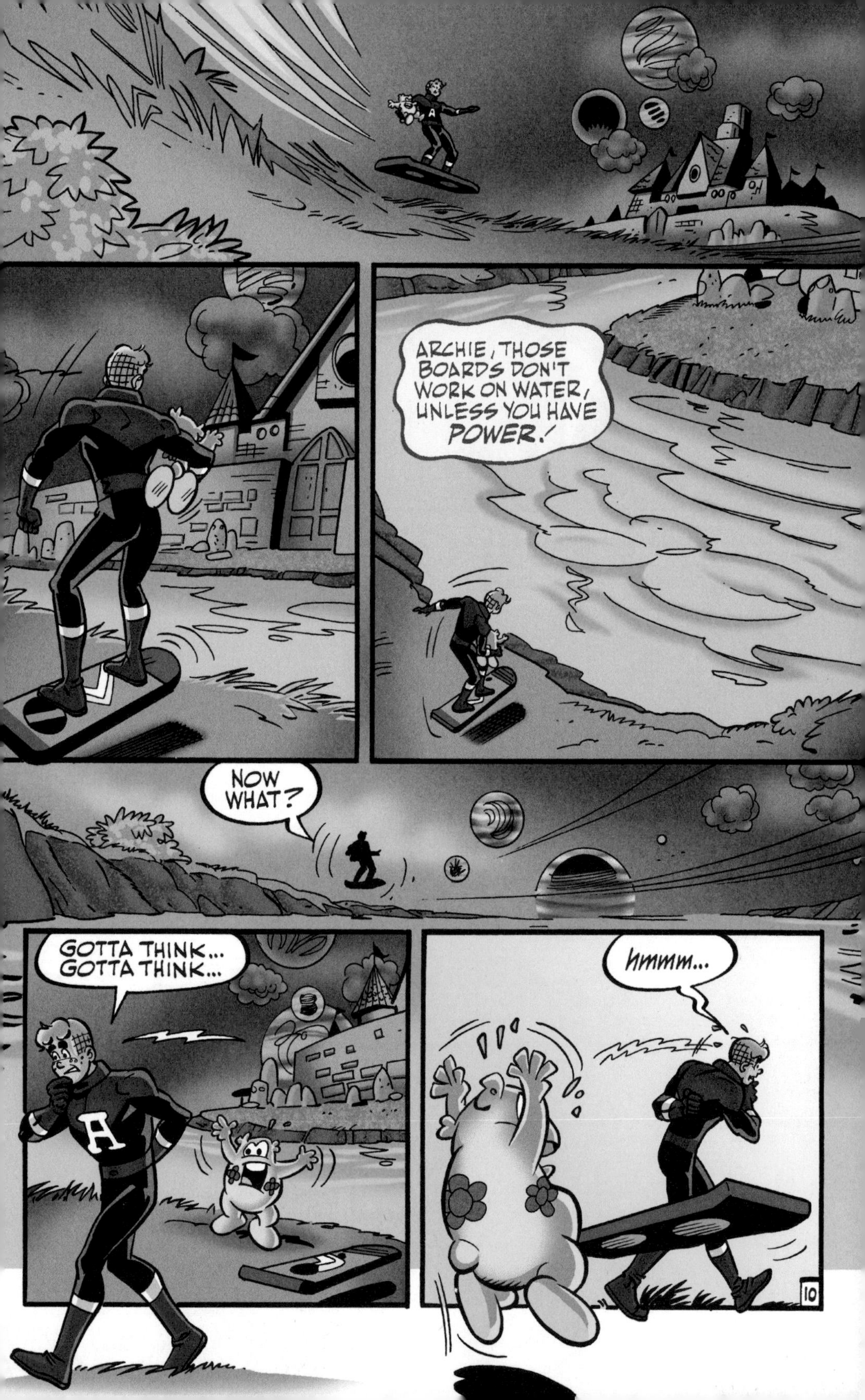
ARCHIE, THOSE BOARDS DON'T WORK ON WATER, UNLESS YOU HAVE POWER.!
NOW WHAT?
GOTTA THINK... GOTTA THINK...
hmmm...

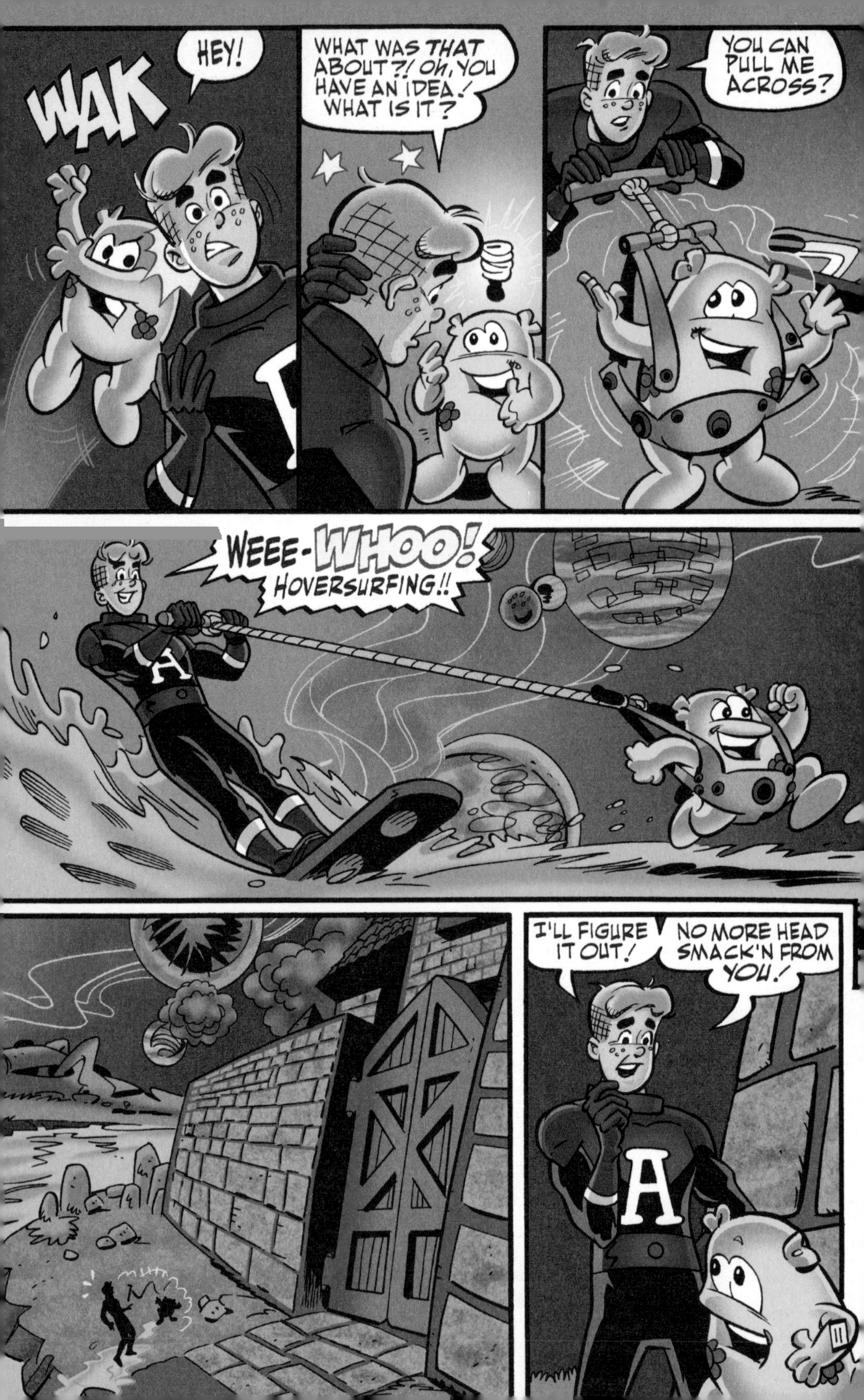
WAK
HEY!
WHAT WAS THAT ABOUT?! OH, YOU HAVE AN IDEA! WHAT IS IT?
YOU CAN PULL ME ACROSS?
WEEE-WHOO! HOVERSURFING!!
I'LL FIGURE IT OUT!
NO MORE HEAD SMACK'N FROM YOU!

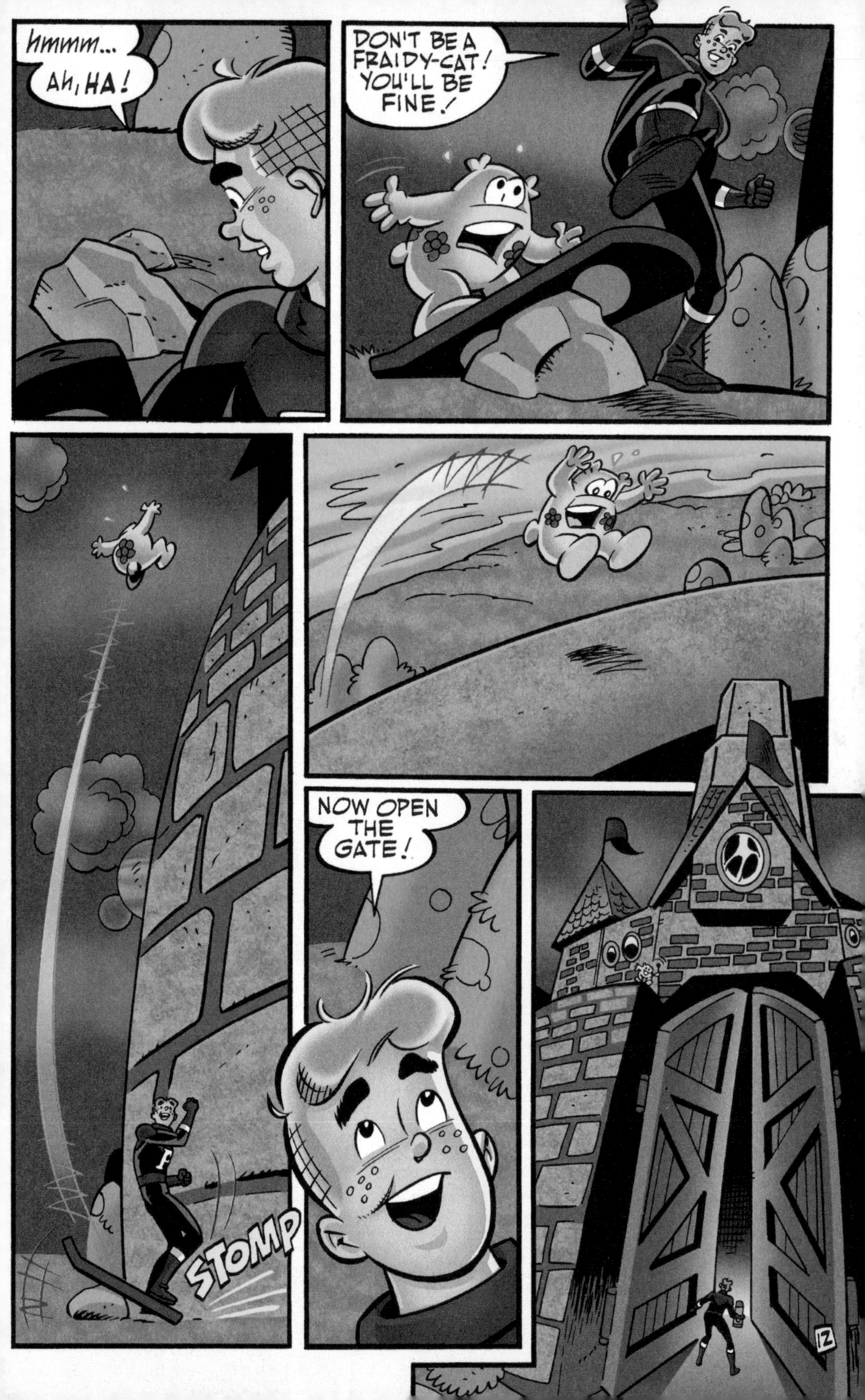
hmmm...
Ah, HA!
DON'T BE A FRAIDY-CAT! YOU'LL BE FINE!
STOMP
NOW OPEN THE GATE!
12

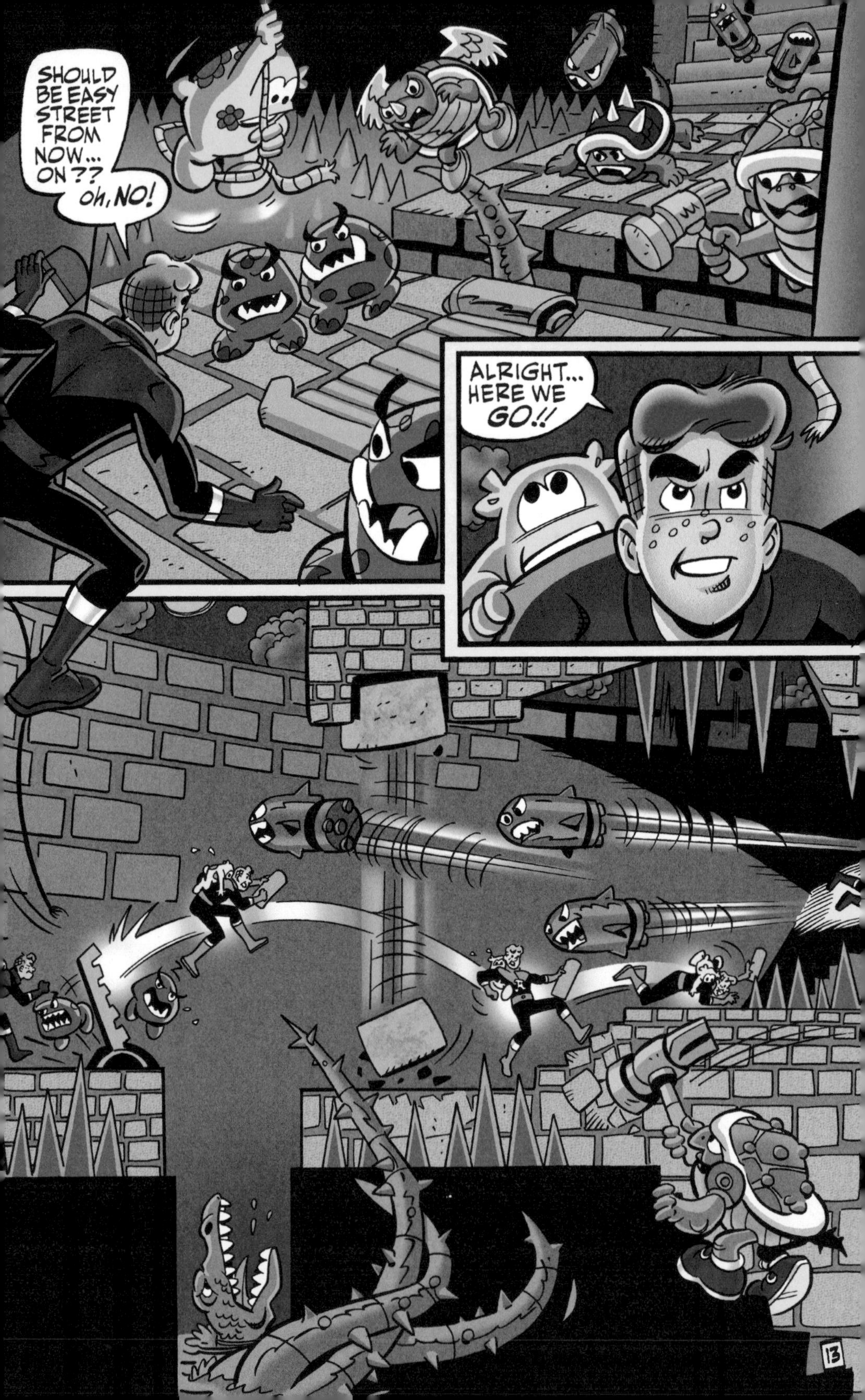
SHOULD BE EASY STREET FROM NOW... ON?? oh, NO!
ALRIGHT... HERE WE GO!!
13

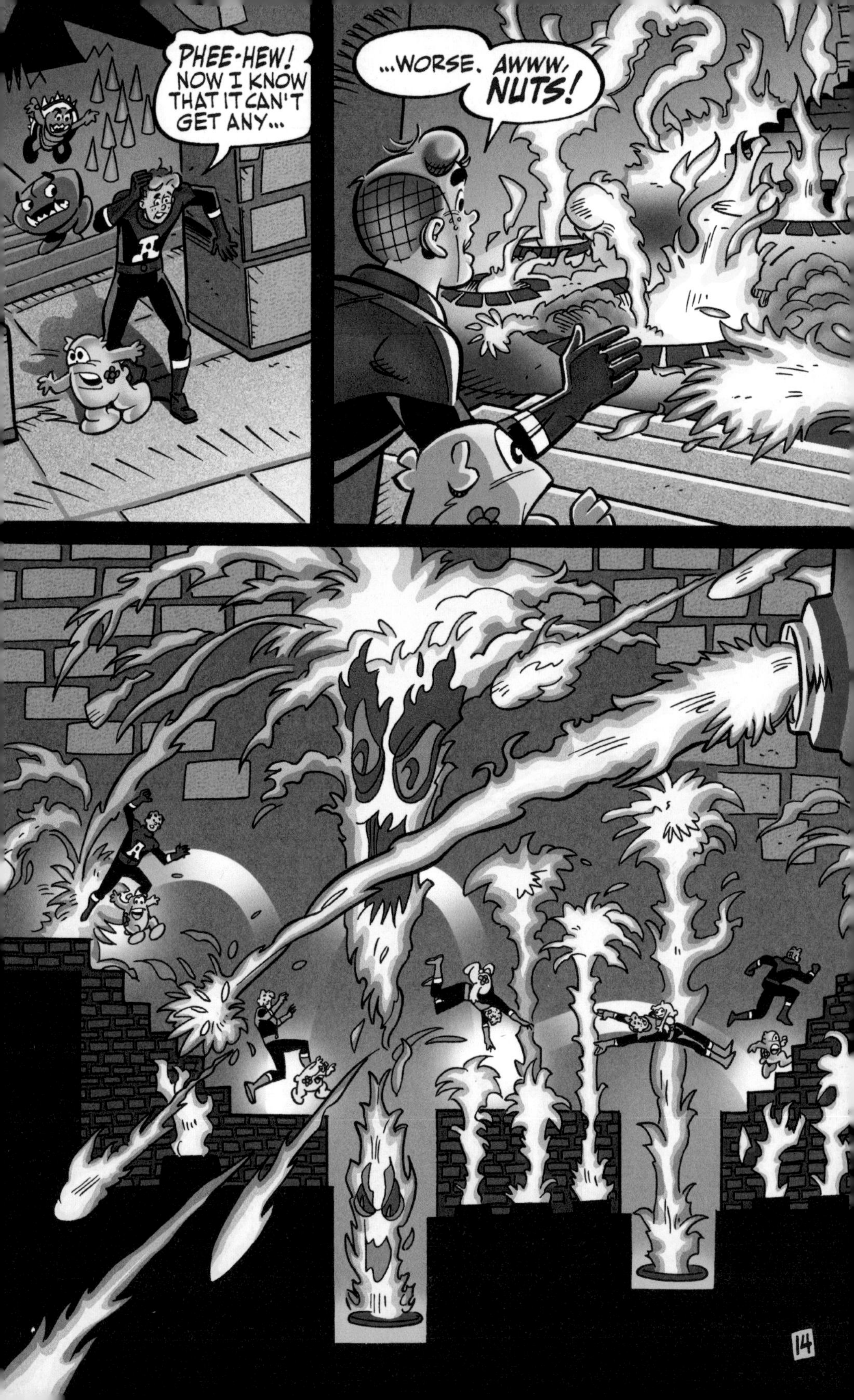
PHEE-HEW! NOW I KNOW THAT IT CAN'T GET ANY...
...WORSE. AWWW, NUTS!

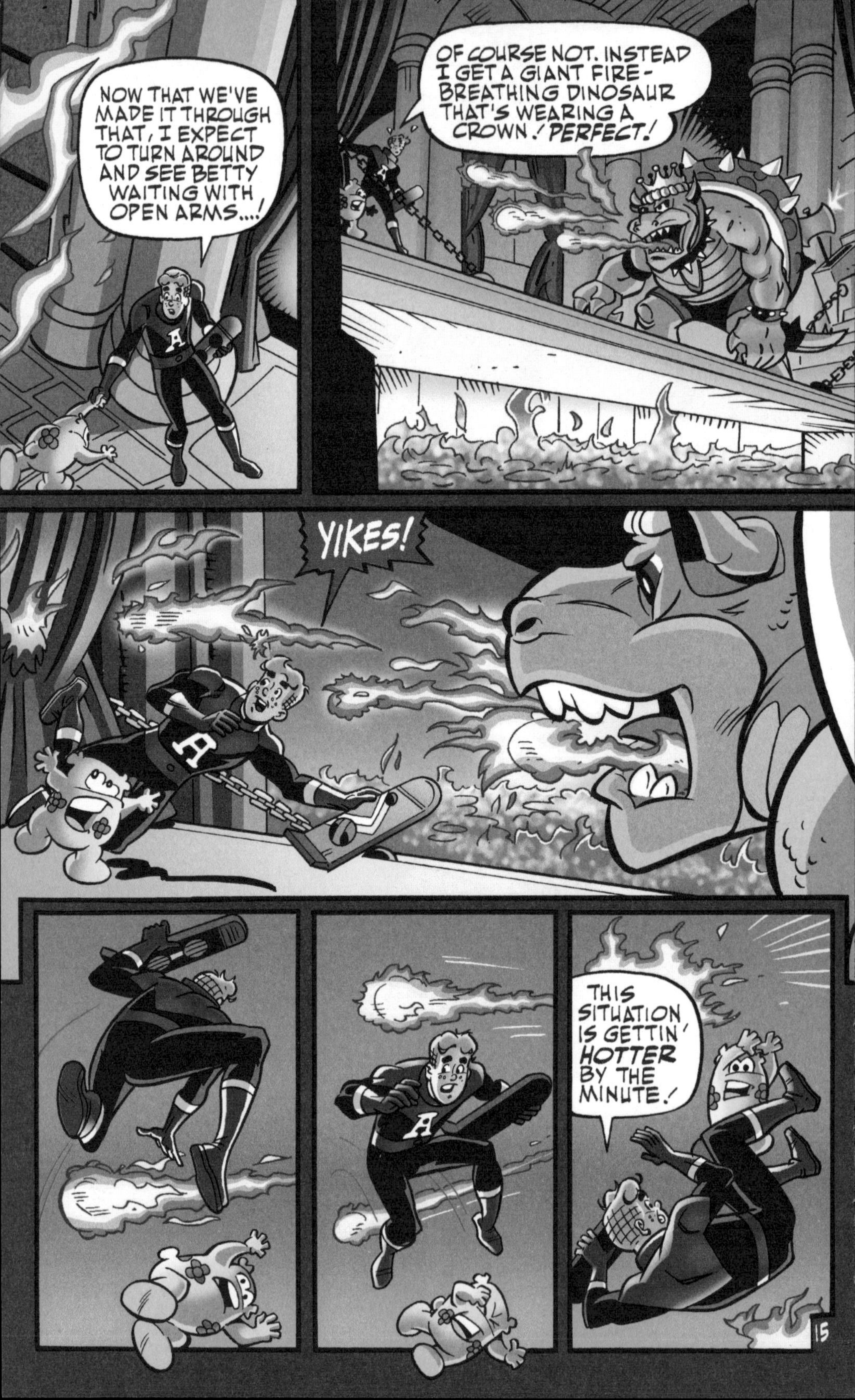
NOW THAT WE'VE MADE IT THROUGH THAT, I EXPECT TO TURN AROUND AND SEE BETTY WAITING WITH OPEN ARMS...!
OF COURSE NOT. INSTEAD I GET A GIANT FIRE-BREATHING DINOSAUR THAT'S WEARING A CROWN! PERFECT!
YIKES!
THIS SITUATION IS GETTIN' HOTTER BY THE MINUTE!

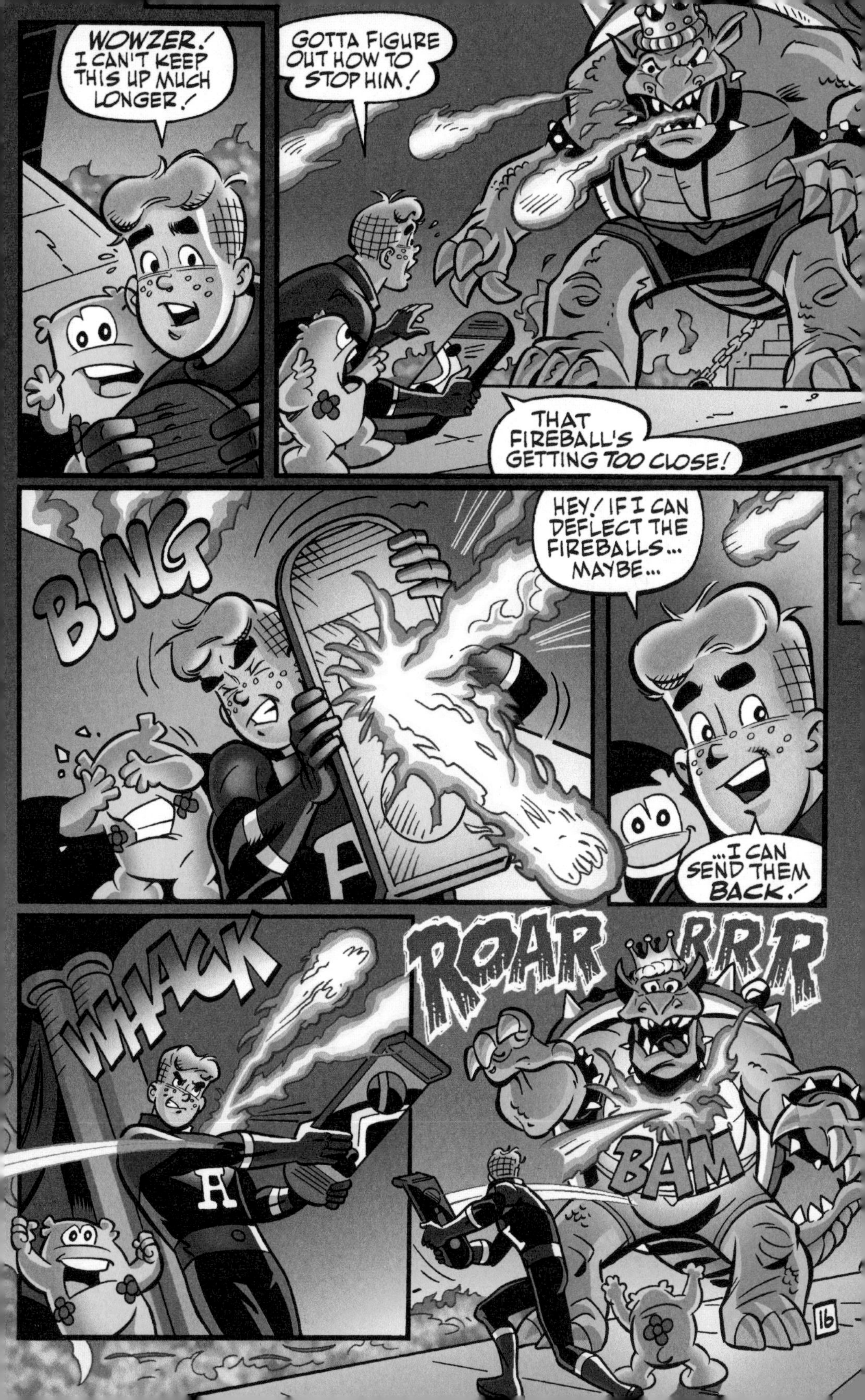
WOWZER! I CAN'T KEEP THIS UP MUCH LONGER!
GOTTA FIGURE OUT HOW TO STOP HIM!
THAT FIREBALL'S GETTING TOO CLOSE!
BING
HEY! IF I CAN DEFLECT THE FIREBALLS... MAYBE...
...I CAN SEND THEM BACK!
WHACK
ROARRRR
BAM
16

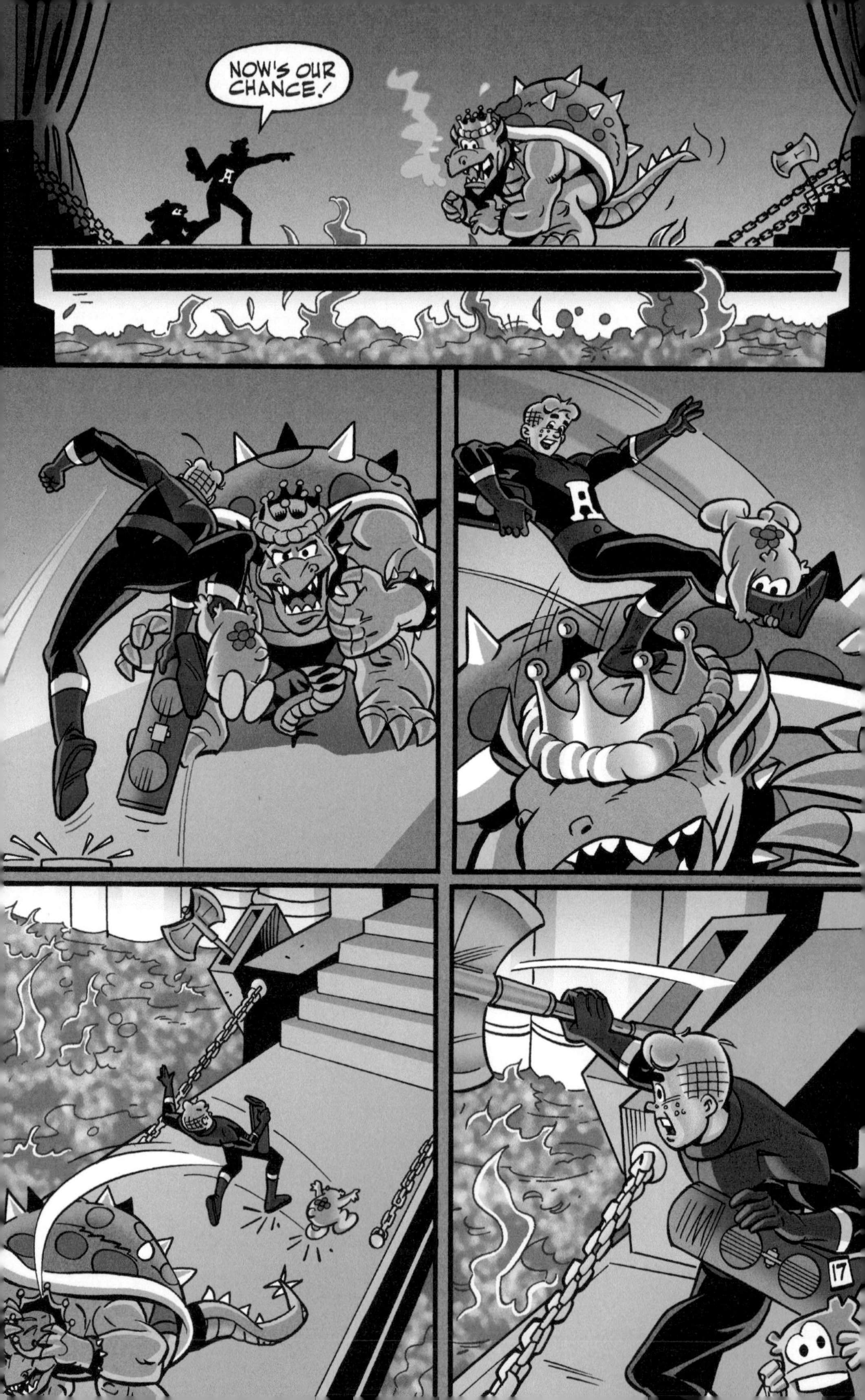
NOW'S OUR CHANCE!

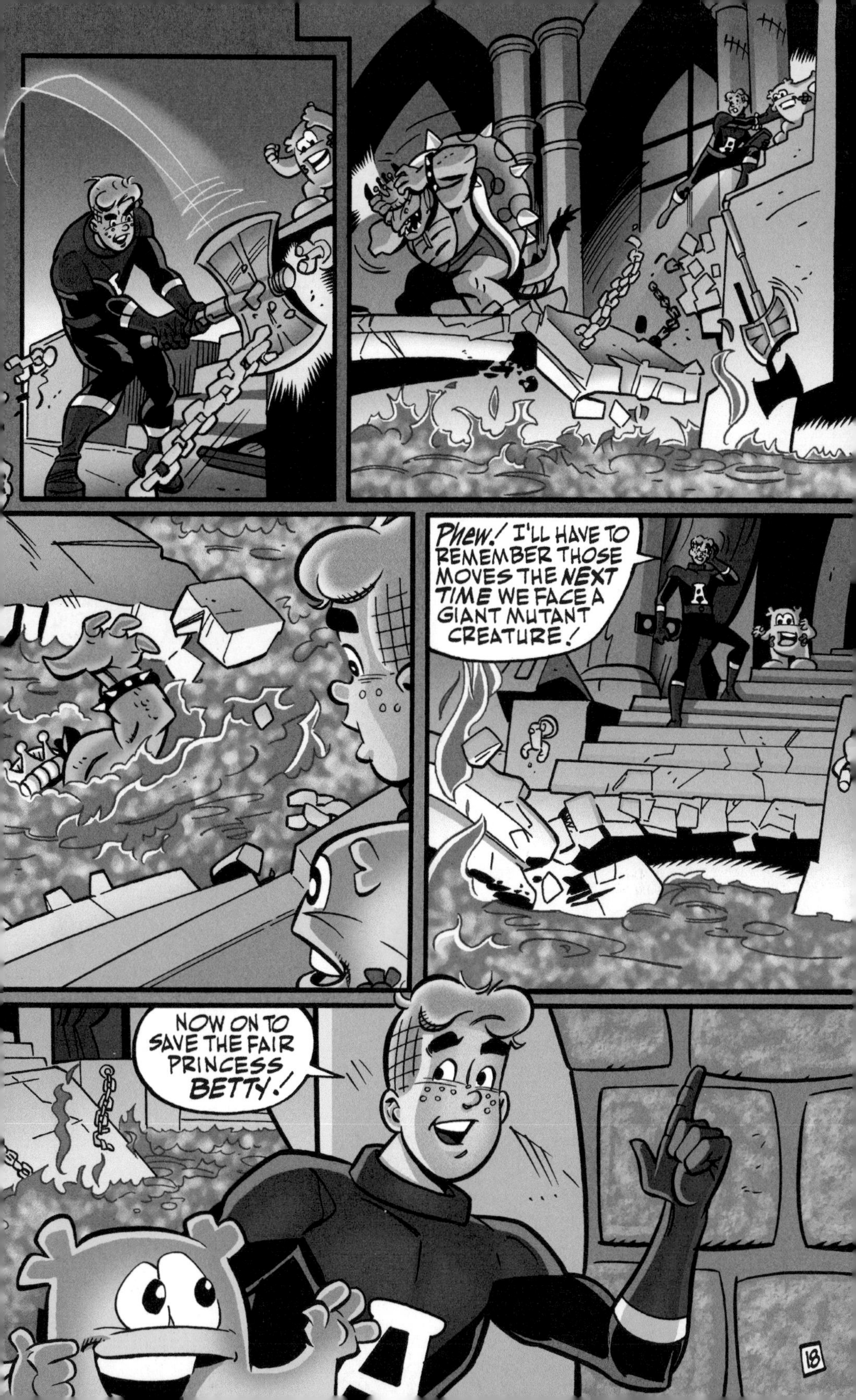
Phew! I'LL HAVE TO REMEMBER THOSE MOVES THE NEXT TIME WE FACE A GIANT MUTANT CREATURE!
NOW ON TO SAVE THE FAIR PRINCESS BETTY!
18

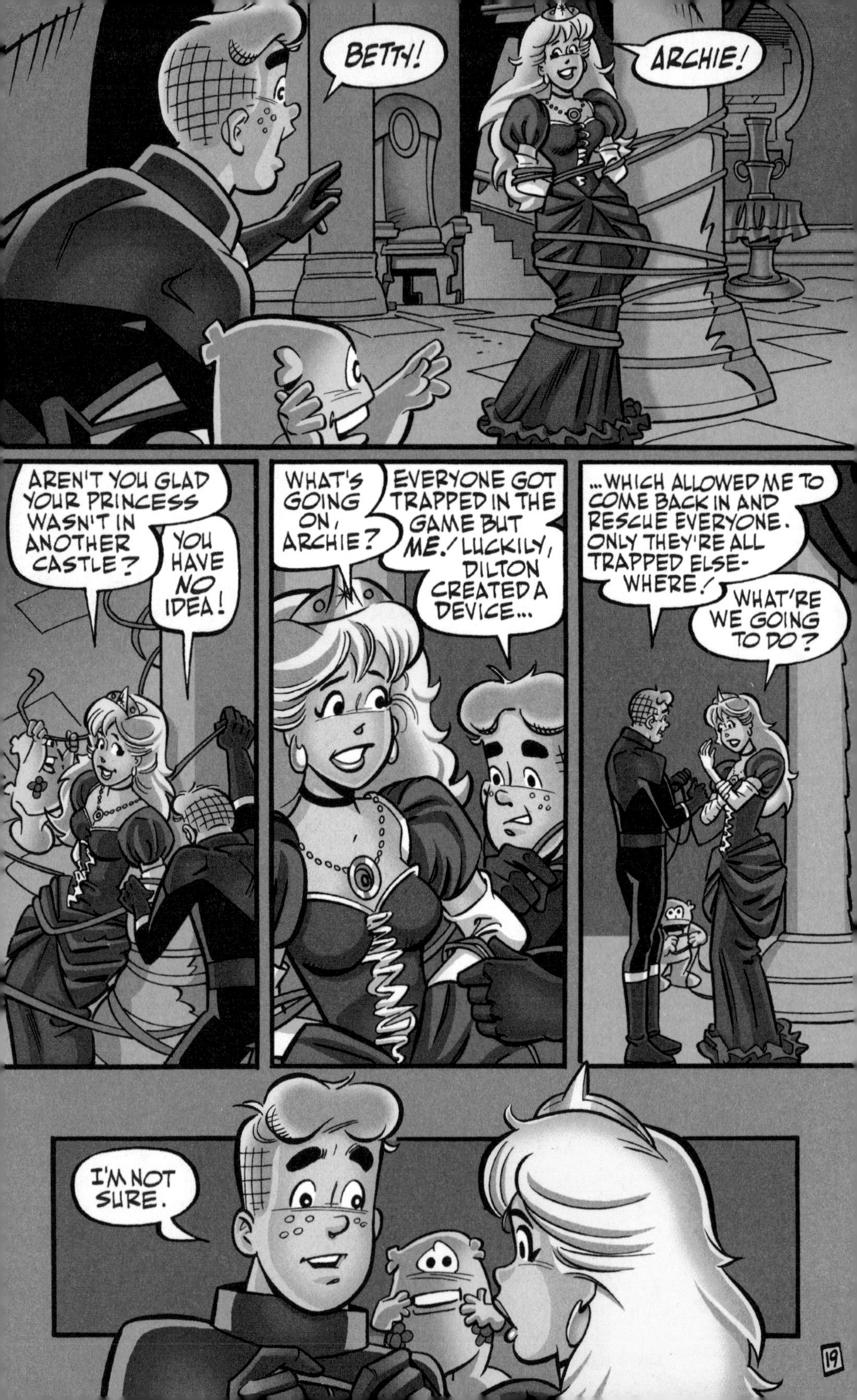
BETTY!
ARCHIE!
AREN'T YOU GLAD YOUR PRINCESS WASN'T IN ANOTHER CASTLE?
YOU HAVE NO IDEA!
WHAT'S GOING ON, ARCHIE?
EVERYONE GOT TRAPPED IN THE GAME BUT ME.! LUCKILY, DILTON CREATED A DEVICE...
...WHICH ALLOWED ME TO COME BACK IN AND RESCUE EVERYONE. ONLY THEY'RE ALL TRAPPED ELSE-WHERE.!
WHAT'RE WE GOING TO DO?
I'M NOT SURE.
19

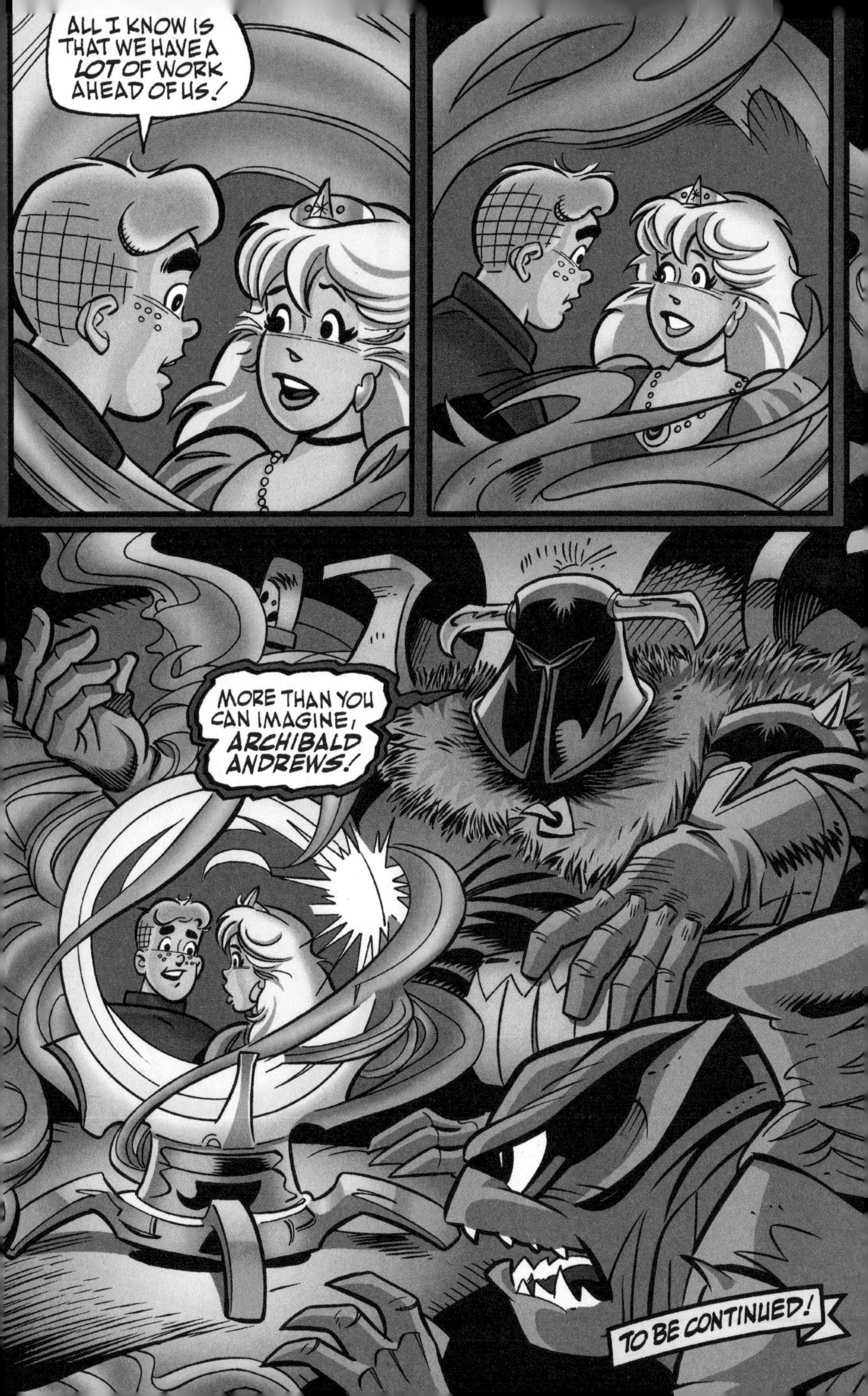
ALL I KNOW IS THAT WE HAVE A LOT OF WORK AHEAD OF US!
MORE THAN YOU CAN IMAGINE, ARCHIBALD ANDREWS!
TO BE CONTINUED!

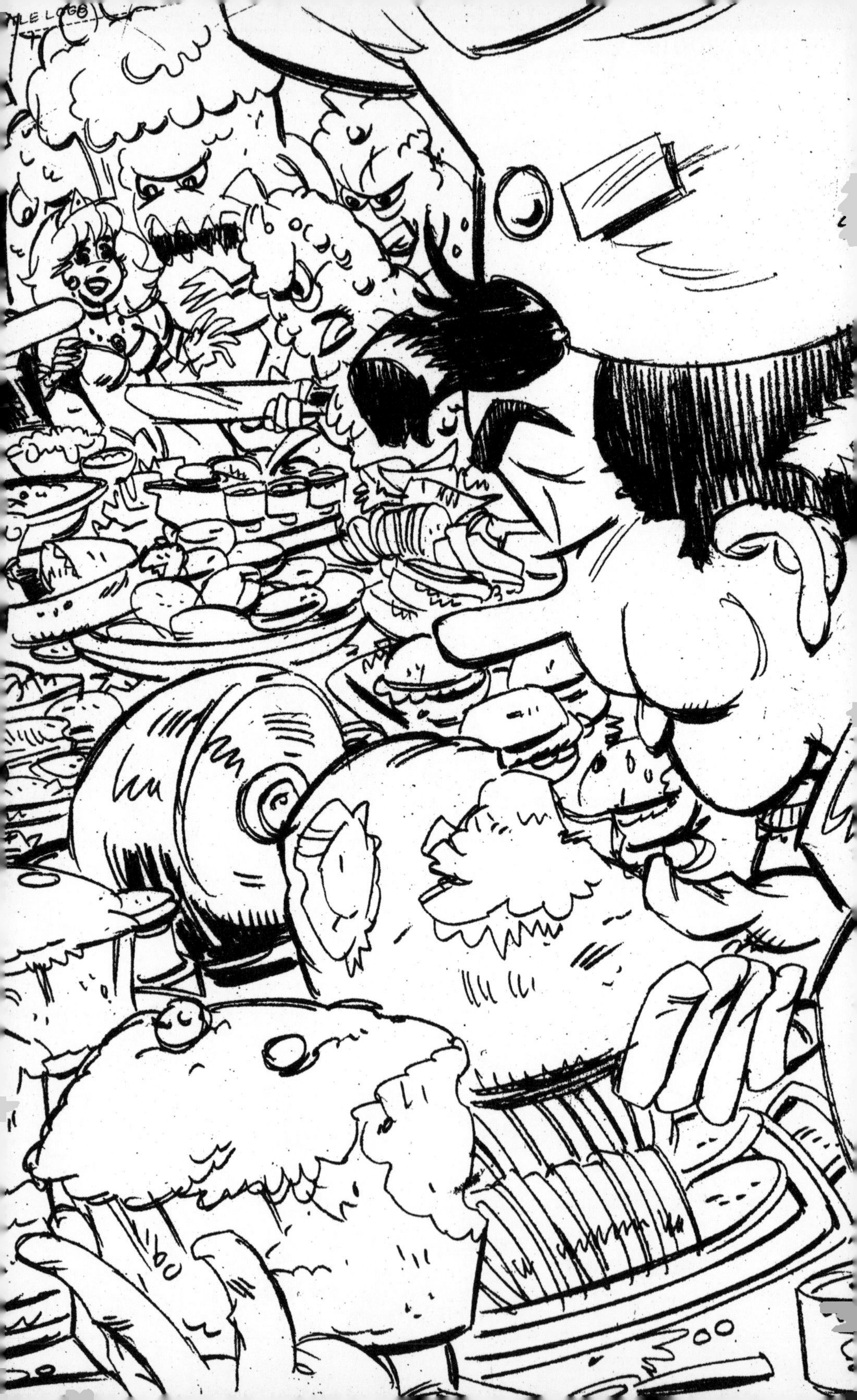
LE LOGO

CHAPTER THREE

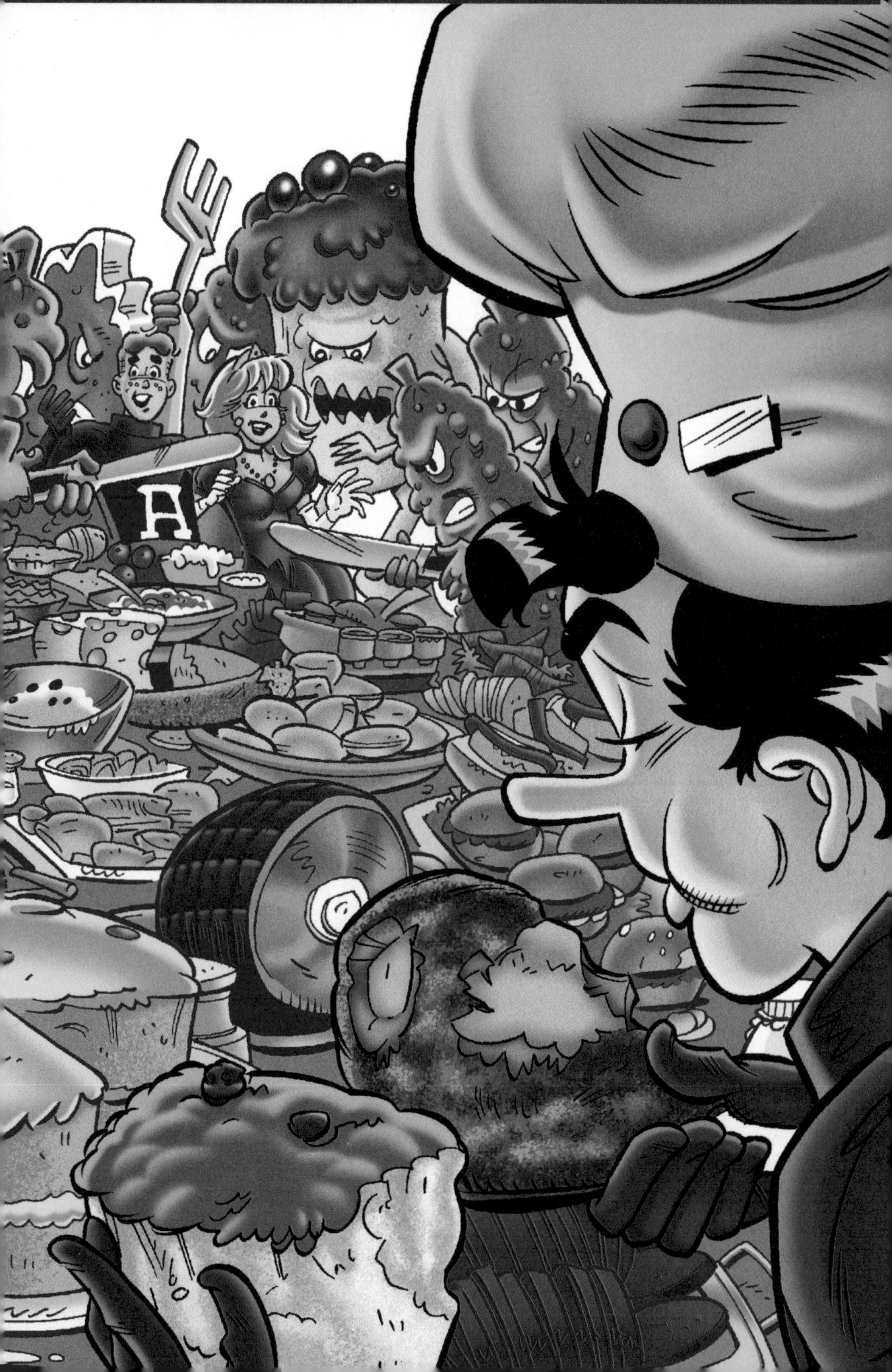

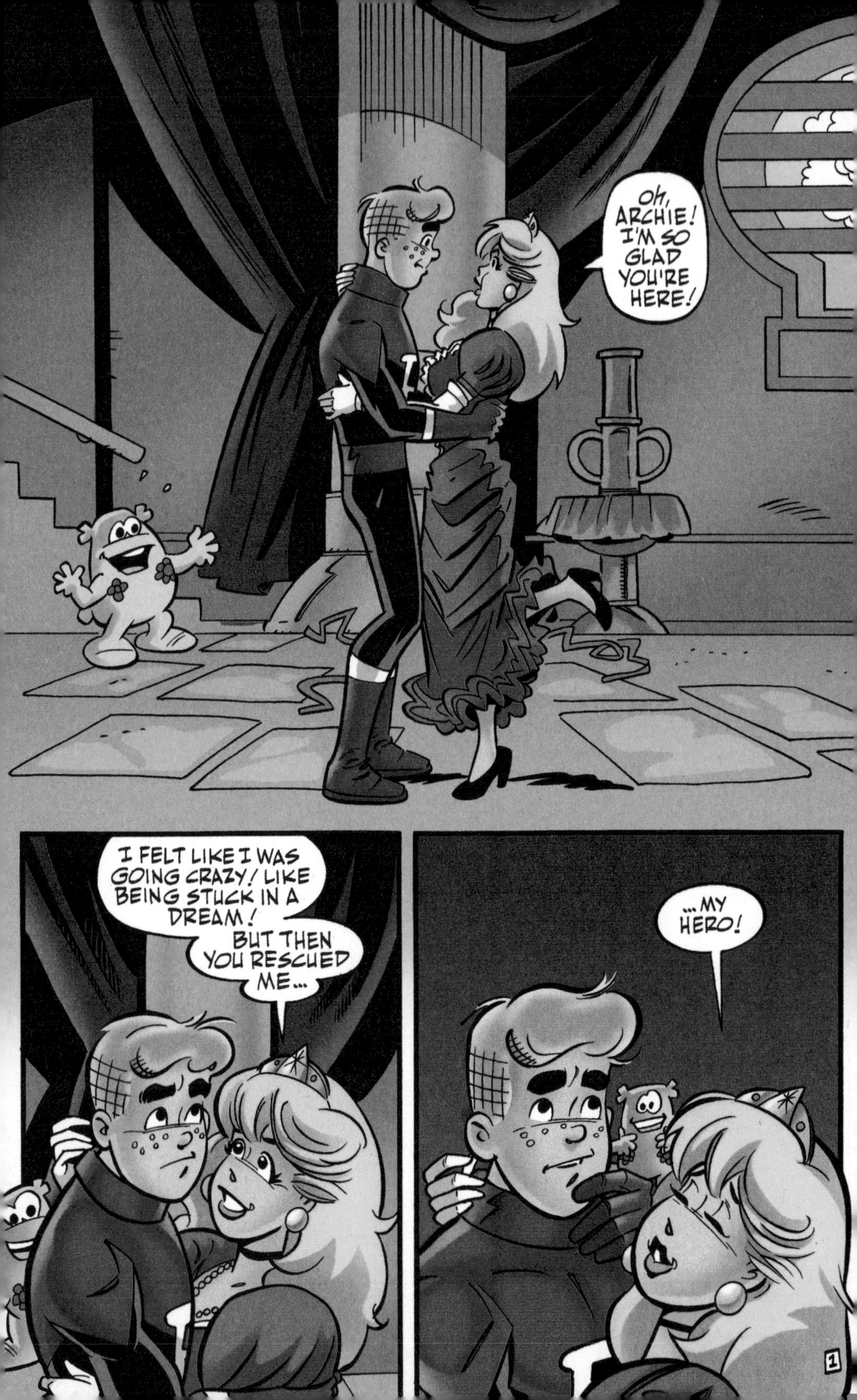
OH, ARCHIE! I'M SO GLAD YOU'RE HERE!
I FELT LIKE I WAS GOING CRAZY! LIKE BEING STUCK IN A DREAM!
BUT THEN YOU RESCUED ME...
...MY HERO!
1

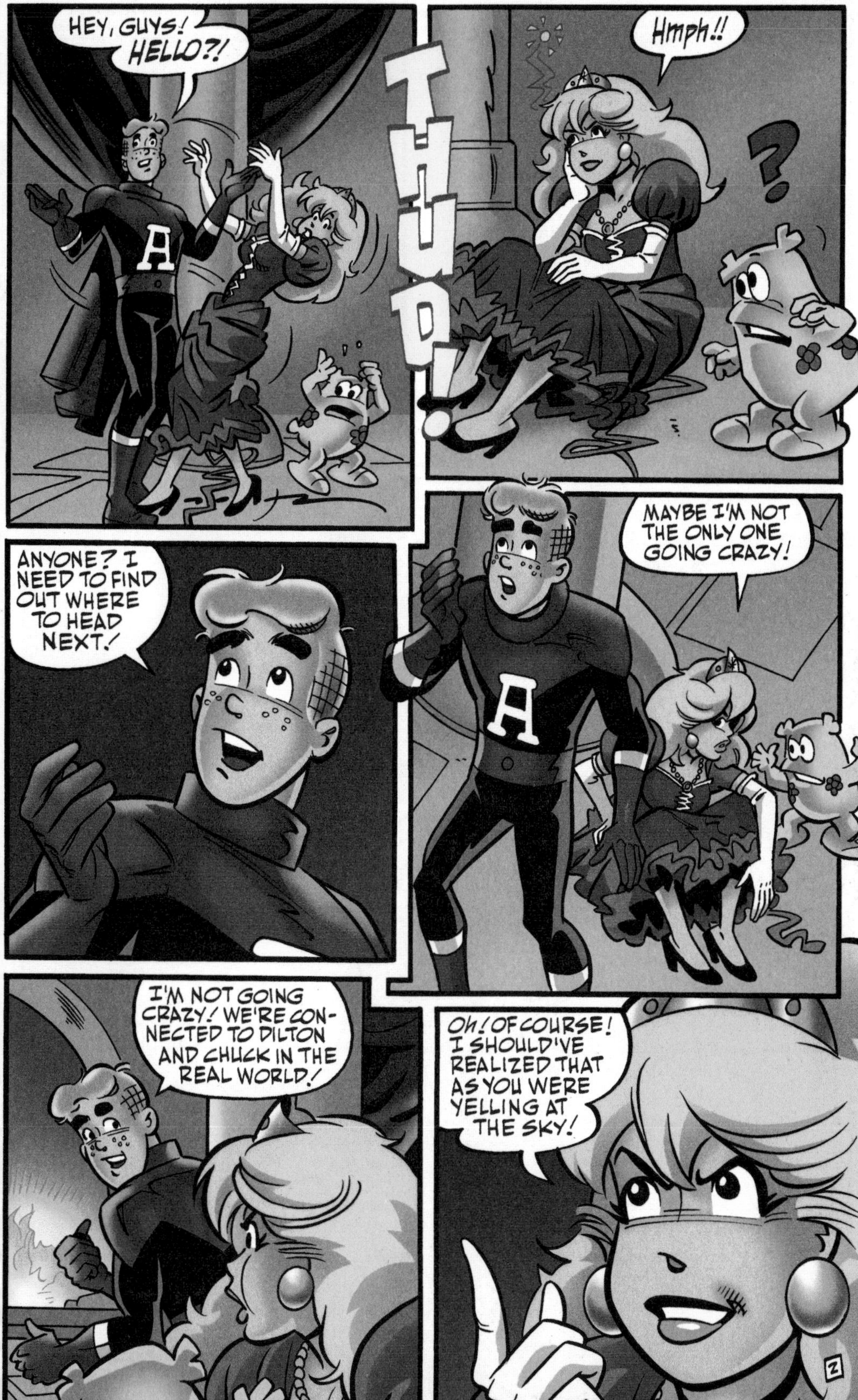
HEY, GUYS! HELLO?!
THUD!!
Hmph!!
?
ANYONE? I NEED TO FIND OUT WHERE TO HEAD NEXT!
MAYBE I'M NOT THE ONLY ONE GOING CRAZY!
I'M NOT GOING CRAZY! WE'RE CON-NECTED TO DILTON AND CHUCK IN THE REAL WORLD!
Oh! OF COURSE! I SHOULD'VE REALIZED THAT AS YOU WERE YELLING AT THE SKY!
2

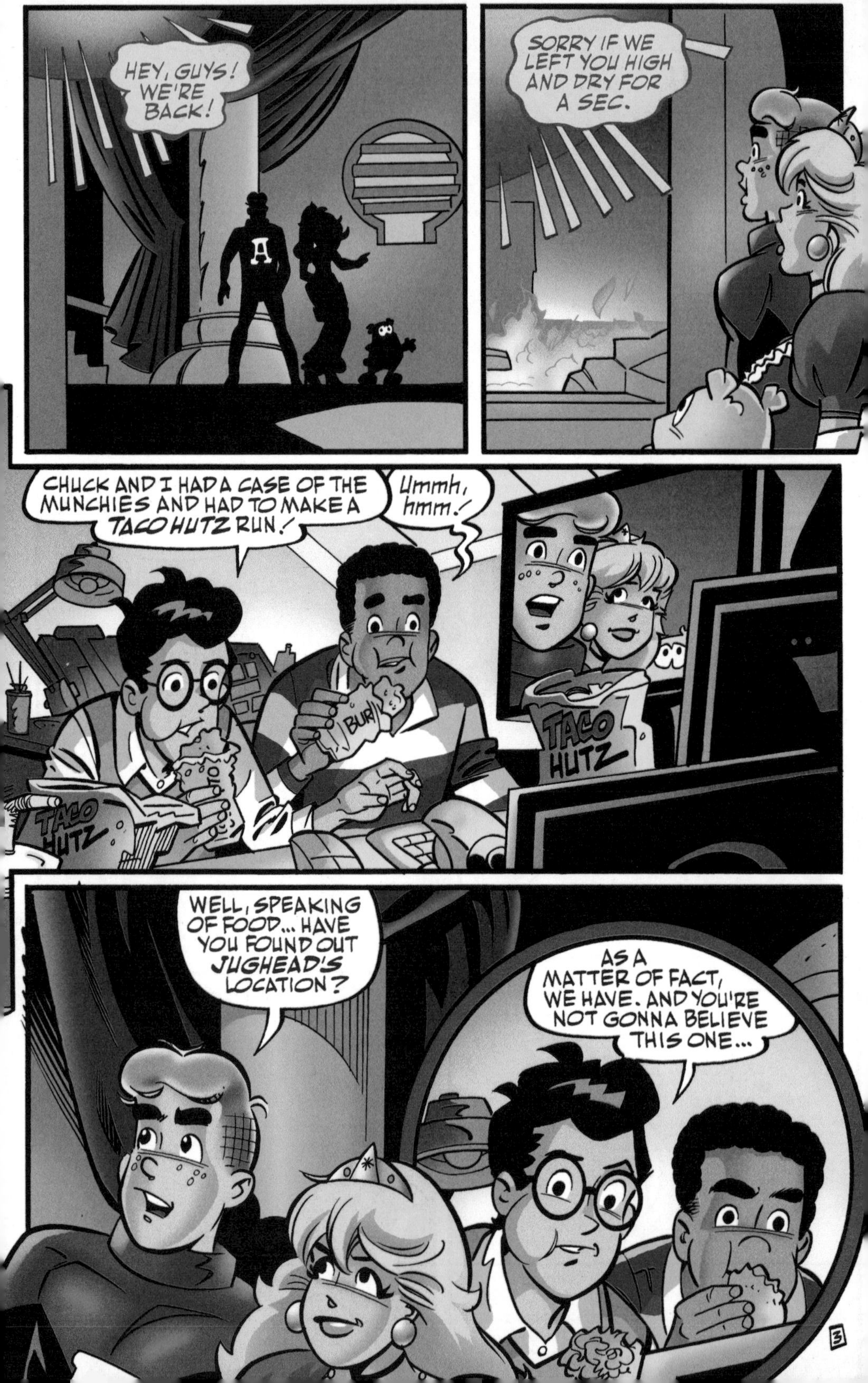
HEY, GUYS! WE'RE BACK!
SORRY IF WE LEFT YOU HIGH AND DRY FOR A SEC.
CHUCK AND I HAD A CASE OF THE MUNCHIES AND HAD TO MAKE A TACO HUTZ RUN!
Ummh, hmm.!
BUR
TACO HUTZ
TACO HUTZ
WELL, SPEAKING OF FOOD... HAVE YOU FOUND OUT JUGHEAD'S LOCATION?
AS A MATTER OF FACT, WE HAVE. AND YOU'RE NOT GONNA BELIEVE THIS ONE...
3

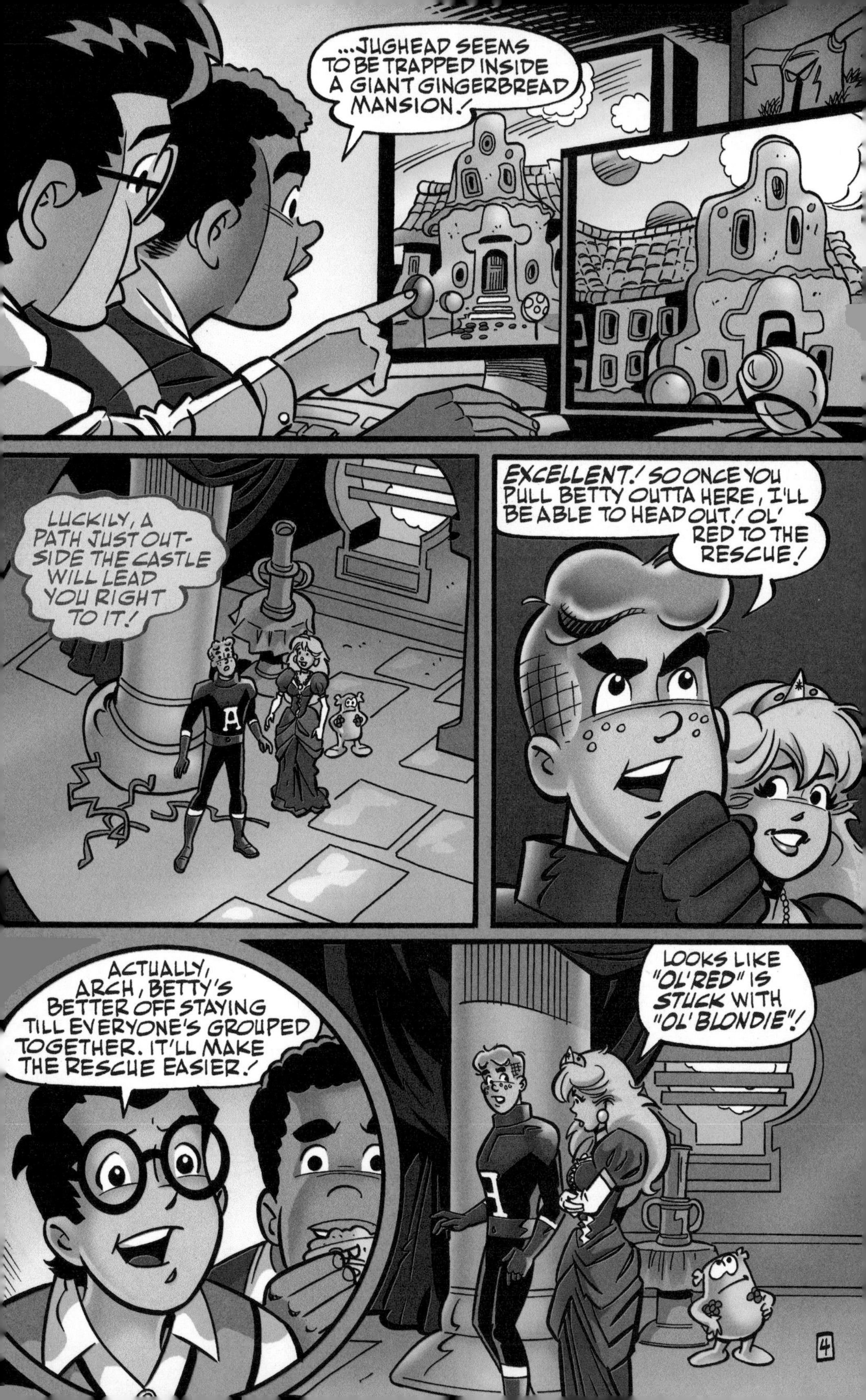
...JUGHEAD SEEMS TO BE TRAPPED INSIDE A GIANT GINGERBREAD MANSION!
LUCKILY, A PATH JUST OUTSIDE THE CASTLE WILL LEAD YOU RIGHT TO IT!
EXCELLENT! SO ONCE YOU PULL BETTY OUTTA HERE, I'LL BE ABLE TO HEAD OUT! OL' RED TO THE RESCUE!
ACTUALLY, ARCH, BETTY'S BETTER OFF STAYING TILL EVERYONE'S GROUPED TOGETHER. IT'LL MAKE THE RESCUE EASIER!
LOOKS LIKE "OL' RED" IS STUCK WITH "OL' BLONDIE"!
4

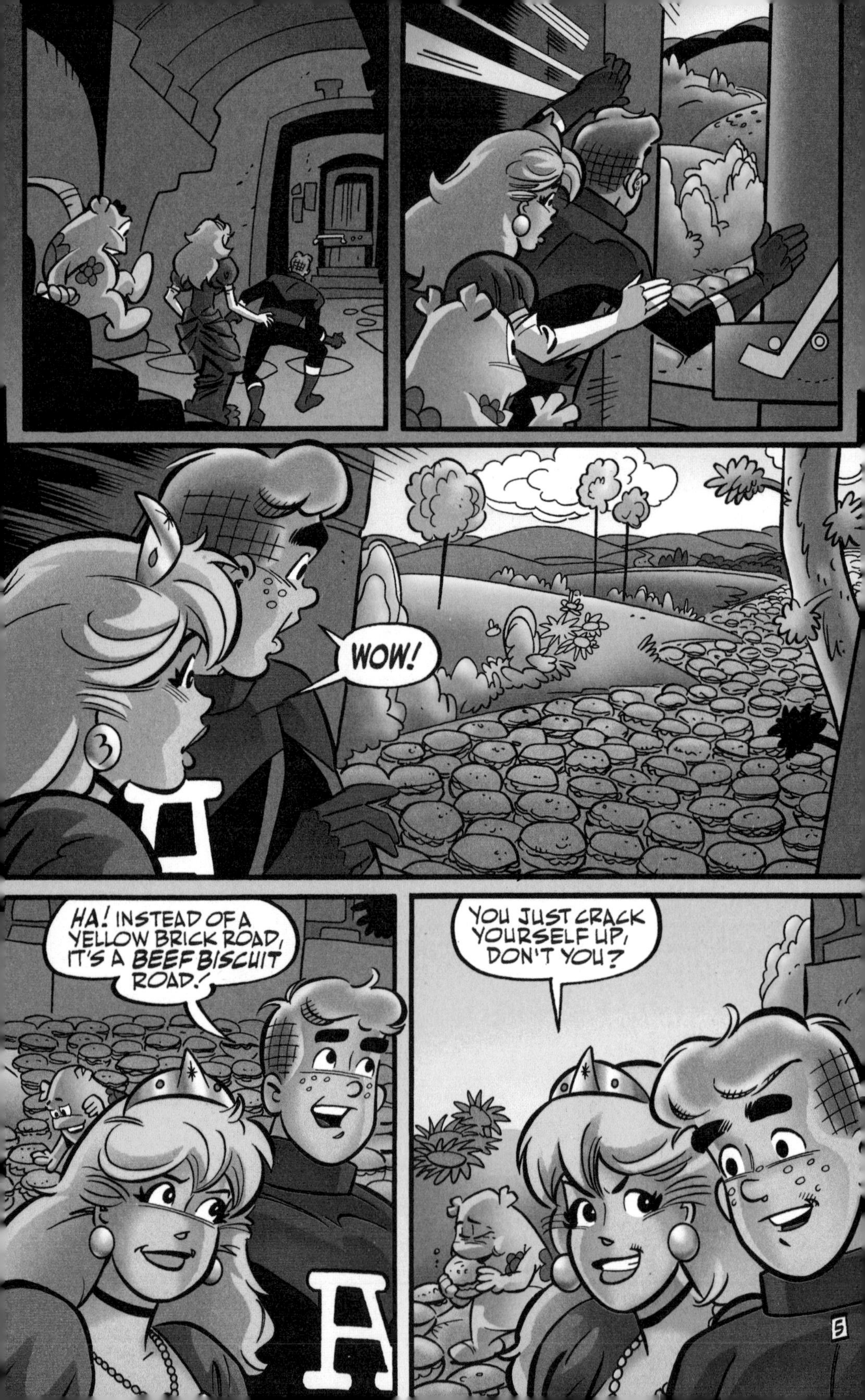
WOW!
HA! INSTEAD OF A YELLOW BRICK ROAD, IT'S A BEEF BISCUIT ROAD!
YOU JUST CRACK YOURSELF UP, DON'T YOU?
5

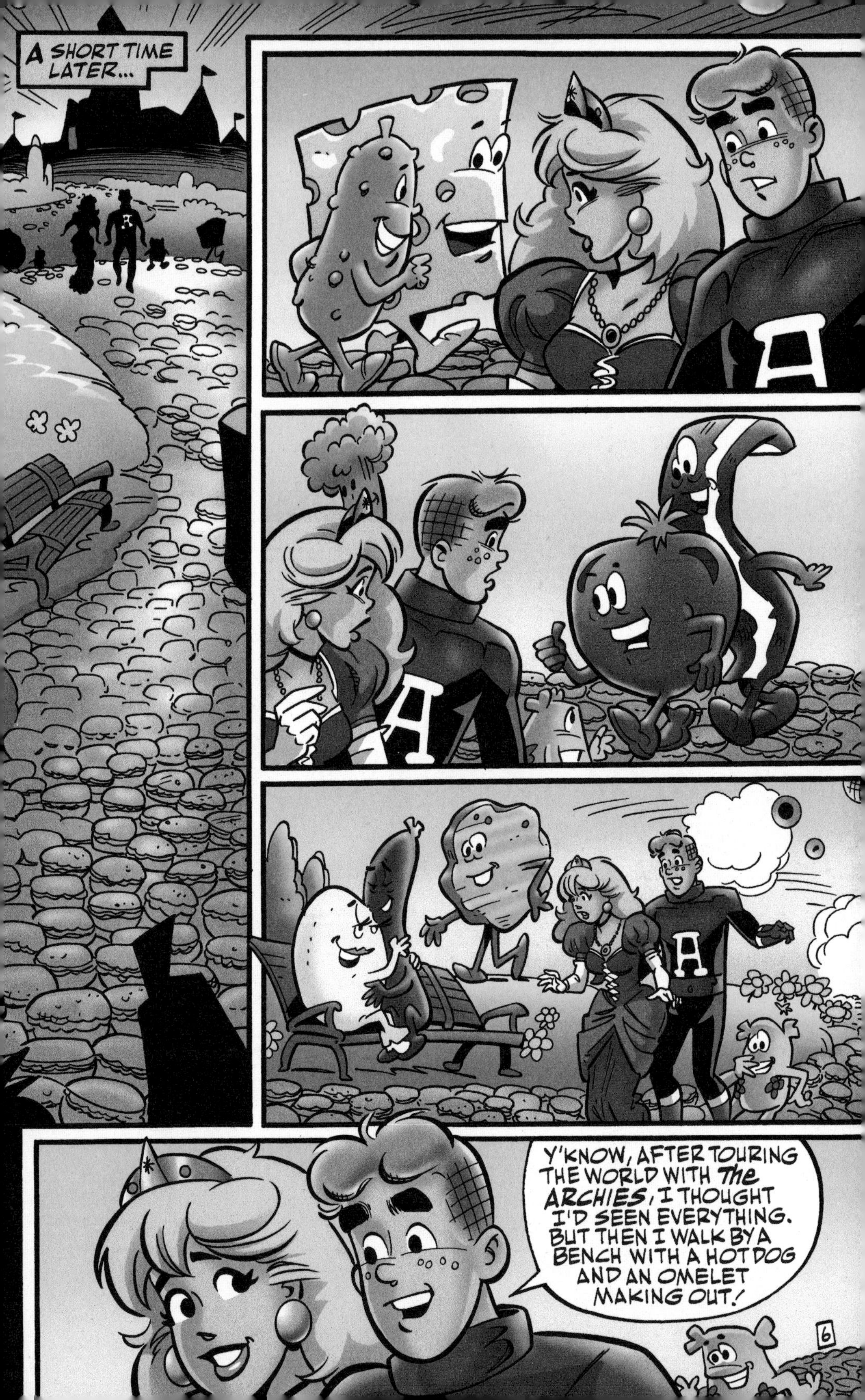

A SHORT TIME LATER...
Y'KNOW, AFTER TOURING THE WORLD WITH *The ARCHIES*, I THOUGHT I'D SEEN EVERYTHING. BUT THEN I WALK BY A BENCH WITH A HOT DOG AND AN OMELET MAKING OUT!
6

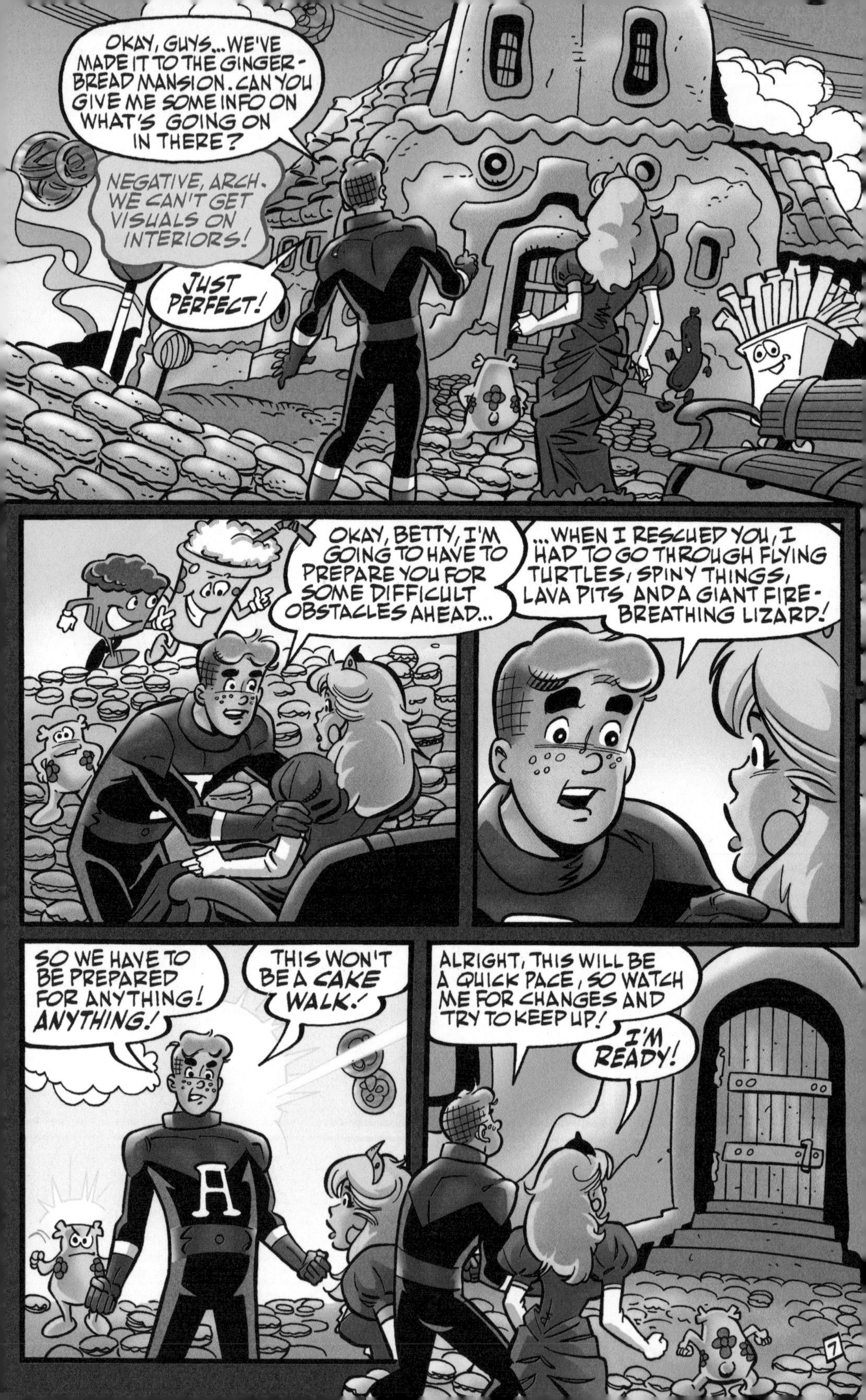
OKAY, GUYS...WE'VE MADE IT TO THE GINGER-BREAD MANSION. CAN YOU GIVE ME SOME INFO ON WHAT'S GOING ON IN THERE?
NEGATIVE, ARCH. WE CAN'T GET VISUALS ON INTERIORS!
JUST PERFECT!
OKAY, BETTY, I'M GOING TO HAVE TO PREPARE YOU FOR SOME DIFFICULT OBSTACLES AHEAD...
...WHEN I RESCUED YOU, I HAD TO GO THROUGH FLYING TURTLES, SPINY THINGS, LAVA PITS AND A GIANT FIRE-BREATHING LIZARD!
SO WE HAVE TO BE PREPARED FOR ANYTHING! ANYTHING!
THIS WON'T BE A CAKE WALK!
ALRIGHT, THIS WILL BE A QUICK PACE, SO WATCH ME FOR CHANGES AND TRY TO KEEP UP!
I'M READY!
7

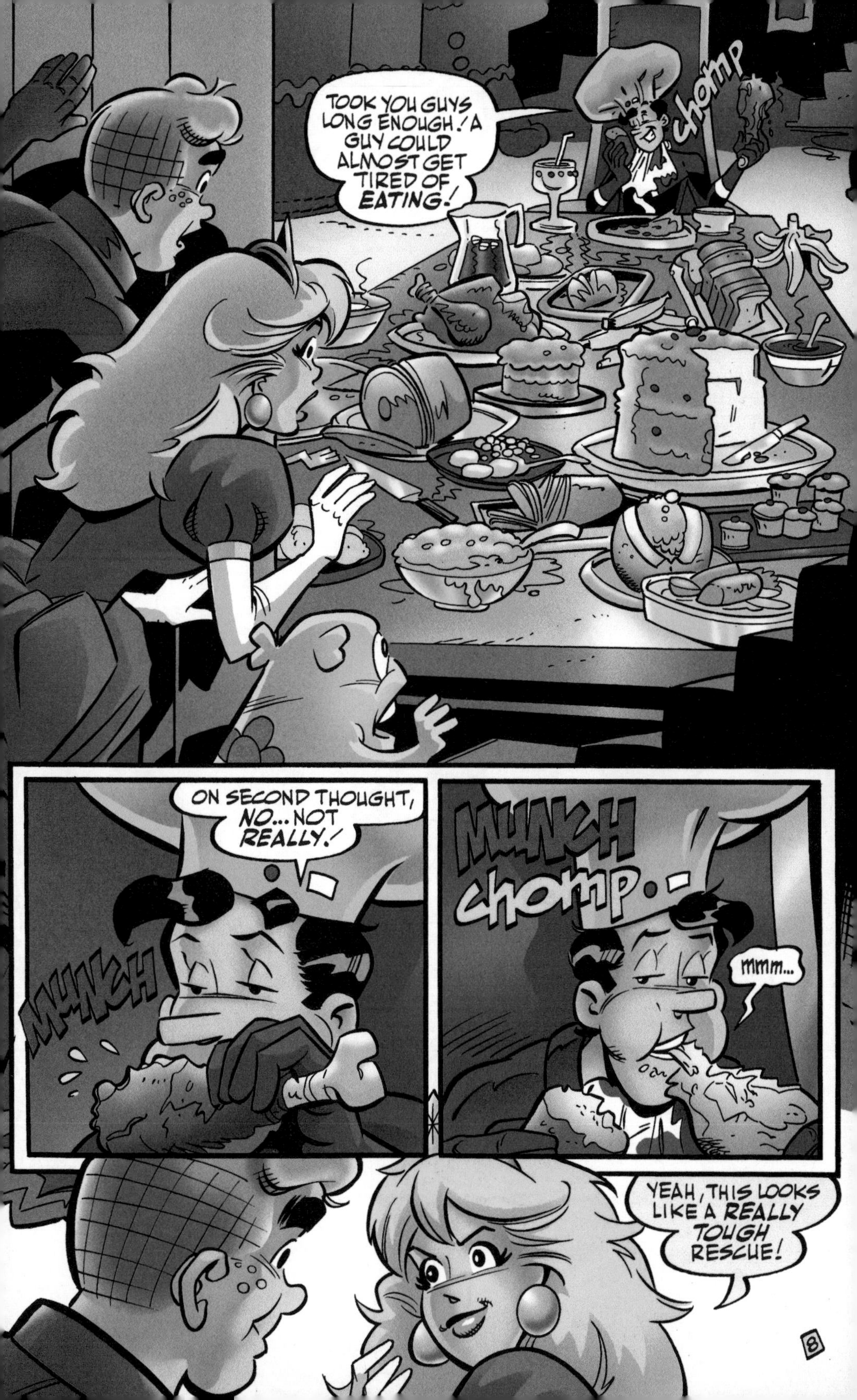
TOOK YOU GUYS LONG ENOUGH! A GUY COULD ALMOST GET TIRED OF EATING!
CHOMP
ON SECOND THOUGHT, NO... NOT REALLY!
MUNCH
MUNCH
CHOMP
MMM...
YEAH, THIS LOOKS LIKE A REALLY TOUGH RESCUE!

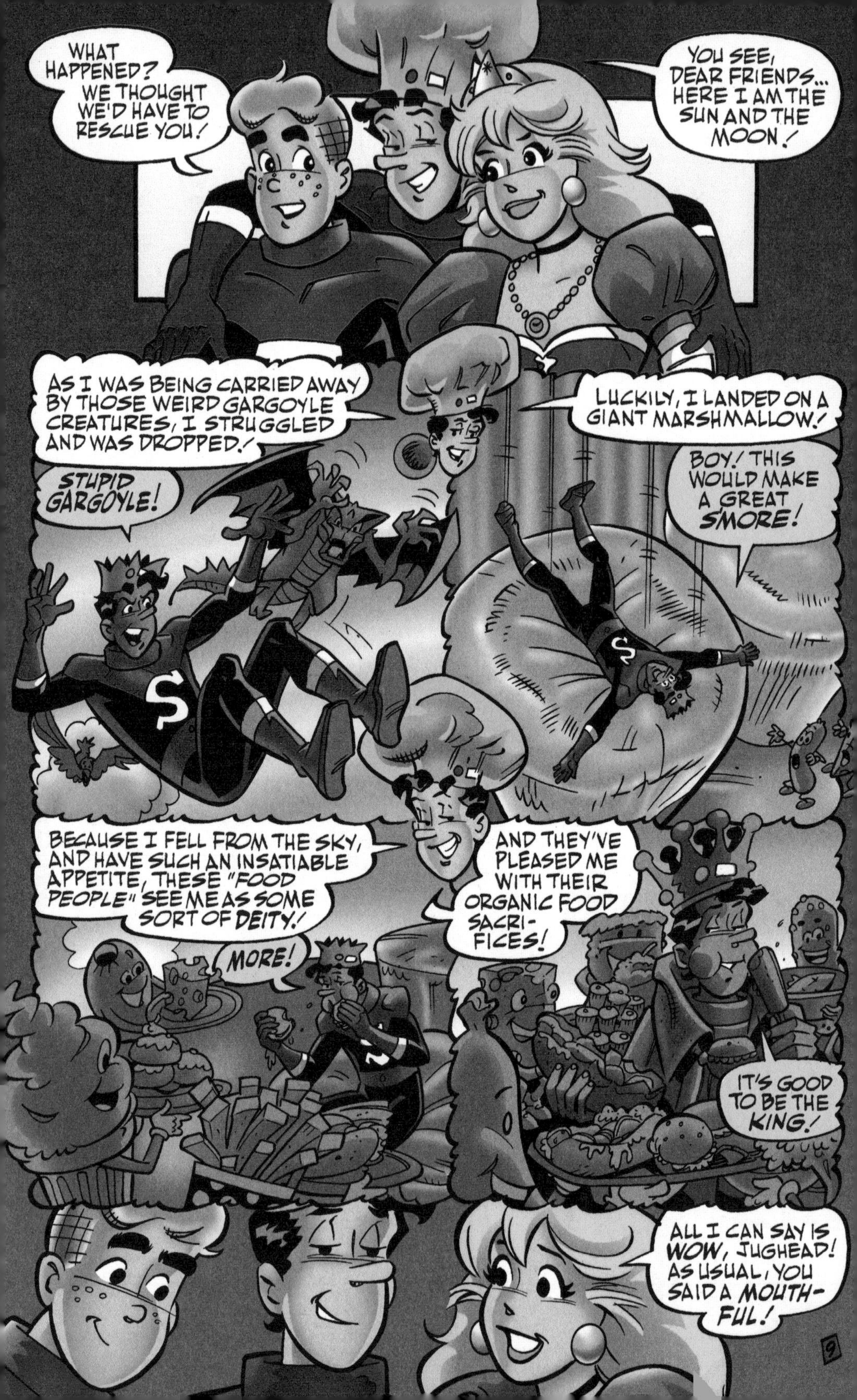
WHAT HAPPENED? WE THOUGHT WE'D HAVE TO RESCUE YOU!
YOU SEE, DEAR FRIENDS... HERE I AM THE SUN AND THE MOON!
AS I WAS BEING CARRIED AWAY BY THOSE WEIRD GARGOYLE CREATURES, I STRUGGLED AND WAS DROPPED!
LUCKILY, I LANDED ON A GIANT MARSHMALLOW!
STUPID GARGOYLE!
BOY! THIS WOULD MAKE A GREAT S'MORE!
BECAUSE I FELL FROM THE SKY, AND HAVE SUCH AN INSATIABLE APPETITE, THESE "FOOD PEOPLE" SEE ME AS SOME SORT OF DEITY!
AND THEY'VE PLEASED ME WITH THEIR ORGANIC FOOD SACRI-FICES!
MORE!
IT'S GOOD TO BE THE KING!
ALL I CAN SAY IS WOW, JUGHEAD! AS USUAL, YOU SAID A MOUTH-FUL!
9

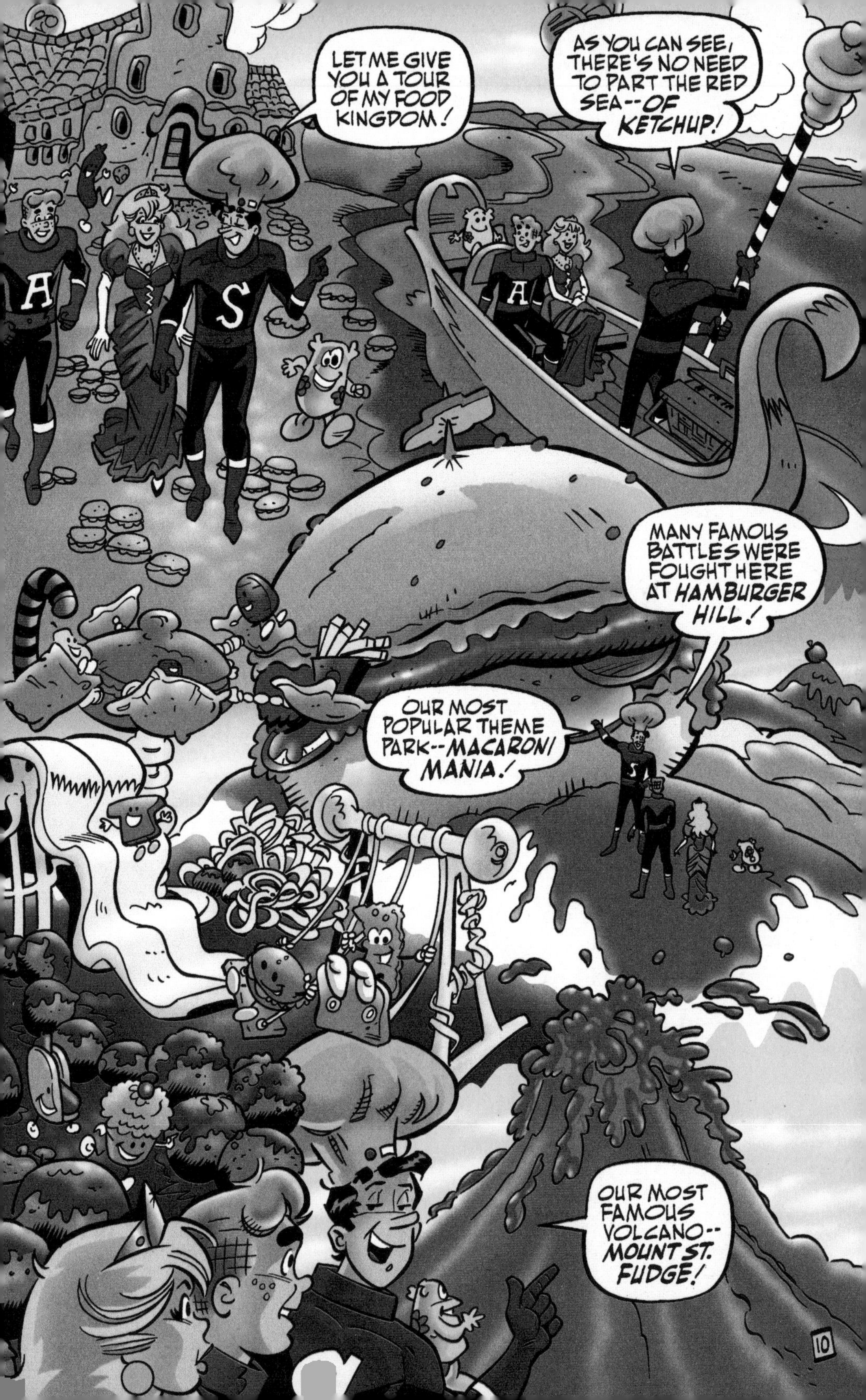
LET ME GIVE YOU A TOUR OF MY FOOD KINGDOM!
AS YOU CAN SEE, THERE'S NO NEED TO PART THE RED SEA--OF KETCHUP!
MANY FAMOUS BATTLES WERE FOUGHT HERE AT HAMBURGER HILL!
OUR MOST POPULAR THEME PARK--MACARONI MANIA!
OUR MOST FAMOUS VOLCANO--MOUNT ST. FUDGE!

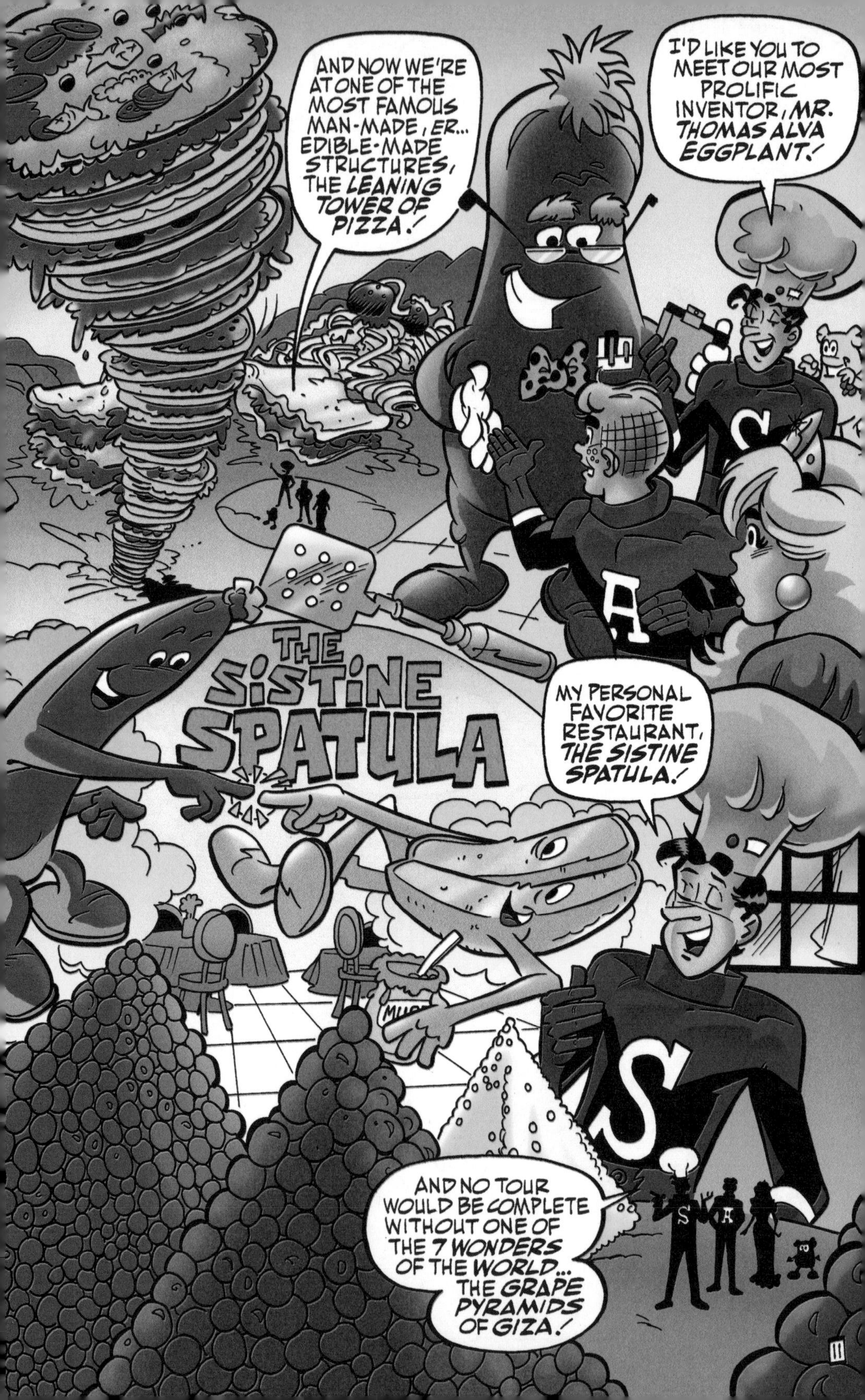
AND NOW WE'RE AT ONE OF THE MOST FAMOUS MAN-MADE, ER... EDIBLE-MADE STRUCTURES, THE LEANING TOWER OF PIZZA!
I'D LIKE YOU TO MEET OUR MOST PROLIFIC INVENTOR, MR. THOMAS ALVA EGGPLANT!
THE SISTINE SPATULA
MY PERSONAL FAVORITE RESTAURANT, THE SISTINE SPATULA!
AND NO TOUR WOULD BE COMPLETE WITHOUT ONE OF THE 7 WONDERS OF THE WORLD... THE GRAPE PYRAMIDS OF GIZA!
11

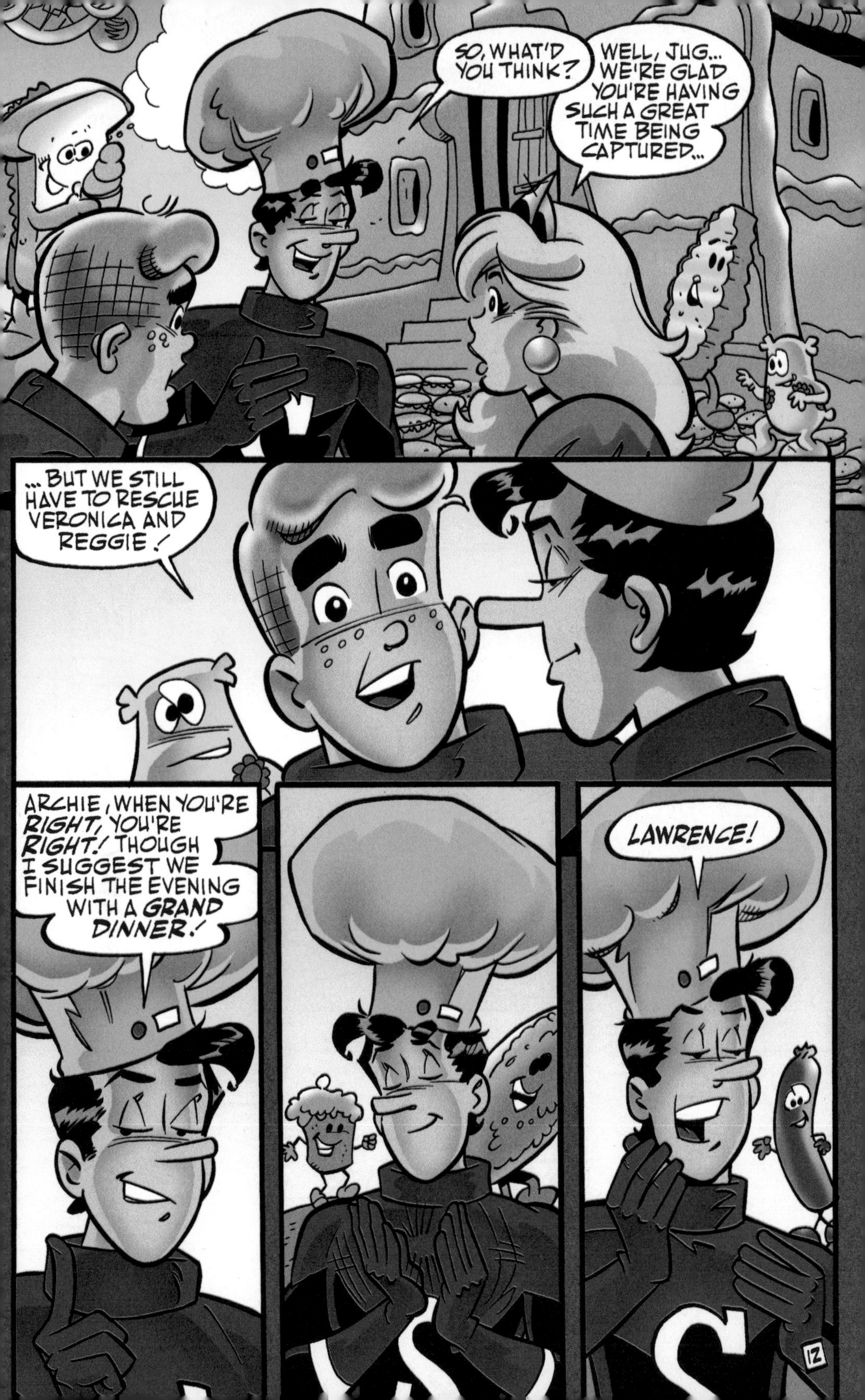
SO, WHAT'D YOU THINK?
WELL, JUG... WE'RE GLAD YOU'RE HAVING SUCH A GREAT TIME BEING CAPTURED...
... BUT WE STILL HAVE TO RESCUE VERONICA AND REGGIE!
ARCHIE, WHEN YOU'RE RIGHT, YOU'RE RIGHT! THOUGH I SUGGEST WE FINISH THE EVENING WITH A GRAND DINNER!
LAWRENCE!
12

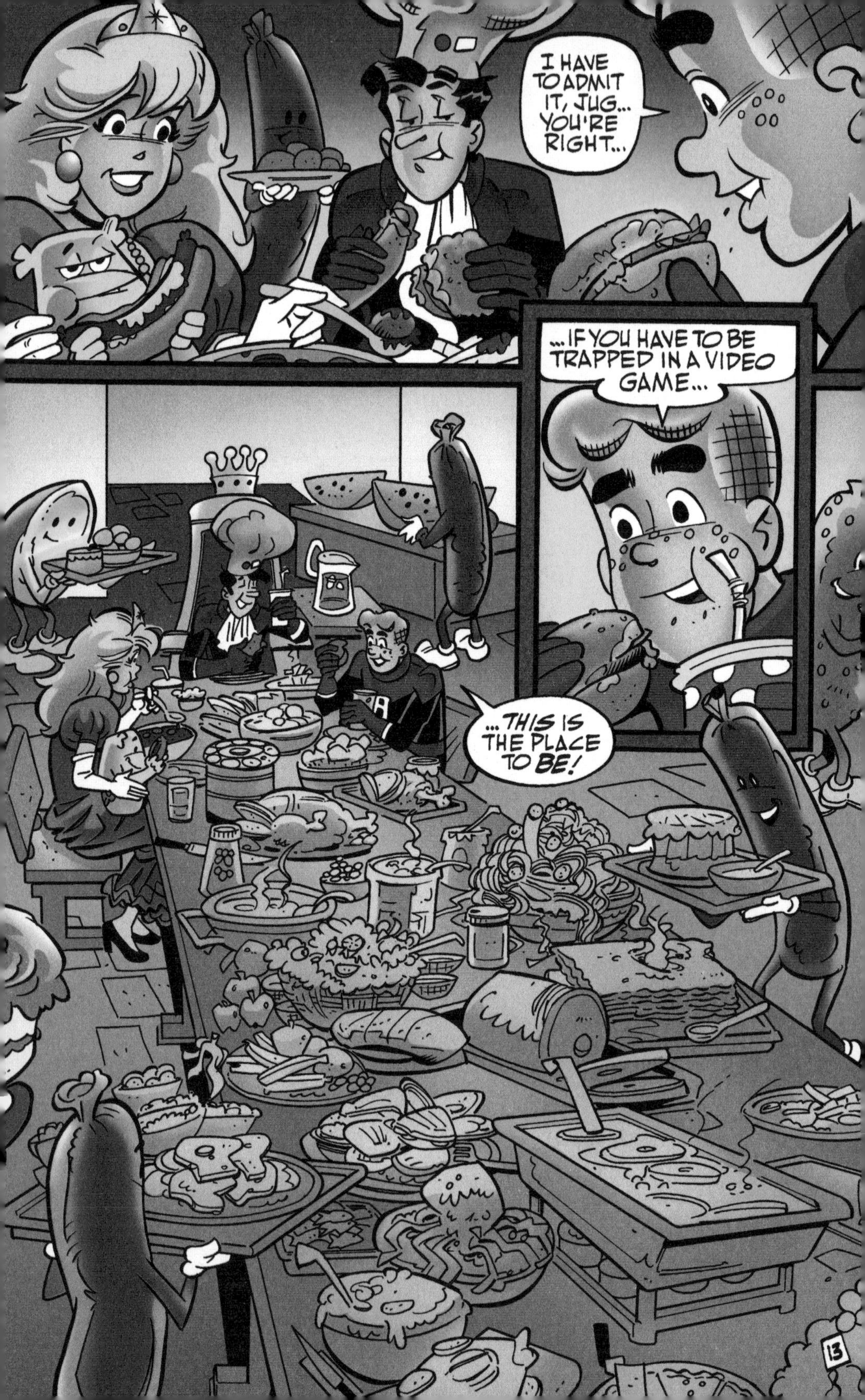
I HAVE TO ADMIT IT, JUG... YOU'RE RIGHT...
...IF YOU HAVE TO BE TRAPPED IN A VIDEO GAME...
...*THIS* IS THE PLACE TO *BE*!

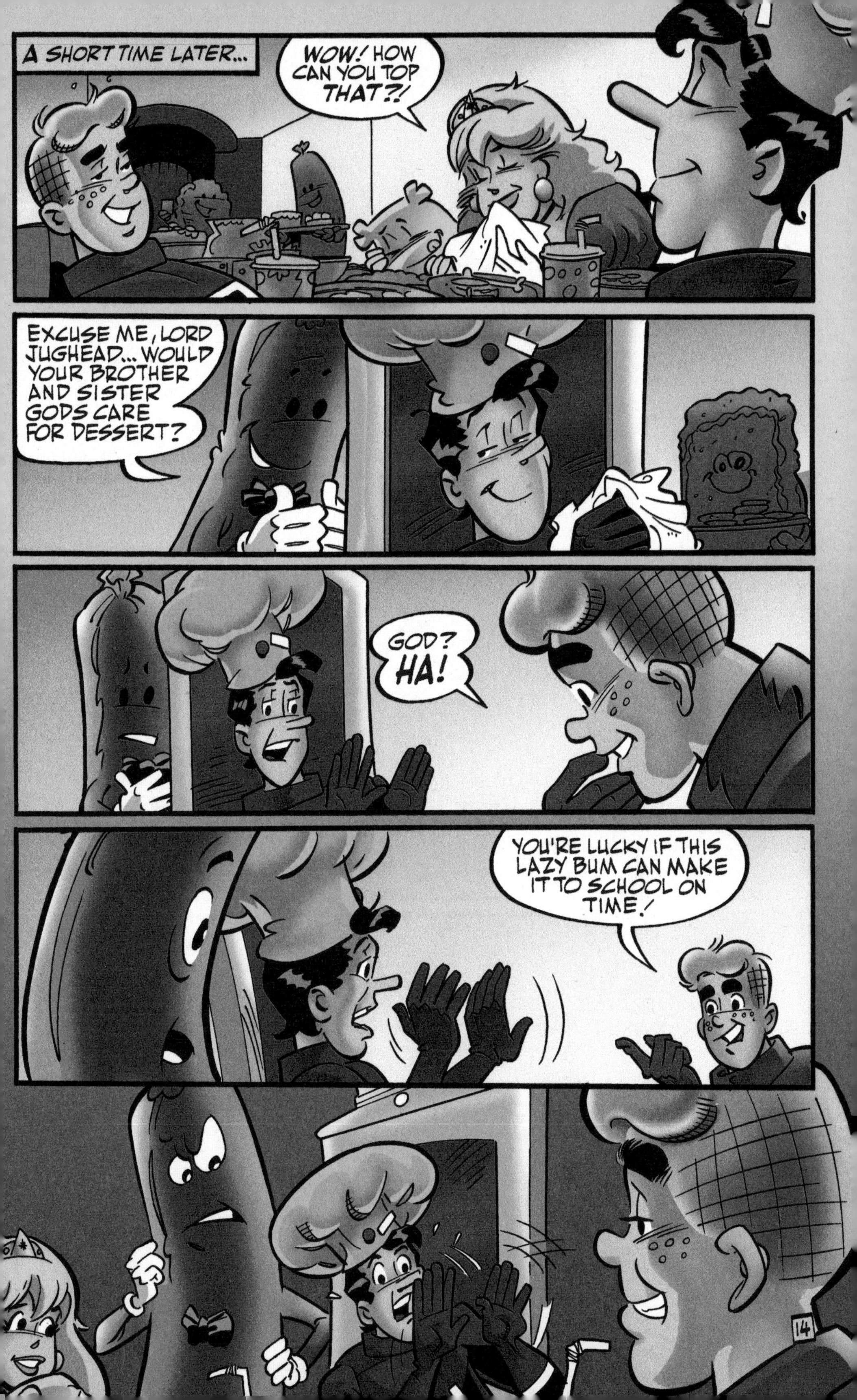
A SHORT TIME LATER...
WOW! HOW CAN YOU TOP THAT?!
EXCUSE ME, LORD JUGHEAD... WOULD YOUR BROTHER AND SISTER GODS CARE FOR DESSERT?
GOD? HA!
YOU'RE LUCKY IF THIS LAZY BUM CAN MAKE IT TO SCHOOL ON TIME!
14

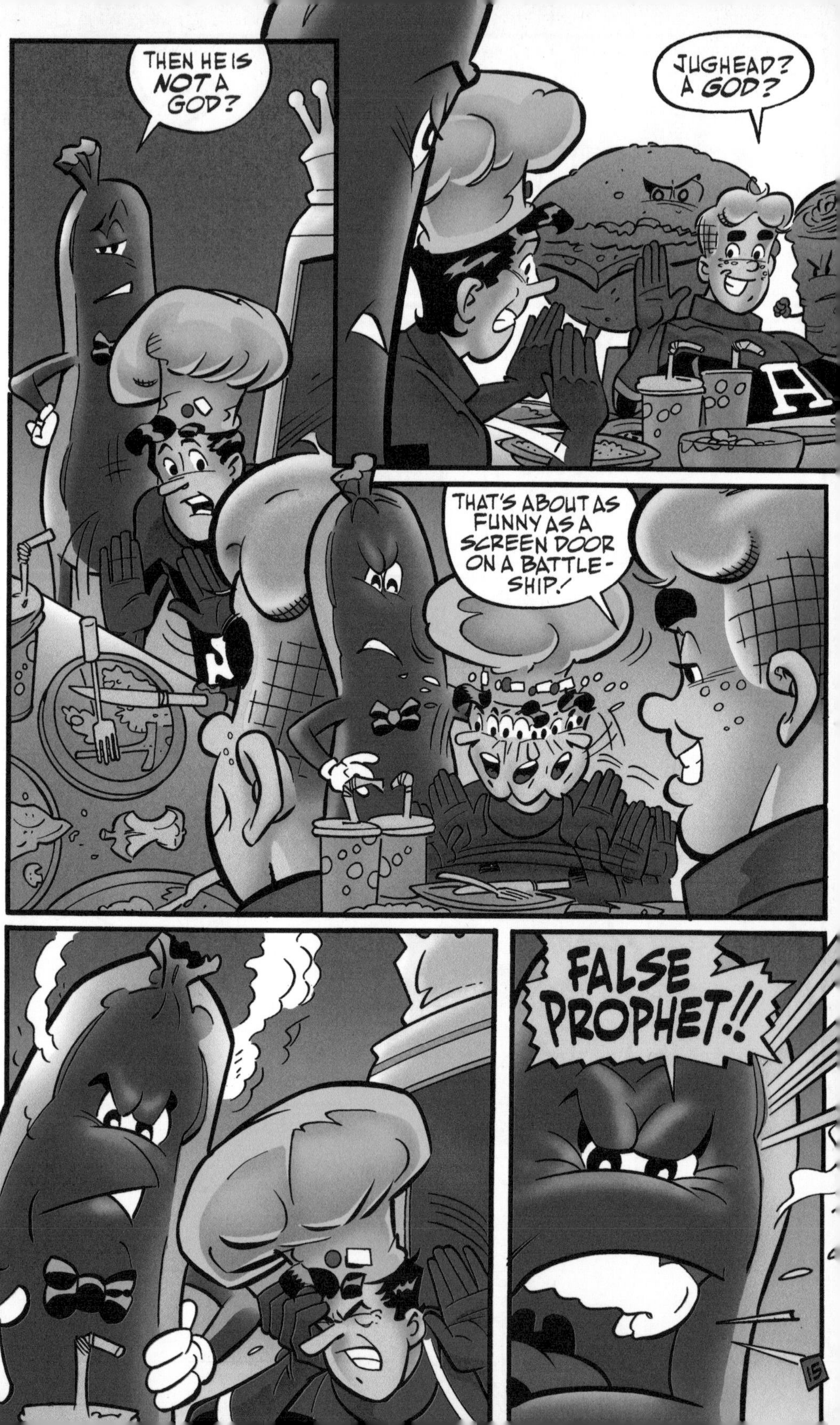
THEN HE IS NOT A GOD?
JUGHEAD? A GOD?
THAT'S ABOUT AS FUNNY AS A SCREEN DOOR ON A BATTLE-SHIP!
FALSE PROPHET!!

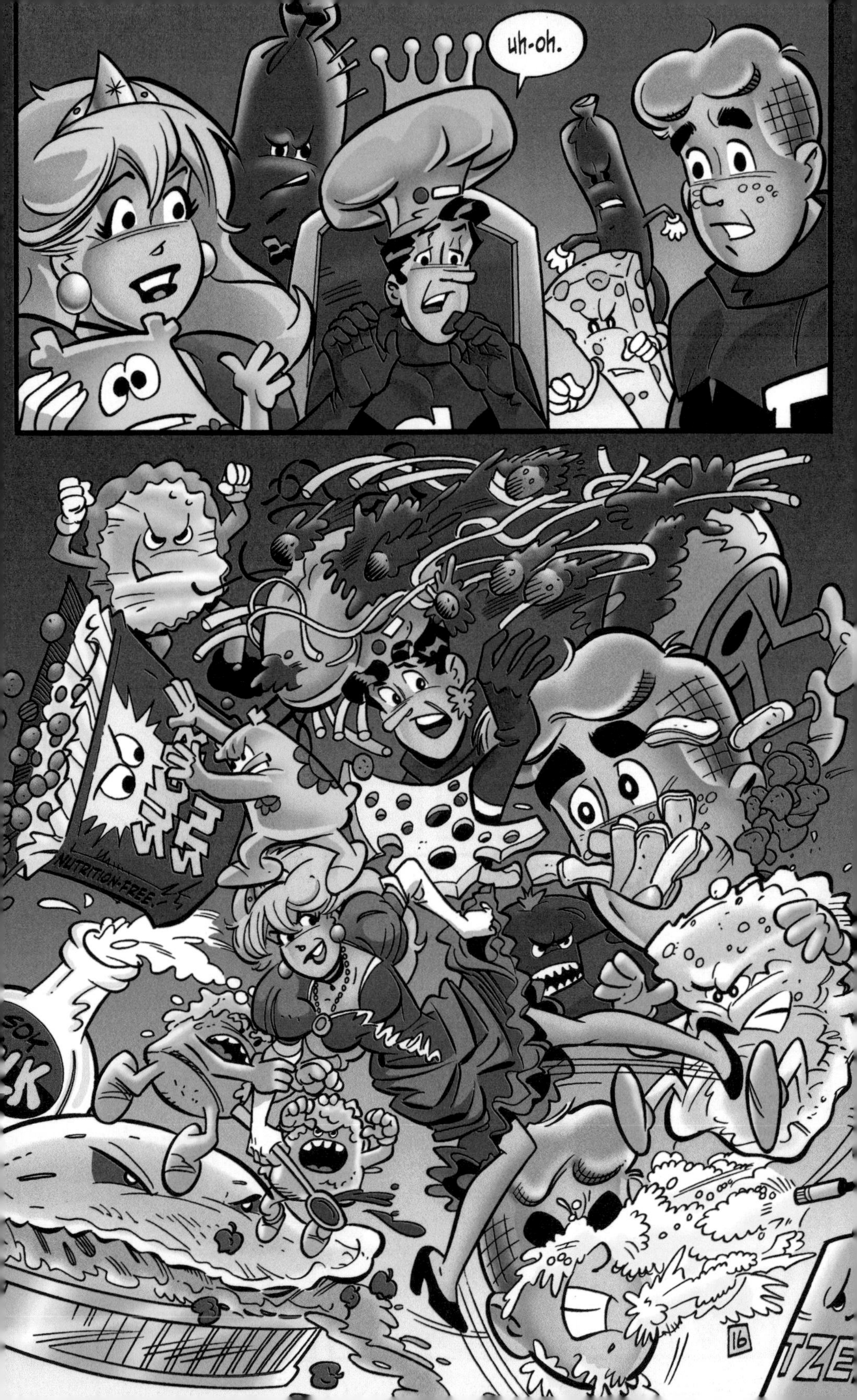
uh-oh.
NUTRITION-FREE.

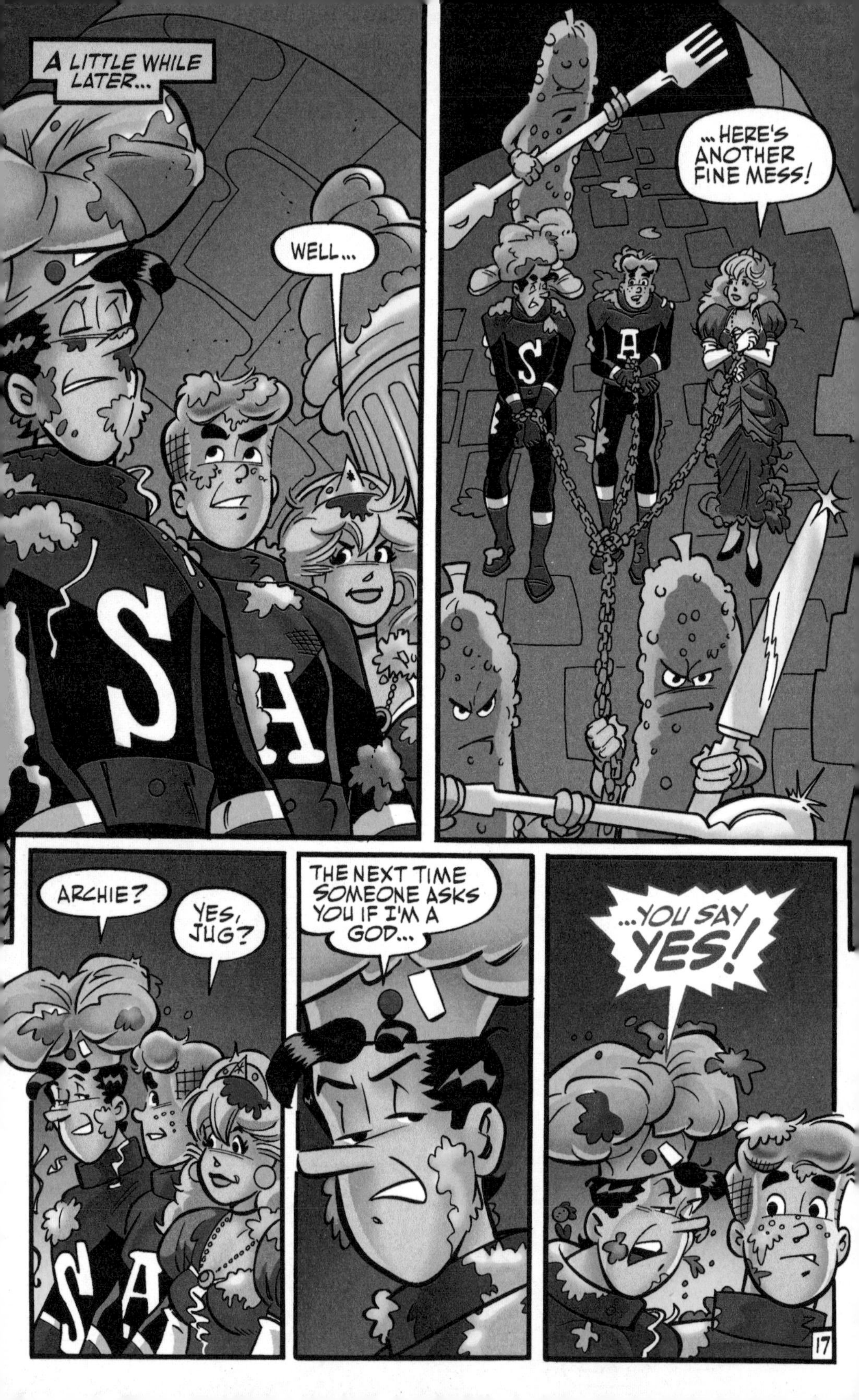
A LITTLE WHILE LATER...
WELL...
...HERE'S ANOTHER FINE MESS!
ARCHIE?
YES, JUG?
THE NEXT TIME SOMEONE ASKS YOU IF I'M A GOD...
...YOU SAY YES!

AREN'T *YOU* SNIPPY WHEN YOUR FACE ISN'T BEING FILLED WITH FOOD!

SORRY, I GET CRANKY WHEN IT'S *PAST MY SNACK TIME!*

IT'S OKAY.

AND DON'T WORRY... I'VE GOTTEN OUT OF TOUGHER SPOTS THAN THIS!

REALLY?

ACTUALLY *NO,* NOT REALLY... IT JUST SOUNDED GOOD!

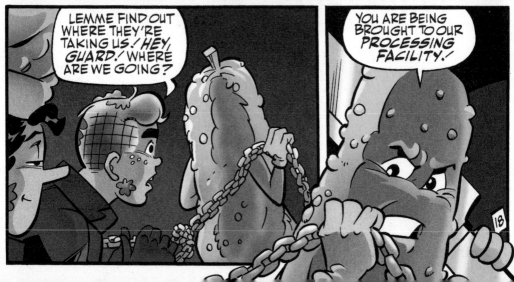

LEMME FIND OUT WHERE THEY'RE TAKING US! HEY, *GUARD!* WHERE ARE WE GOING?

YOU ARE BEING BROUGHT TO OUR *PROCESSING FACILITY!*

18

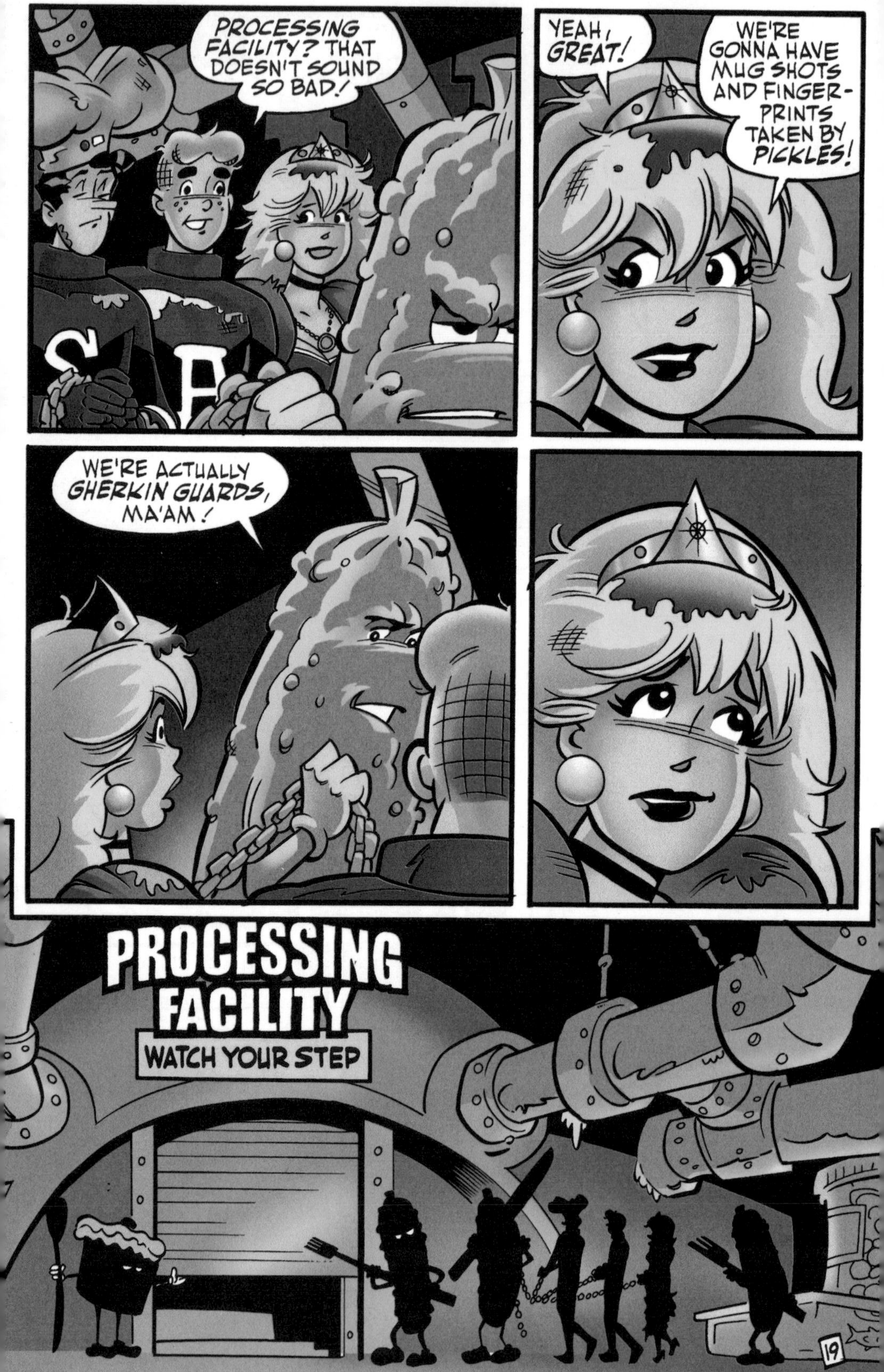
PROCESSING FACILITY? THAT DOESN'T SOUND SO BAD!
YEAH, GREAT!
WE'RE GONNA HAVE MUG SHOTS AND FINGER-PRINTS TAKEN BY PICKLES!
WE'RE ACTUALLY GHERKIN GUARDS, MA'AM!
PROCESSING FACILITY
WATCH YOUR STEP
19

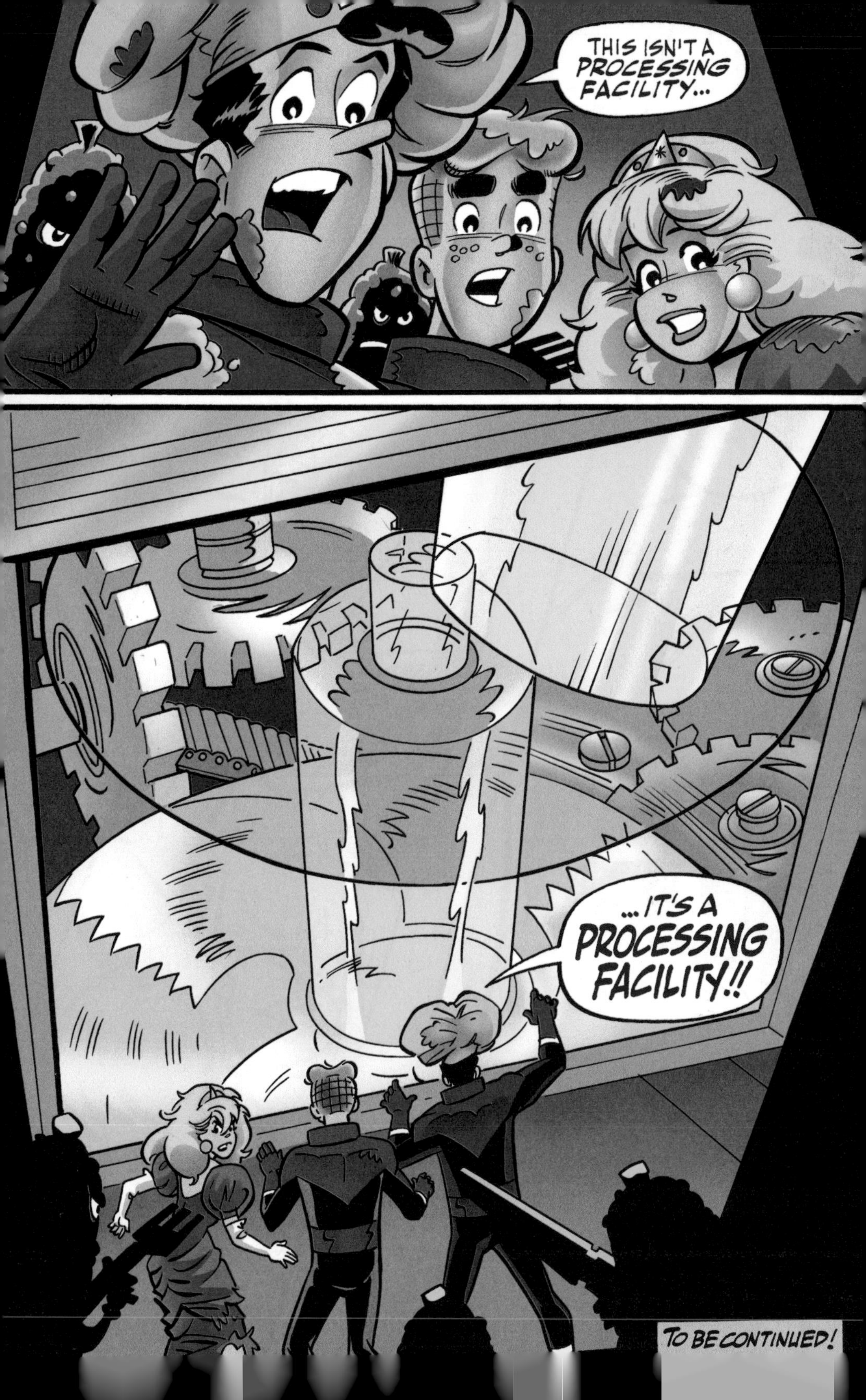
THIS ISN'T A PROCESSING FACILITY...
...IT'S A PROCESSING FACILITY!!
TO BE CONTINUED!

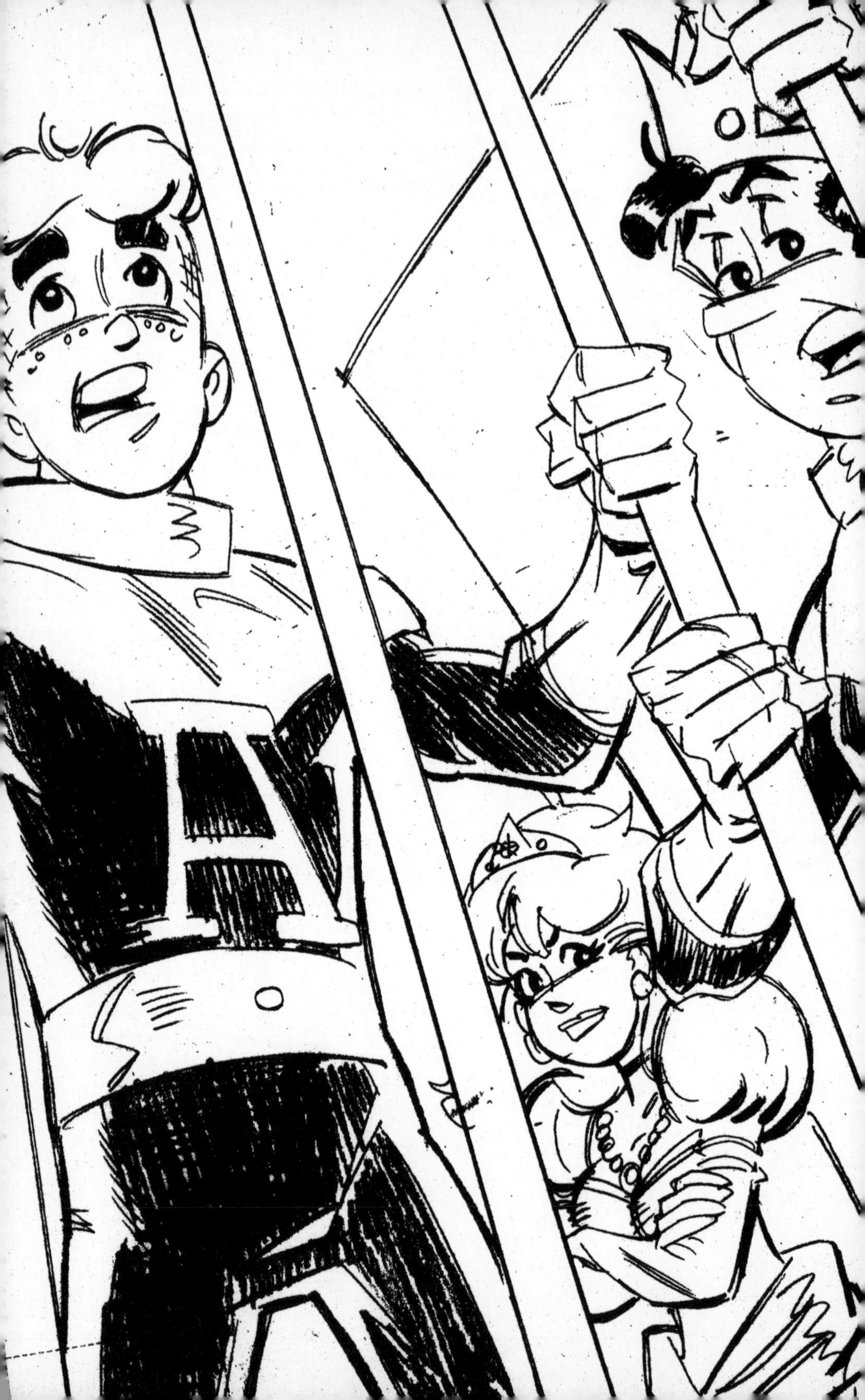

CHAPTER FOUR

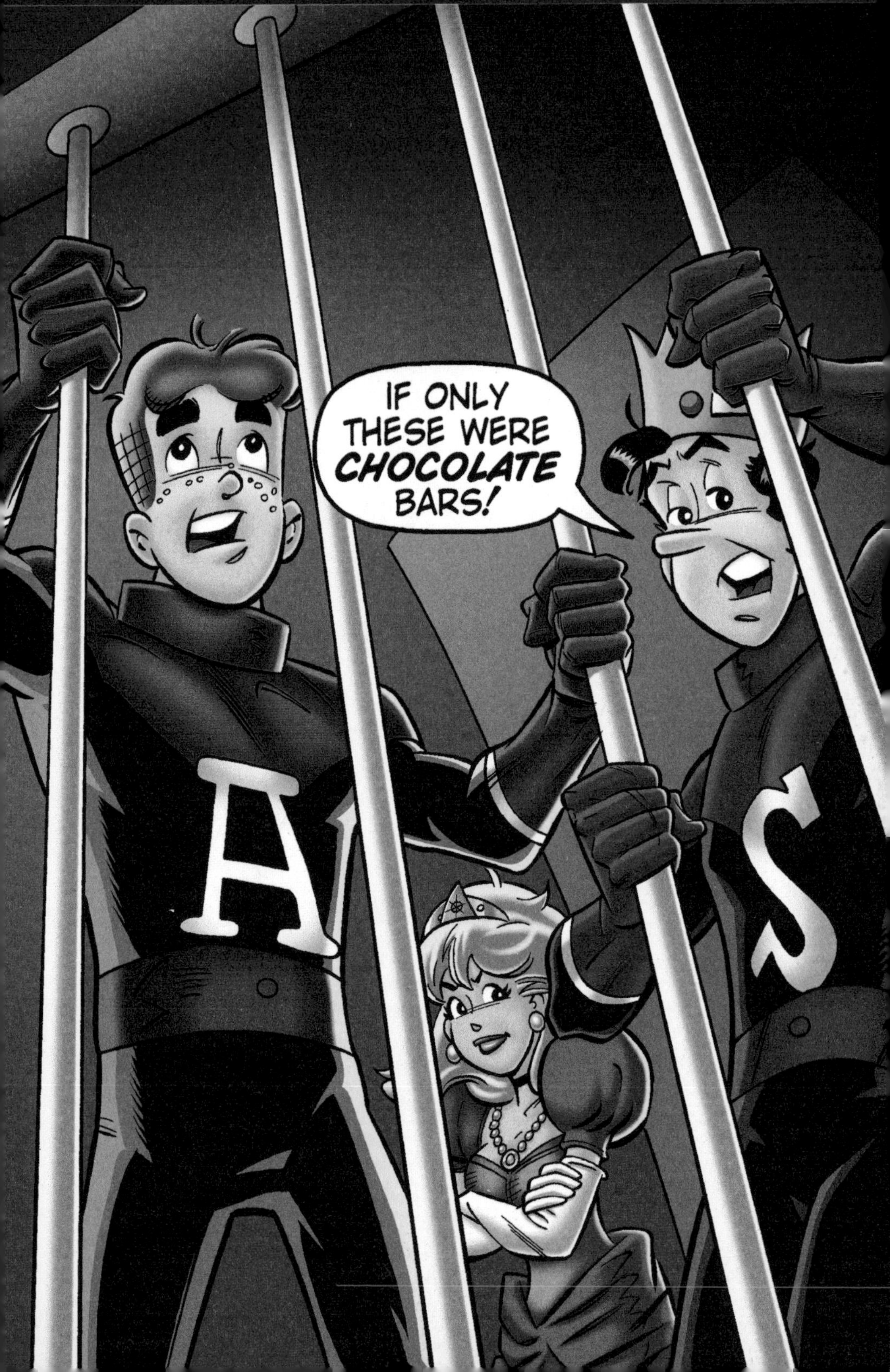
IF ONLY THESE WERE CHOCOLATE BARS!

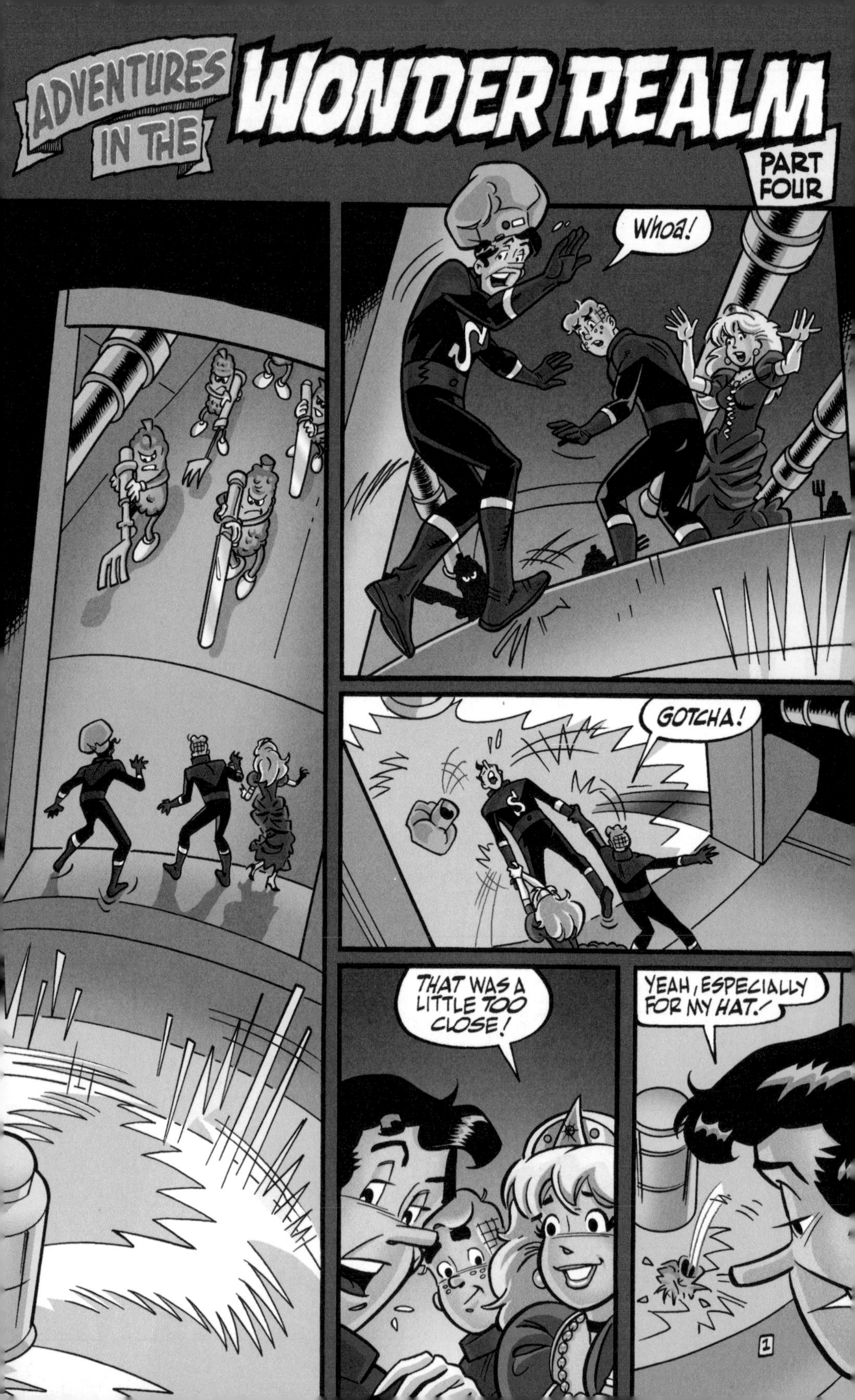
ADVENTURES IN THE
WONDER REALM
PART FOUR
Whoa!
GOTCHA!
THAT WAS A LITTLE TOO CLOSE!
YEAH, ESPECIALLY FOR MY HAT.
1

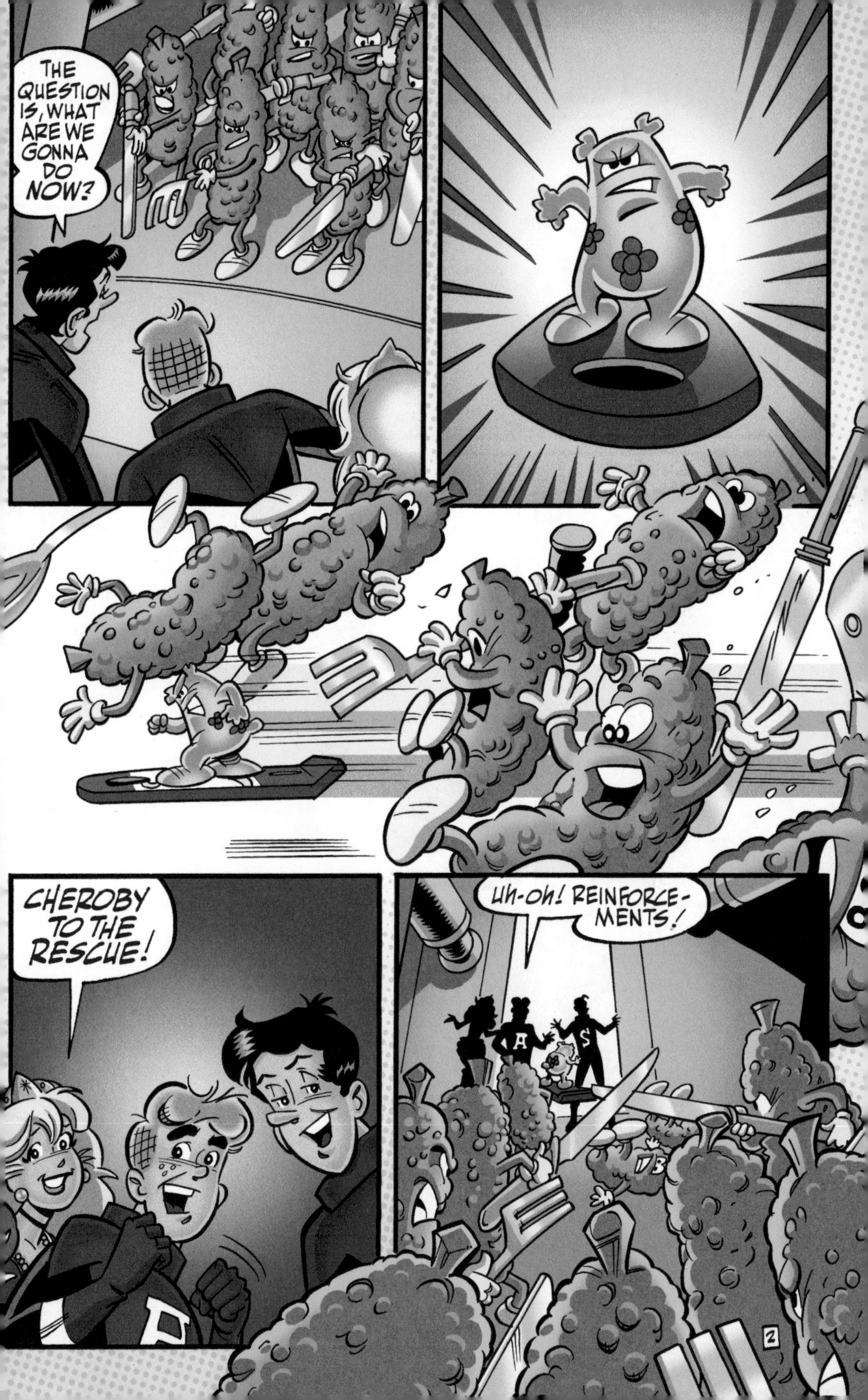
THE QUESTION IS, WHAT ARE WE GONNA DO NOW?
CHEROBY TO THE RESCUE!
UH-OH! REINFORCE-MENTS!
2

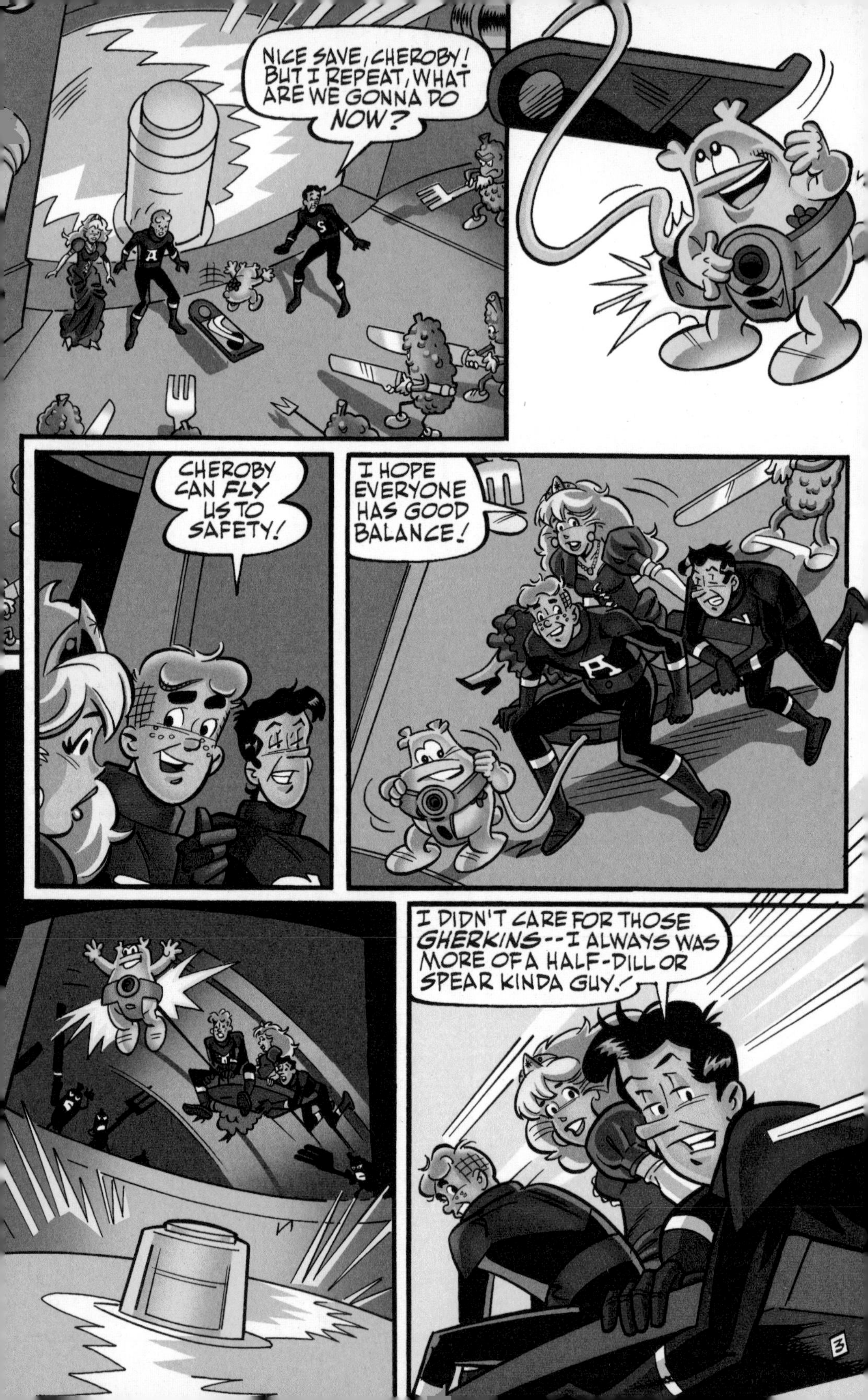
NICE SAVE, CHEROBY! BUT I REPEAT, WHAT ARE WE GONNA DO NOW?
CHEROBY CAN FLY US TO SAFETY!
I HOPE EVERYONE HAS GOOD BALANCE!
I DIDN'T CARE FOR THOSE GHERKINS-- I ALWAYS WAS MORE OF A HALF-DILL OR SPEAR KINDA GUY.
3

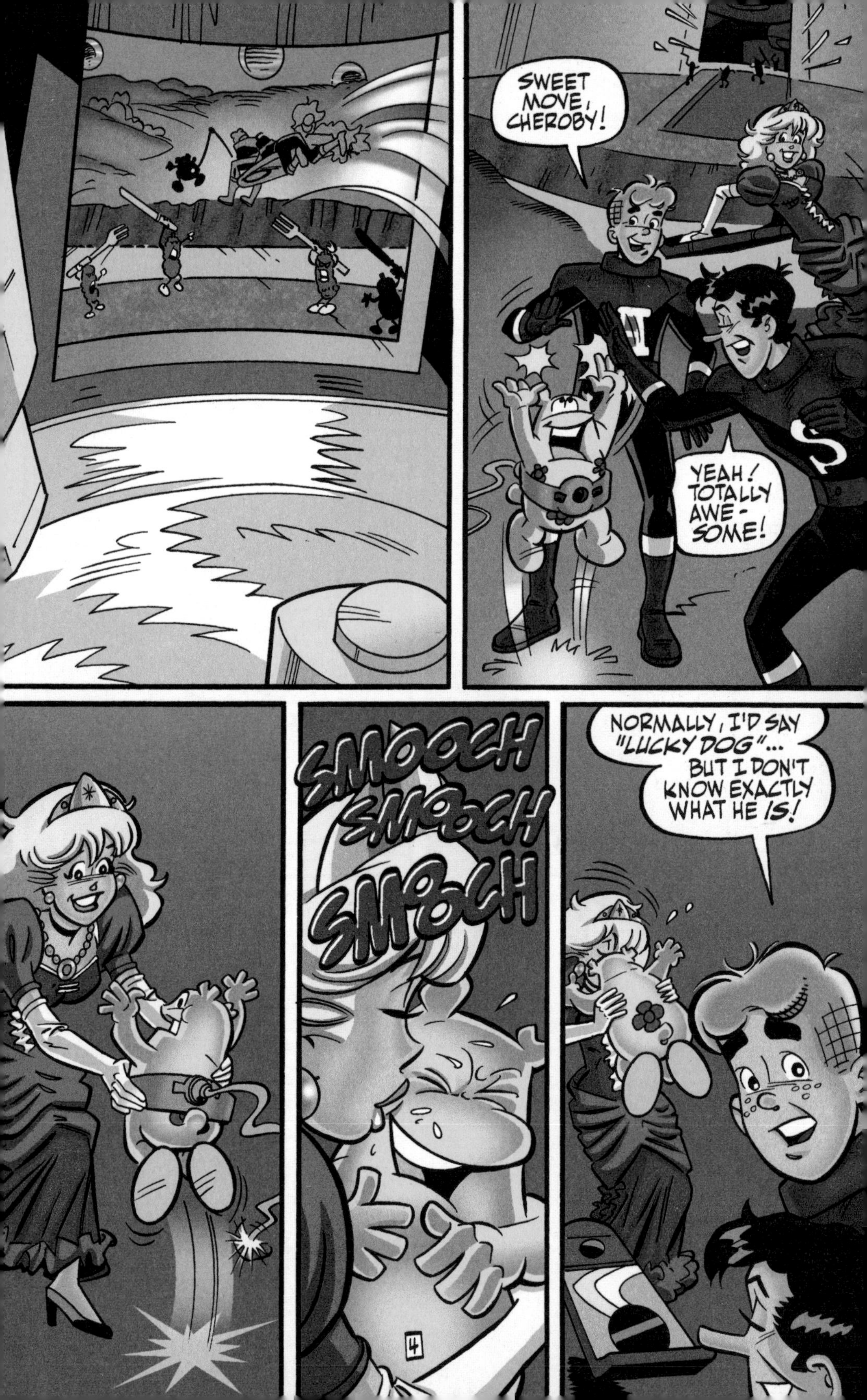
SWEET MOVE, CHEROBY!
YEAH! TOTALLY AWE-SOME!
SMOOCH
SMOOCH
SMOOCH
NORMALLY, I'D SAY "LUCKY DOG"... BUT I DON'T KNOW EXACTLY WHAT HE IS!
4

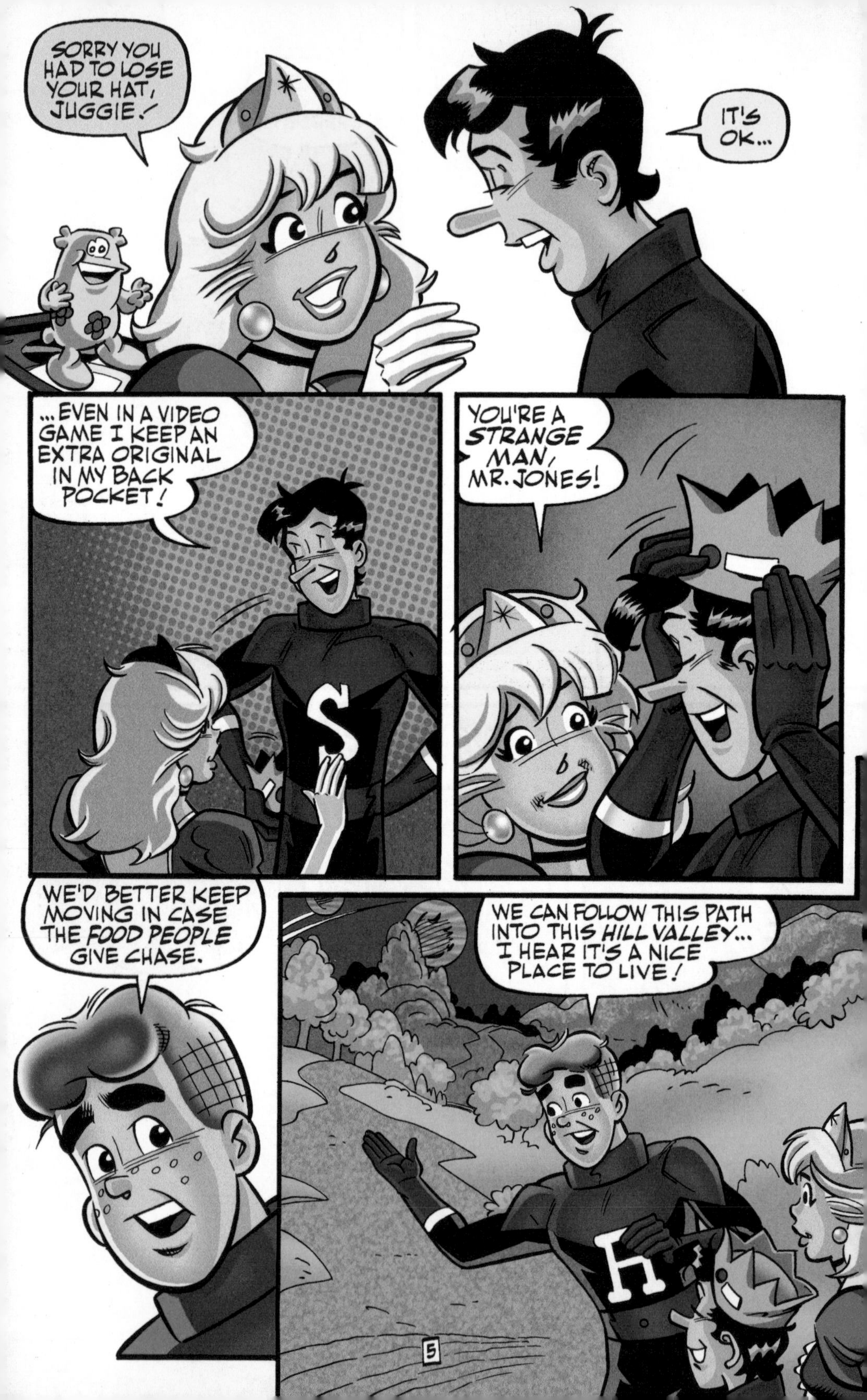
SORRY YOU HAD TO LOSE YOUR HAT, JUGGIE!
IT'S OK...
...EVEN IN A VIDEO GAME I KEEP AN EXTRA ORIGINAL IN MY BACK POCKET!
YOU'RE A STRANGE MAN, MR. JONES!
WE'D BETTER KEEP MOVING IN CASE THE FOOD PEOPLE GIVE CHASE.
WE CAN FOLLOW THIS PATH INTO THIS HILL VALLEY... I HEAR IT'S A NICE PLACE TO LIVE!
5

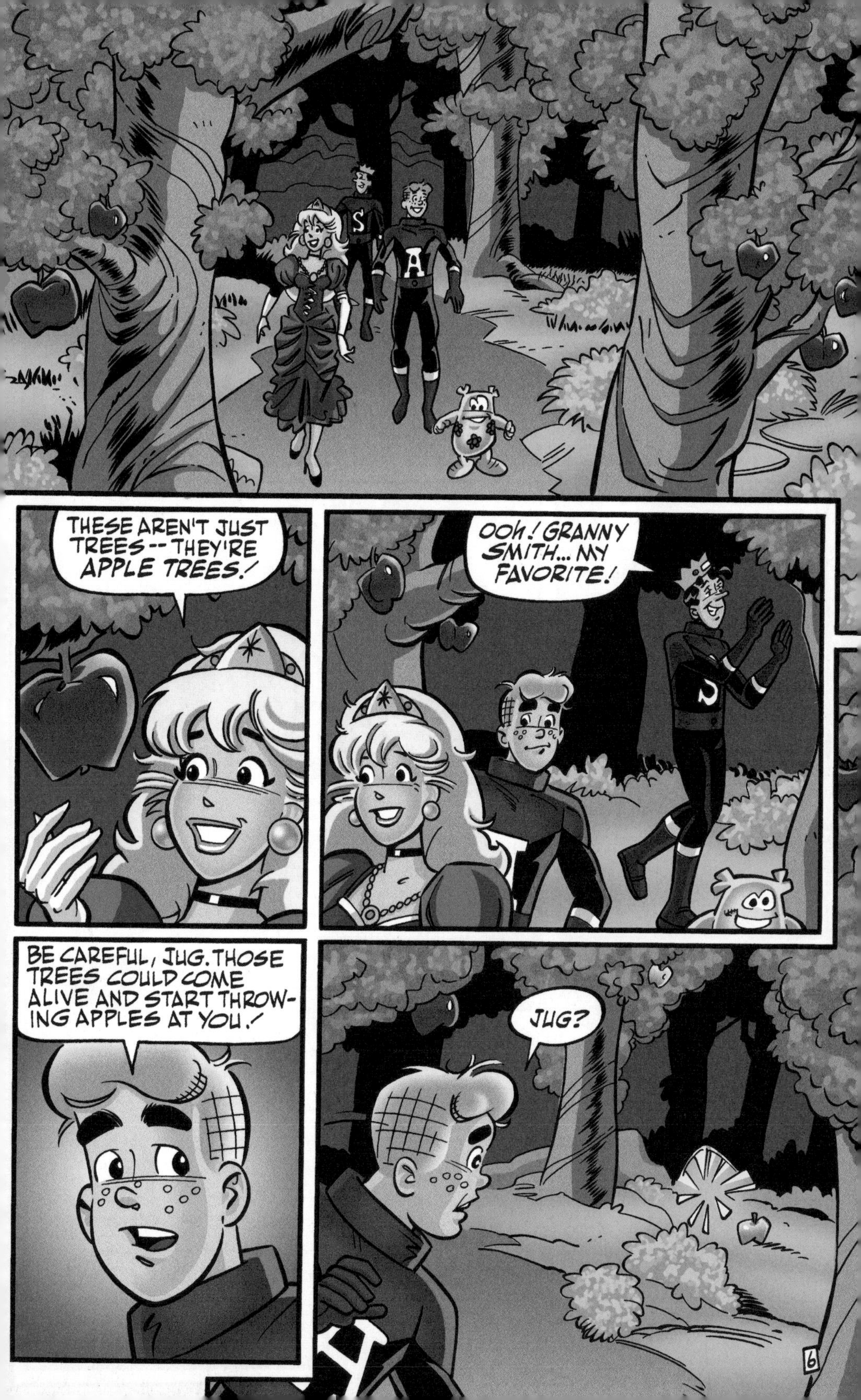
THESE AREN'T JUST TREES -- THEY'RE APPLE TREES!
OOH! GRANNY SMITH... MY FAVORITE!
BE CAREFUL, JUG. THOSE TREES COULD COME ALIVE AND START THROWING APPLES AT YOU!
JUG?
6

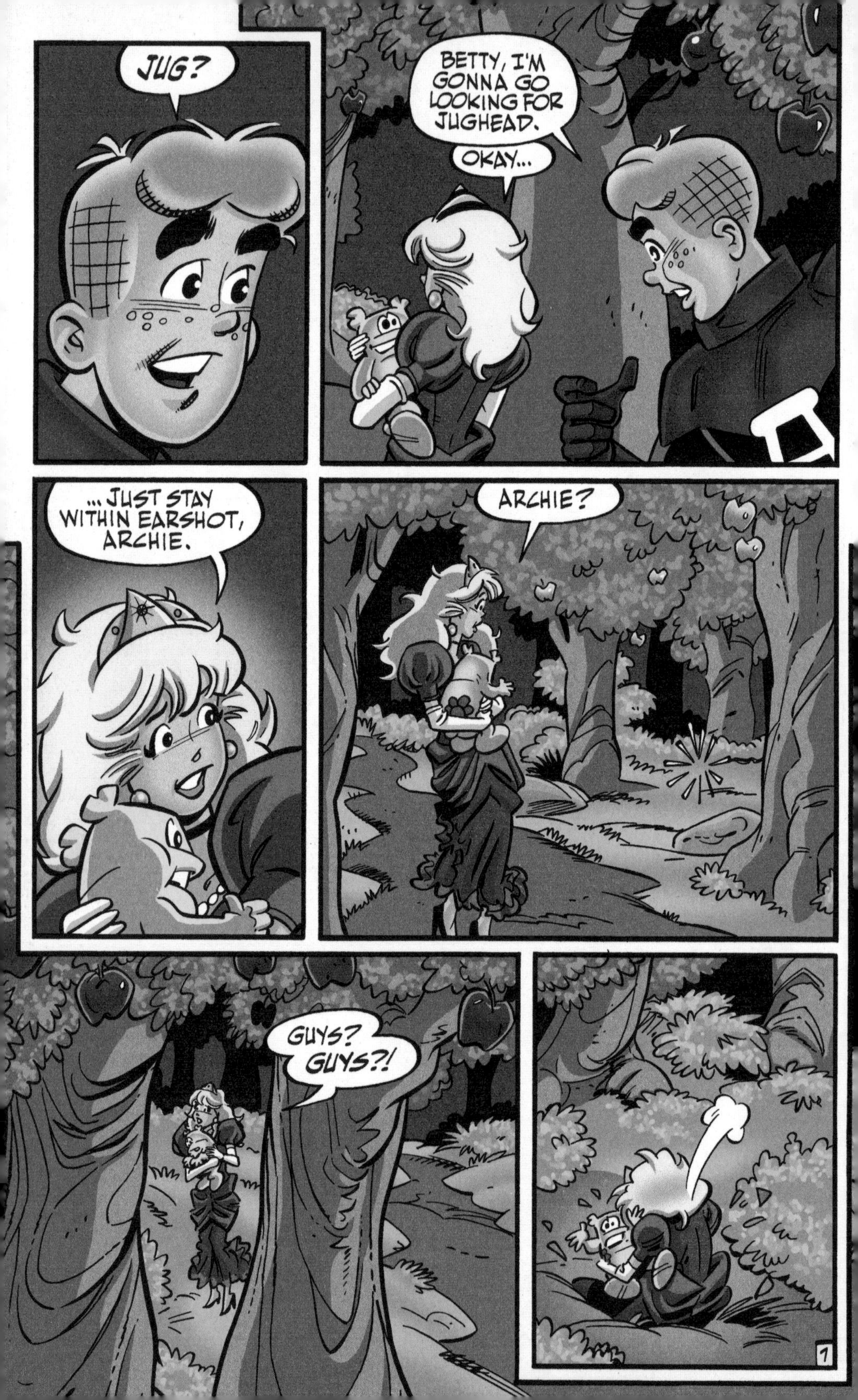
JUG?
BETTY, I'M GONNA GO LOOKING FOR JUGHEAD.
OKAY...
... JUST STAY WITHIN EARSHOT, ARCHIE.
ARCHIE?
GUYS? GUYS?!

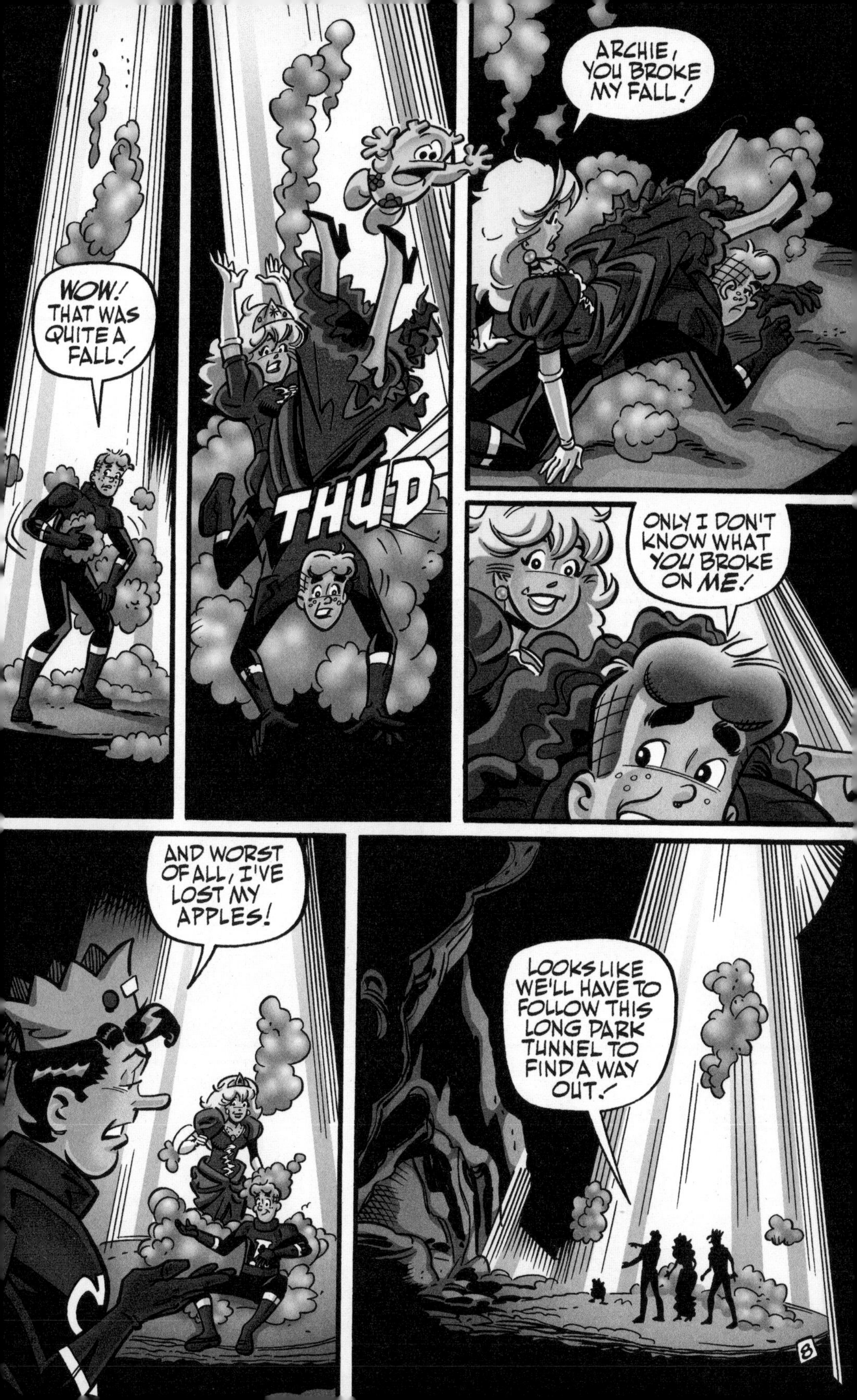

WOW! THAT WAS QUITE A FALL!
THUD
ARCHIE, YOU BROKE MY FALL!
ONLY I DON'T KNOW WHAT YOU BROKE ON ME!
AND WORST OF ALL, I'VE LOST MY APPLES!
LOOKS LIKE WE'LL HAVE TO FOLLOW THIS LONG PARK TUNNEL TO FIND A WAY OUT!
8

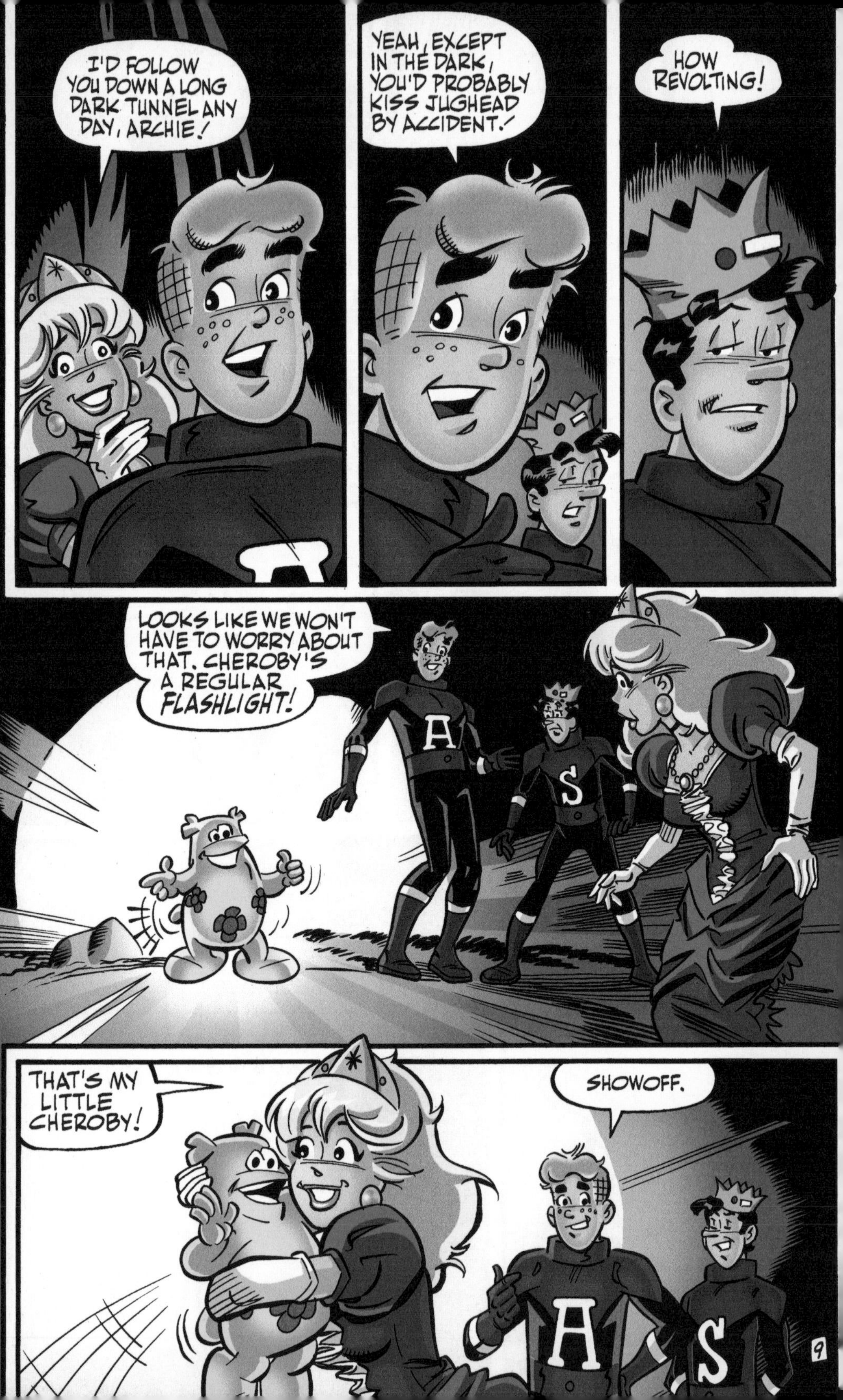
I'D FOLLOW YOU DOWN A LONG DARK TUNNEL ANY DAY, ARCHIE!
YEAH, EXCEPT IN THE DARK, YOU'D PROBABLY KISS JUGHEAD BY ACCIDENT!
HOW REVOLTING!
LOOKS LIKE WE WON'T HAVE TO WORRY ABOUT THAT. CHEROBY'S A REGULAR FLASHLIGHT!
THAT'S MY LITTLE CHEROBY!
SHOWOFF.

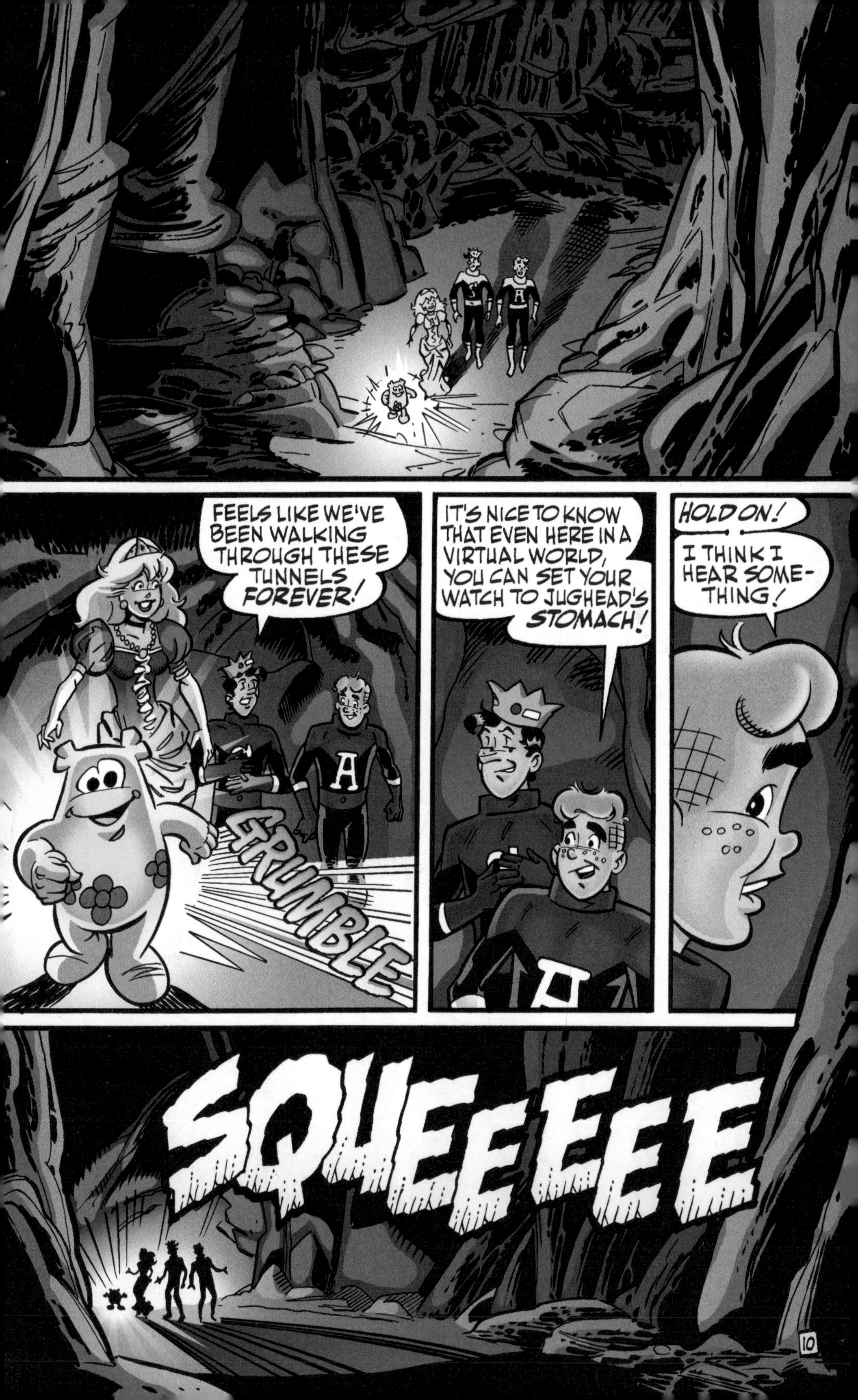
FEELS LIKE WE'VE BEEN WALKING THROUGH THESE TUNNELS FOREVER!
GRUMBLE
IT'S NICE TO KNOW THAT EVEN HERE IN A VIRTUAL WORLD, YOU CAN SET YOUR WATCH TO JUGHEAD'S STOMACH!
HOLD ON!
I THINK I HEAR SOMETHING!
SQUEEEEE

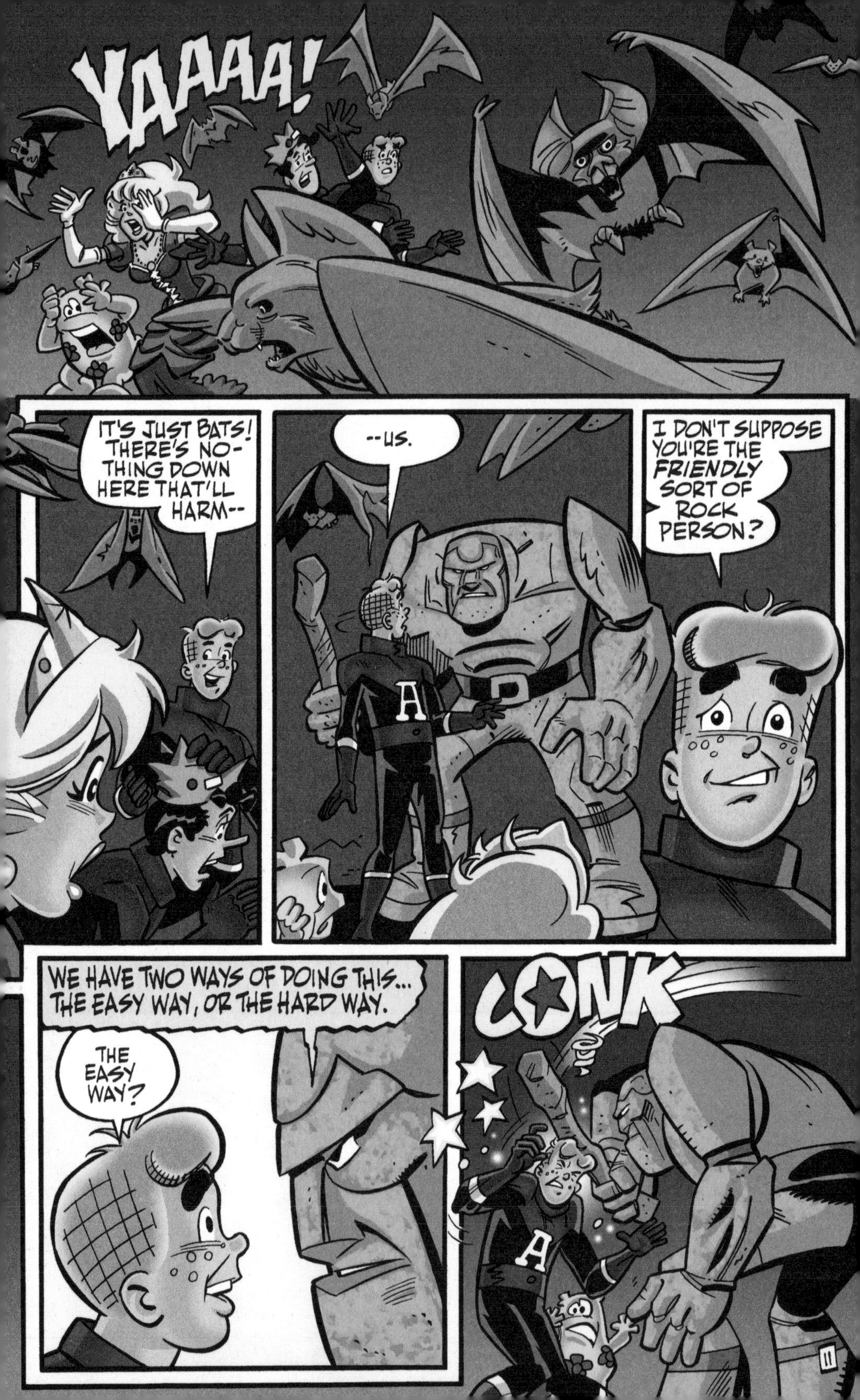
YAAAA!
IT'S JUST BATS! THERE'S NOTHING DOWN HERE THAT'LL HARM--
--US.
I DON'T SUPPOSE YOU'RE THE FRIENDLY SORT OF ROCK PERSON?
WE HAVE TWO WAYS OF DOING THIS... THE EASY WAY, OR THE HARD WAY.
THE EASY WAY?
CONK
11

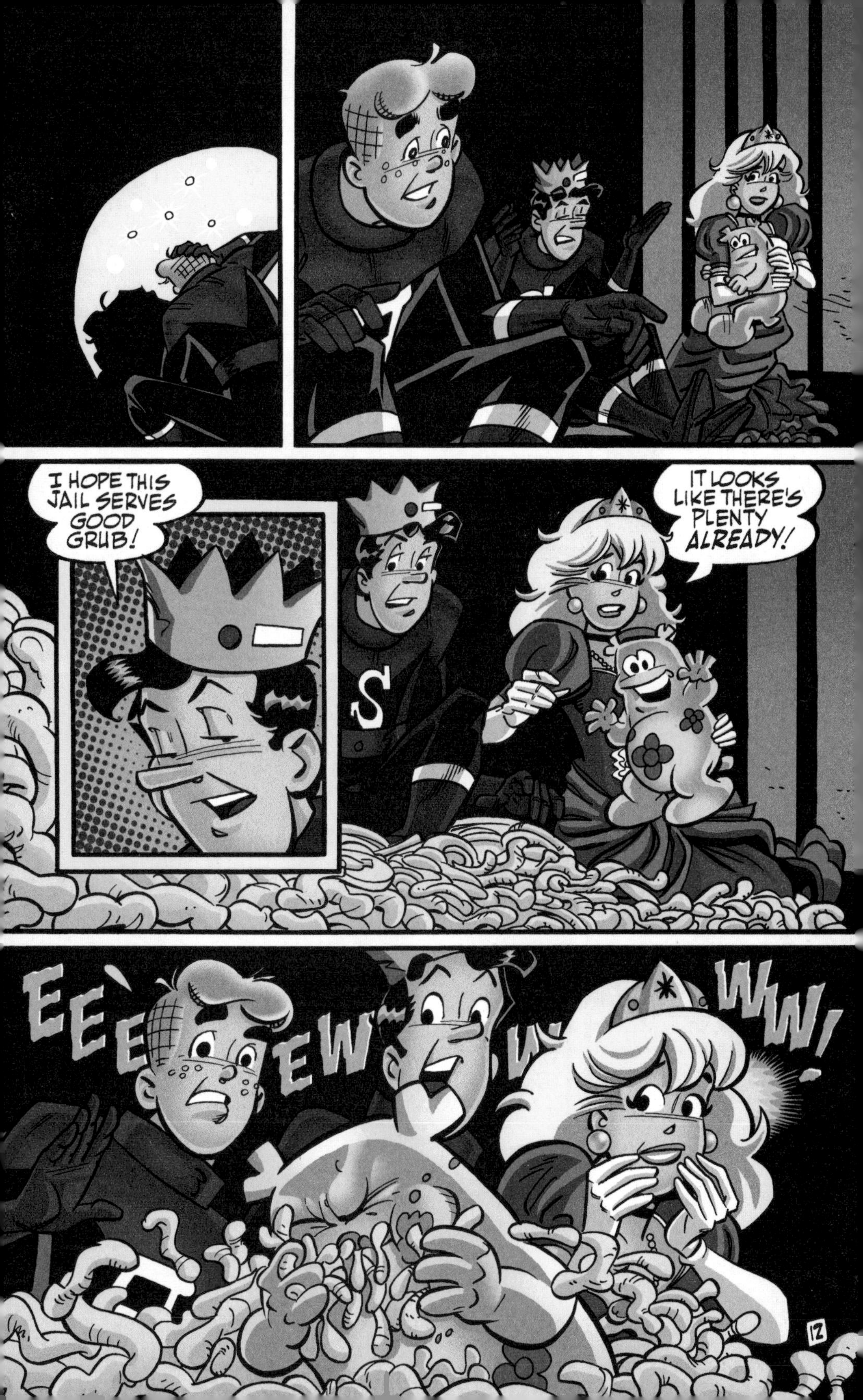
I HOPE THIS JAIL SERVES GOOD GRUB!
IT LOOKS LIKE THERE'S PLENTY ALREADY!
EEEEW WW!

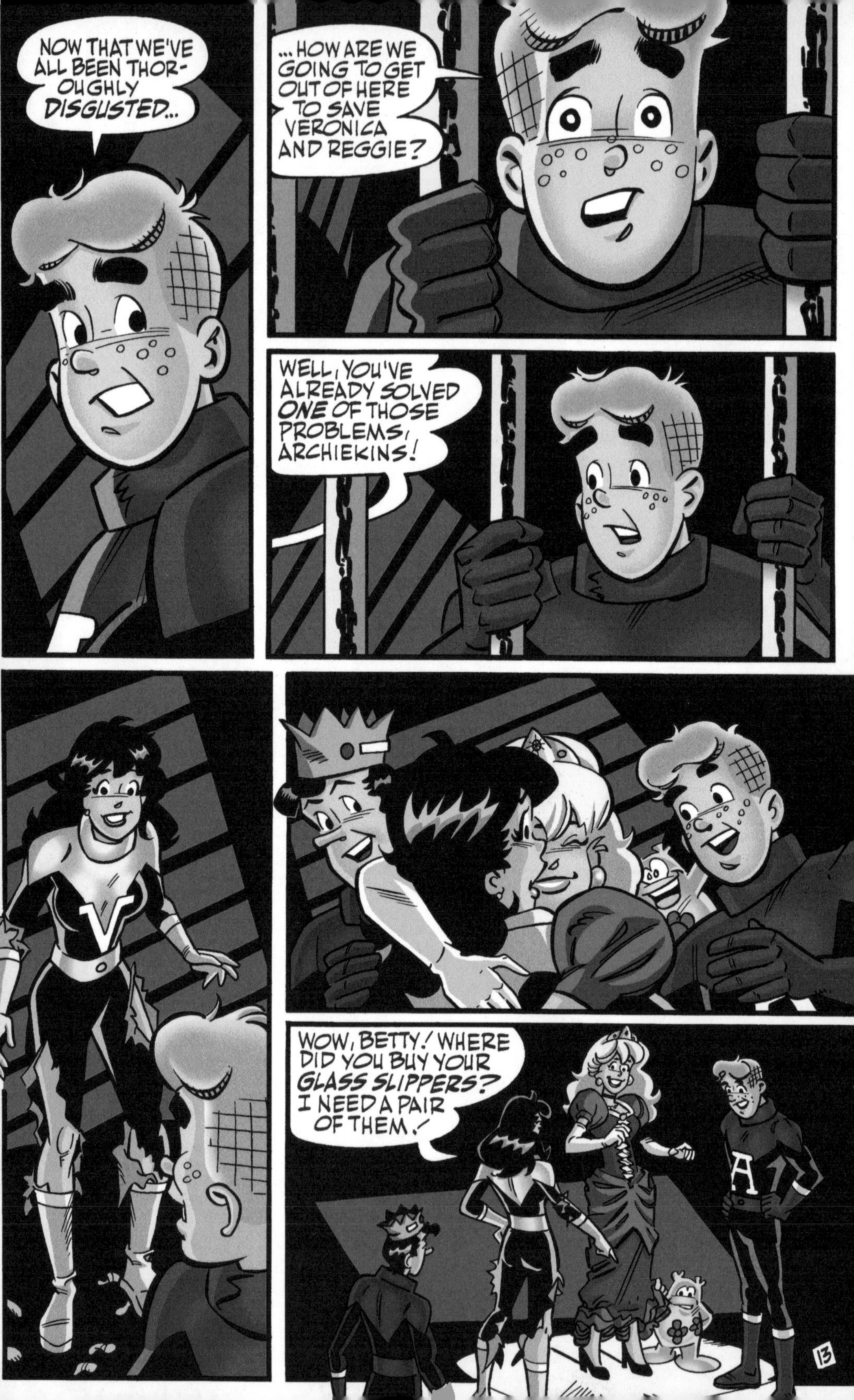
NOW THAT WE'VE ALL BEEN THOROUGHLY DISGUSTED...
...HOW ARE WE GOING TO GET OUT OF HERE TO SAVE VERONICA AND REGGIE?
WELL, YOU'VE ALREADY SOLVED ONE OF THOSE PROBLEMS, ARCHIEKINS!
WOW, BETTY! WHERE DID YOU BUY YOUR GLASS SLIPPERS? I NEED A PAIR OF THEM!

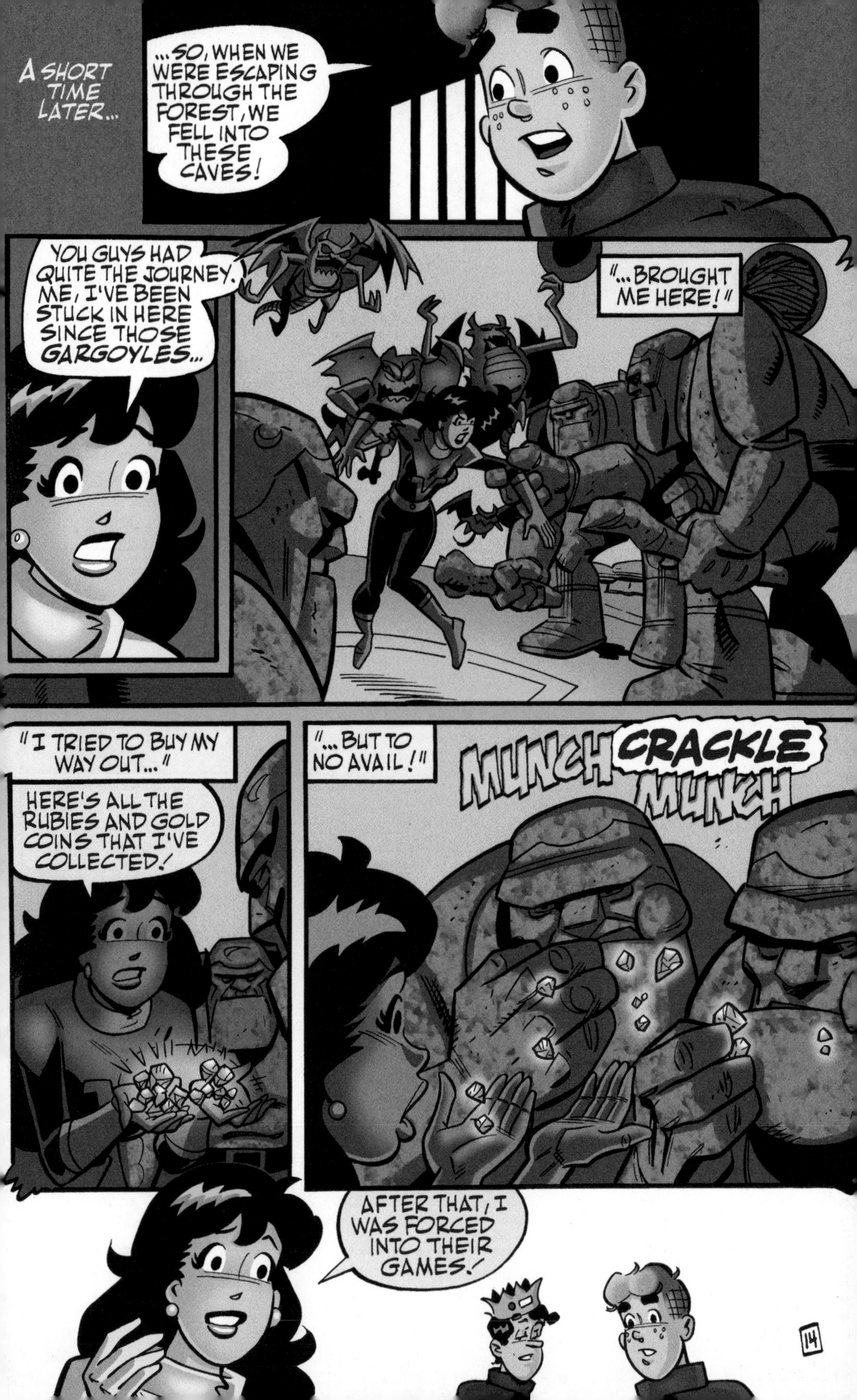
A SHORT TIME LATER...
...SO, WHEN WE WERE ESCAPING THROUGH THE FOREST, WE FELL INTO THESE CAVES!
YOU GUYS HAD QUITE THE JOURNEY. ME, I'VE BEEN STUCK IN HERE SINCE THOSE GARGOYLES...
"...BROUGHT ME HERE!"
"I TRIED TO BUY MY WAY OUT..."
HERE'S ALL THE RUBIES AND GOLD COINS THAT I'VE COLLECTED!
"...BUT TO NO AVAIL!"
MUNCH
CRACKLE
MUNCH
AFTER THAT, I WAS FORCED INTO THEIR GAMES!
14

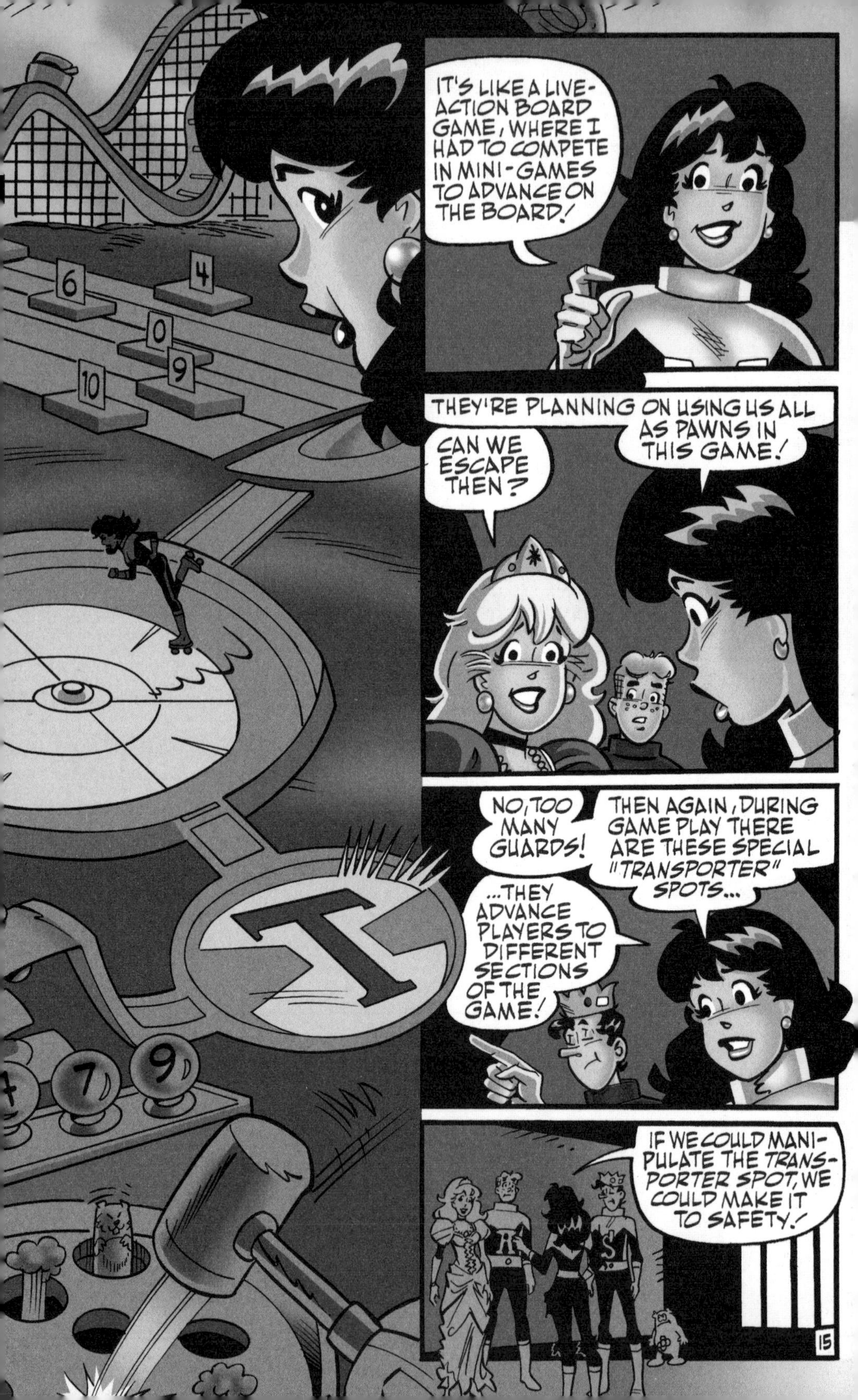
IT'S LIKE A LIVE-ACTION BOARD GAME, WHERE I HAD TO COMPETE IN MINI-GAMES TO ADVANCE ON THE BOARD!
THEY'RE PLANNING ON USING US ALL AS PAWNS IN THIS GAME!
CAN WE ESCAPE THEN?
NO, TOO MANY GUARDS!
THEN AGAIN, DURING GAME PLAY THERE ARE THESE SPECIAL "TRANSPORTER" SPOTS...
...THEY ADVANCE PLAYERS TO DIFFERENT SECTIONS OF THE GAME!
IF WE COULD MANIPULATE THE TRANSPORTER SPOT, WE COULD MAKE IT TO SAFETY!
15

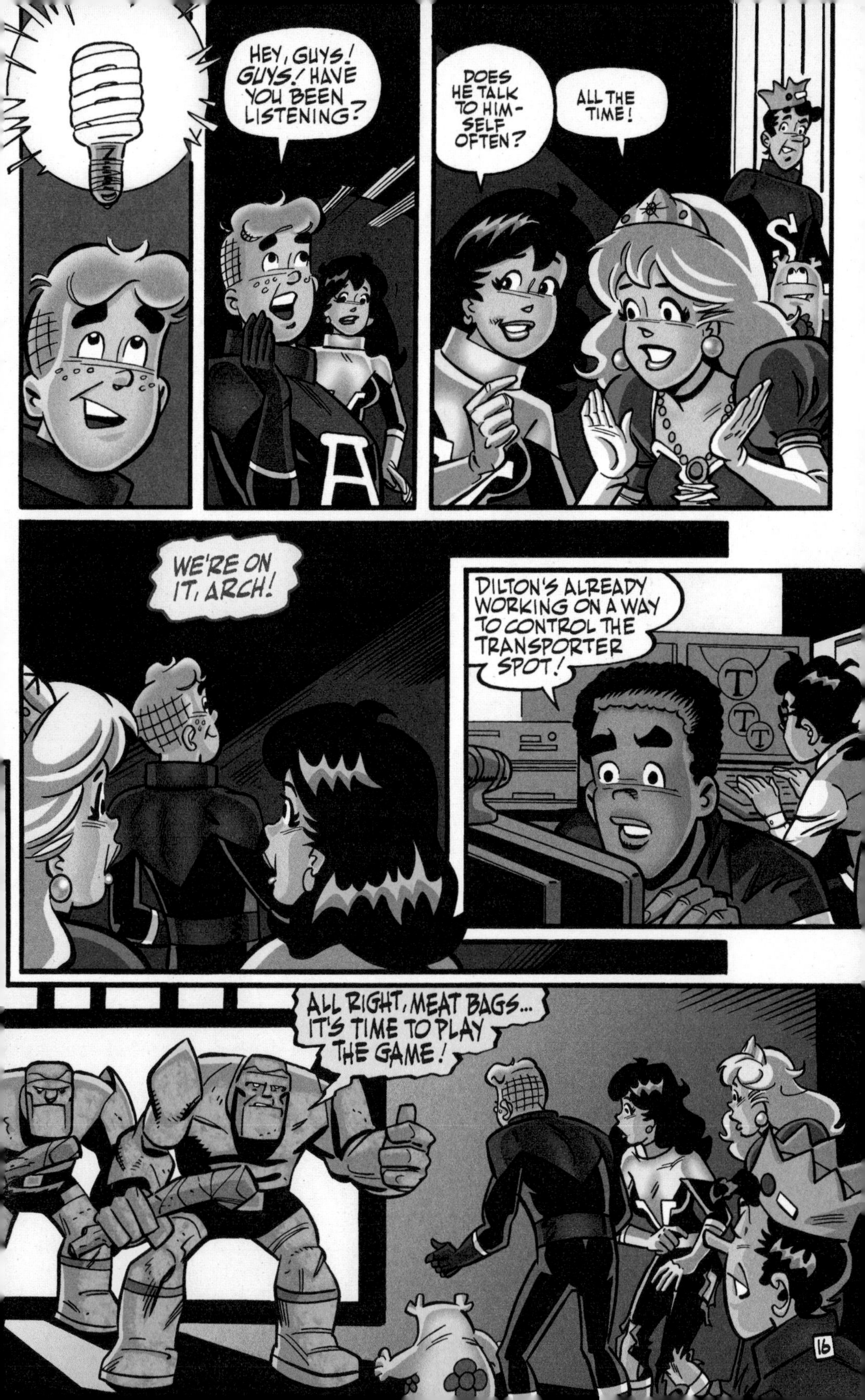
HEY, GUYS! GUYS! HAVE YOU BEEN LISTENING?
DOES HE TALK TO HIM-SELF OFTEN?
ALL THE TIME!
WE'RE ON IT, ARCH!
DILTON'S ALREADY WORKING ON A WAY TO CONTROL THE TRANSPORTER SPOT!
ALL RIGHT, MEAT BAGS... IT'S TIME TO PLAY THE GAME!

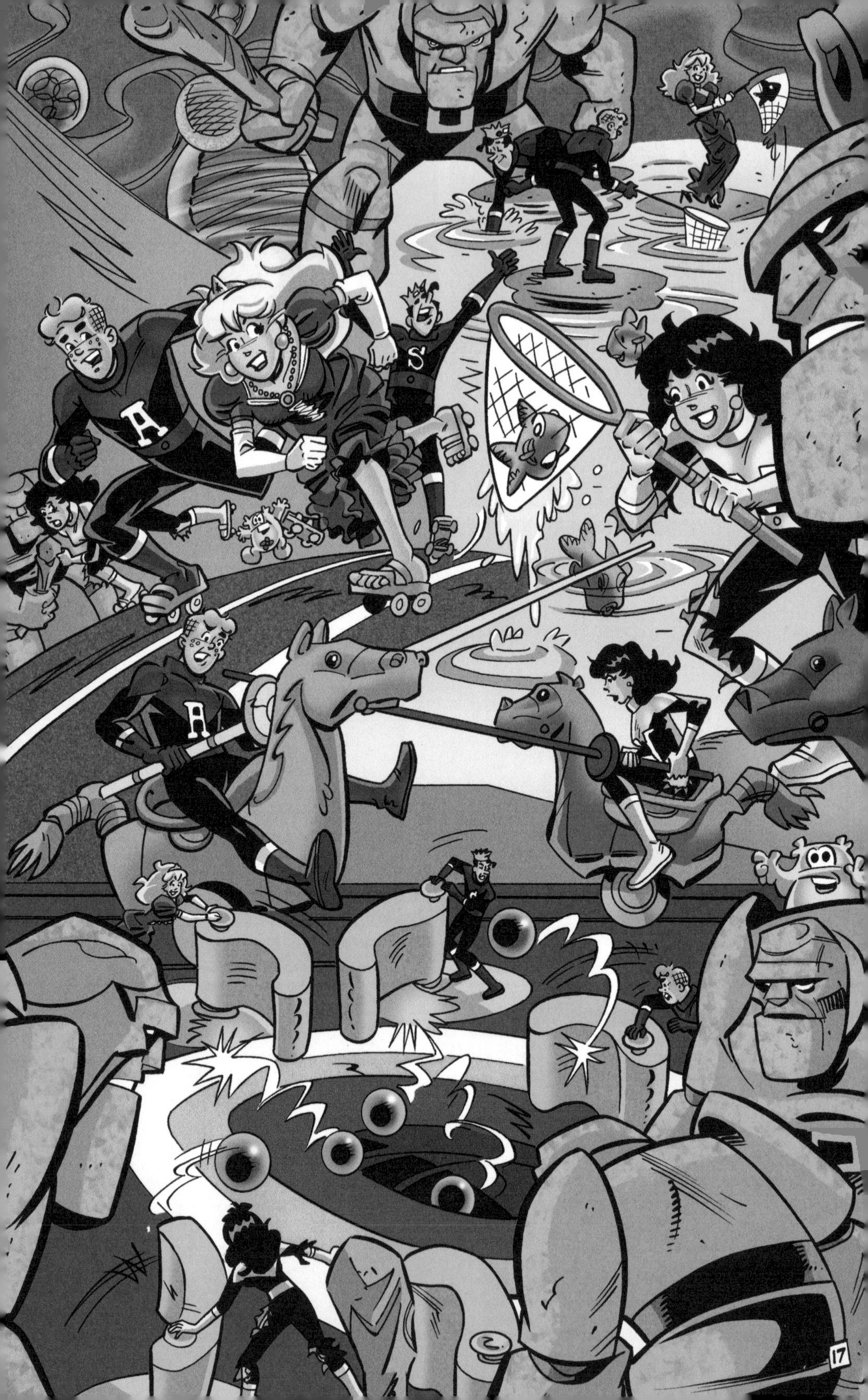

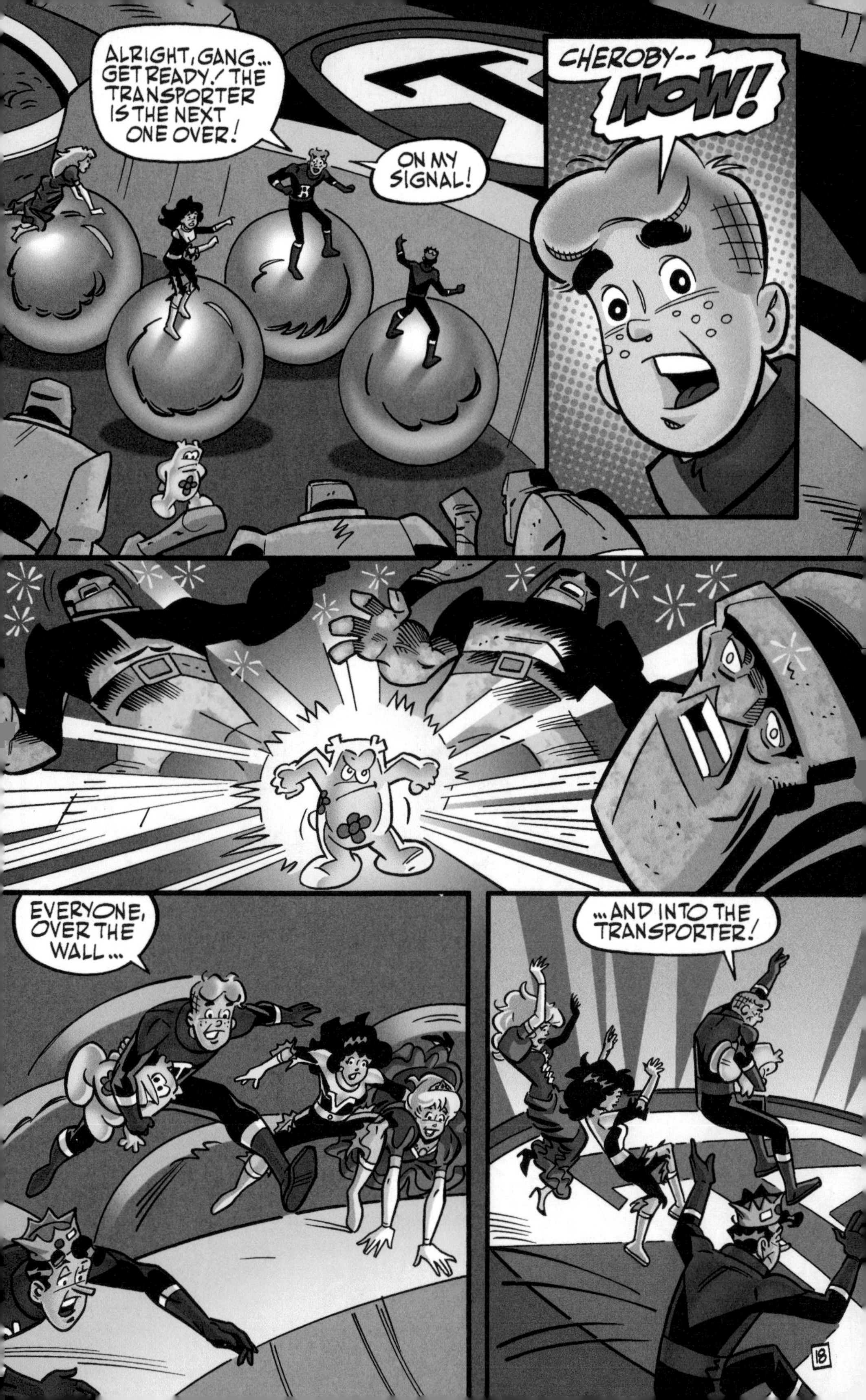

ALRIGHT, GANG... GET READY! THE TRANSPORTER IS THE NEXT ONE OVER!
ON MY SIGNAL!
CHEROBY-- NOW!
EVERYONE, OVER THE WALL...
...AND INTO THE TRANSPORTER!
18

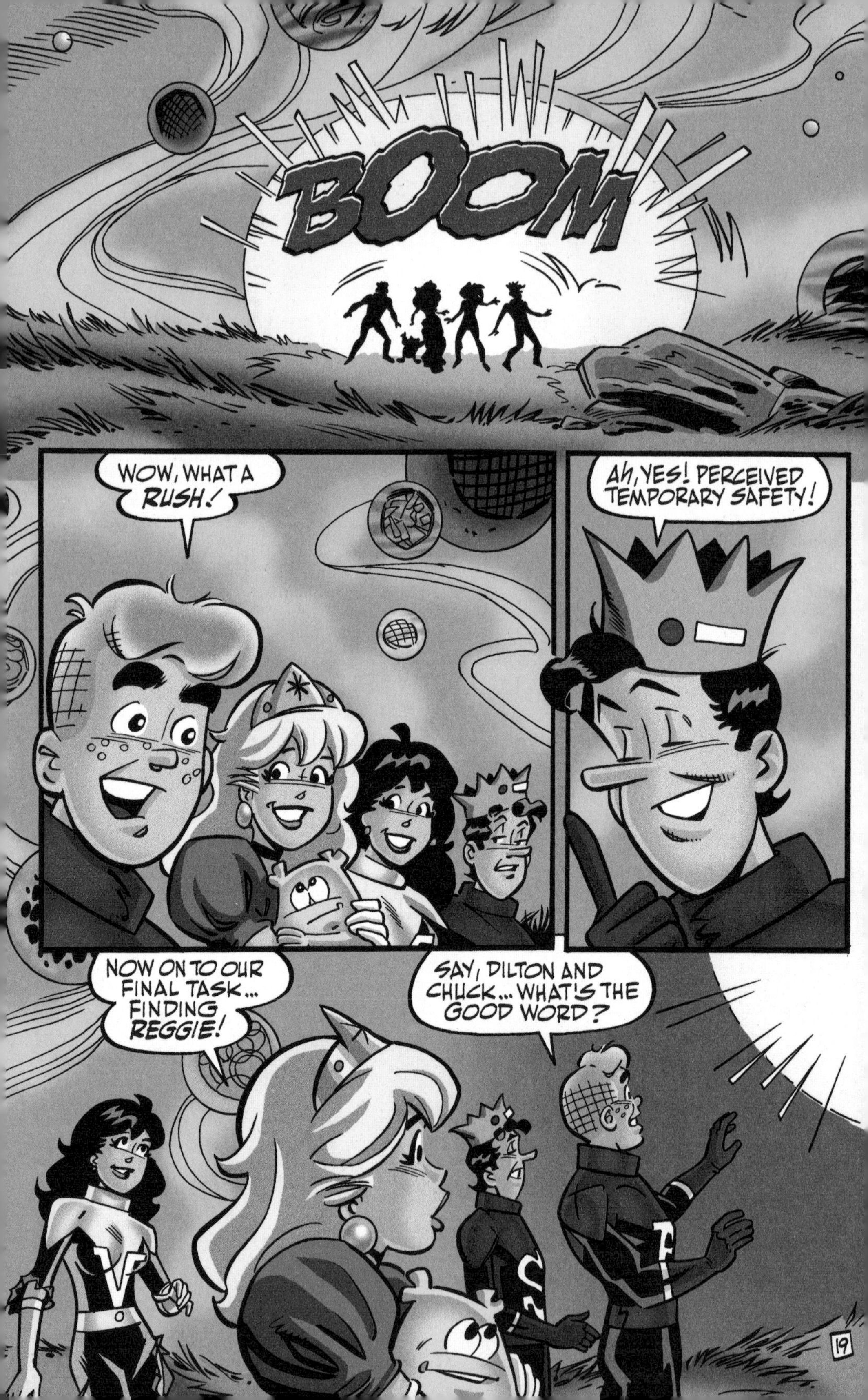

BOOM
WOW, WHAT A RUSH!
AH, YES! PERCEIVED TEMPORARY SAFETY!
NOW ON TO OUR FINAL TASK... FINDING REGGIE!
SAY, DILTON AND CHUCK... WHAT'S THE GOOD WORD?

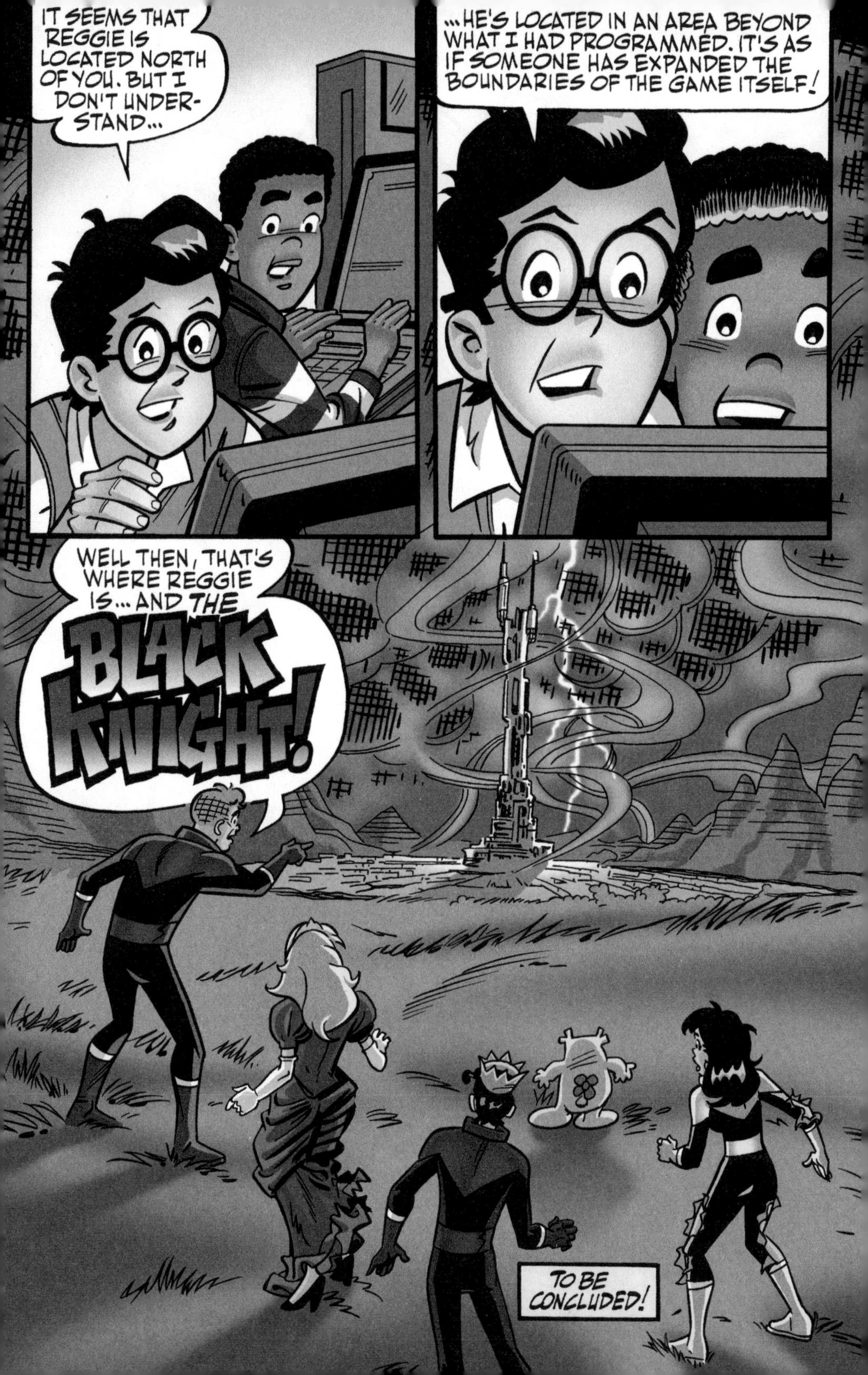
IT SEEMS THAT REGGIE IS LOCATED NORTH OF YOU. BUT I DON'T UNDER-STAND...
...HE'S LOCATED IN AN AREA BEYOND WHAT I HAD PROGRAMMED. IT'S AS IF SOMEONE HAS EXPANDED THE BOUNDARIES OF THE GAME ITSELF!
WELL THEN, THAT'S WHERE REGGIE IS... AND THE BLACK KNIGHT!
TO BE CONCLUDED!

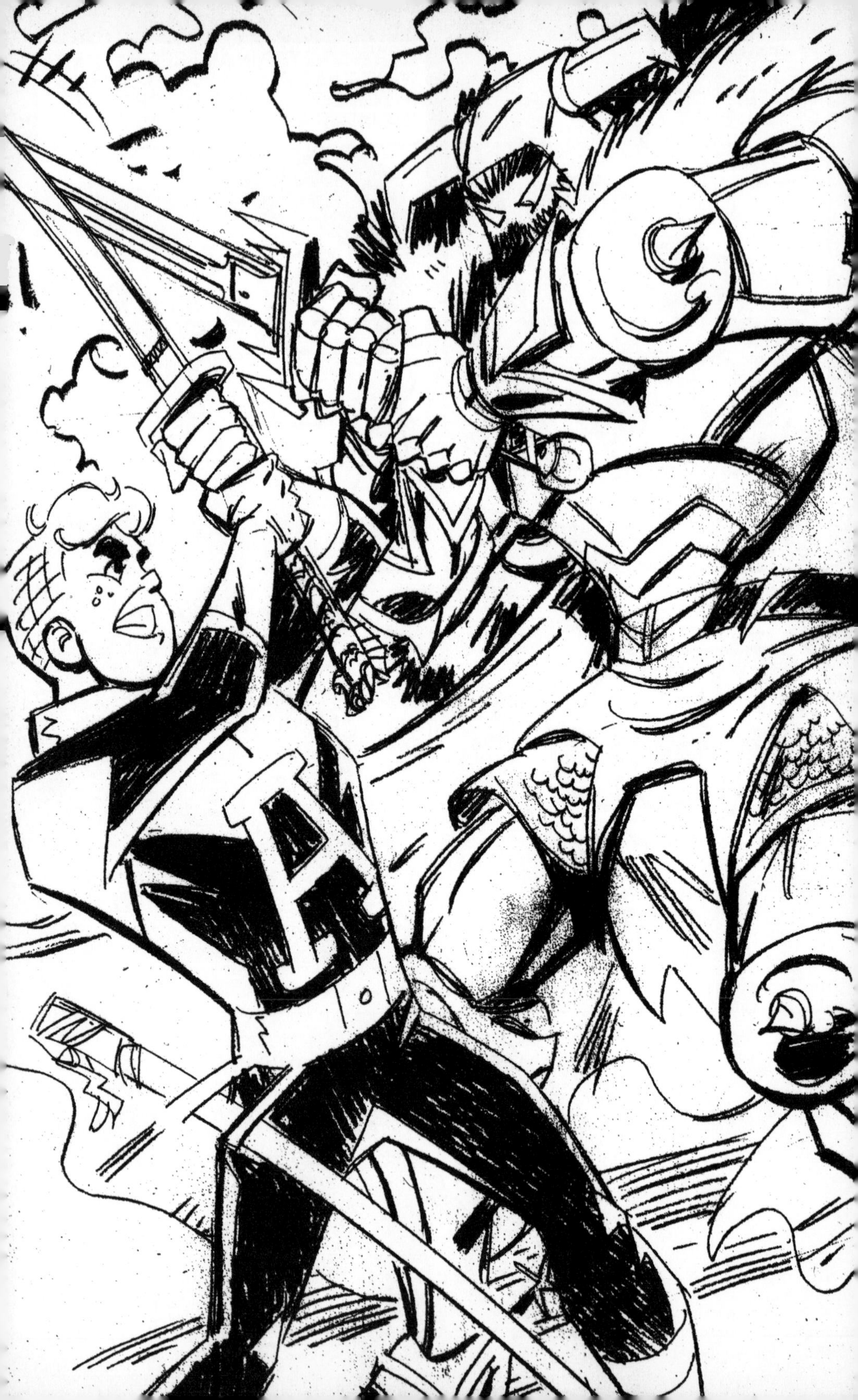

CHAPTER FIVE

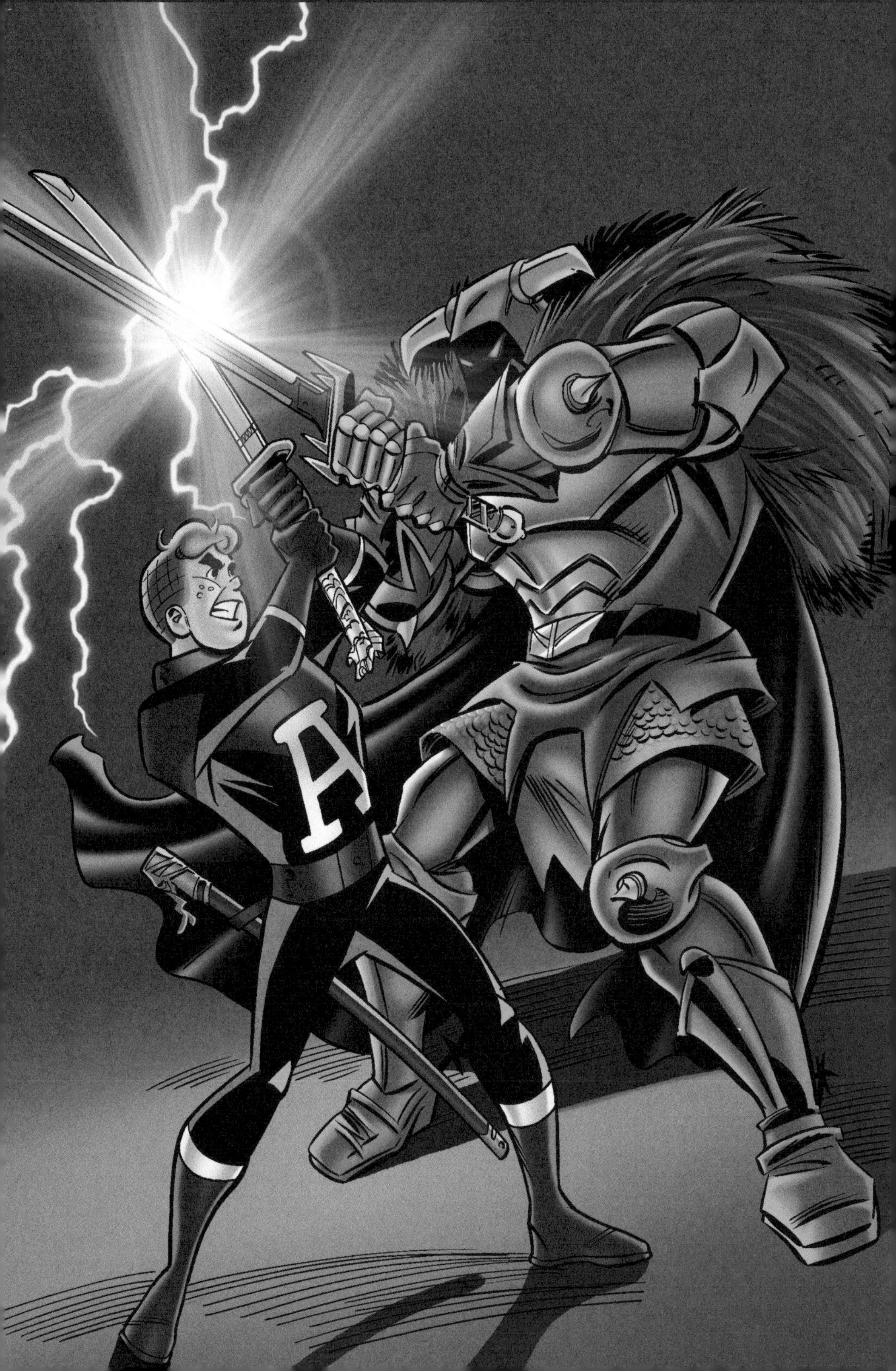

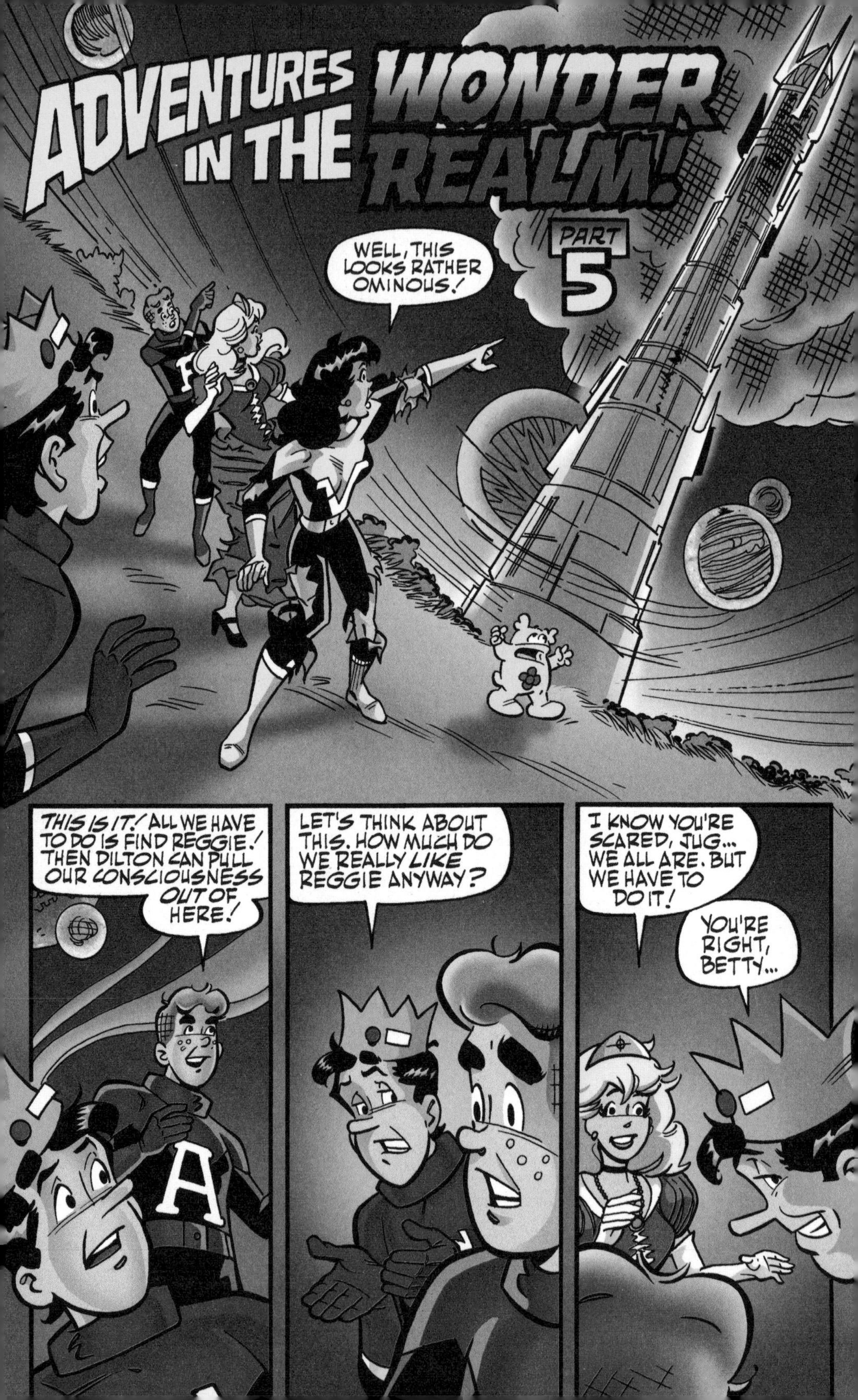
ADVENTURES IN THE WONDER REALM!
PART 5
WELL, THIS LOOKS RATHER OMINOUS!
THIS IS IT! ALL WE HAVE TO DO IS FIND REGGIE! THEN DILTON CAN PULL OUR CONSCIOUSNESS OUT OF HERE!
LET'S THINK ABOUT THIS. HOW MUCH DO WE REALLY LIKE REGGIE ANYWAY?
I KNOW YOU'RE SCARED, JUG... WE ALL ARE. BUT WE HAVE TO DO IT!
YOU'RE RIGHT, BETTY...

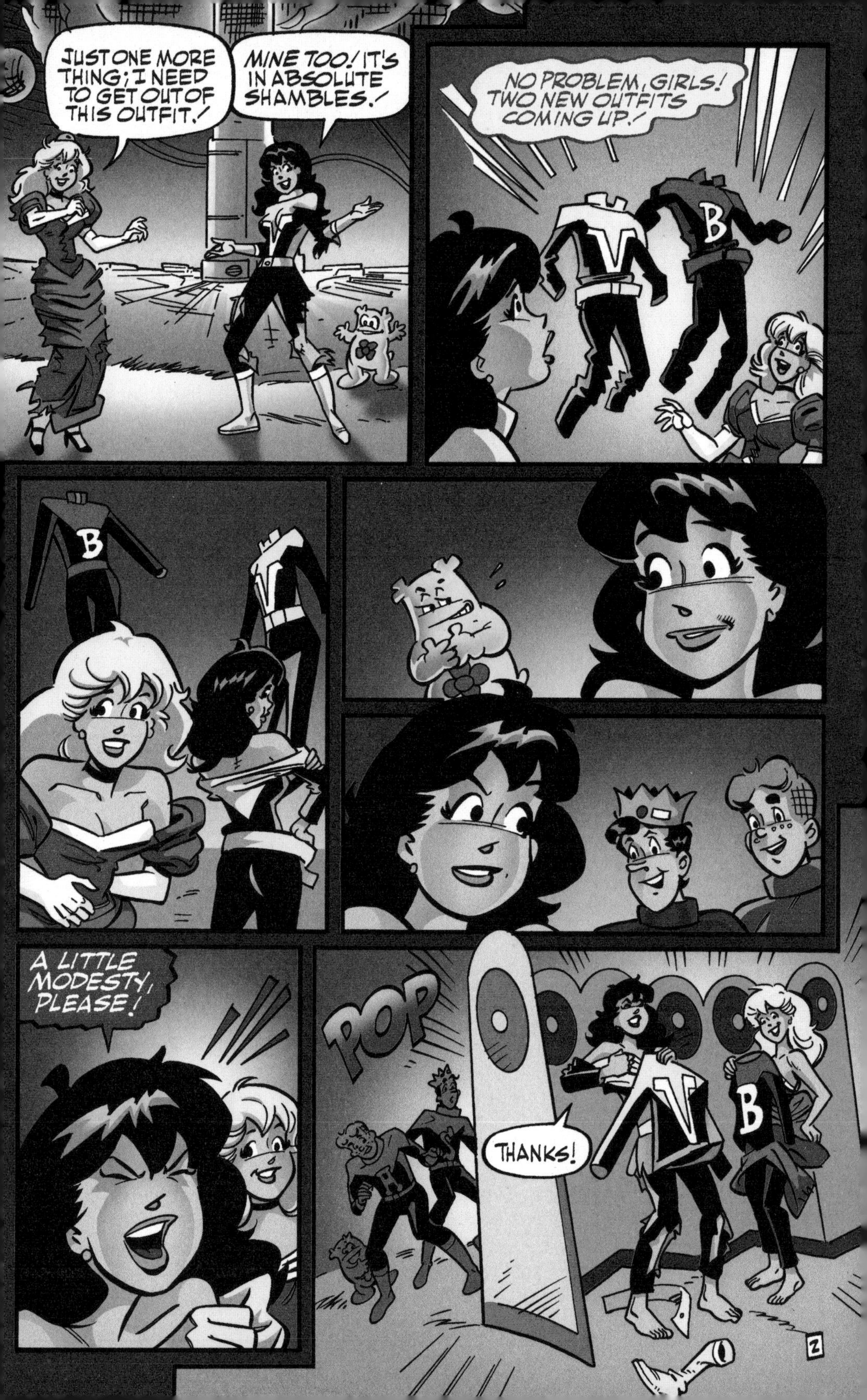
JUST ONE MORE THING; I NEED TO GET OUT OF THIS OUTFIT!
MINE TOO! IT'S IN ABSOLUTE SHAMBLES!
NO PROBLEM, GIRLS! TWO NEW OUTFITS COMING UP!
A LITTLE MODESTY, PLEASE!
POP
THANKS!
2

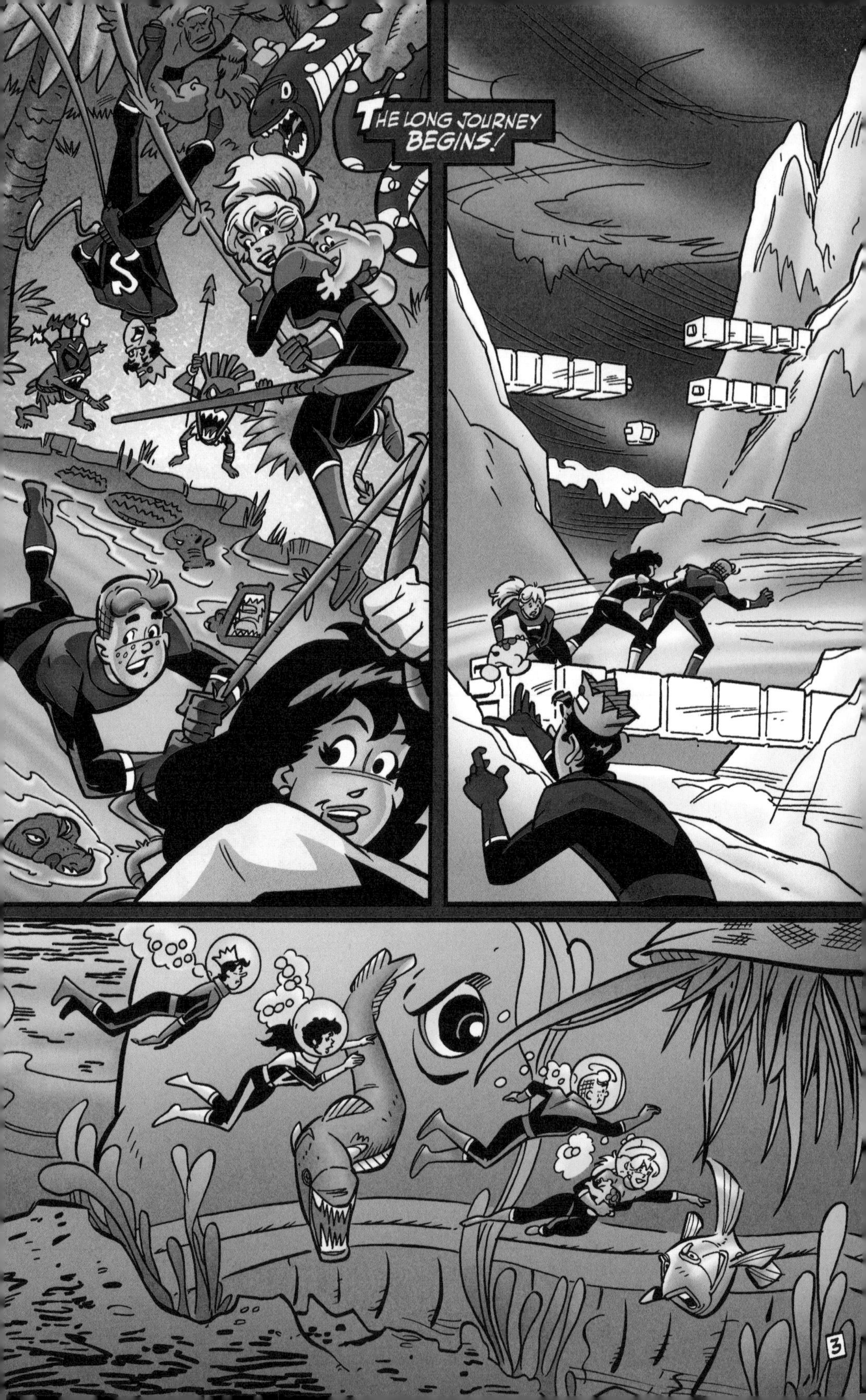
THE LONG JOURNEY BEGINS!

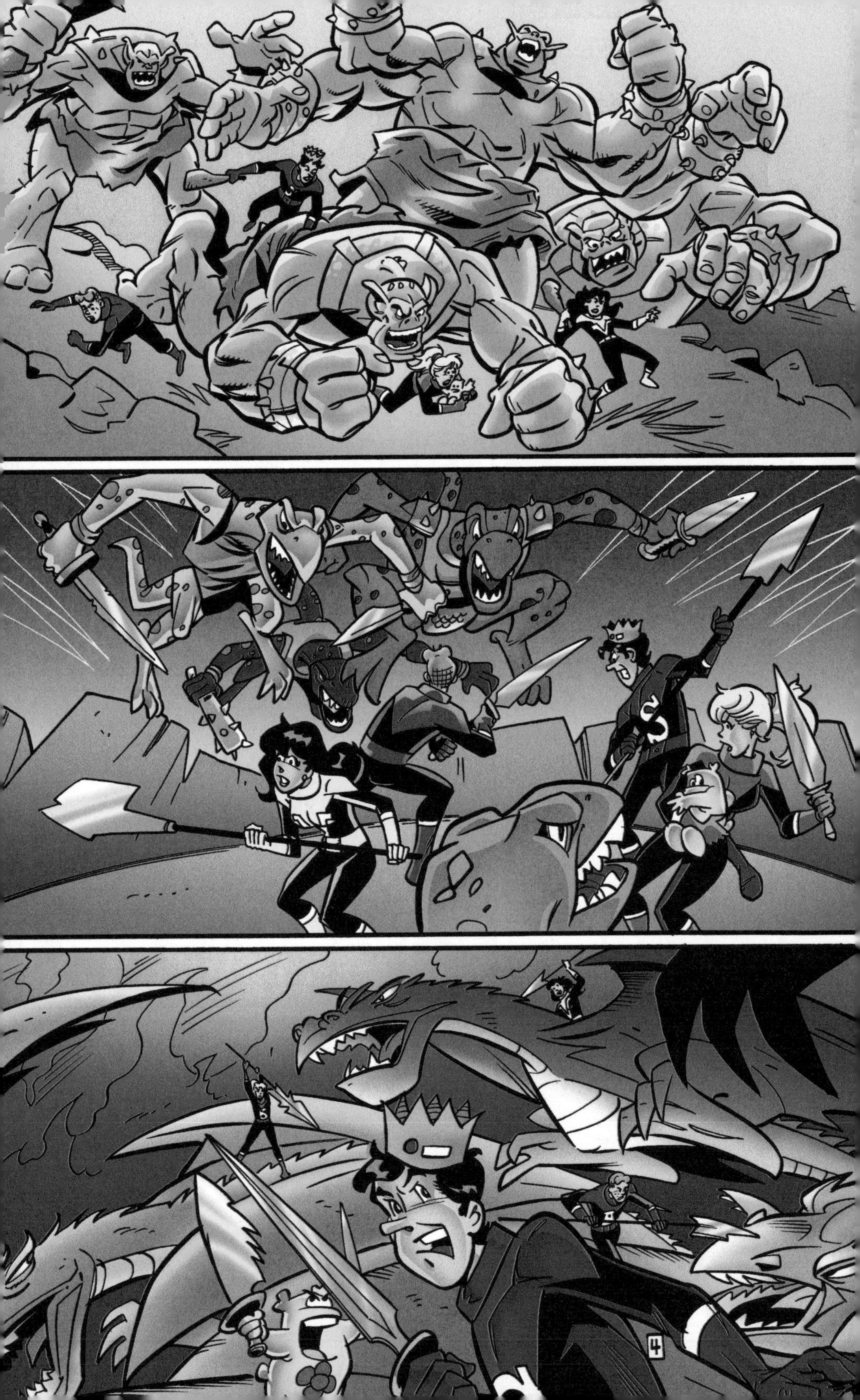
4

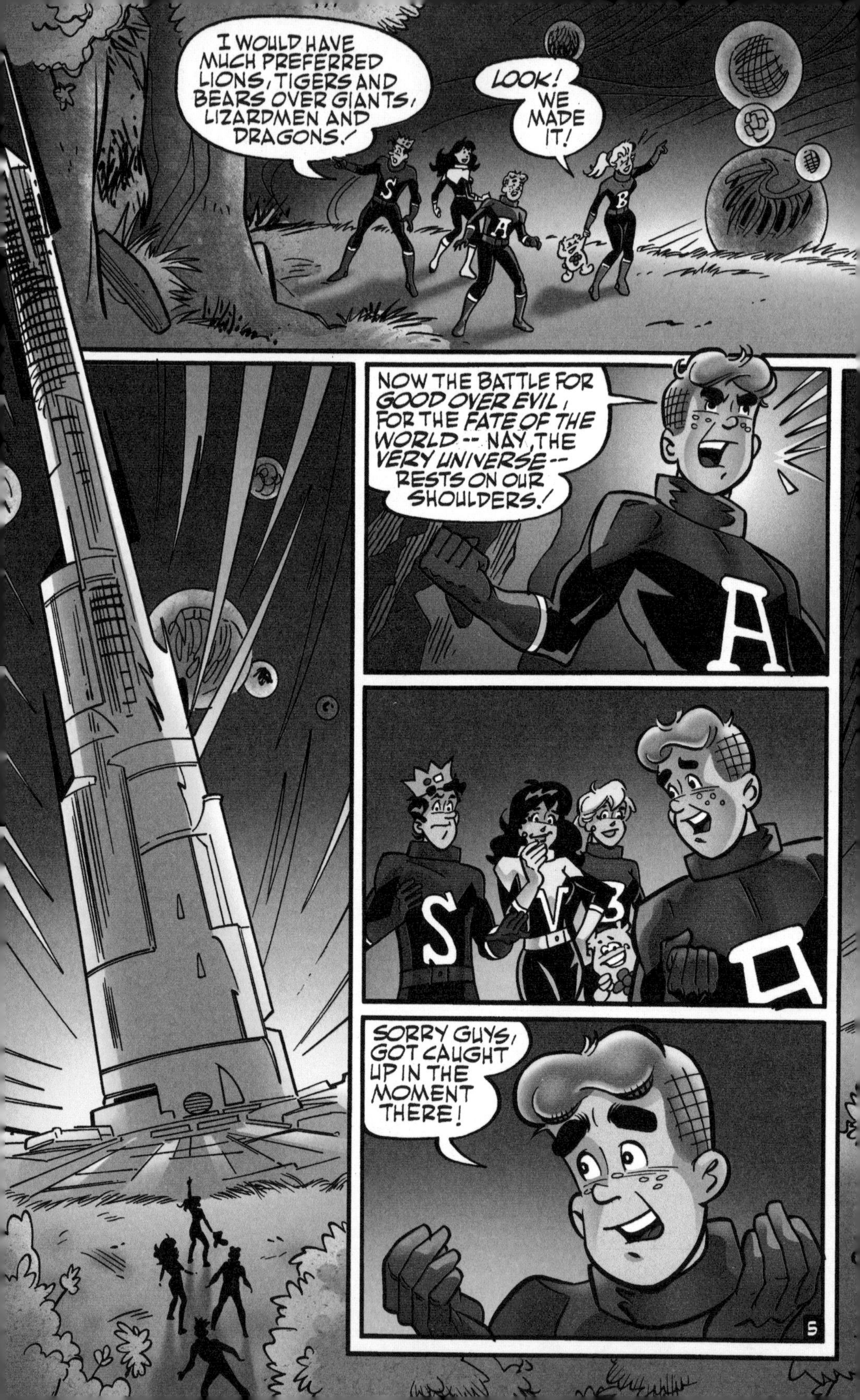
I WOULD HAVE MUCH PREFERRED LIONS, TIGERS AND BEARS OVER GIANTS, LIZARDMEN AND DRAGONS!
LOOK! WE MADE IT!
NOW THE BATTLE FOR GOOD OVER EVIL, FOR THE FATE OF THE WORLD -- NAY, THE VERY UNIVERSE -- RESTS ON OUR SHOULDERS!
SORRY GUYS, GOT CAUGHT UP IN THE MOMENT THERE!

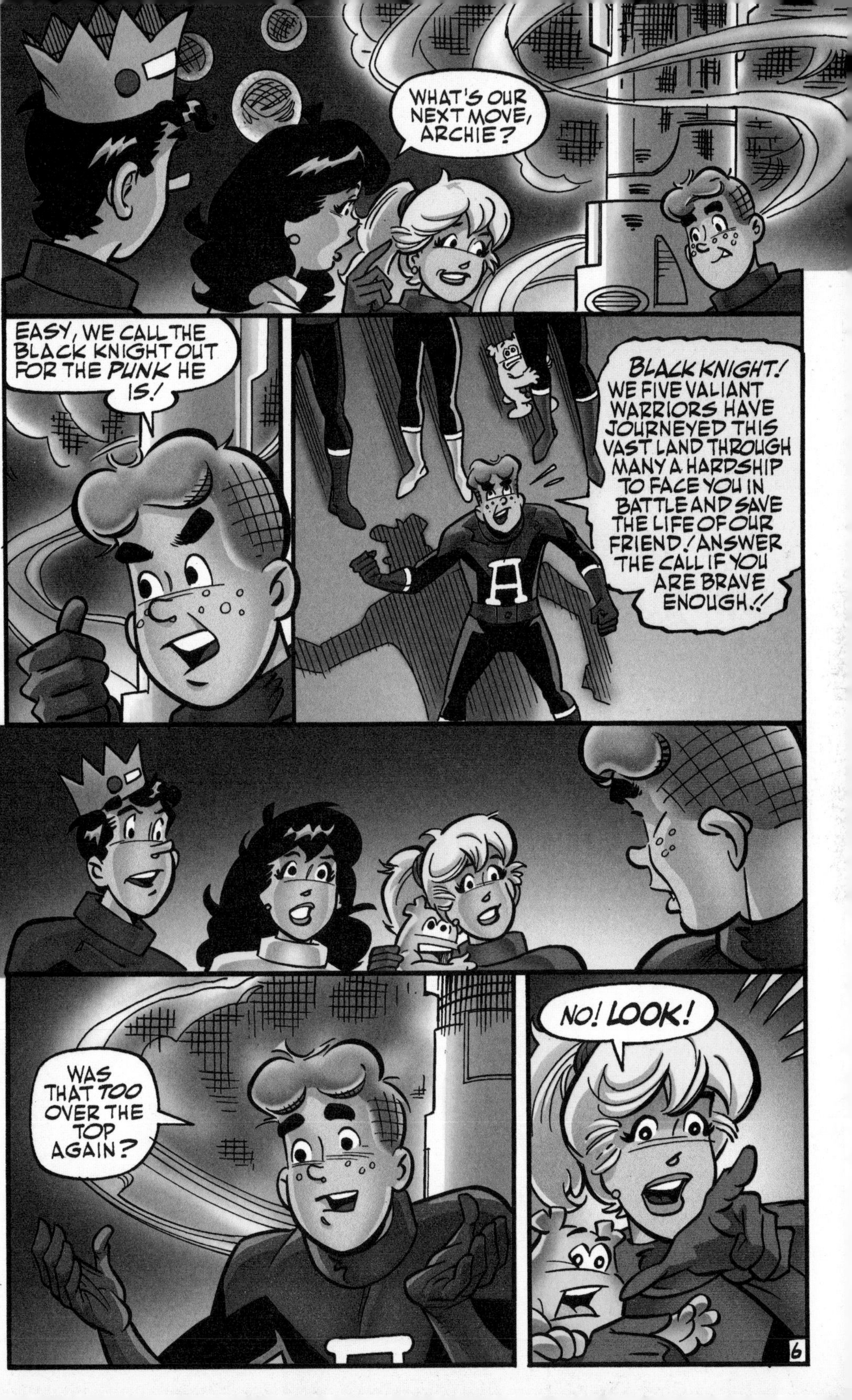
WHAT'S OUR NEXT MOVE, ARCHIE?
EASY, WE CALL THE BLACK KNIGHT OUT FOR THE PUNK HE IS!
BLACK KNIGHT! WE FIVE VALIANT WARRIORS HAVE JOURNEYED THIS VAST LAND THROUGH MANY A HARDSHIP TO FACE YOU IN BATTLE AND SAVE THE LIFE OF OUR FRIEND! ANSWER THE CALL IF YOU ARE BRAVE ENOUGH!!
WAS THAT TOO OVER THE TOP AGAIN?
NO! LOOK!
6

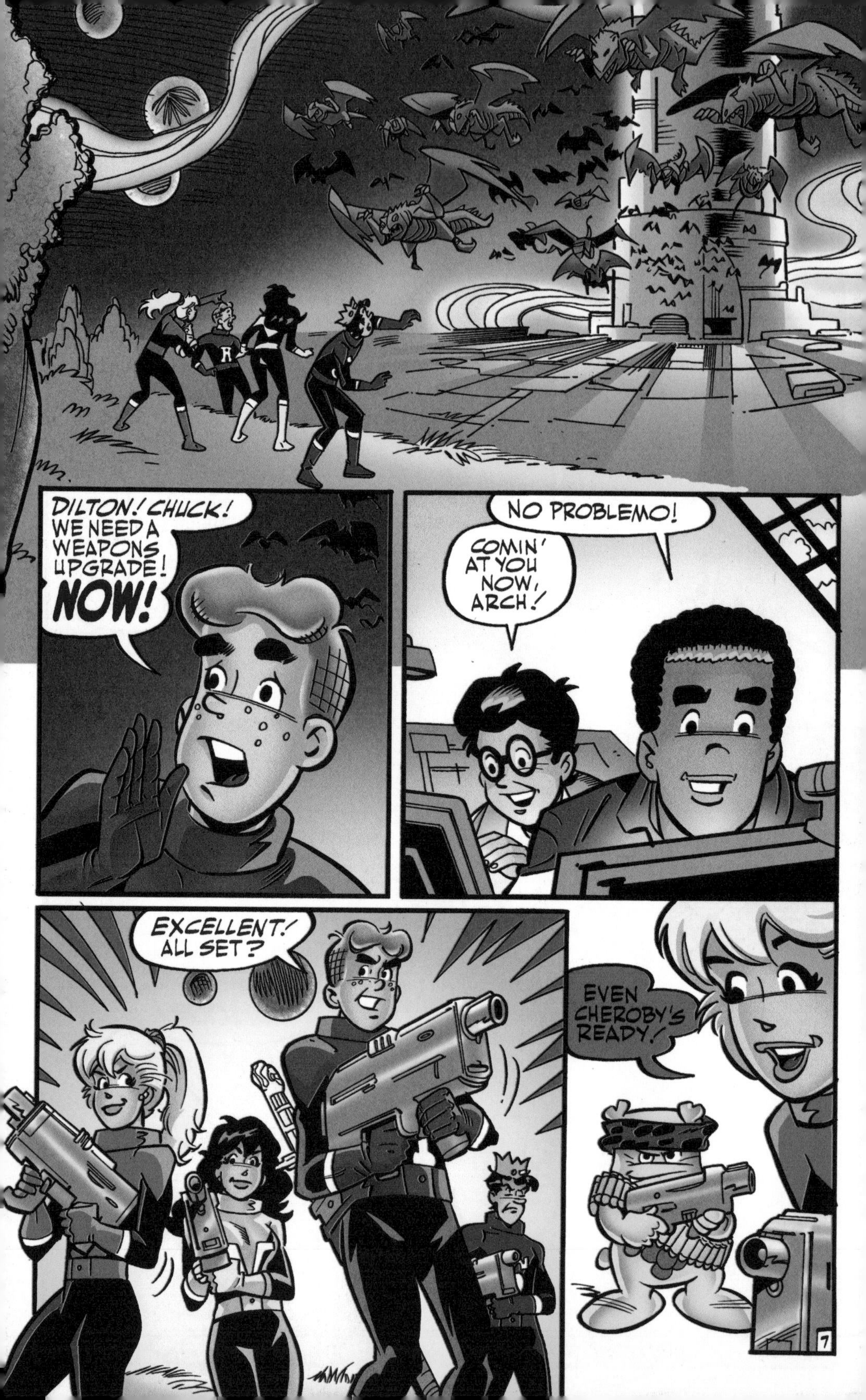
DILTON! CHUCK! WE NEED A WEAPONS UPGRADE! NOW!
NO PROBLEMO!
COMIN' AT YOU NOW, ARCH!
EXCELLENT! ALL SET?
EVEN CHEROBY'S READY!
7

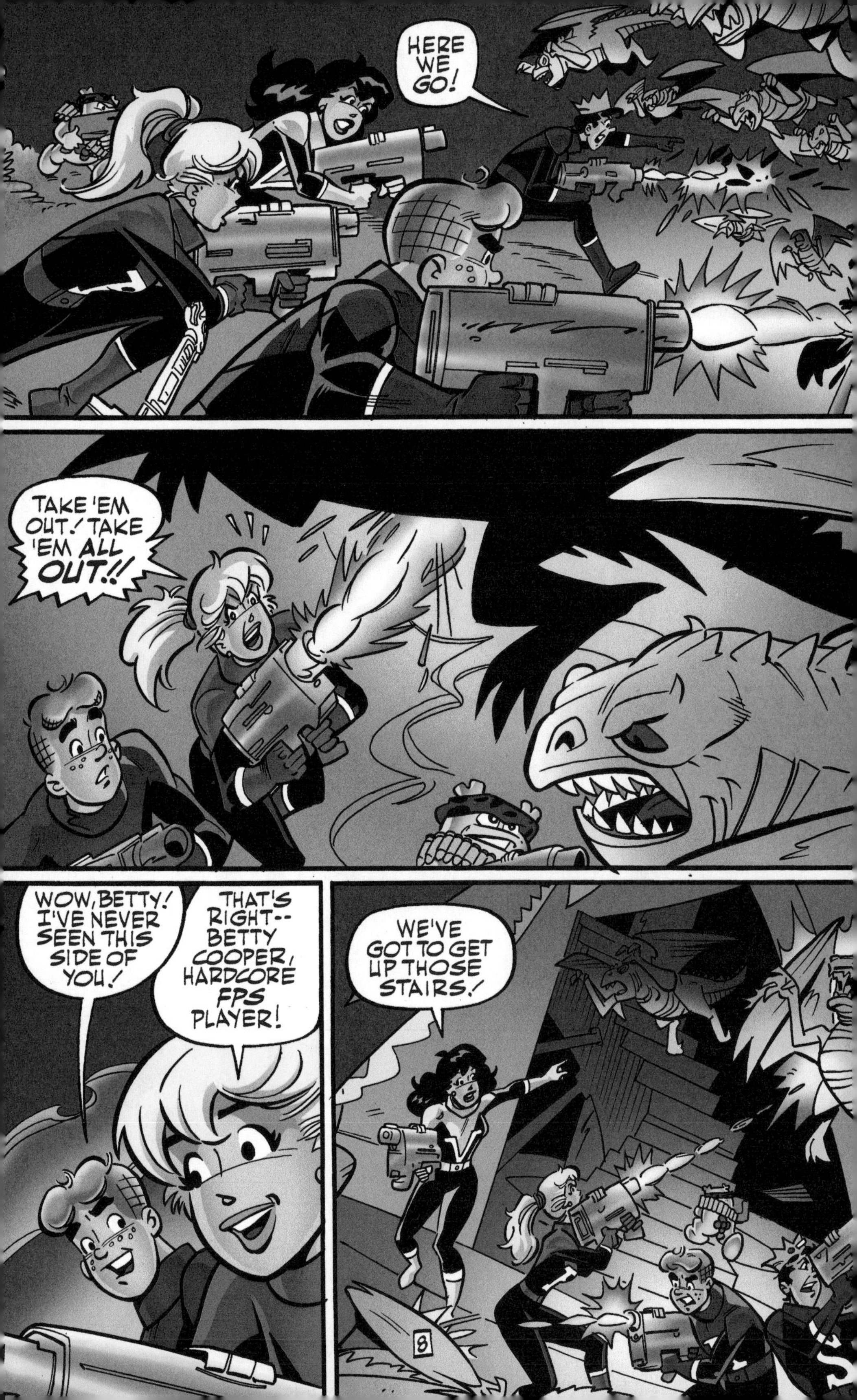
HERE WE GO!
TAKE 'EM OUT! TAKE 'EM ALL OUT!!
WOW, BETTY! I'VE NEVER SEEN THIS SIDE OF YOU!
THAT'S RIGHT-- BETTY COOPER, HARDCORE FPS PLAYER!
WE'VE GOT TO GET UP THOSE STAIRS!

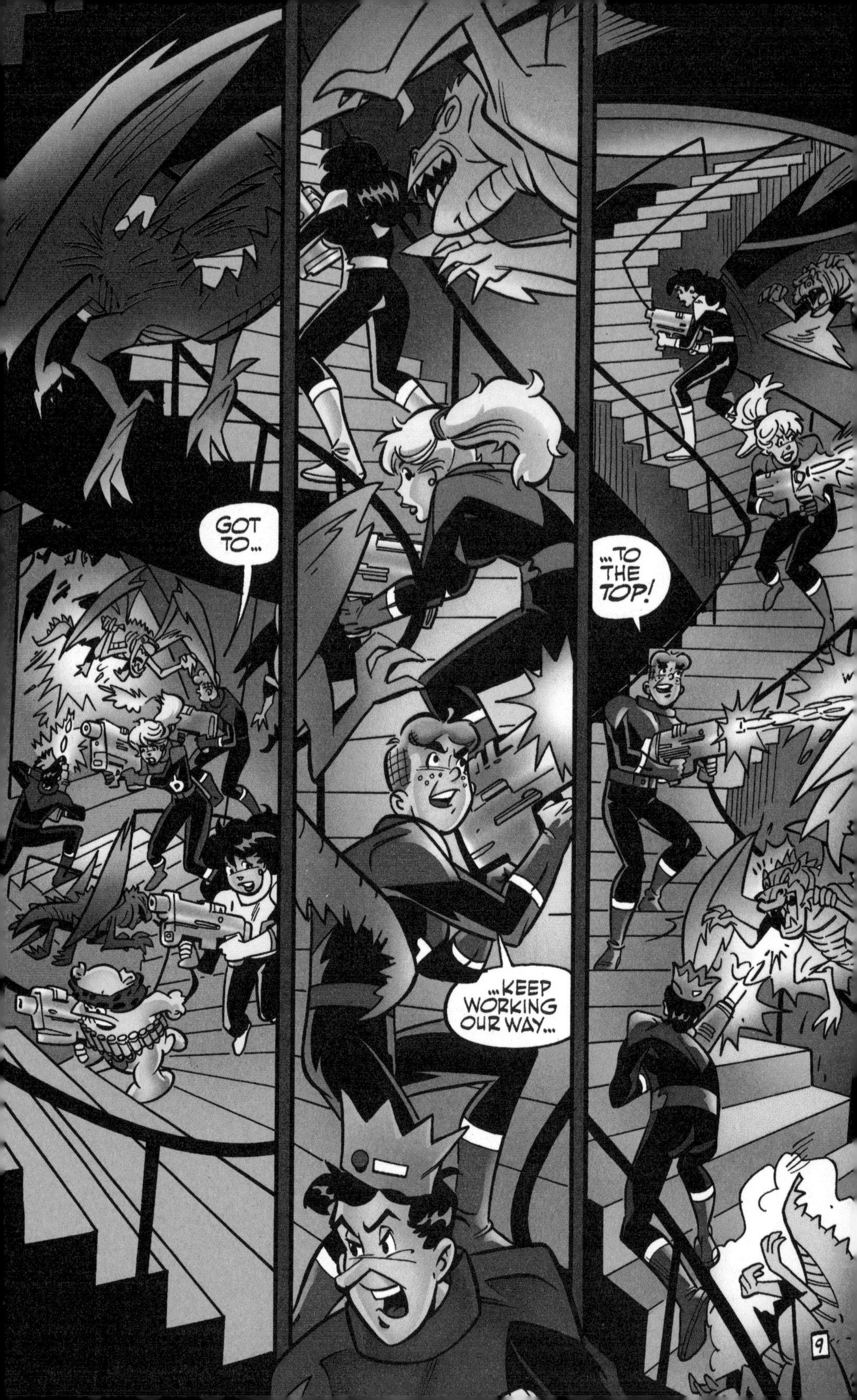
GOT TO...
...KEEP WORKING OUR WAY...
...TO THE TOP!
9

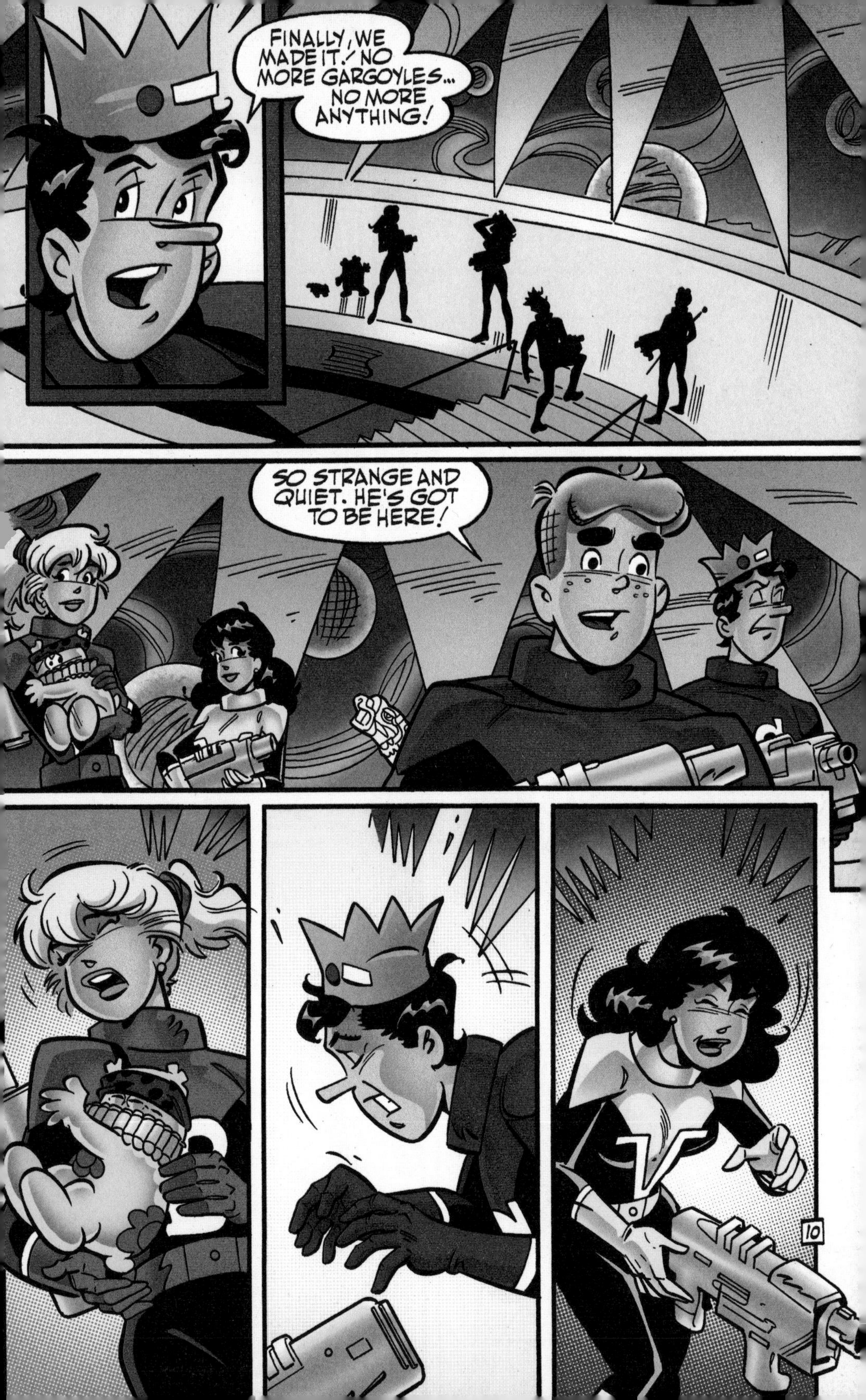
FINALLY, WE MADE IT! NO MORE GARGOYLES... NO MORE ANYTHING!
SO STRANGE AND QUIET. HE'S GOT TO BE HERE!
10

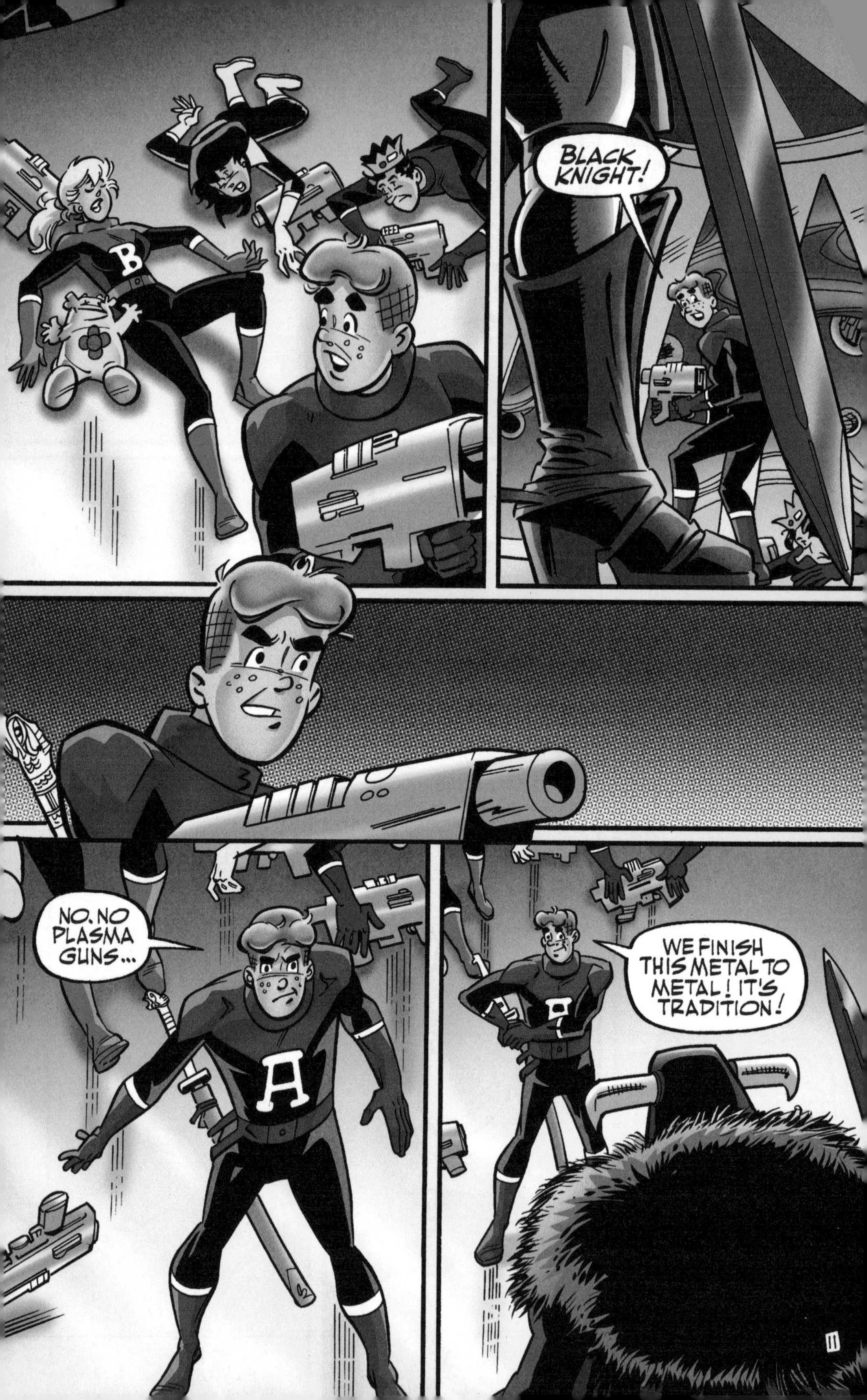
BLACK KNIGHT!
NO. NO PLASMA GUNS...
WE FINISH THIS METAL TO METAL! IT'S TRADITION!

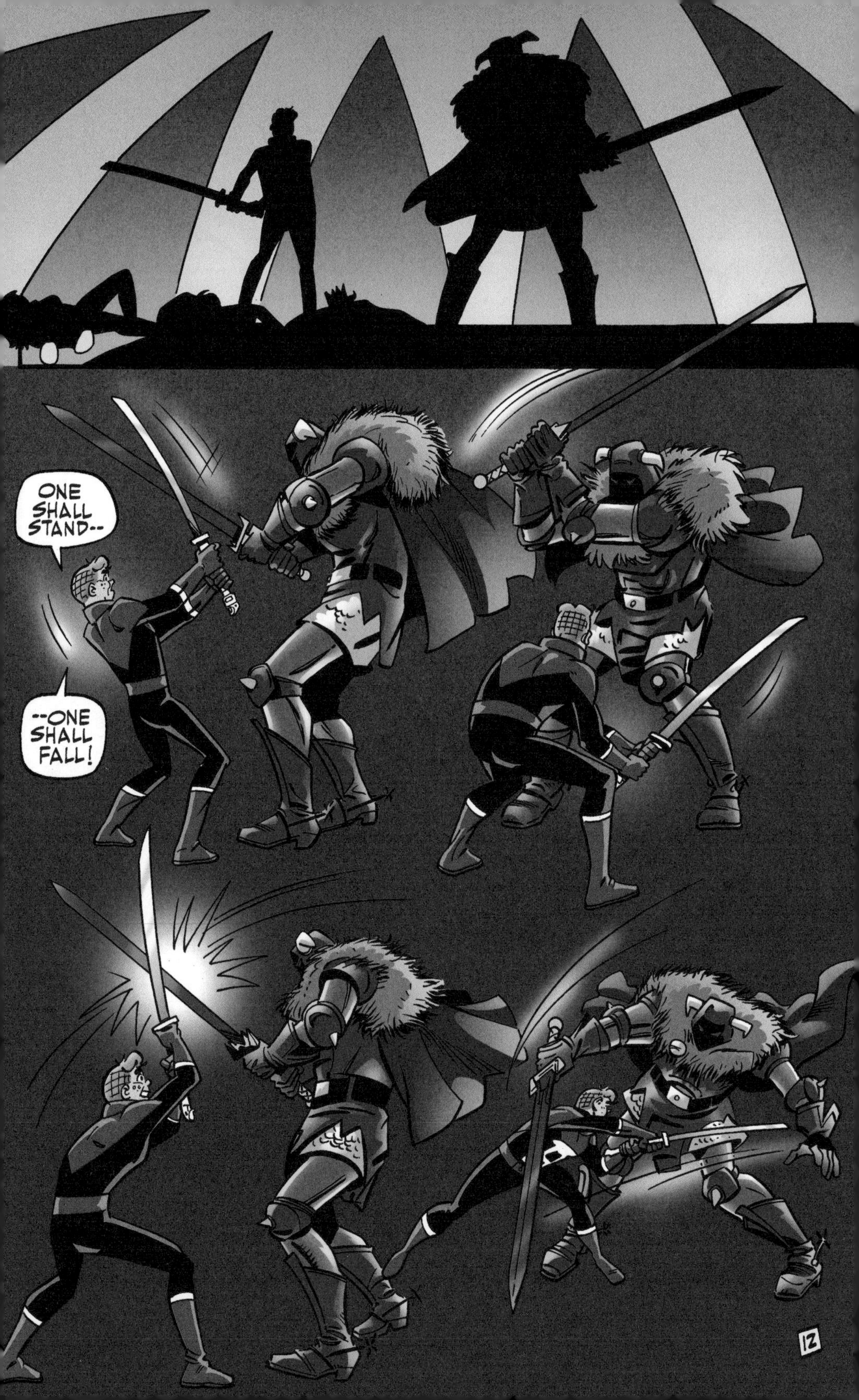
ONE SHALL STAND--
--ONE SHALL FALL!
12

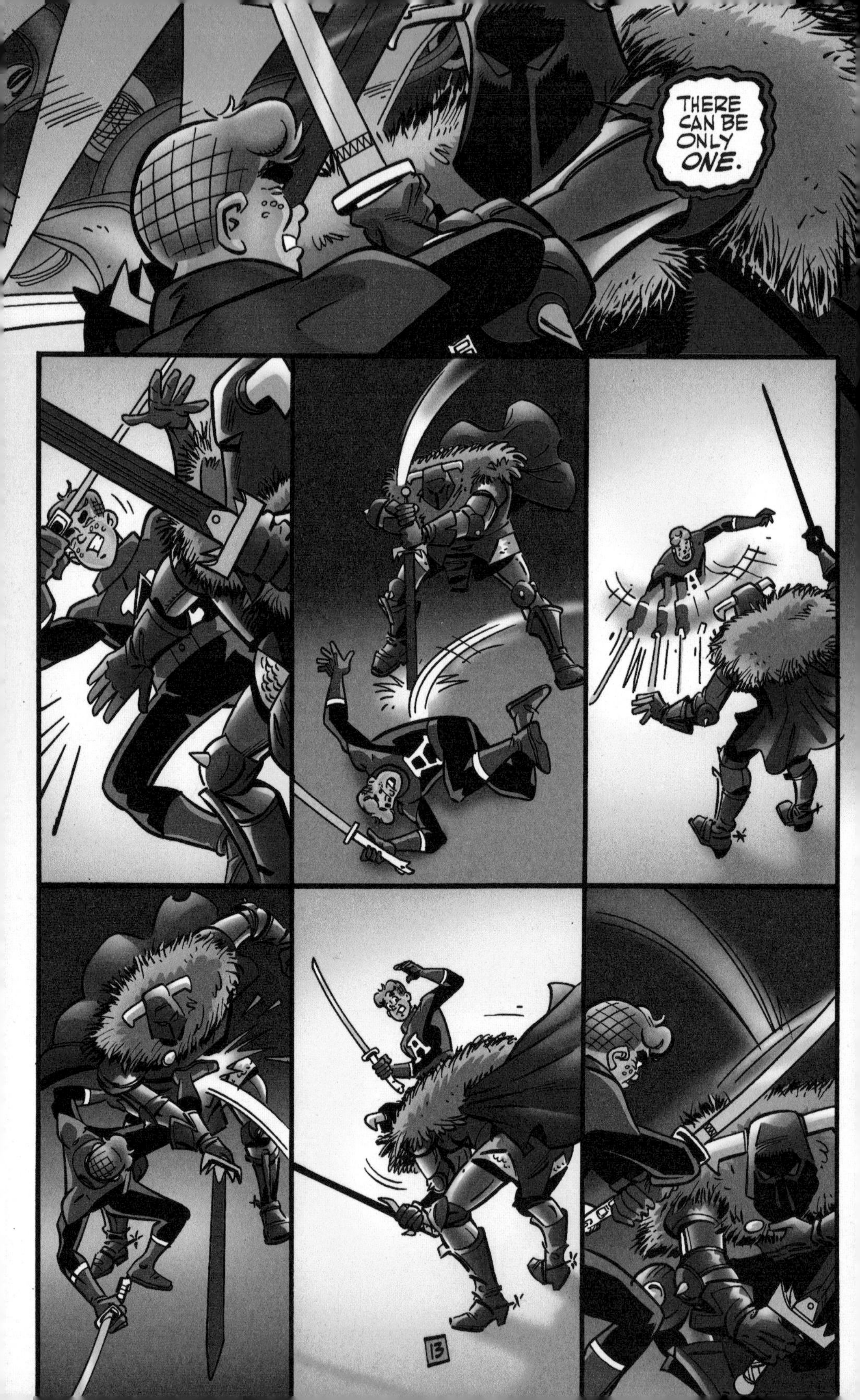
THERE CAN BE ONLY ONE.
13

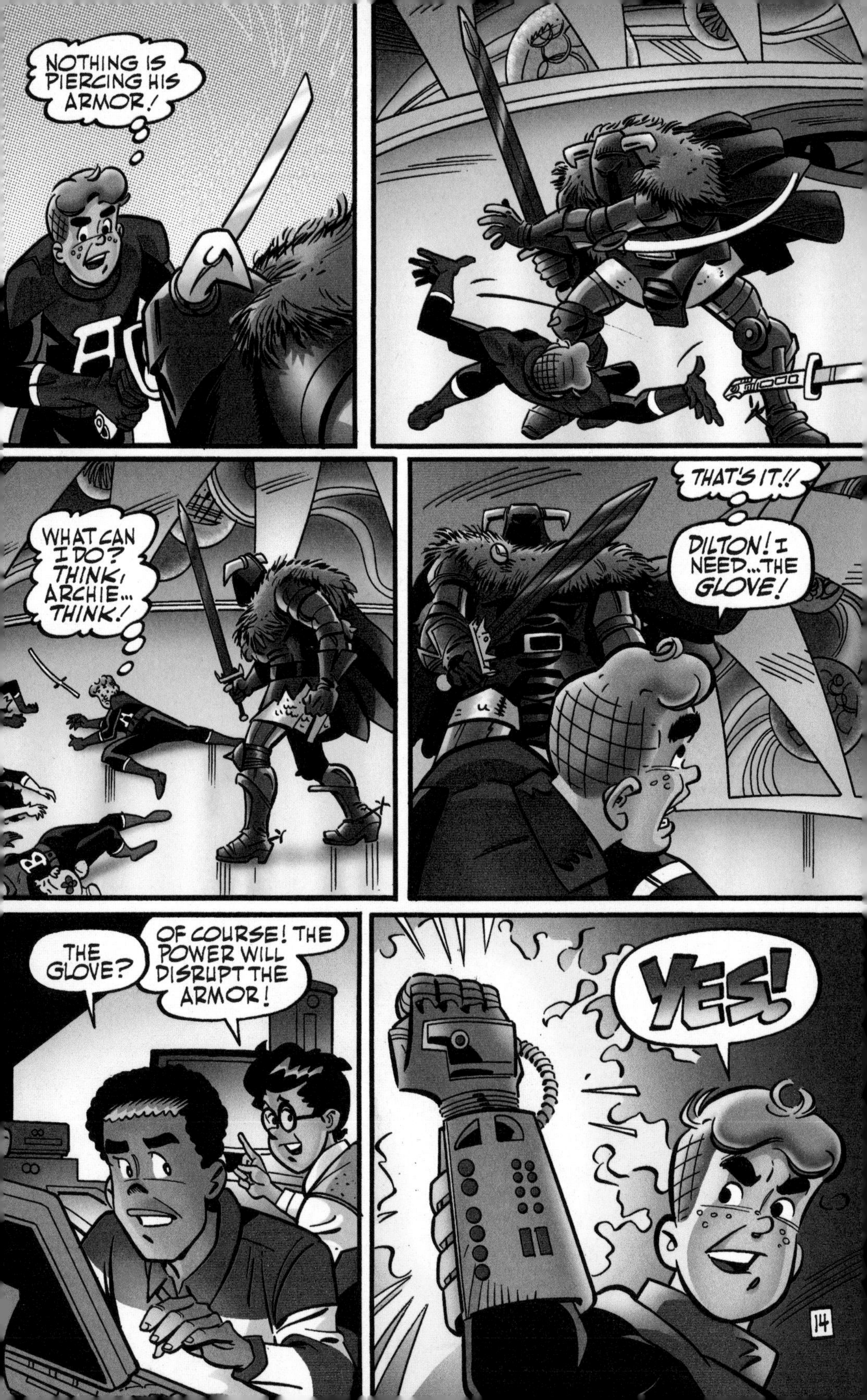
NOTHING IS PIERCING HIS ARMOR!
WHAT CAN I DO? THINK, ARCHIE... THINK!
THAT'S IT!!
DILTON! I NEED... THE GLOVE!
THE GLOVE?
OF COURSE! THE POWER WILL DISRUPT THE ARMOR!
YES!

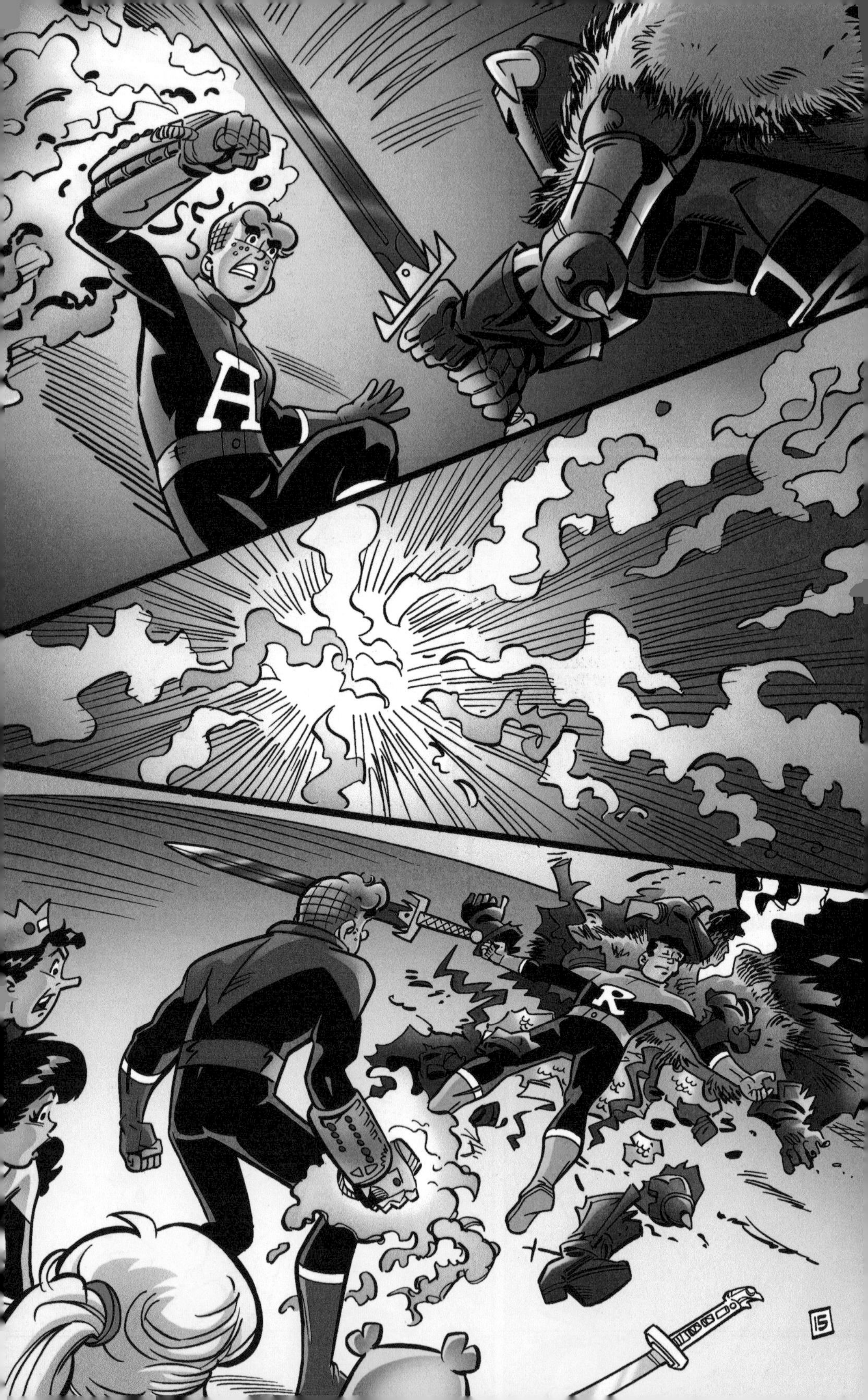

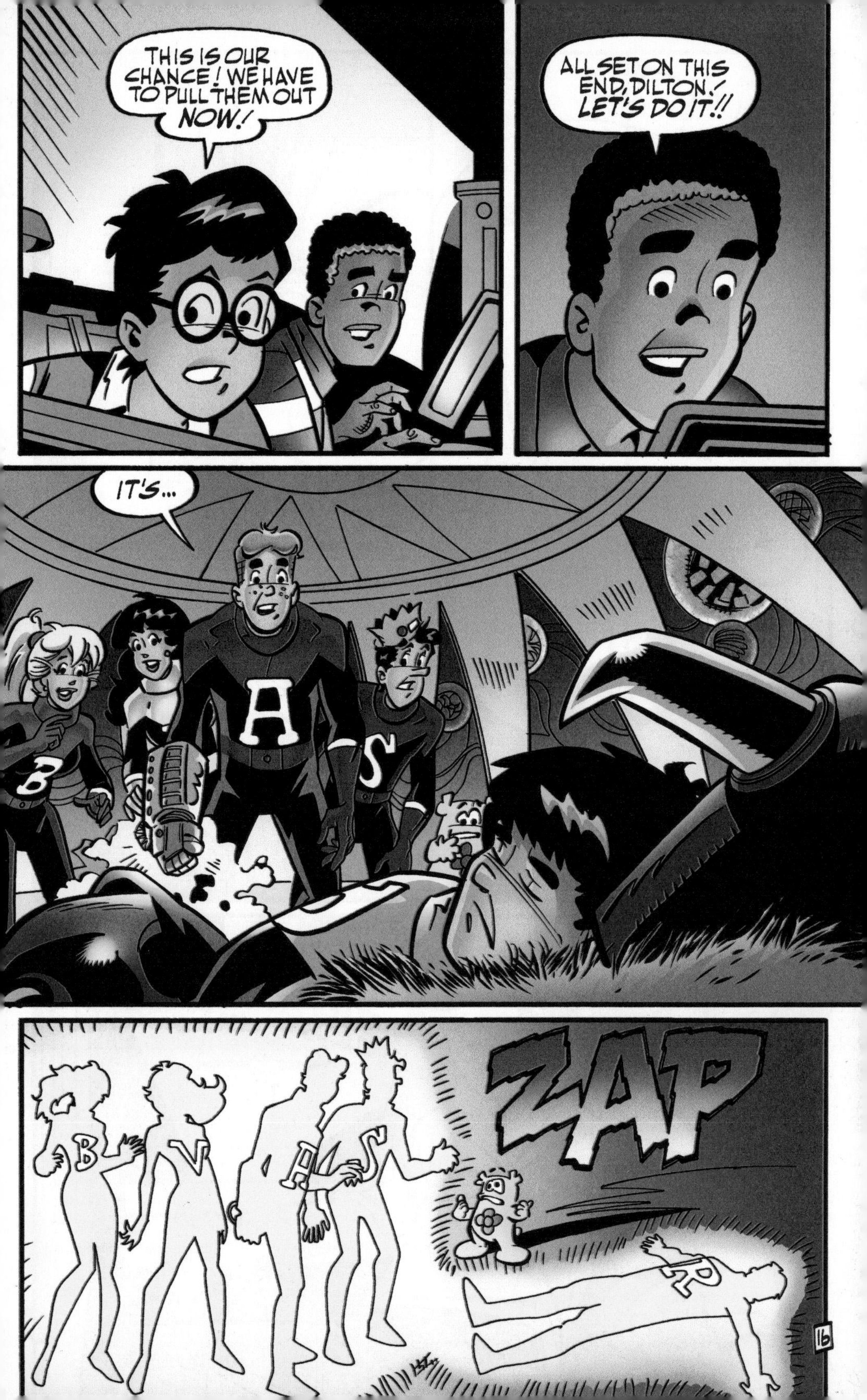
THIS IS OUR CHANCE! WE HAVE TO PULL THEM OUT NOW!
ALL SET ON THIS END, DILTON! LET'S DO IT!!
IT'S...
ZAP
16

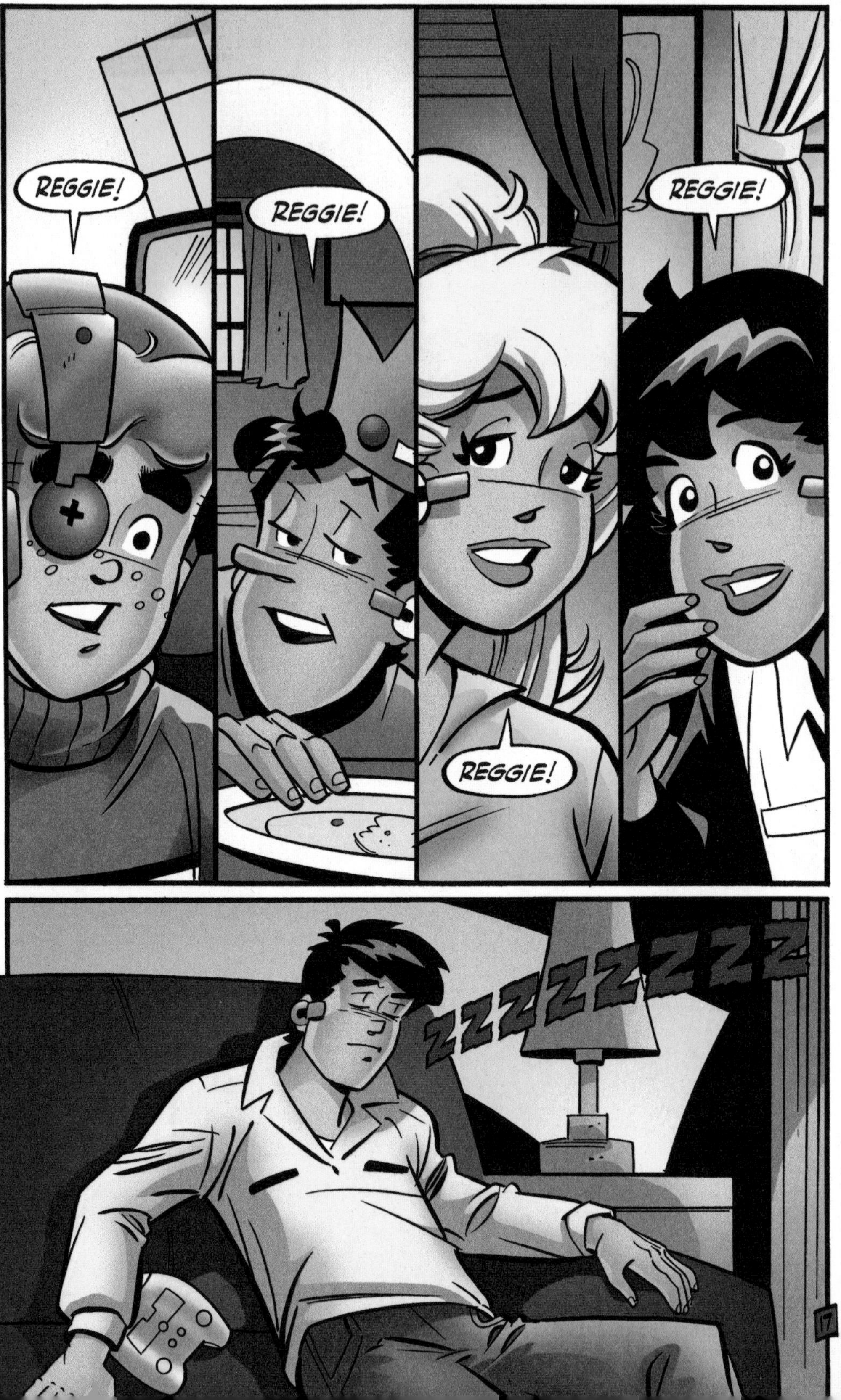
REGGIE!
REGGIE!
REGGIE!
REGGIE!
ZZZZZZZZZZ

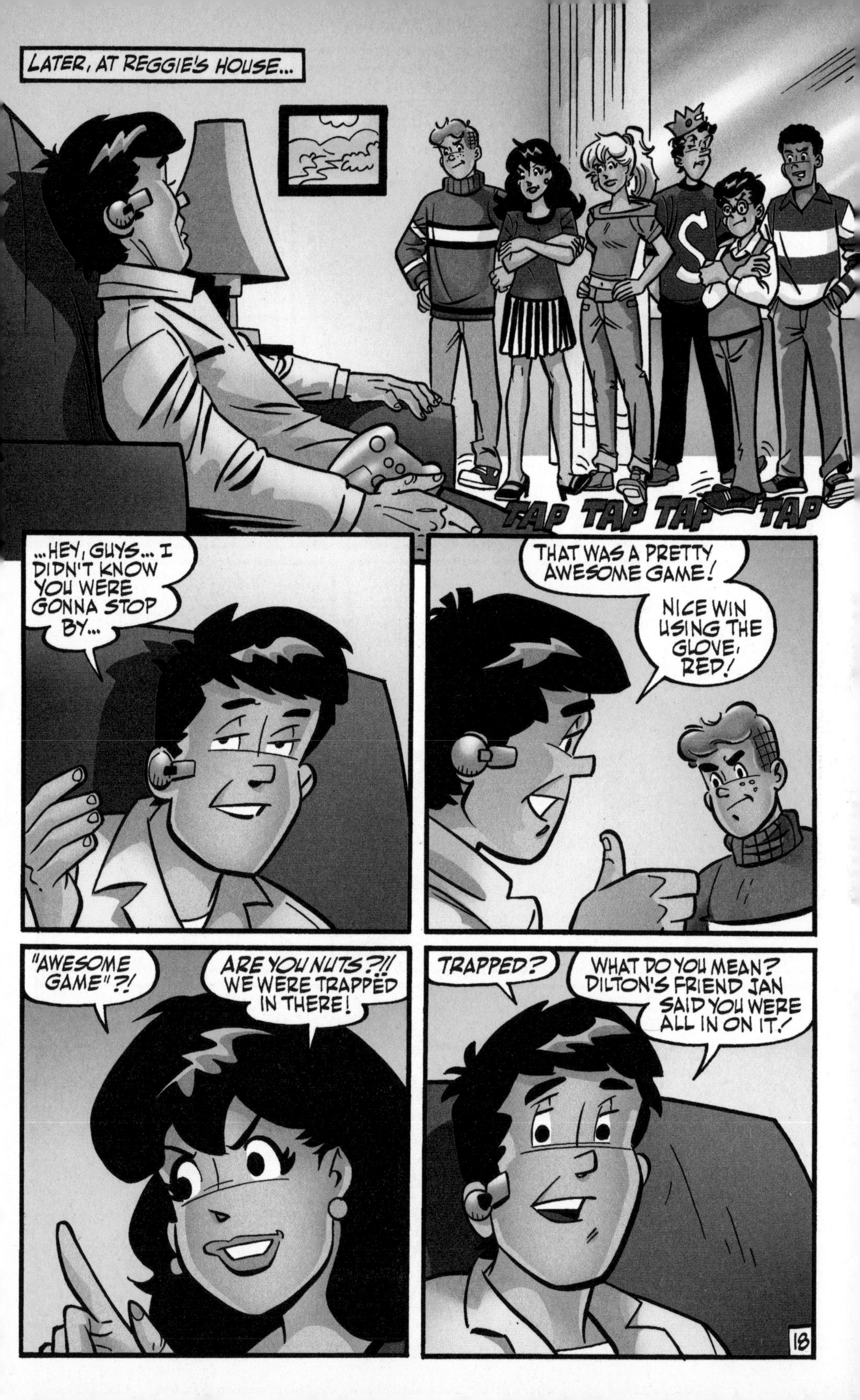
LATER, AT REGGIE'S HOUSE...
TAP TAP TAP TAP
...HEY, GUYS... I DIDN'T KNOW YOU WERE GONNA STOP BY...
THAT WAS A PRETTY AWESOME GAME!
NICE WIN USING THE GLOVE, RED!
"AWESOME GAME"?!
ARE YOU NUTS?!! WE WERE TRAPPED IN THERE!
TRAPPED?
WHAT DO YOU MEAN? DILTON'S FRIEND JAN SAID YOU WERE ALL IN ON IT!
18

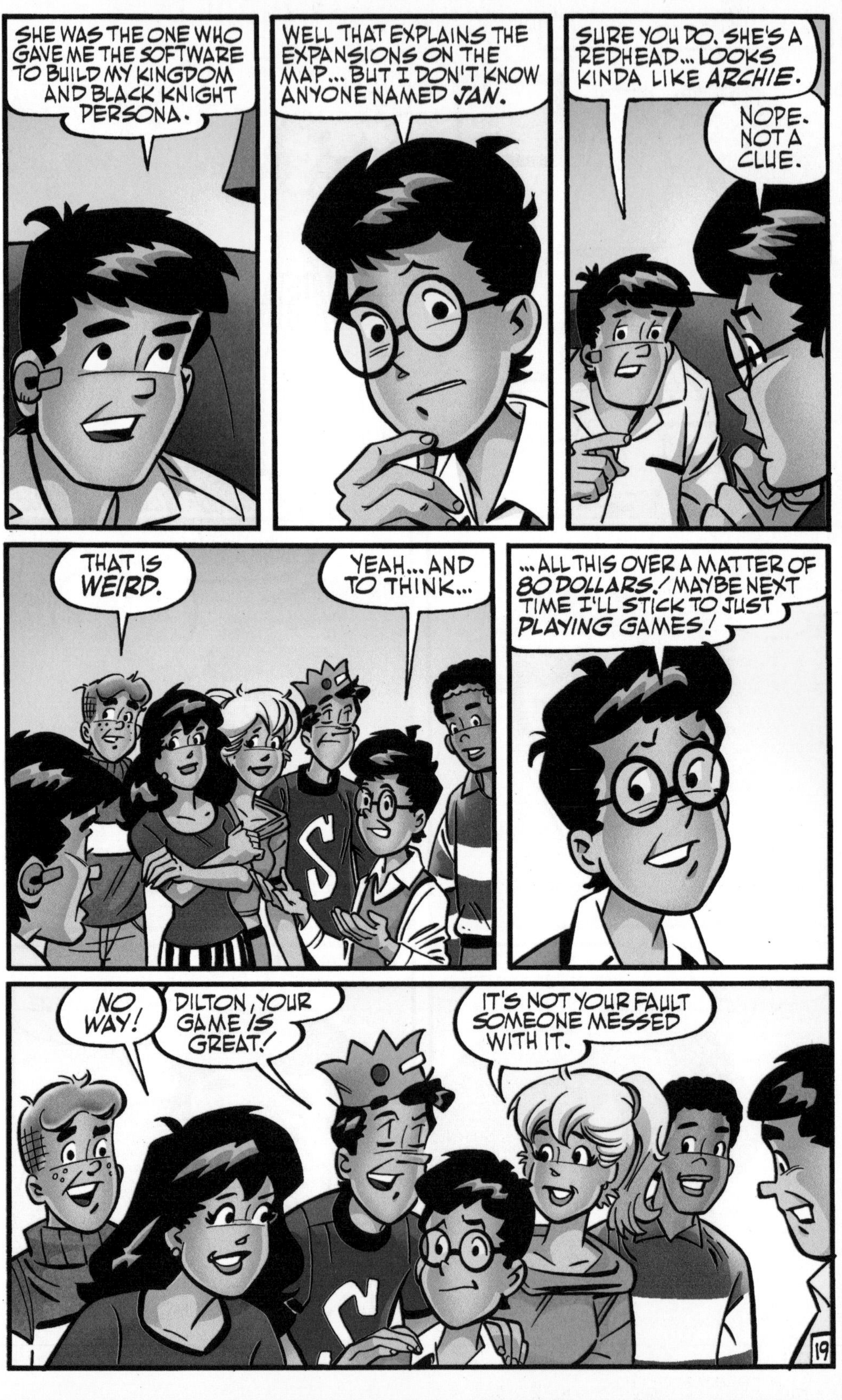
SHE WAS THE ONE WHO GAVE ME THE SOFTWARE TO BUILD MY KINGDOM AND BLACK KNIGHT PERSONA.
WELL THAT EXPLAINS THE EXPANSIONS ON THE MAP... BUT I DON'T KNOW ANYONE NAMED JAN.
SURE YOU DO. SHE'S A REDHEAD... LOOKS KINDA LIKE ARCHIE.
NOPE. NOT A CLUE.
THAT IS WEIRD.
YEAH... AND TO THINK...
...ALL THIS OVER A MATTER OF 80 DOLLARS! MAYBE NEXT TIME I'LL STICK TO JUST PLAYING GAMES!
NO WAY!
DILTON, YOUR GAME IS GREAT!
IT'S NOT YOUR FAULT SOMEONE MESSED WITH IT.
19

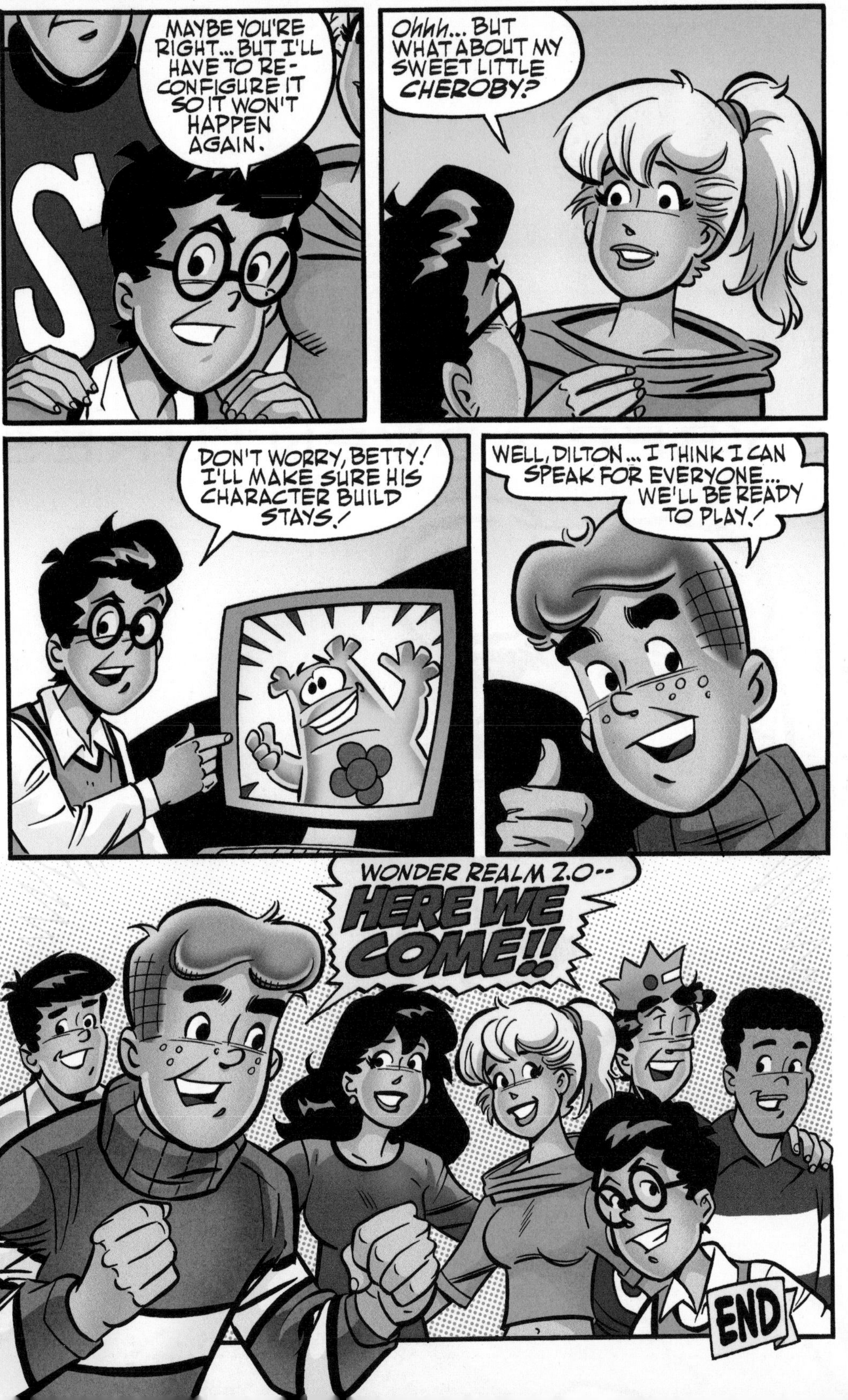
MAYBE YOU'RE RIGHT... BUT I'LL HAVE TO RE-CONFIGURE IT SO IT WON'T HAPPEN AGAIN.
Ohhh... BUT WHAT ABOUT MY SWEET LITTLE CHEROBY?
DON'T WORRY, BETTY! I'LL MAKE SURE HIS CHARACTER BUILD STAYS!
WELL, DILTON... I THINK I CAN SPEAK FOR EVERYONE... WE'LL BE READY TO PLAY!
WONDER REALM 2.0-- HERE WE COME!!
END

Archie®

CYBER ADVENTURES

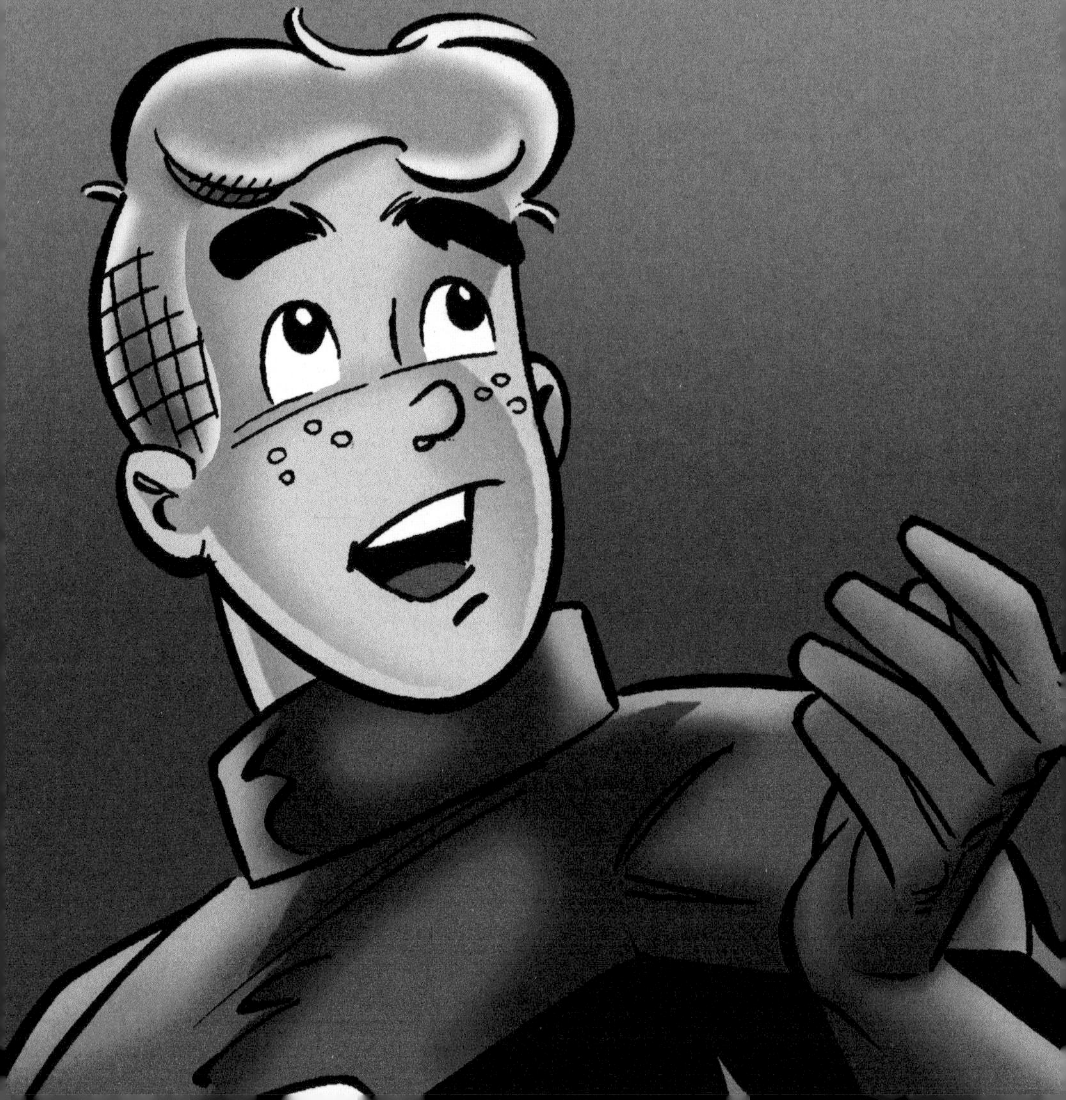

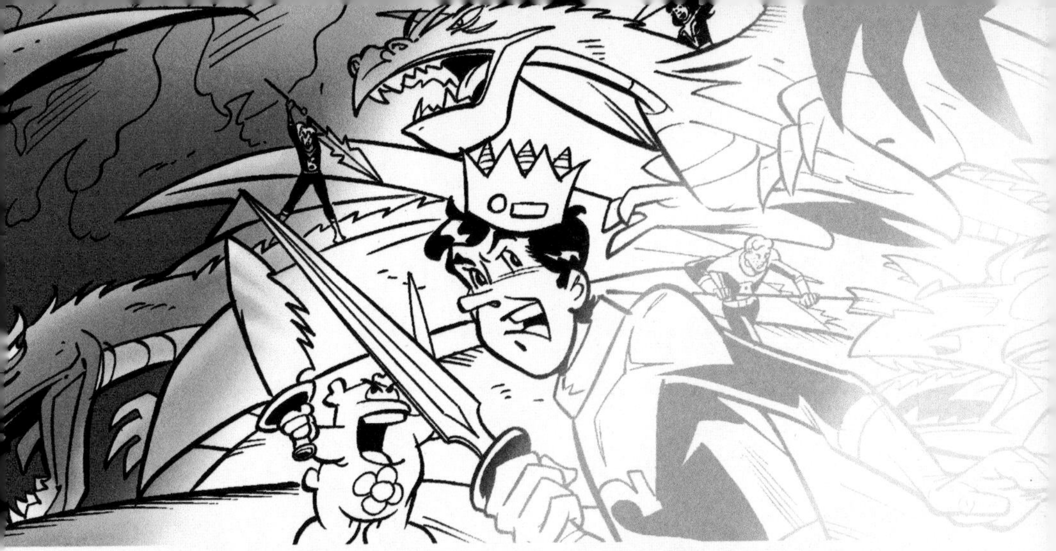

SKETCHBOOK

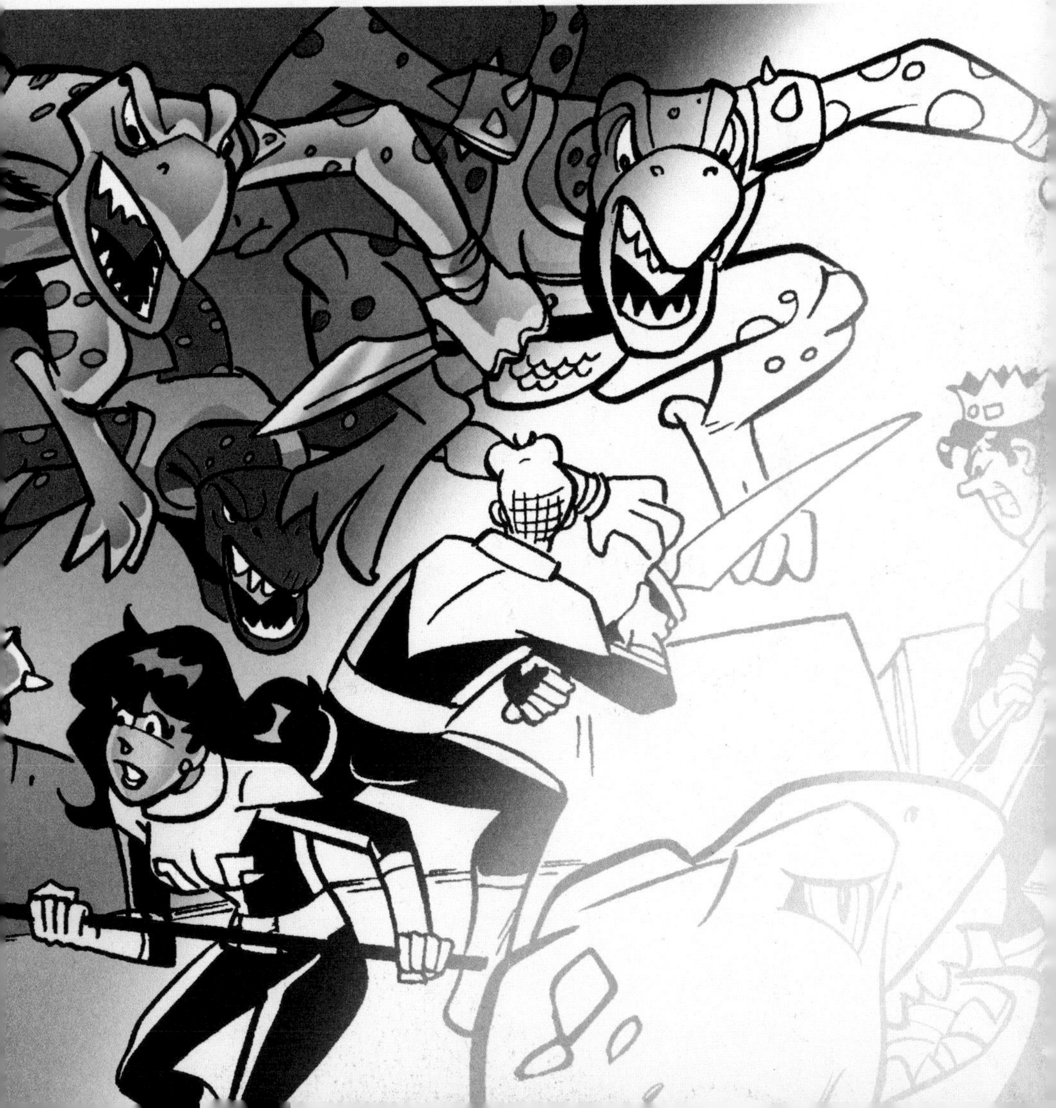

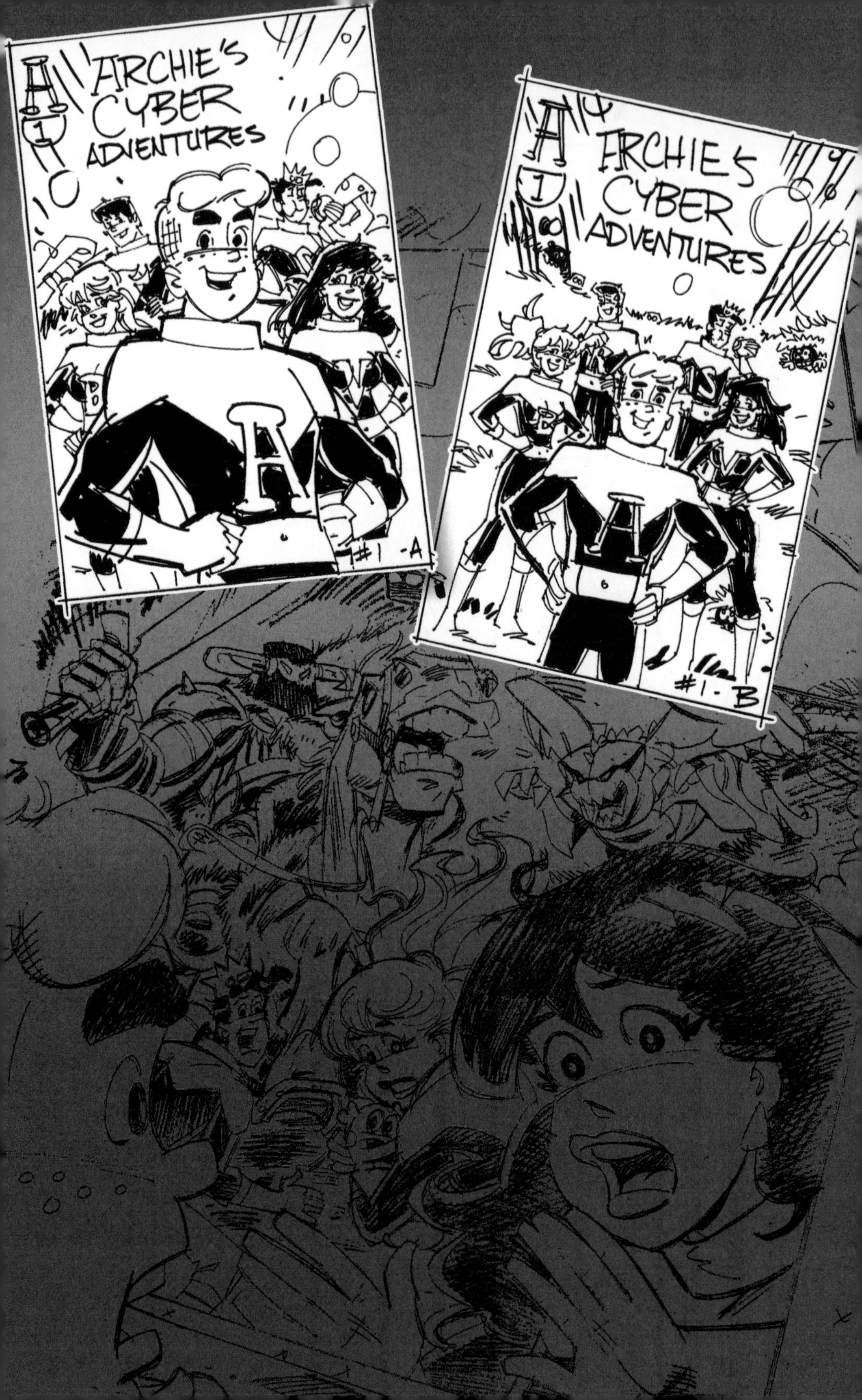

A
1
ARCHIE'S
CYBER
ADVENTURES
#1 -A
A
1
ARCHIE'S
CYBER
ADVENTURES
#1 - B

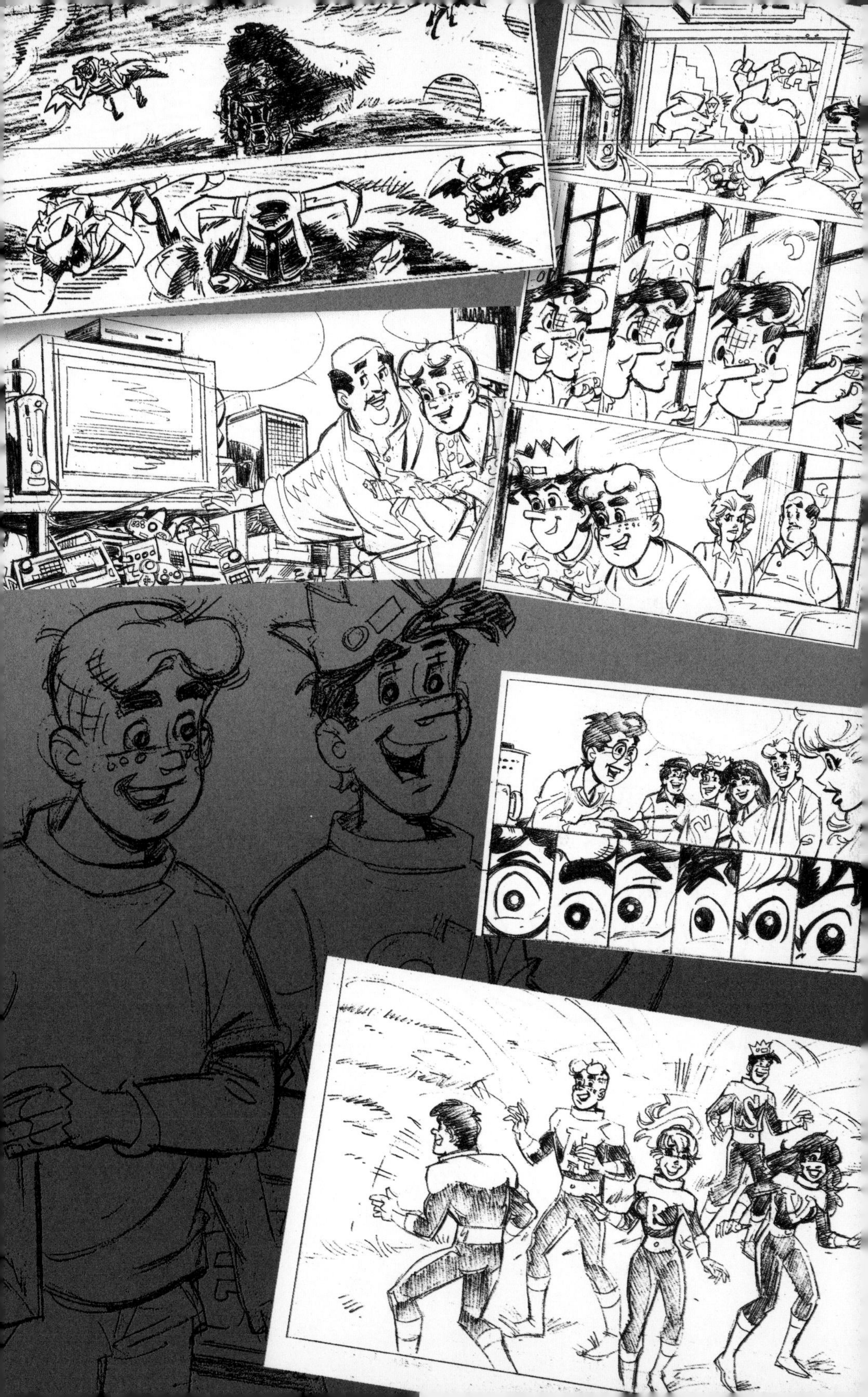

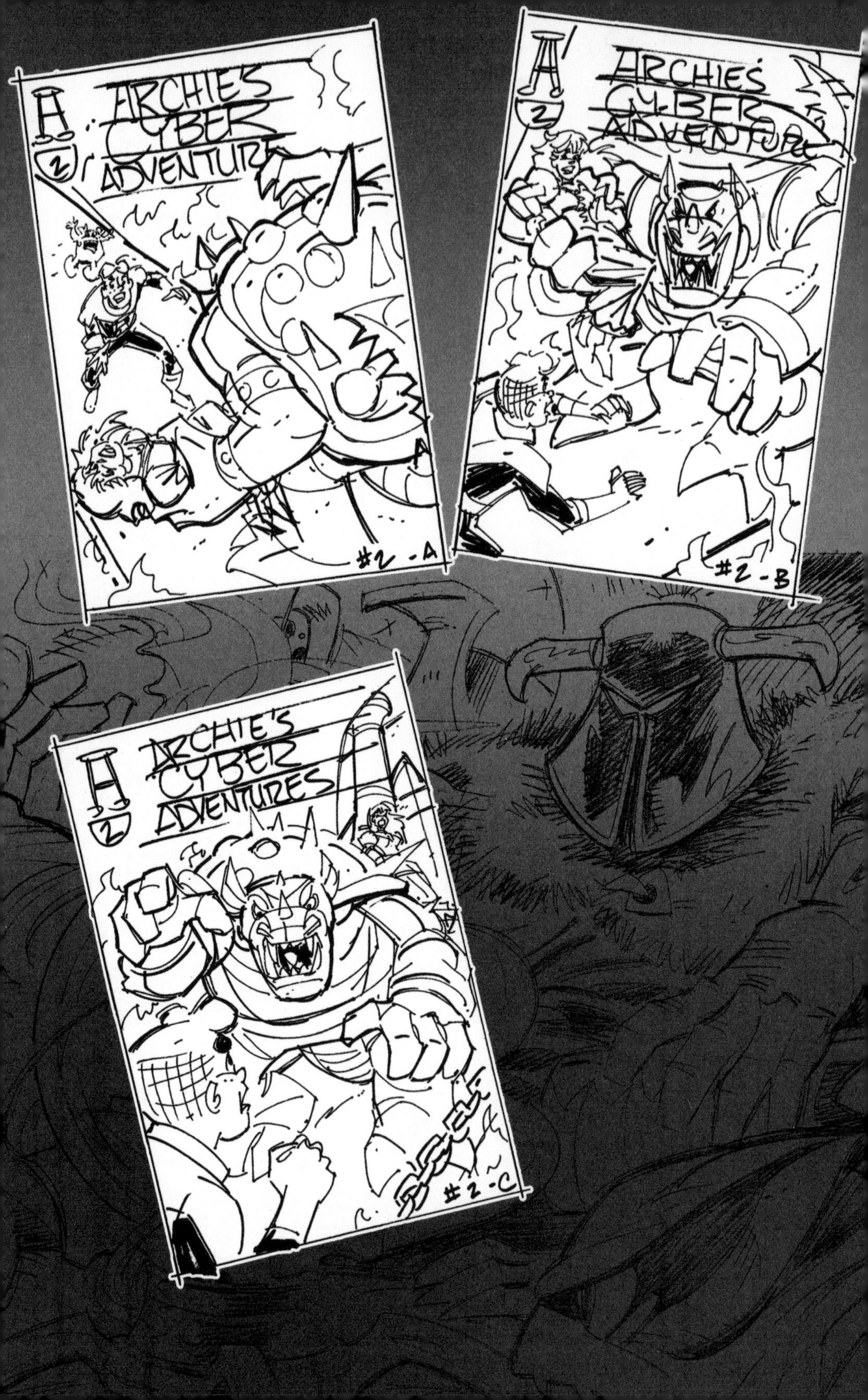
ARCHIE'S CYBER ADVENTURE
#2-A
ARCHIE'S CYBER ADVENTURE
#2-B
ARCHIE'S CYBER ADVENTURES
#2-C

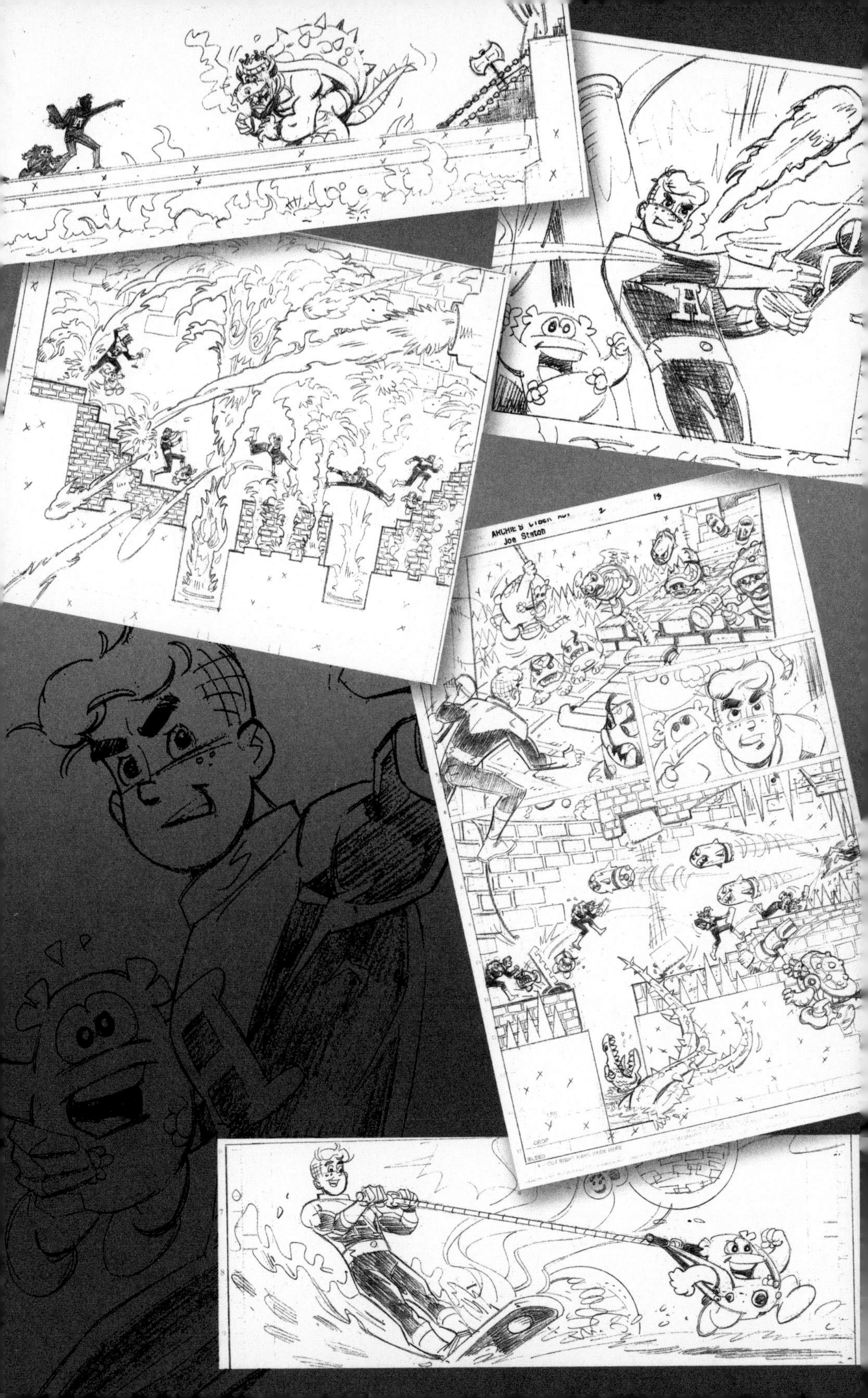
2
13
Joe Staton

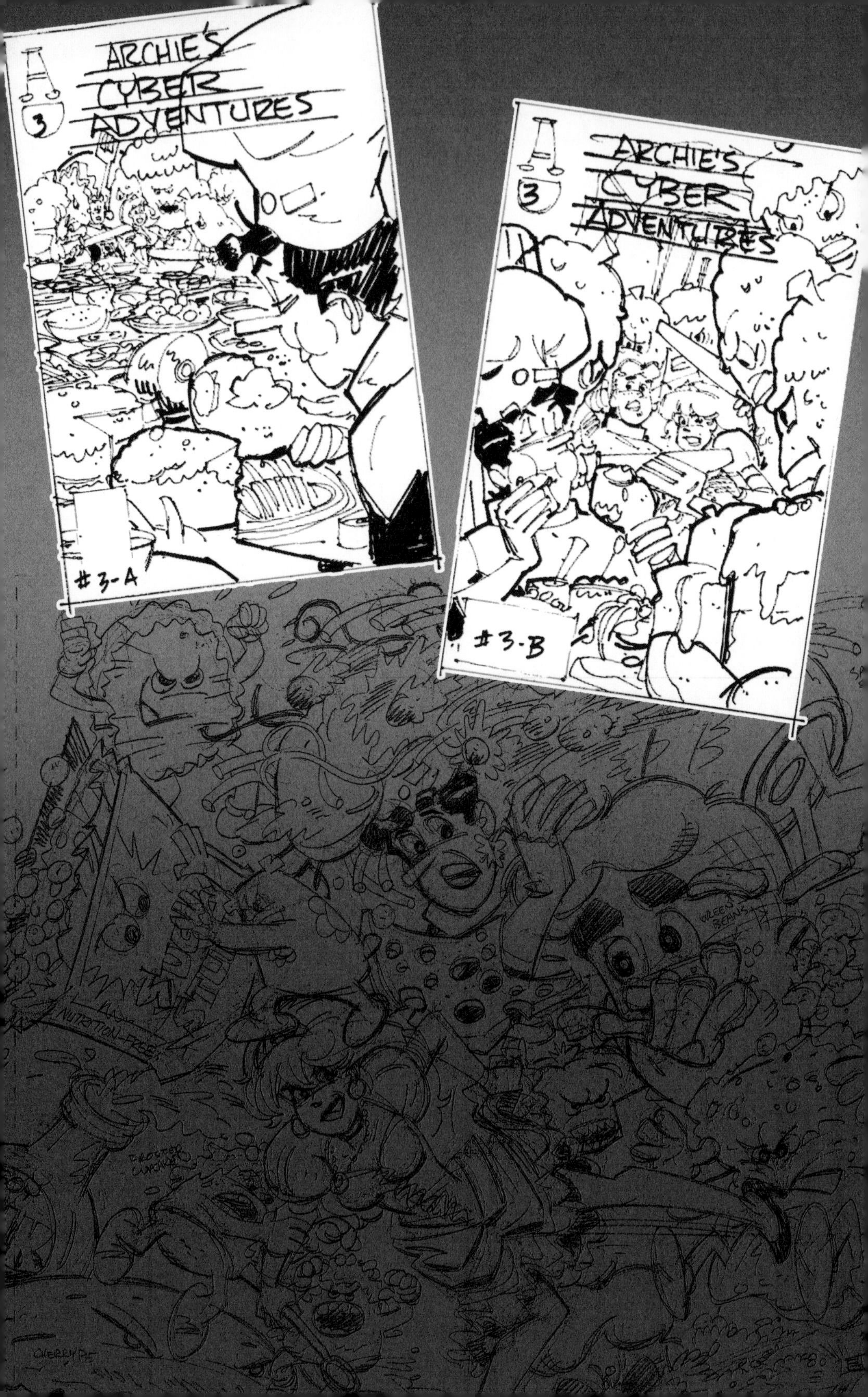
ARCHIE'S CYBER ADVENTURES
3
#3-A
ARCHIE'S CYBER ADVENTURES
3
#3-B
NUTRITION-FREE
GREEN BEANS

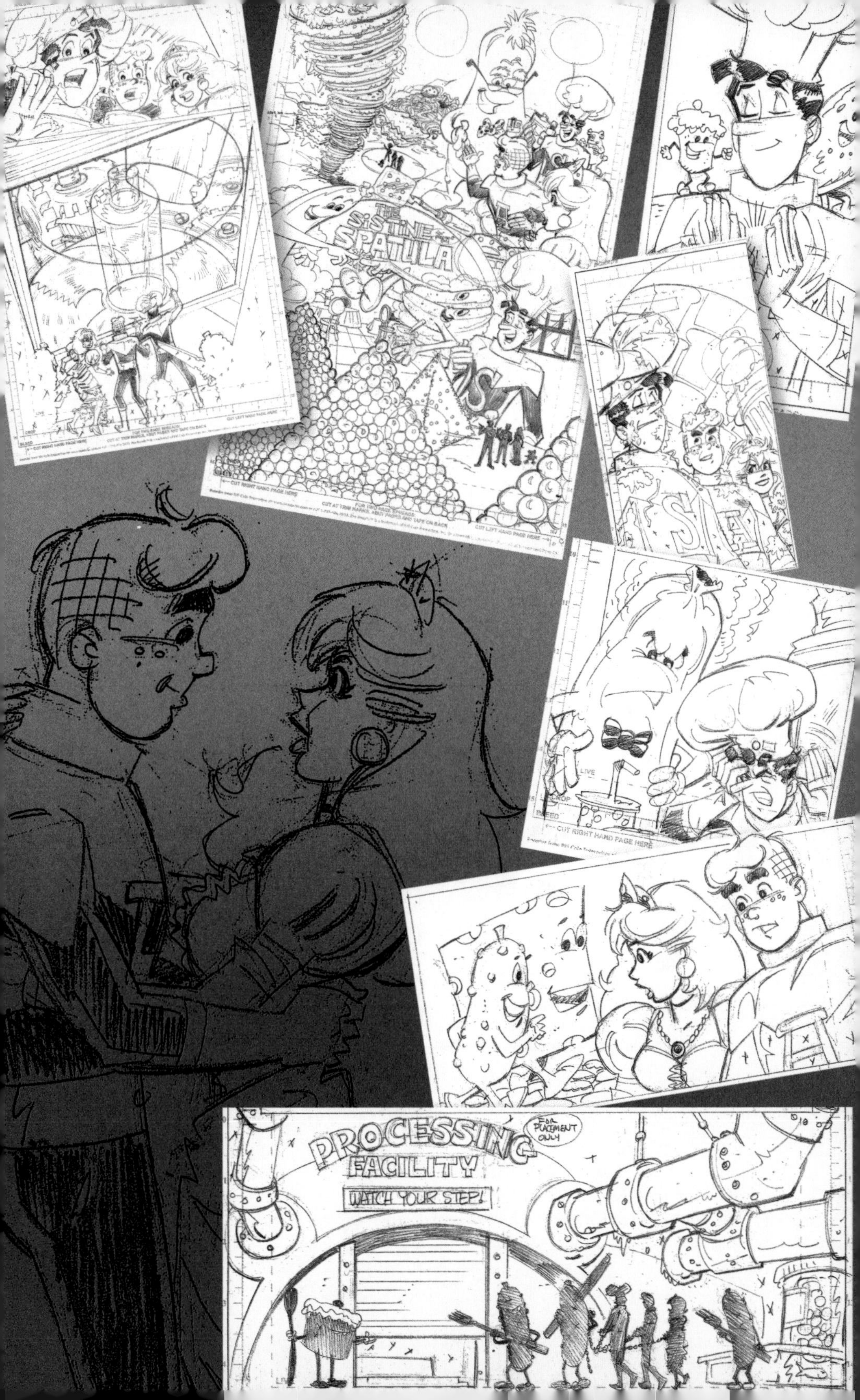
THE SISTINE SPATULA
CUT RIGHT HAND PAGE HERE
CUT LEFT HAND PAGE HERE
PROCESSING
FACILITY
WATCH YOUR STEP!
FOR PLACEMENT ONLY

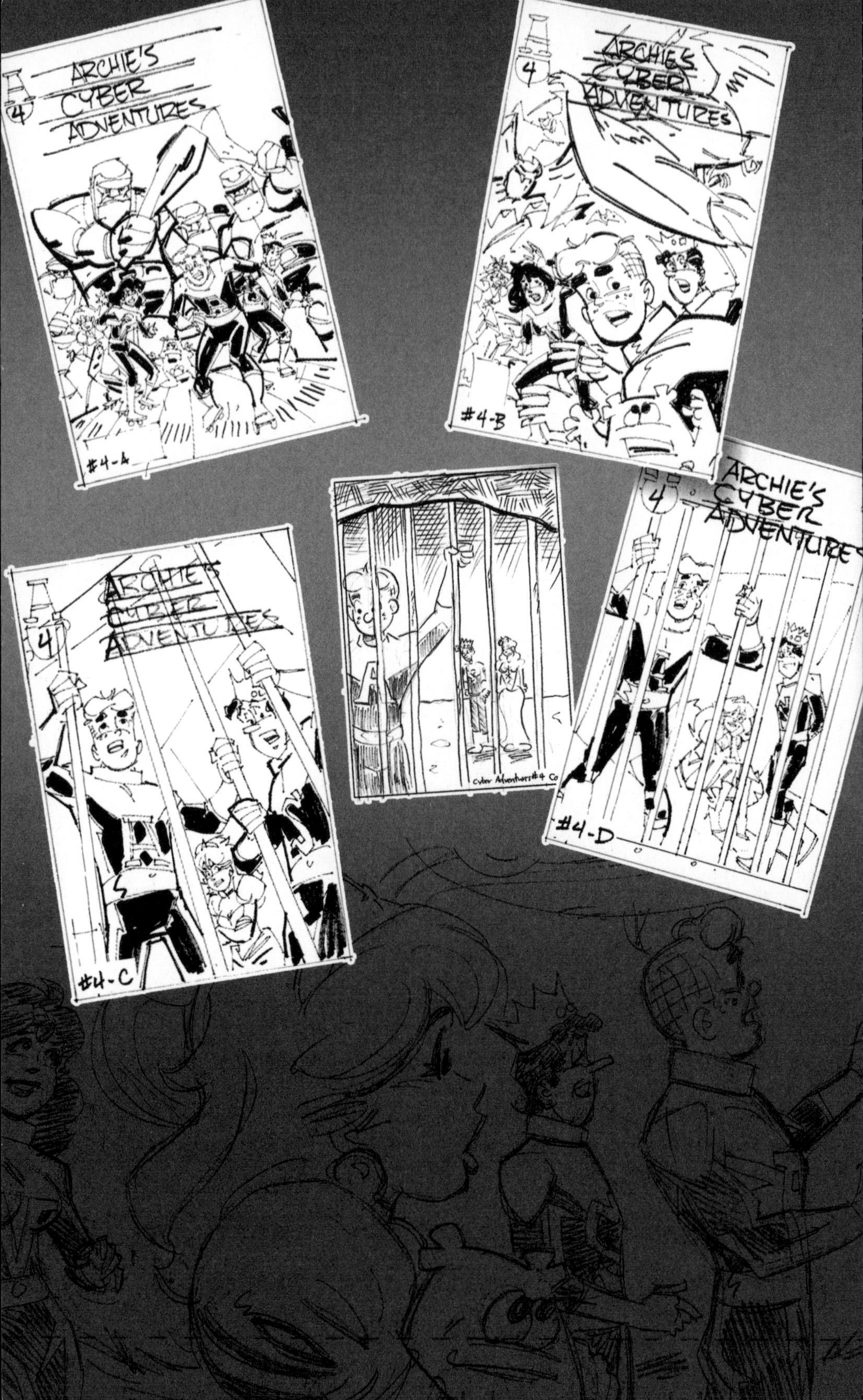

4
ARCHIE'S
CYBER
ADVENTURES
#4-A
4
ARCHIE'S
CYBER
ADVENTURES
#4-B
4
ARCHIE'S
CYBER
ADVENTURES
#4-C
Cyber Adventures #4
4
ARCHIE'S
CYBER
ADVENTURES
#4-D

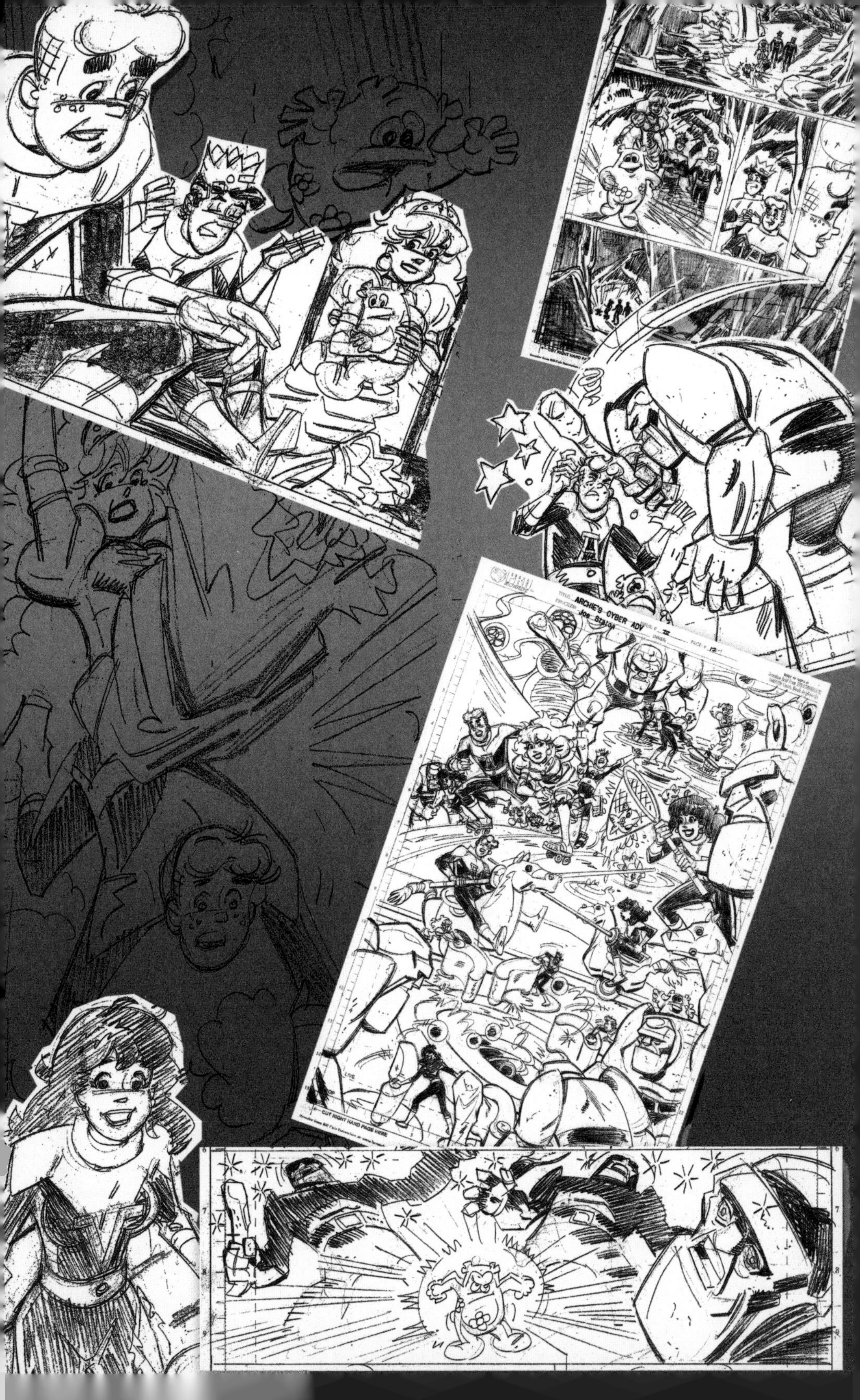
TITLE ARCHIE'S CYBER ADV
PENCILER Joe Staton
ISSUE # II
INKER
PAGE #

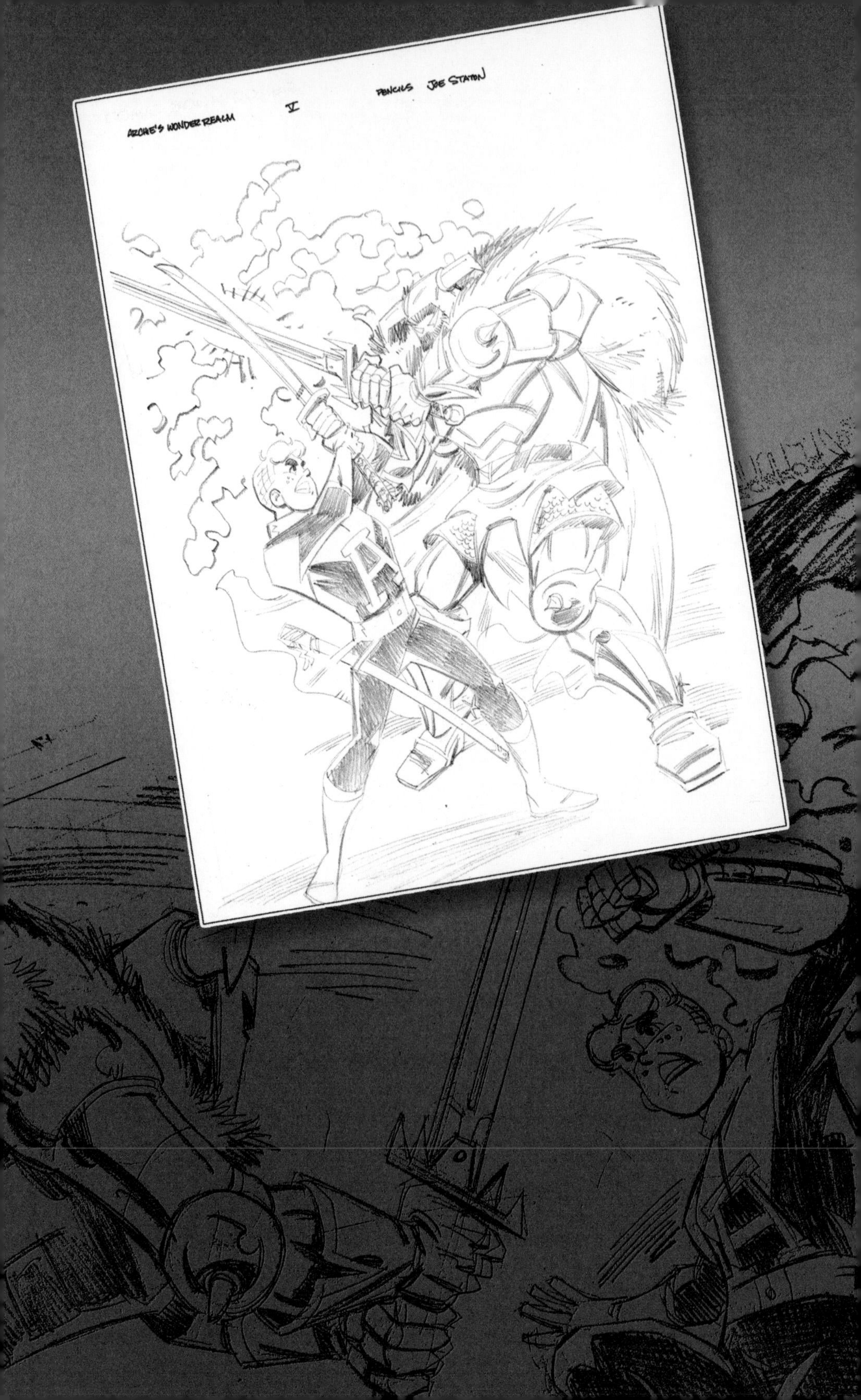

ARCHIE'S WONDER REALM
V
PENCILS JOE STATON

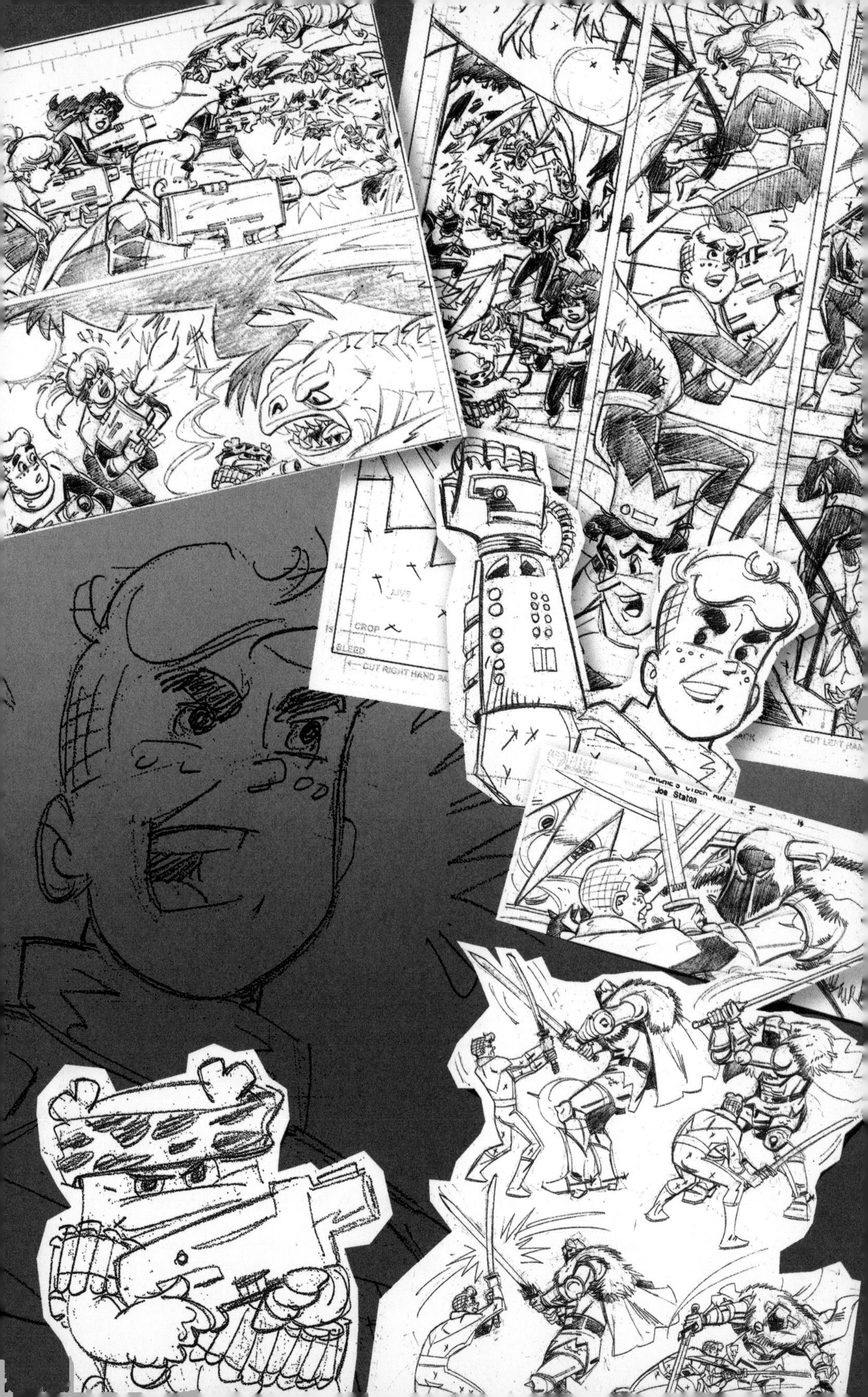
CROP
BLEED
Joe Staton

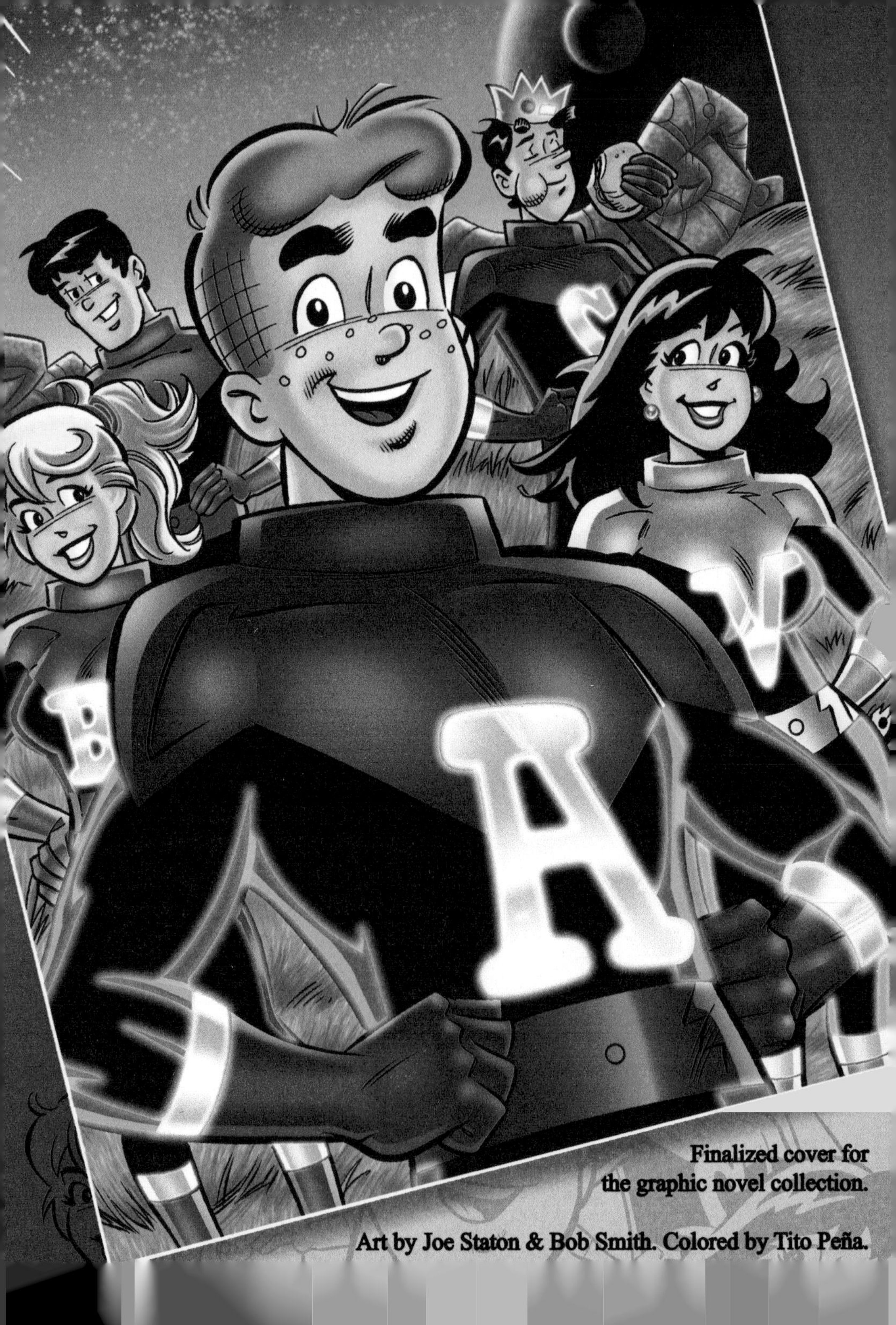
A
B
V

Finalized cover for
the graphic novel collection.

Art by Joe Staton & Bob Smith. Colored by Tito Peña.

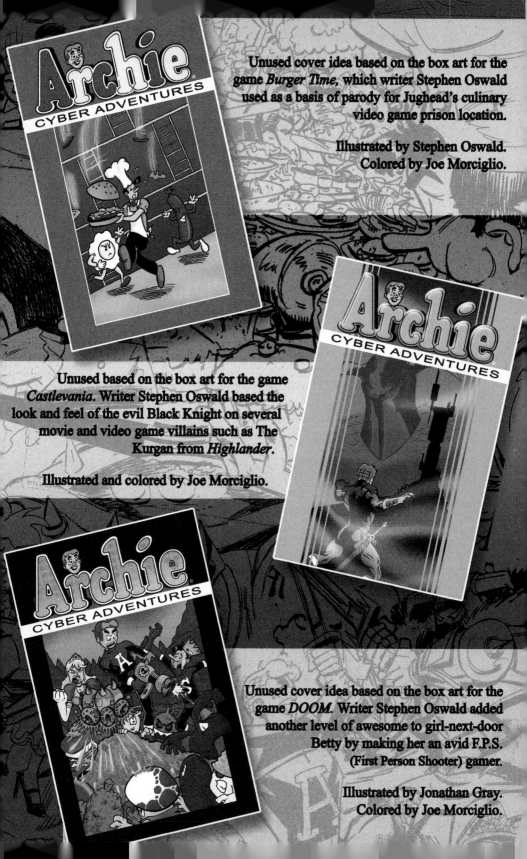

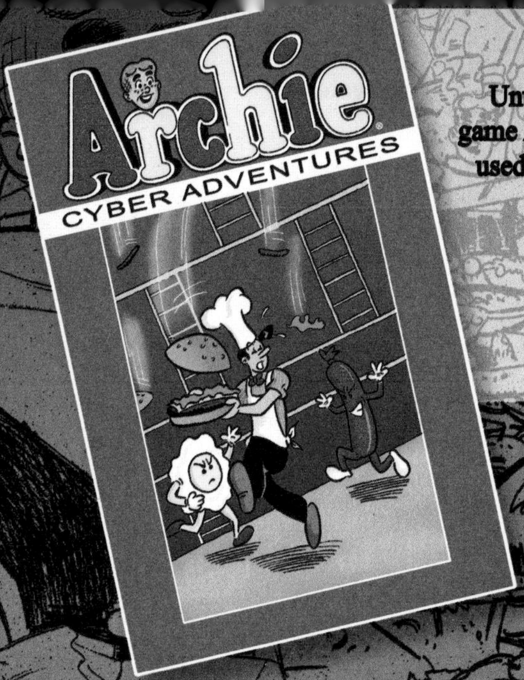
Archie
CYBER ADVENTURES

Unused cover idea based on the box art for the game *Burger Time*, which writer Stephen Oswald used as a basis of parody for Jughead's culinary video game prison location.

Illustrated by Stephen Oswald.
Colored by Joe Morciglio.

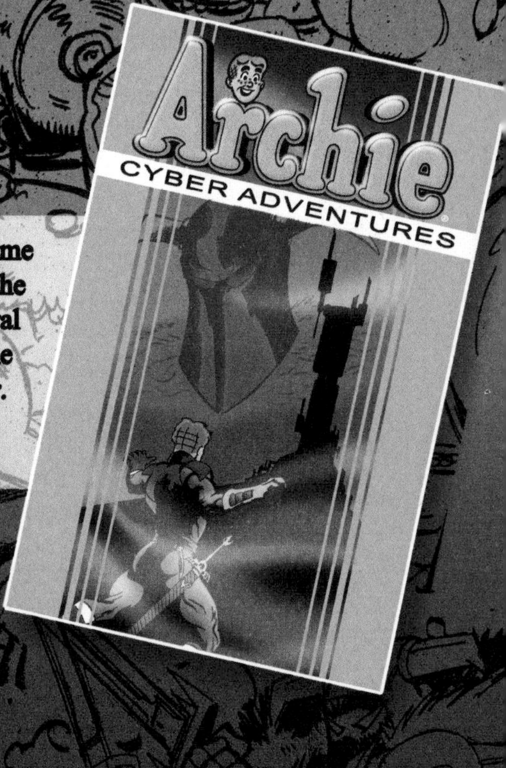
Archie
CYBER ADVENTURES

Unused based on the box art for the game *Castlevania*. Writer Stephen Oswald based the look and feel of the evil Black Knight on several movie and video game villains such as The Kurgan from *Highlander*.

Illustrated and colored by Joe Morciglio.

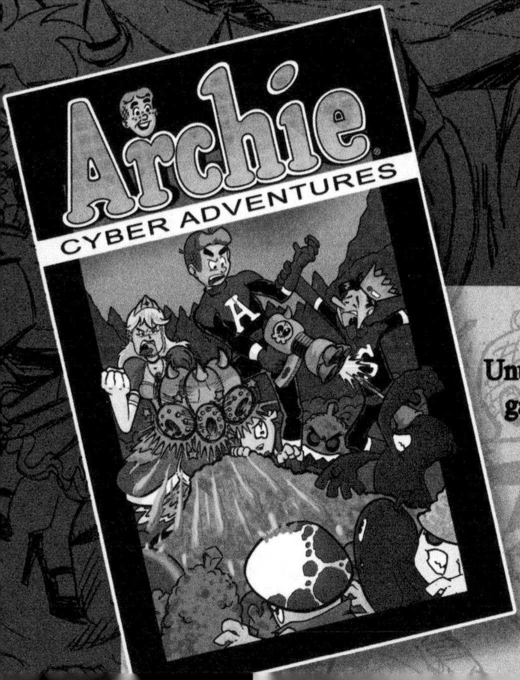
Archie
CYBER ADVENTURES

Unused cover idea based on the box art for the game *DOOM*. Writer Stephen Oswald added another level of awesome to girl-next-door Betty by making her an avid F.P.S. (First Person Shooter) gamer.

Illustrated by Jonathan Gray.
Colored by Joe Morciglio.

THE ARCHIE WEDDING
Archie
in WILL YOU MARRY ME?

The Archie Wedding: Will You Marry Me?

Archie has finally chosen! The winner is... BOTH OF THEM!

ISBN: 978-1-879794-51-1

Archie's Weird Mysteries

Strange things are happening in a little town called Riverdale. ***Based on the hit animated series!***

ISBN: 978-1-879794-74-0

Archie's
WEIRD MYSTERIES

THE Archie BABIES

The Archie Babies

Before they ruled the halls of Riverdale High, Archie and his pals were kings and queens of the playground!

ISBN: 978-1-879794-72-6

Archie & Friends: Night at the Comic Shop

Classic comic characters leave their four-color worlds to wreak havoc on Riverdale!

ISBN: 978-1-879794-69-6

Archie & FRIENDS
NIGHT AT THE COMIC SHOP

Archie
FRESHMAN YEAR BOOK TWO
THE HIGH SCHOOL CHRONICLES BOOK TWO
GREETINGS
FRESHMAN COMICS
CHUCK'S LAST STAND?

Archie: Freshman Year Book 2

The coolest freshmen at Riverdale High are back for an all-new semester of hilarity!

ISBN: 978-1-879794-71-9

Archie: World Tour

Archie and friends go on a globe-trotting expedition full of excitement and adventure!

ISBN: 978-1-879794-73-3

Archie
WORLD TOUR

Best of JUGHEAD
CROWNING ACHIEVEMENTS
American Idle

Best of Jughead: Crowning Achievements

Get ready for a buffet of comedy with everyone's favorite foodie. Jughead! Bon appétit!

ISBN: 978-1-879794-67-2

Archie: The Man from R.I.V.E.R.D.A.L.E.

Archie suits up for adventure as he takes on some of the world's most diabolical ne'er-do-wells!

ISBN: 978-1-879794-68-9

Archie
THE MAN FROM R.I.V.E.R.D.A.L.E.

Archie® COMICS

LOOK FOR THESE AND OTHER GRAPHIC NOVELS AT COMIC SHOPS AND BOOKSTORES EVERYWHERE!

ALSO AVAILABLE ONLINE AT ARCHIECOMICS.COM

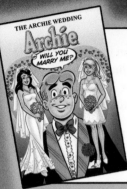

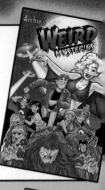

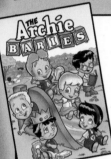

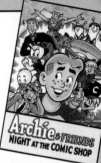

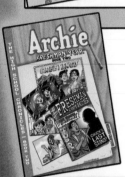

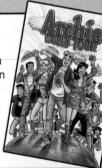

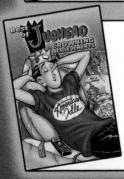

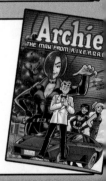

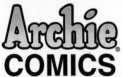